*Berkley Sensation titles by Kaki Warner*

*Blood Rose Trilogy*

PIECES OF SKY
OPEN COUNTRY
CHASING THE SUN

*Runaway Brides Novels*

HEARTBREAK CREEK
COLORADO DAWN
BRIDE OF THE HIGH COUNTRY

*Heroes of Heartbreak Creek*

BEHIND HIS BLUE EYES
WHERE THE HORSES RUN

# Where the Horses Run

## KAKI WARNER

BERKLEY SENSATION, NEW YORK

**THE BERKLEY PUBLISHING GROUP**
Published by the Penguin Group
Penguin Group (USA) LLC
375 Hudson Street, New York, New York 10014

USA • Canada • UK • Ireland • Australia • New Zealand • India • South Africa • China

penguin.com

A Penguin Random House Company

WHERE THE HORSES RUN

A Berkley Sensation Book / published by arrangement with the author

Berkley Sensation Books are published by The Berkley Publishing Group.
BERKLEY SENSATION® is a registered trademark of Penguin Group (USA) LLC.
The "B" design is a trademark of Penguin Group (USA) LLC.

For information, address: The Berkley Publishing Group,
a division of Penguin Group (USA) LLC,
375 Hudson Street, New York, New York 10014.

ISBN: 978-0-425-26327-3

PUBLISHING HISTORY
Berkley Sensation mass-market edition / July 2014

PRINTED IN THE UNITED STATES OF AMERICA

10  9  8  7  6  5  4  3  2  1

Cover art by Judy York.
Cover design by Lesley Worrell.

*I dedicate this book to . . .*

*Henry, the littlest prince and thief of my heart.*

*To Miss Charm and Miss Belle, happily fox-trotting
through the fields of heaven, tails high and
mischief in their eyes.*

*And especially to all those lucky enough to have
their lives enriched by that magnificent, courageous,
loyal creature called the horse.*

My heartfelt thanks to . . .

Bob and Janet Boyce for patiently answering all
    my horse questions.
Regan Walker for her insightful comments and
    helpful suggestions.
And of course, Cyndi Thomson . . . friend,
    listener, neighbor, and fellow horse lover.
Y'all are the best.

                                                    K

# *Prologue*

"America?" Josephine Cathcart set down her goblet so abruptly water sloshed over the rim of the cut crystal. She looked in surprise at the single other diner, seated on her left at the head of the twenty-five-foot-long table.

Flushed. Red-rimmed eyes. That belligerent thrust to his chin.

Although the footmen had just set their soup course before them, Father was well into his second bottle of wine. She had expected a difficult meal when he had informed her earlier that they would be dining in the formal dining room this evening, and Jamie would not be included. She had prepared herself for another lecture about her selfishness in not accepting their neighbor's suit. Instead, her father made this startling announcement. "Why would you go to America?"

"To see a man about an auger. Might be useful at the mine."

Even though she knew little about mining, Josephine was well aware that the mine that had built Father's fortune was producing less and less coal each month. Could this auger improve that? Or was it just another desperate attempt to slow their steady slide toward financial ruin?

She sipped a spoonful of tepid leek and parsnip soup that was far too salty—Cook's retaliation, no doubt, for the latest delay in her wages—then returned her spoon to her soup plate.

She wasn't ignorant of their circumstances. She knew they

couldn't continue this week-to-week existence much longer. People weren't getting paid, and of late, the merchants in Penrith looked at her with even more disdain than they had in the past. "Is there no more artwork to sell?"

"I've sent too much to the auction house as it is. I don't want to raise doubts among my investors."

They already had doubts. Especially those who had lost substantial sums in Father's other ventures. A sense of inevitability weighted her down. "There must be something else we can do."

"There is." In the light of the branched silver candelabra, his dark eyes glittered in a way that reminded her of a cornered animal trapped in a burrow.

She shook her head. "I'll not marry Mr. Huddleston, Father." A widower twice over with six unruly daughters, Ezra Huddleston was so desperate for a son he was willing to overlook her "deplorable morals and lack of social status," in deference to her fine figure and proven breeding ability. Such a romantic.

"By damn, girl!" Father's broad palm hit the table with enough force to make his spoon clatter on his soup plate. "You'll do what I tell you!"

She clenched her hands in her lap. "I'm nearly twenty-six and well past my girlhood, Father." When he started to argue, she glanced pointedly at the footmen standing against the wall like frozen statues.

Catching the warning, he waved a hand in dismissal. "Take this swill away and leave us. And, Rogers, bring me another bottle."

The footmen quickly cleared. As they hurried out, the head footman hurried back in with a new bottle of wine. Within moments only the two of them remained in the cavernous room. Father sipped wine and studied her, tension humming between them.

She wondered how they had drifted so far apart. Was it his fear of being thrust back into poverty that made him so distant and cold? Or perhaps he still simmered over the scandal and taint of Jamie's illegitimacy. Still, he had allowed them to continue living here, and even if he hadn't warmed toward his grandson, he never mentioned the shame his birth had caused him. So he must still love her a little.

"Huddleston's offer is a good one."

Josephine doubted it. Their neighbor was only a country squire. He hadn't the resources to help Father out of the financial hole into which he'd so carelessly plunged them. So why was Father insisting on this match?

"He's thirty years older than I am, Father. Why would he seek to take on the added expense of a wife this late in his life?"

"He wants a son. And having an attractive young wife on his arm is a boost to any man, no matter his age. That he'll even consider offering for you is an indication of the depth of his interest."

Josephine shuddered, well aware of the *depth* of Huddleston's interest. He had cornered her in the conservatory twice this month. "He won't take Jamie."

"I'll keep the boy here. You can visit him whenever you want."

*The boy* was his grandson, yet Father could scarcely say his name. "No."

"And if we lose everything, Josephine? What will happen to you and the lad then? A life on the streets? Don't you understand I'm trying to save you?"

She almost smiled. Save *me*? Perhaps.

If anything, Father was a practical man, having learned the brutal necessities of survival in the deep coal mines of Cumberland. And even though he had long since clawed his way out of the black bowels of the earth to become a person of consequence and wealth, he still applied the same lessons to his life.

Survival. At any cost.

Yet it took a great deal of money to survive in society. And as the coal in his mine had played out, so had his wealth. He had tried to recoup his losses with risky ventures, high-stakes gambling, quietly selling off the valuable artwork he had bought to impress, yet had never understood or appreciated. But still, the money flowed through his hands like water.

So now it was Josephine's turn on the auction block. She was his last hope, and as such, was less a cherished daughter than a handy tool to be used. At one time she would have done his bidding without question. But with motherhood, her loyalties had shifted. Now, she was less concerned with pleasing her father than in doing what was best for her son. Jamie came first. Always.

Appetite gone, she carefully folded her napkin and placed it beside her tableware. "I will not marry him."

"Fine. Then I'll take you with me to America."

"Why?" Although in her heart, she knew. As had happened so many times in the past, she would be his lure—the pretty face and warm smile—drawing investors to the latest scheme he was brewing. Having run through his prospects here, he was off to drum up new capital in America.

Josephine was weary of it. Sick of watching him fritter away what assets still remained, when liquidation would clear all his debts and still leave enough for a comfortable life.

Sadly, she would never convince him of that. So she was faced with a choice: stay in this monstrosity of a house until the servants left and it sank into disrepair or the debt collectors' hands—or find a way to build a safer, saner future for herself and her son.

Realizing she was twisting her hands, she straightened her fingers and pressed them flat against her thighs. "And what about Jamie?" If she took him with her to America, she might be able to spirit him away. She could pretend to be a widow; Jamie's paternity need never come into question. She had already begun replacing her jewelry with paste copies. If she sold off the rest, it might provide enough to make a fresh start.

Could she truly leave all she knew and loved? For Jamie, yes.

"He can stay here with his nanny. He'll only be a distraction."

Her head snapped up. "A distraction? From what?" Then understanding came in a rush, and she sat back, unable to hide her surprise. "This trip isn't only about a piece of mining equipment, is it? You're taking me to America in hopes of finding me a rich husband, aren't you?" She had to laugh. Didn't he understand that no American would marry her simply because she was English? Without a title, she had no value, especially in view of her Great Indiscretion.

The flush on his ruddy cheeks darkened. "The Brownlea girl caught a railroad financier, didn't she? And she's got a face that would curdle milk."

"Her father also has connections to railways here," she reminded him.

"With your beauty and brains, daughter," he pressed on, "you could grace any man's table. God knows I spent a fortune preparing you for such a purpose."

"And what about my son? Am I to keep quiet about him and pretend he doesn't exist?" Jamie was the greatest blessing in her life. To deny him would be to tear out her own heart.

"Just don't flaunt him. That's all I ask. Set the hook first."

Feeling faintly ill, Josephine listened to rain ping against the panes of the French doors onto the terrace and wondered how her life had come to this . . . trying to trick rich men into offering marriage, despite the fact that she was past her prime, the mother of an illegitimate son, impoverished, and impossibly tall. It was ludicrous. Disgusting.

And yet . . .

What if she did find a decent man who would accept both her and her son? What if the life she'd thought no longer available to her was truly a possibility?

At any rate, what were her other options? Stay here until they lost everything and ended up on the street? Or marry Huddleston.

Surely, an American couldn't be as bad as either of those.

# *One*

Sound travels far in dry, open country, and Rayford Jessup was still a quarter of a mile away from the Hendricks place when he heard the screaming.

He nudged his horse into a gallop.

A hundred yards closer and he could tell it was animal, not human.

A horse.

By the time he splashed across the small creek running beside the house and barn, the noise had escalated to whinnies, crashes, and shouted curses. He tensed, more easily able to tolerate shouts of anger than screams of rage or fear from a distressed horse. What were they doing to the poor animal?

His own horse snorted, head up, ears pricked, his steps sidling and hesitant. Feeling the beginnings of a shy, Rafe murmured softly and ran a hand along the chestnut's neck, reminding the young gelding he wasn't alone, and he needed to pay attention to his rider, not what was going on in the barn.

He reined in beside an odd sheepherder's-style wagon parked in front of the house. Giving the restive gelding a moment to settle down, he kept his hands and legs still, his voice calm and unhurried as he looked around.

Like most of the scattered holdings in the dry mesquite and cactus country along the Texas-Mexico border, the Hendricks place was a grit-scoured collection of warped wood corrals, rough outbuildings, and sagging lean-tos bleached by the sun to the color of pitted pewter. That it survived at all was due to the narrow muddy creek that fed the single, wind-damaged cottonwood shading the adobe house. Rafe supposed there was some appeal in the endless expanse of open sky, but he much preferred the rolling grass and cedar-dotted hills farther north, or the bluebonnet fields in central Texas.

Sensing no immediate danger, his horse began to relax, even though he remained alert to the shouts and whinnies that continued to come from the barn. Rafe praised him with more pats, then dismounted as two men and a huge dog came out of the double barn doors.

One man was tall—probably as tall as Rafe, but leaner—with the rolling loose-hipped gait of a lifelong horseman. The other man was older, short, and stocky. James Hendricks, the man who had sent word for Rafe to come.

"Glad you made it, Jessup," Hendricks called, angling toward him. "Got a real mess going here."

Rafe didn't give a response, since none was required. After looping the reins around the hitching rail in front of the house, he studied the dog, then the stranger approaching him.

Both had gray hair. He didn't know how old the dog was, but the man didn't look much older than Rafe's thirty-two. Probably ex-cavalry. In addition to the tight buff-colored trousers tucked into knee-high, polished boots, and the small military-style case attached to his belt, he had a commanding way about him and a directness in his green gaze that hinted at either a background as a military officer, or one in the law. Having been a Deputy U.S. Marshal for several years, Rafe recognized the probing look, and knew when he was being assessed.

The dog—a wolfhound, judging by the size and rough coat—bounded forward to do its own assessing, sniffing Rafe from every angle. When he offered no menace, Rafe reached out and rested a hand on the big, rough-coated head. The dog accepted it, gave a quick lick, then flopped in the dirt by Rafe's boot.

"That's Tricks," Hendricks said, walking up. "This is his owner, Angus Wallace, although he says most call him Ash because of his hair. Ash, this here's Rayford Jessup, the man I told you about."

"The wizard with horses." Wallace spoke with a strong

Scottish accent, offering a firm handshake and a broad smile. "You'll be needing magic, so you will, to deal with the lad tearing up the barn."

"Ash is looking to start a horse-breeding ranch up in Colorado," Hendricks explained. "Heard at the fort I had mustangs, so he and the wife came by to see what was available."

Rafe didn't have much admiration for Hendricks's horses. Mostly scrubs. All the decent mustangs had been rounded up years ago, except for a few small herds that roamed back and forth across the border between Texas and Mexico. If the Scotsman was thinking to build a stable with these pickings, he wasn't as knowledgeable about horses as Rafe had surmised.

Hendricks flinched when he heard a guttural whinny followed by a series of loud thuds and men yelling. "Well, come along," he said, waving them toward the barn. "Best see if there's anything you can do."

As they walked, Hendricks explained that two sage rats had brought in the mustang several days ago. "Nice-looking stud horse. Or was. Animal's tore up good and mad at the world. We barely got him locked in the stall before all hell broke loose. For two days, he kicked and screamed and snapped at anyone who dared open the stall door to throw him food. Wouldn't eat or drink. Still won't eat. Quieted down some yesterday, so I figured we'd try again." He gave a snort of disgust. "You can hear how well that's going."

When they moved out of the glare of the midday sun and into the barn, the air cooled and grew thick with the odors of hay and sweet feed and manure. Comforting, familiar smells that reminded Rafe of his early years on the farm in Missouri. When his eyes adjusted to the gloom, he saw two men standing well back from a stall at the other end of the open center aisle. The stall had a divided door, but as they approached, Rafe could see splintered wood in the bottom half, and blood smears on the upper half where the door hung askew on a broken hinge.

Another shriek, more thuds rattling the timbers and sending puffs of hay dust sifting down through the gaps in the planked loft floor overhead.

"Don't get too close," Hendricks warned. "He's already taken a bite out of one of my men. *Vamoose*," he said to the two Mexican watchers. "See if any more new foals dropped today."

As the ranch workers left, Rafe stepped up to the broken door. Staying out of kicking or biting range, he peered into the darkened stall.

Crazed eyes stared back.

The animal was a mess. Blood on his mouth where he had gotten splinters from biting chunks out of the door. Scraped knees, hind legs skinned, pasterns red with blood. It was a wonder the horse hadn't shattered a hoof kicking the walls. Having seen enough, Rafe stepped back, almost bumping into Wallace, who had moved up beside him.

"Puir beast," the Scot muttered, pulling the curious hound away from the bloody stall door. "I dinna think he'll last much longer."

Rafe didn't, either. "What are your plans for him?" he asked, turning to Hendricks.

"Figure to breed him to my mares. Or sell him, if I can get a good price. But I can't do either unless he's at least broke to halter. That's why I sent for you." He met Rafe's frown with a shrug. "Heard you could break a green colt without raising a hand. Thought maybe you could settle this one."

Rafe doubted it. The mustang was too mature, too accustomed to running wild to ever be biddable. As for breeding, neither his conformation nor his attitude would make him a decent stud. Some horses were best left alone. This was one of them. Reaching into his vest pocket, he fingered the few half-eagles he'd brought with him. "How much do you want for him?"

Hendricks named a price that was more than double what the mustang was worth. Even if the animal survived being broken, Rafe doubted he would attract many buyers.

"I'll pay you half that," Wallace cut in.

Rafe looked at him in surprise, wondering if the man knew he was offering top dollar for a poor animal. He had thought the Scotsman had horse savvy, but apparently he didn't. Frowning, he stepped back as the two men negotiated.

A wasted trip. He had hoped to pick up enough money to head north, maybe sign on with one of the big ranches along the Chisholm Trail, or find work at the stockyards in Abilene, Kansas. Then once he had enough set by, he'd look for a patch of land in Wyoming Territory where he could plant his stake and start over. Now that he was recovered and strong enough to do hard labor again, he was anxious to put Texas and all the bad memories behind him.

"You'll stay for supper?" Hendricks asked Rafe as he walked past toward the front doors, several eagles and half-eagles clinking in his palm.

Rafe shook his head. "Thanks anyway."

"Tell my wife we'll be leaving, too," the Scotsman called after him. "I'll be in directly to help her pack her equipment."

Seeing Rafe's curious look, he grinned proudly. "That's her wee wagon by the house. I drive her around in it so she can take her pictures. A.M. Wallace. She's a famous photographer. You've heard of her, no doubt."

Rafe hadn't, but rather than admit it, he asked Wallace what he intended to do with the mustang. "He won't go easy."

"Aye. He's a wild one, so he is." As he spoke, the Scotsman led the wolfhound inside an empty stall, locked the door, then returned to the stallion's. Watching the horse warily, he reached for the slide bar on the battered stall door. "Mind your feet, Jessup," he warned in a calm voice. "He'll come out fast."

"You're turning him loose?"

"He's too proud to bend, and I'll no' break a horse I dinna need. He'll find his way home. Stand clear."

Rafe stepped out of the horse's pathway to escape.

Wallace slid the bolt, eased open the top and bottom doors, then stood against the wall and waited.

At first, nothing. Then a snort.

Then the mustang burst out of the stall at a dead run, kicking up straw and dirt clods as he raced toward the light at the open end of the barn. A moment later, he was tearing through the brush, tail up, head raised in a triumphant whinny.

Free. Unencumbered. As he was meant to be.

It was a moving sight. One that made Rafe want to race along with him, just to feel the wind in his face and see what was over the next rise. He watched in silent envy until the horse topped the ridge, then turned to Wallace, who stood beside him with his newly freed dog. "You did a good thing, turning him loose."

Those green eyes studied him. "You would have done differently?"

"No."

"I thought not." With a chuckle, the Scotsman threw his

arm across Rafe's shoulders and steered him toward the house. "So, lad. Where now? Back to the family?"

"No family. North, probably."

"As free as the wind, are you?"

Wallace made it sound exciting and purposeful, rather than the aimless flight of a man trying to outrun a past too painful to face. "Mostly looking for work."

"If 'tis work you seek, I can offer it. As Hendricks said, I'm putting together a herd."

"Of mustangs?"

"Thoroughbreds."

Rafe stopped so abruptly the Scotsman's arm slid off his shoulder. "In Colorado?" Thoroughbreds were magnificent animals. He'd seen less than a handful of them this side of the Mississippi.

"Aye. In a wee mountain town called Heartbreak Creek. But first, I need a wrangler to go with me to get them."

"Go where?"

"To God's own heaven." A rumble of laughter and a flash of pure delight in those moss-colored eyes. "To Northbridge, in the Highlands of Scotland."

"Scotland? The country?"

"Is there any other? We'll start in England. I've already contacted several stables there. But first, we'll go to Heartbreak Creek so you can see the stable I'm building. Then we head east, leaving out of New York in four months. If you care to learn more, you can ride along with me and the countess as we head home."

He must have seen Rafe's surprise. "Oh, I forgot to tell you. I carry a Scottish title. Earl of Kirkwell. The lass is my countess. We avoid the titles when in America, but since we'll be going to Britain . . ." He shrugged, a crafty grin showing a wealth of white teeth. "I ken it's a bother. But it gets me free drinks, so I dinna complain. And I can play my pipes at ceremonial events."

"What am I supposed to call you?" Rafe wouldn't "my lord" any man.

"In America, Ash. My wife will tell you to call her Maddie—she hates pretense. In public, just Kirkwell for me, and Lady Kirkwell for her." That assessing look again. "So, are ye coming with me, lad? I'll pay ye well."

Steady work, steady pay, and thoroughbreds. How could he not? "Seems you've got yourself a wrangler."

SEPTEMBER 1871, MANHATTAN

What the Scot didn't tell Rafe was that in addition to his wife— a nice lady that Rafe liked right off—accompanying them to England would be the wolfhound, a foul-tempered manservant named Pringle, who had as much contempt for his employer as his employer had for him, and a Cheyenne Dog Soldier named Thomas Redstone. Rafe had met them all during his time in Heartbreak Creek when he had worked with several of the local men to track down a murderer terrorizing the town.

The Indian had been a late addition to their traveling group. Initially, he was only to take the train as far as Indiana, where he planned to stop off to see a woman named Prudence Lincoln. But something happened between the two of them, and without explanation, he had reboarded the train just as they were leaving and continued on with them to New York.

Generally, Rafe didn't have a problem with Indians, especially ones who didn't drink or steal. But he did have a problem nursemaiding one. Upon arrival in New York, the Scot had asked Rafe to keep an eye on the Cheyenne until their steamer sailed . . . a more difficult task than Rafe had anticipated, since the redskin had a tiresome habit of wandering off whenever the mood struck him.

One-quarter white and three-quarters savage, Redstone had a dry sense of humor and a smile that women seemed to admire. And he had presence. Perhaps it was the utter confidence in the way he spoke and moved and looked at the world. Heads would always turn when he came into a room because, without saying a word, he dominated it. Like Ash and the other men Rafe had met in Heartbreak Creek, the Cheyenne was a strong, resourceful, intelligent man. But with Thomas, there was something more. An unknown element. One never quite knew what he would do if pushed too far.

Definitely a law unto himself. And even after Thomas ordered a barber in New York to cut off his topknot so he would look more white, anyone who looked into those dark eyes knew

Thomas Redstone was a man to reckon with. Rafe was curious to see how folks in England and Scotland would deal with the Dog Soldier. Or how Thomas would deal with them.

He would find out soon enough, since he was sharing a room with the fellow on the voyage to Liverpool. And in a first-class stateroom next to the Kirkwells, no less. That way, Ash had explained when he'd given them their room assignment, it would be more convenient for Rafe to keep an eye on the Cheyenne, since "we canna let the savage wander around by himself in steerage."

A convenience that came with a high price: being in first class meant he and Thomas were required to wear fancy clothes to dinner. Ash had them sewn by his own tailor in New York—which was another nursemaiding nightmare, trying to convince the Indian to let the terrified tailor fit him.

But finally, here they were. Stepping past his trunk that the steward had delivered to their stateroom earlier, Rafe studied the luxurious accommodations. Two tidy beds, a private lavatory with a tub that boasted hot and cold running water, an electric bell to summon the steward, bureaus, a built-in closet with a mirror, and a promenade deck right outside their window.

Impressive.

He had read the brochure that had come with the tickets, and knew that at only six months old, the *Oceanic* was the latest design in oceangoing steamships. In addition to the stateroom amenities and promenade deck, it also carried four masts for auxiliary sails, twelve boilers, a four-cylinder compound engine, and had an iron hull. They were traveling in style.

Thomas was less impressed. "Is that the only window?"

"Better than below deck in steerage with Pringle and the other single men. They don't have any windows." Opening the trunk, Rafe began transferring clothing and books to the bureau built into the wall beside his bed.

Thomas peered through the window at the chairs lined up along the open deck. "I will sleep out there."

"Not allowed." As he unpacked, Rafe watched the Cheyenne pace the small cabin. He knew it was difficult for the Indian to give up the freedom he was accustomed to, and could only guess at how difficult it must be to straddle two cultures. But Thomas had chosen to join the white world—which shouldn't be too difficult with his greater height, slightly paler skin, and more refined features than most full-blooded Cheyenne—and Rafe was determined to make the transition as painless as possible, as much for himself as for Thomas. He didn't want to listen to him pace all night. "I thought you wanted to act white."

Thomas turned to look at him.

"I'm assuming you figure that will make you more acceptable to Prudence Lincoln."

That shutter dropped over the swarthy face. "We will not speak of her."

"All right, we won't. But being white means sleeping indoors, and wearing proper clothes, and following the rules. Can you do that?"

Muttering in Cheyenne, Thomas slouched onto the bed against the far wall.

Ignoring the glare in those dark eyes, Rafe resumed unpacking. He respected Thomas. Liked the man's steadfast loyalty and assured manner. But he had a feeling this whole "white" thing was destined to failure. What would happen to Thomas then?

A loud blast from the ship's foghorn and an increase in pitch and yawl indicated they had cleared the shelter of the harbor and were heading into open seas. The movement beneath his feet felt odd to Rafe, but not troublesome. He wondered how Ash was handling it. The Scotsman's earlier crossing, when he'd come to America seeking his runaway wife, had been difficult, coming so soon after the explosion that had ended his military career and left him plagued with dizzy spells. Hopefully the tin of ginger and raspberry tea that the doctor in Heartbreak Creek had mixed for him would make this crossing easier.

He glanced at Thomas. "Does the movement bother you?"

Thomas gave him a puzzled look.

"Never mind."

After he emptied the trunk, Rafe set it in the closet, then stretched out on his bed with one of the books he'd brought—*Rob Roy*, a historical adventure novel by Sir Walter Scott. It was difficult to read because a lot of the dialogue was in Scottish dialect, and he frequently had to flip to the glossary in back to get the meaning of the words. But since he would be visiting Scotland, he thought it might be interesting to get a feel for the people.

"You brought many books," Thomas said after a while.

Rafe nodded absently. Then an idea came to him and he lowered the book. "Can you read, Thomas?" Maybe if the Cheyenne had something to occupy his mind, he wouldn't be so restless during the time they would be stuck at sea.

There was a long pause before the Indian answered. "When Black Kettle was my chief, white missionaries came to our village with a book about your Christian god. They offered to teach us to read it. I tried. But I was young, and thought the lessons were boring, so I stopped going.

"Then later, the bluecoats came with papers they called 'treaties.' They said the papers would keep the People safe. We soon learned that the words written there were false. The killing has not stopped, and with every passing season, the number of Cheyenne grows less. Then Prudence Lincoln came."

He looked toward the window, sadness pulling down the lines of his face. "When I saw how important books were to her, I tried to learn again. I was a much better student with her as my teacher." He shrugged and faced Rafe again. "But none of her books spoke of the People. So I have not read since she left."

"But you did learn your letters?" Rafe persisted.

"And numbers. But because I have no interest in such things, it is hard."

Rafe rose from the bed and went to the bureau. After studying the titles, he pulled one from the stack—*The Last of the Mohicans*, by James Fenimore Cooper. "You might like this one." He handed the book to Thomas. "It's about an Indian of the Mohican tribe and a white scout who fought together against the French many years ago."

"Did they win?"

"Read it and see."

Grudgingly, Thomas took the book.

Twenty minutes before the dinner hour, a knock sounded on their door. Rafe opened it to find Lord and Lady Kirkwell standing in the hall.

They were both finely attired. The countess wore a purple ruffled gown with narrow shoulder sleeves, and a low, square neckline that Rafe worked hard not to admire. The earl was dressed in similar fashion to Rafe and Thomas—black trousers with an open waistcoat, a winged collared dress shirt, and a white neckerchief, which Ash called a cravat.

"You look magnificent," Lady Kirkwell gushed, clasping her gloved hands in delight. "Don't they look handsome, Ash?"

"Thomas, why are you no' wearing shoes?"

The Cheyenne held up the knife he usually wore in a sheath laced to the outside of his tall leather moccasin. "I do not know where to put this."

"In the bluidy bureau. We're going to dinner. No' a buffalo hunt."

"Let me help you with that tie," the countess offered, crossing to Thomas before mayhem erupted.

While she retied the neckerchief the Cheyenne had mangled, the earl said to Rafe, "We'll be dining at the captain's table tonight. A British coal merchant named Horatio Cathcart, and his daughter, Miss Josephine Cathcart, will be there. I met him years ago when I was with the Hussars and we needed remounts. Back then, he had an excellent stable of thoroughbreds. But he was also quite a gambler, so I dinna ken if that holds true today. As I recall, he bought the horses for his daughter, who was reputed to be a fine rider. See if you can find out from her the condition of the Cathcart stable, while I talk with her father. We'll compare notes later."

Rafe frowned. "You want me to talk to her."

"Aye."

"But I'm not a talker."

"Bollocks. You talk to my wife well enough."

"That's different. She has a sweet spot for me."

Ash ignored that. "Ask her a few questions, then let her do the talking. That's what women like best."

Rafe grinned, just to goad him. "Not with me. You must be doing something wrong."

Ash punched his shoulder then feigned innocence when his wife glared at him. "Just behave," he muttered. "And mind that the heathen doesna stab or choke anyone. March."

With a sigh, Rafe fell in behind Thomas as the four of them left the cabin.

First a fancy suit of clothes, now a fancy dinner and stilted conversation with the high and mighty. It promised to be a long, awkward evening. His collar already felt too tight and his hands were sweating.

*Maybe she'll be plain and a giggler.* With coal black hair

instead of sun-streaked brown, and a cross-eyed squint rather than eyes the color of dark clover honey. Maybe he wouldn't think of Miranda once all night.

He was wrong.

On all counts.

# Two

Head high, her gait uneven as she battled the rolling motion of the ship, Josephine Cathcart descended with her father down the broad staircase to the *Oceanic* dining room. Her gloved palm left a damp smear on the brass handrail, her knees felt wobbly, and aversion burned like acid in her stomach.

It was not to be borne. Being put on display once again. The impoverished Englishwoman, only slightly used but attractive enough to preside over any wealthy man's table, and available to the highest bidder.

It was the vilest of clichés.

Father's grip on her arm tightened, his blunt fingers digging into the flesh above her elbow. "Smile." A hint of his thick Cumberland coal miner's accent shadowed the admonition as he dipped his head and added, "Chin up, love. It's only business. Nothing more."

Josephine clung to the railing and struggled to even her breathing.

The whole trip to America had been a waste. In addition to learning that the auger was unsuitable for mining in Cumberland, it seemed Father's reputation for pushing questionable ventures had preceded him. Not that they were treated poorly—the American reputation for hospitality was well founded. But there were no new capital investments, and no offers of marriage. Nothing had changed, other than the loss of the substantial funds spent on this unsuccessful trip. Now, with only a few days left to parade his daughter past wealthy travelers and make new business connections in the gentlemen's smoking lounge, Father was making the most of the opportunity.

There was little chance of success as far as she was concerned. Rich Americans did not wed impoverished, untitled Englishwomen any more than sons of impoverished barons married coal miners' naive daughters, no matter how much they professed to love them. She had learned that the hard way. But Father still couldn't seem to understand that here on the surface, far above the black coal that had made him rich, an entirely new set of rules for survival applied.

"Two men are joining us tonight," he said. "I want you to pay special attention to them."

Josephine's stomach twisted. Was her father now her procurer?

"I've arranged for them to be seated near you," he went on, his whisky-laced breath hot in her ear. "A Mr. Calhoun, who is unmarried and considered quite a catch. Something to do with lumber. And another man you met when you were seventeen, although you may not remember him. A Scot named Angus Wallace. He was with the Hussars then and came to look at our horses."

She had been so in love with William at the time, she had scarcely been aware of anyone else. But she did vaguely recall a tall man with dark hair and a strong Scots brogue. "What do you hope to achieve, Father?" she murmured. "I read he's married now. What could he possibly want from us?"

"Same as before. Horses."

Josephine stumbled. If she hadn't had the handrail on one side, and her father on the other, she might have tumbled headlong down the stairs. "You're selling our horses?"

"Keep your voice down," he growled through a strained smile.

Her mind reeled. *The horses* . . . "Surely not Pembroke's Pride, too?"

"Since you've failed to snare a rich husband, what choice do I have?"

He had always had choices. He had simply made the wrong ones.

*Pems. Dear heaven.* The stallion and Jamie were the greatest joys in her life. "But he's still recovering from his injury. He's not ready."

"He looks sound enough. That's all that matters. Now you'll

be nice, daughter," he warned as they reached the landing. "He's an earl now, and wealthy. You'll paint him a fine picture so he'll buy our horses at a dear price. It's either that, or Huddleston, or putting on a grand smile for Mr. Calhoun."

Josephine wanted to scream at him. *I'm not a whore! I never was, nor will I be one for you!* Instead, she struggled to keep her voice bland, knowing a show of temper would only make him more truculent.

"Father, please—"

"We'll speak of it no more, girl. Smile. Good evening, Captain," he said in a jovial voice to the uniformed man approaching them. "Hope we're not late."

"Not at all, Mr. Cathcart. Miss Cathcart. Welcome."

Numbly, Josephine nodded to the ship's captain and the other diners staring back at her over the sumptuous table. She saw an empty place no doubt saved for her. On one side, rising at her approach, was a well-favored man with deep brown eyes and a knowing smile that sent prickles of awareness up her spine. On the other stood a tall, stern-faced man with eyes as expressionless as polished blue steel. Across the table, standing beside another empty chair, was a green-eyed man who looked vaguely familiar, except now he had gray hair and a beautiful woman at his side, who greeted Josephine with a bright welcoming smile.

She felt like vomiting.

She would have drawn Rafe's eye in any case. He might have been celibate throughout his long recovery, but he wasn't dead, and he enjoyed looking at attractive women.

But it wasn't her fine features, or the richness of her deep brown hair, or the two bright spots of color on her otherwise ashen face that caught his attention. It wasn't even her surprising height.

It was her eyes—one brown, the other half-brown and half-blue, as if in infancy they had started to change, then had stopped partway through—and the emotion he saw reflected there.

Memories sent his mind spiraling.

He had seen that look before—in startled babies, trapped animals, in a doe bleeding on the ground, watching the hunter approach. And a year ago, in that instant before she turned to flee, he had seen it in Miranda's honey-colored eyes.

Utter panic.

He stood frozen until Ash's cough broke the hold of the past. Clumsily, he nodded in welcome as the newcomers were introduced. Seeing the woman come around to the open seat beside his, he reached down to pull out her chair, but saw that the fellow seated on her left had beaten him to it. He pasted on a smile to cover his confusion.

She didn't even look at him, but sank stiffly into the chair, her face so lacking in animation, it seemed carved from stone.

While introductions continued around the table, Rafe struggled to corral his scattered thoughts. It was disconcerting that after he'd blocked that memory for almost a year, a chance expression on another woman's face should send it bursting into his mind. He looked around, wondering if anyone had noticed his discomfiture, and saw Thomas, seated diagonally at the other end of the table, watching him.

As usual, the Cheyenne's face revealed nothing of his thoughts, and folding his arms across his broad chest he resumed staring straight ahead, obviously having no interest in the goings-on around him.

"Excuse me," a soft voice in a British accent murmured.

Rafe turned to see Miss Cathcart looking past him at Thomas. "Is that man an American Indian?"

Rafe was glad to see that the frantic look was gone from her eyes, although her expression of weary defeat wasn't much of an improvement. "Yes. He's a Cheyenne Dog Soldier. Or was."

"Is he dangerous?"

Rafe wasn't certain how to answer. In Heartbreak Creek, he had heard rumors about the leather pouch Thomas had once worn beneath his war shirt that had purportedly contained the blunted bullet that had killed his wife and son. The Cheyenne had vowed to return it to the trapper who had fired it . . . by shoving the piece of metal into the man's beating heart.

Vengeance. Rafe was familiar with it. Revenge was something he'd seen often as a U.S. Marshal. No one knew if Thomas had carried out that threat, but one day the pouch was gone. When questioned about it, he had simply shrugged.

"He can be," Rafe finally said.

He was saved from further discussion by the arrival of their first course. Happy to eat rather than attempt conversation,

Rafe picked up his fork. Then noting that none of the other diners had begun eating, he set it back down.

"He's traveling to Scotland with you and Lord and Lady Kirkwell?" Miss Cathcart asked.

"Yes." Rafe watched her remove her gloves, one finger at a time, and saw that despite the slight tremble, there was surprising strength in her hands. Then he remembered what Ash had said about her interest in horses. Realizing this was his chance to learn more about the Cathcart stable, he said, "I believe we'll be visiting you and your father in Penrith on our way."

"So I hear." Picking up her fork, she stabbed with unnecessary vigor at a shrimp curled on a bed of greens. "Although I doubt you have as much interest in visiting us as in assessing the quality of our stable."

Hearing the rebuke in her tone, Rafe dropped the subject.

The meal progressed through the early courses. In no mood for further rebukes, Rafe kept his head down, half listening to Ash's discussion with Mr. Cathcart about the thoroughbred's ability to adapt to rough terrain, and wondering when the woman beside him would finish chatting with the man on her left, so he could start a conversation with her.

Idle chitchat wasn't his strong point. And after spending most of the last year inside his own head, he had lost the knack for it. It wasn't that he was shy—he was simply more of an observer than a talker. Which was probably why he was good with animals. He took the time to study them, learn what they feared and liked and disliked. If he was patient and waited long enough, they would eventually show him what they wanted and needed, too. Sometimes, all it took was a touch.

Same with women. Except once a comfortable level of understanding was reached, they wanted to talk about it. Endlessly. Complicating a simple thing by beating it to death with words.

He figured the woman beside him would be more complicated than most. He sensed she was angry. And afraid. And maybe if he waited long enough, she would tell him why, then he'd know what to do. Probably offer advice on the cut of her dress or some other such nonsense. In his experience, pretty women done up as fine as Miss Cathcart was worried more about clothes and doodads and gossip than anything substantial.

It wasn't until the lull before the meat courses arrived that Miss Cathcart finally turned to speak to him. "What are your plans for them?"

Rafe looked at her. And couldn't look away. Those astonishing eyes trapped him, pulled him in. Made him forget what she'd asked him.

"Is something wrong?" she asked, breaking the awkward silence.

"Your eyes are different colors." *Hell.* Had he actually said that aloud?

"Indeed?" Without taking her gaze from his, she slid a dainty forkful of something green into her mouth.

Did all women's lips do that when they chewed? Purse, relax, then purse again, as if contemplating—no, *preparing* for—a kiss? How had he never noticed that before?

She swallowed, further scattering his thoughts. "I never noticed."

Realizing his blunder, he tried to cover it. "I saw a horse once with different-colored eyes." *Worse.* Wiping his sweating palms on the napkin draped over his thigh, he cleared his throat. "He was very smart."

"Ah. Well." She tilted her head slightly, as if to allow the eye with the blue splash to study him better. "That makes all the difference."

Wisely, he kept his mouth shut.

She didn't. "I've never before been compared to a horse." One corner of her mobile mouth lifted into a comma of a smile. "I rather like it."

Relieved—and resolved never to speak again—Rafe picked up his fork.

"So what are your plans for the horses?" she pressed.

Realizing the cursed conversation would continue, he put down his fork again. "Lord Kirkwell is building a thoroughbred stable in Colorado Territory."

"For what purpose? Racing?" Anger vibrated in her voice.

"Not to my knowledge."

"Oh?" A brittle smile. "That is some comfort, I suppose."

"You don't approve of horse racing?"

"I don't mind a good run." She frowned down into the round, unblinking eye of the baked trout the server set before her. "But I will never approve of any sport that routinely causes injury, or even death, to horses."

"Nor would I."

"Then you must be the exception." With a look of distaste, she poked at the fish with her fork as if to assure herself it was dead. "I have yet to meet a man who isn't a steeplechase enthusiast, regardless of the toll it takes on the fine animals forced to participate."

Rafe waited for the server to set his plate in front of him before he spoke. "I've never seen a steeplechase race. But if it's as dangerous for the horses as you say, then I doubt I would ever have a liking for it." Swiveling toward her, he stuck out his right hand. "Rayford Jessup. The exception. Pleased to make your acquaintance, Miss Cathcart."

She stared at his hand. Dark brown brows furrowing into a frown, she lifted her gaze until those striking eyes met his. Rafe sensed it was the first time she had looked directly at him, rather than through him. He wondered what she saw.

But before he could find out, the man on her left recaptured her attention, leaving Rafe to continue his meal in blessed silence.

With a deep sigh, Ash settled into the leather armchair across from Rafe's in the gentlemen's smoking lounge. "Well?"

Rafe eyed the Scotsman's glass. "Shouldn't you be drinking your tea instead of whisky?" The earl traveled with his own brew—Northbridge Scotch Whisky, a rare and potent blend that could set a man on his heels in no time.

"There's tea in here. No' enough to ruin the flavor, of course, but 'tis there. So what did you learn from Miss Cathcart?"

Rafe sipped from his own glass, pausing to let the alcohol lay a warm trail down his throat. "She hates steeplechase races, and she doesn't like fish served with the head still on."

"That's it?"

Rafe thought for a moment. "One of her eyes is both brown and blue, and she's got a nice smile. Strong hands, too."

Ash stared at him.

"She did wonder if Thomas was dangerous, which I thought was pretty astute. And she's angry about selling the horses."

"Bluidy hell."

"I told you I wasn't much of a talker."

Laughing, Ash waved the comment aside. "The horses are hers, no' Cathcart's. If she's angry, he must be selling them off without her blessing, which might mean he's desperate enough for money to accept a reasonable offer. You did well, lad."

Then why did he have a vague feeling that he'd betrayed a confidence?

"Did she say aught about their stallion, Pembroke's Pride?"

Rafe shook his head.

"I heard he'd been injured. If he's still usable, I'd like to have him. He was only a colt when I was through Penrith before, but he showed great promise." They sat in silence for a time, then Ash looked around. "Where's the savage?"

"Reading."

"Thomas? Reading? Isna that carrying this white thing a bit far?"

Rafe knew about the Scotsman's difficulty with reading and writing, and the "affliction" that scrambled the letters on the page into gibberish. He could sense the frustration it must cause a man as intelligent as Wallace. One of Rafe's duties on this trip was to look over any sales contracts or written materials before the earl signed his name. A mark of trust from a man he admired. It made up for a lot of the self-doubt Rafe has suffered over the last year.

The room filled as late diners wandered in. Gradually, companionable silence gave way to the clink of glasses and low male voices. Cigar smoke rose to collect against the ornate plaster ceiling.

"Why isn't she married?" Rafe asked after a while.

"Who?"

"Miss Cathcart." Seeing the grin spread across the Scot's face made Rafe regret he'd asked.

"Have an eye for her, do you, lad?"

Rafe gave him a warning look.

Ash laughed. "Aye, and well you should. She's an attractive lady. I dinna ken why she never married. When I was in Penrith—must be eight or so years ago now—I think she was maybe seventeen at the time—I heard whispers about her and some weak-chinned Englishman. Her father was in a fine state about it."

"Yet they never married."

"She's a commoner's daughter. He was a baron's son."

"That matters?"

"Aye. In Britain, it does. But I'll admit after spending near two years away from such distinctions, I see little sense in it now."

"That's why you don't use your title in America?"

"That, and I dinna like the reminder." Ash stared into his drink. "I wasna born to it, and I never aspired to it, nor does it sit well that every man in my family had to die for me to become the Earl of Kirkwell. I'd happily trade the title and all that goes with it to have my brothers back, so I would."

Rafe nodded in understanding. He knew the Scot felt caught between the life he was building in America and his duties back in Scotland, and he respected the man for trying to earn his way by his own efforts, rather than the circumstances of his birth. Rafe was glad he didn't suffer the weight of such responsibility. Having learned the hard way that with connections come obligations, he preferred the solitary life instead.

"My lord," a nasal voice cut in.

Rafe looked up to see Pringle standing stiffly beside Ash's chair.

Pointedly ignoring the smirking old man who had been foisted on him by Mrs. Throckmorton, the cantankerous guardian of the wife of one of the wealthiest and most influential men in Heartbreak Creek, Ash pulled a silver flask from his pocket, poured into his glass, recapped, and returned the flask to his jacket. "What is it, Pringle?" he finally asked with a deep sigh.

"If I might be so bold to interrupt your evening debauch, your lordship, will you need me to help prepare you for bed?"

Ash glared at him. "Dinna even try, ye fumble-handed deviant. I've dressed myself since I was a bairn, and I'll do so until I die. Go. Return to whatever it is ye do that doesna include me. Dismissed."

Top lip curled in disapproval, Pringle gave a smirking bow. "Of course, sir. Thank you, your lordship. Should you have need of me, I shall be in my small, cramped cubby belowdecks, scraping manure off your boots."

Ash rounded on him with a snarl. "I was forced to bring you to Scotland, you simpering sod, but that doesna mean ye'll arrive safely. Do ye ken?"

Pringle's nostrils flared. His faded blue eyes narrowed mutinously below his bushy white brows. "I do indeed *ken*. Your lordship."

"Then if you must approach me, you will do so with proper respect or I'll have Thomas give you instruction. Do ye *ken* that?"

His terror of the Cheyenne evident, Pringle looked around, eyes wide. When he saw the Indian wasn't present, he returned to his belligerent self. "Yes, your lordship." Another smirking bow. He started to turn, then hesitated. "Oh," he added, as if only then remembering. "Lady Kirkwell requests your attendance. Apparently dinner didn't agree with her."

Ash's glass hit the side table so hard liquid spattered on the polished wood. "She's been ill?"

"Several times, I believe. And on some of your belongings, it seems." Pringle could barely hide his delight at imparting such news.

"Why dinna you tell me?" Not waiting for an answer, Ash rose.

"Shall I bring your libation, milord?" But the earl was already out the door. Pringle looked longingly at the glass.

"Go ahead," Rafe said. "No use letting good liquor go to waste."

"Thank you, sir, but that would be improper."

"Suit yourself."

"But since you insist."

Before Rafe could point out that he hadn't insisted on anything, the old man grabbed the glass, downed the contents in a single gulp, then erupted in a coughing fit. "Judas," he choked out once he caught his breath. "What was that?"

"Ginger and raspberry tea," Rafe guessed. "Laced with Northbridge Scotch Whisky." Tossing back the last of his own drink, he rose, thinking he ought to go check on Thomas and make sure he wasn't sending smoke signals off the deck. Then after changing out of his fancy clothes, he might take a stroll along the deck. Perhaps he'd come across Miss Cathcart and they could resume the conversation he hadn't been able to pursue over dinner.

He liked the way she talked. And that teasing tone when she chided him. Her accent was different from that of the countess. Softer. Yet with an edge to it that let him know she wouldn't be easy to fool or intimidate. He admired that.

And those beautiful mismatched eyes.

# Three

An interesting pair, Josephine thought, watching from the shadows of her wooden chaise as the two men, deep in conversation, strolled slowly along the railing of the promenade deck.

Mr. Jessup was taller than his companion, and blond to his Indian friend's shoulder-length black hair. Both were stern-faced men with weathered skin and a way of moving that drew the eye. Relaxed. Athletic. Confident. Neither seemed bothered by the constant pitch and yawl of the ship. Everything about them, from the way they walked, to the set of their shoulders, to the intensity with which they viewed their surroundings, proclaimed them men of experience, not all of which had come easily.

They had changed clothes since she'd last seen them at dinner, and seemed more comfortable in the less formal attire.

Mr. Jessup wore a shirt with no collar, dark trousers, and a long unbuttoned canvas coat similar to those worn by coachmen, but which in America was called a duster. Mr. Redstone was dressed in like fashion except in place of the coat, he wore a vest, and the long, fringed leather footwear favored by the few Indians she had seen during her brief trip from Boston to New York. She could easily imagine either man transported into one of the Western paintings she frequently saw in the London art gallery windows.

The two men stopped, spoke for a moment, then Mr. Redstone

went back inside. Mr. Jessup stayed. Resting his elbows on the railing, he looked out over the rolling sea, his profile highlighted by a lantern affixed to a nearby support post.

She studied him, taking in the long length of his legs, the strength and slope of his back, the thrust of his jaw as he tipped back his head to study the night sky.

There was something intimate about watching a man who didn't know you were there . . . especially a man as guarded as Rayford Jessup. What was he thinking to put such a pensive, almost sad, expression on his chiseled face?

He had surprised her at dinner when he'd stuck out his hand and introduced himself. At first, she'd been confused, then had realized he was referring back to her own words. That had surprised her even more. A man who actually listened. She hadn't known such a thing existed. But just as she began to warm up to him, he had suddenly gone silent and had scarcely spoken for the rest of the meal.

Odd, that. Most men of her acquaintance were only too happy to talk about themselves, revealing far more than she cared to know about their hunting or riding prowess, their luck—or lack of it—at the gaming tables, their drinking escapades. Mr. Calhoun certainly had.

But she had learned little from Mr. Jessup.

That had infuriated Father. Which was why he had sent her to search him out after dinner in an attempt to gather more information about the earl's true purpose in coming to Penrith.

Instead, she had come here, to the darkest, most sheltered part of the deck, to enjoy the windy silence, broken only by the rhythmic rumble of the giant steam engine several decks below and the occasional snap of the auxiliary sails overhead.

It was a solitude she rarely experienced at home.

Sensing someone's approach, she turned just as a familiar voice from dinner said, "Lucky me. My quarry sitting alone in the dark."

Mr. Calhoun stopped at the end of her chaise and smiled down at her. In the faint light of the lanterns bolted along the promenade, his large square teeth gleamed like polished piano keys. "Were you waiting for me, Miss Cathcart?"

She repressed a shiver, not sure why the man put her vaguely on edge. He had been polite and attentive over dinner—quite the opposite of the American seated on her right—and was certainly pleasant to look at.

"Actually, I was waiting for a falling star." She nodded toward the endless star-studded vista reaching down to the gently rolling horizon line. "The last stragglers of the Leonid meteor shower."

"I fear you've missed it."

"I fear you're right."

"Could I interest you in a stroll, instead?" He held out his hand.

She hesitated then, remembering Father's admonitions to put on a smile, accepted his offer. As she rose and took his arm, she was aware that Mr. Jessup had turned to watch them, and was relieved when Mr. Calhoun suggested walking in the opposite direction of the tall man standing at the rail.

As they strolled—lurched was more like it—the swells having risen as the wind strengthened—they spoke of nonsensical things, trying not to bump into each other as they made their way around the promenade. There were few other passengers out this late, and she began to worry about being in such a dark, secluded place with a man she scarcely knew.

"I spoke to your father earlier," he said, breaking a long silence. "He says you're quite unattached, which I find both puzzling and encouraging."

She looked levelly at him, as they were both nearly the same height. "Oh?" No telling what Father had said. He was far too blunt sometimes.

Mr. Calhoun's teeth showed in a wide smile. "You're much too beautiful to be alone. A woman as alluring as you should always have a man at her side."

Unsure how to respond to that, she said nothing.

As they came around the corner after a full circuit, she saw that Mr. Jessup was still there, elbows resting on the rail, staring out over the water.

"Are you looking for someone, Josephine?" Mr. Calhoun murmured.

Startled, she drew back when he leaned closer to whisper into her ear, "Someone to chase away the loneliness? Bring a smile to your lovely face? Return passion to your life?"

She froze, too astounded to respond.

Which he seemed to take as encouragement. "I can be that

man, my dear. I'm rich. I can shower you with gifts, show you the world, give you the companionship you seek."

She jerked her hand from his arm. "What exactly did my father tell you?"

He blinked in surprise. "That you were open to an offer."

"Of marriage?"

He laughed. "Lord, no. The last thing I need is a wife."

A ringing began in her ears. She couldn't seem to catch her breath. *A whore.* He thought her a whore. And her father had planted that impression.

His smile faded. He stepped back. "I can see I have offended you. But really, Miss Cathcart. It's no secret that . . . well, your situation is well known. I'm an important man. I have a reputation to consider. I can offer you protection and companionship, but not my name. I'm sure you understand."

A searing pain knifed through her chest. Years of being snubbed, whispered about, treated with disdain and contempt, hardened into a single burning point of fury. Without thought, she lashed out. The sound of her palm striking his cheek was unnaturally loud in the stillness. "How dare you!"

He stumbled back. "What was that for?"

Unable to curb the rage consuming her, she drew her arm back to strike him again.

He caught her wrist in a bruising grip. "What's wrong with you?"

"Let her go," a deep voice ordered.

Through a blur of tears, Josephine saw a tall, imposing figure move up to Mr. Calhoun's shoulder.

"I said let her go. Now."

Calhoun released her arm. Muttering under his breath, he stomped away.

The rush of fury dissipated, leaving her so shaky that when the ship pitched, she almost lost her balance.

A hand gripped her elbow, steadying her. "Are you all right, Miss Cathcart?"

She opened her mouth to answer, but no sound came out.

"Come sit down." He led her to a nearby chaise. She sank onto the cold wooden slats, her nerves in such disarray she feared she might faint. Leaning back, she draped an arm over her burning eyes and struggled to get herself in hand. She rarely cried. And certainly not over some snide remark. But for some reason, this time . . .

How could Father have exposed her to that?

She heard the creak of wood as Mr. Jessup sat on the chaise beside hers. Taking her arm away, she saw that instead of settling back as she had, he sat facing her, leaning forward, his arms folded atop his bent knees. "Feeling better?"

She wasn't sure. Here she sat in the dark with another man she scarcely knew. Yet in Mr. Jessup she sensed no threat. "Yes. Thank you for coming to my aid. It was foolish of me to be out here alone."

"Why were you?"

She took a deep breath and let it go. Fear and tension went with it. But anger at her father remained. "Actually, I was sent to find you."

That seemed to startle him. "Why?"

"My father"—the word tasted bitter on her tongue—"wants me to convince you that our horses are worth the outrageous price he intends to ask for them."

He studied her for a moment, a fall of sun-bleached hair shadowing his eyes so she couldn't read his expression. "Are they?"

"They are to me. But then, I've known most of them since birth. I've walked them when they were colicky, wrapped their sore legs, brushed and bathed them. I've mixed warm mash for them when they were sick, and consoled them when they were weaned. They're like . . . family, I suppose."

"And now you have to sell them."

New tears rose. But rather than let him see them, she looked out to the distant horizon. "Yes."

It was a moment before he spoke again. "The earl will pay a fair price. No more, no less. But if he does buy your horses, Miss Cathcart, no harm will come to them."

She turned her head and looked at him. "You're certain of that?"

"I am. He's a good man. And he appreciates horses. In fact, rather than have a deaf gelding destroyed, he brought him all the way from Ireland to America out of loyalty to an animal that had been injured in his service. If you must part with your horses, they could be in no better care than with Kirkwell."

Emotion clogged her throat. It was a moment before she trusted her voice enough to speak. "Thank you for telling me that."

"Is there anything else you'd like to know?"

She heard the smile in his voice. It made her smile, too. "All I've seen of your country is a few big cities on the Northeastern coast, and the artwork of George Winter, and the fascinating illustrations Karl Bodmer made during his travels into the interior. Are the Western mountains as grand as they say?"

"Grander. Tell me about the horses."

She laughed aloud. Another first: a man who didn't enjoy the sound of his own voice. But because he seemed genuinely interested in what she had to say, and because—other than Jamie—horses were her passion, she did as he requested.

"We have six proven brood mares, descended from the finest thoroughbred lines in England, and three fillies that will be ready over the next few years. This spring we welcomed six new foals, two of them sturdy colts, all sired by a young stallion we have never used before."

"Why didn't you use Pembroke's Pride?"

How had he learned about Pems? She considered ignoring the question, then realized if he was coming to Penrith, he would find out soon enough. "He was injured last year and is still recovering."

"Injured how?"

"In a fall." She quickly added, "But Mercury's bloodlines are every bit as strong. And he's younger, so we may not use Pembroke's Pride again."

To deter further questions on that subject, she rambled on about this year's foals, the health of their dams, the strengths of their sire.

He listened without interruption. In fact, he scarcely even moved, but continued to sit facing her, his big hands loosely clasped between his bent knees. His stillness was a noticeable thing. And slightly unsettling. How long had it been since a man was as attentive to her words as he was to her face or her father's supposed wealth?

Yet his calm quietness reassured her, and despite the unaccustomed novelty of having a man's entire focus on her as if every word she spoke was of utmost importance, she began to lose some of the wariness she normally felt in the company of strangers. Mr. Jessup knew little about her and nothing about Jamie, so she had no fear of another tawdry proposal. Nor did she question his motives since he showed little interest in Father's reputed fortune—or lack of it now. He simply wanted to know about her beloved horses.

So she told him, relishing the chance to sit in the shadows away from prying eyes and enjoy the company of a handsome man she scarcely knew and would probably never speak to alone after this night. It was a gift he was giving her . . . the freedom to just *be*. No games. No hidden purposes. No intent other than to share a common love of horses.

It wasn't until she saw a deck steward turning down the oil lamps that she realized how late it was. "Mercy. I must have rambled on for hours." She sat up.

He immediately rose and held out a hand to assist her.

It was a big hand, rough with calluses, his long fingers engulfing hers. Neither of them wore gloves, and the warmth of his skin against hers felt alien and intimate.

"I'm sorry you have to sell your horses," he said, looking into her eyes, his hand still gripping hers. "But if they come into my care, I promise they'll be treated well."

"Your care? You're the earl's groom?"

A wry smile pulled his lips up on one side. "Wrangler. And I don't mistreat animals."

She saw the steadiness in his dark blue eyes, heard the conviction in his voice, and believed him. "I'm glad."

He gave her fingers a gentle squeeze, then released them. "I've enjoyed talking with you, Miss Cathcart. Perhaps we'll dine together again."

"Perhaps."

But she doubted it. Since this crossing was Father's last chance to catch the attention of possible investors, or snare a husband for her, he would make certain they sat with different diners each night to make the most of the opportunity. And anyway, Mr. Jessup would be coming to Penrith soon. She would have many chances to speak to him there.

The idea lightened her mood.

Which underscored in a pathetic way how lonely her life truly was.

*    *    *

Thomas didn't glance up from his book when Rafe returned to their cabin. Moving quietly so he wouldn't disturb his reading, Rafe hung his coat on a peg in the closet, then flopped down atop his bed along the opposite wall.

Clasping his hands behind his head, he stared at the ceiling, picturing Miss Cathcart's face there, with the salty breeze tugging long tendrils of dark hair loose from the scarf tied around her head, and that shy way she had of looking up at him from beneath the long curve of her lashes. He'd been wrong about her. She wasn't the flighty, high-stepper he had imagined. And she had a temper. He smiled, remembering how she'd struck Calhoun, and wondering what the man had done.

"You talked to her for a long time," Thomas said.

Startled out of his reverie, Rafe looked over at him.

"The woman watching from the shadows."

"You knew she was there?"

Thomas shrugged. "I am Cheyenne."

Hoping to change the subject, Rafe nodded to the book in Thomas's hands. "How's your book?"

"I do not like it. And I do not understand why these white people fight each other over lands that are not theirs."

"Probably for the same reason Indians fight other tribes over hunting grounds that aren't theirs. Greed."

The Cheyenne glared at him.

"Everybody wants more of something, Thomas. Food, land, wealth, women. Greed is what moves the world."

"What is it you want, Rayford Jessup?"

Rafe thought for a moment. "Peace. And a patch of ground with good grass and water."

"In Heartbreak Creek?"

"Maybe."

"Will you fight for it?"

"I'll buy it."

"And who will you buy it from, *ve'ho'e*—white man?"

Seeing from the Indian's expression that this discussion was headed into a dead end, Rafe gave up and held out his hand. "Sorry you don't like the book. Give it back and I'll try to find one more to your liking."

Thomas shook his head. "I want to know who wins." He started to say more when the door opened and Ash walked in.

Rafe could tell by his expression that something was troubling him. Sitting up, he swung his feet to the floor. "What's wrong?"

"My wife. The lass says nothing is amiss, but I can see her food isna sitting well and she sleeps too much. Tricks is faring no better. Puir lad doesna like being cooped up in the hold. It was selfish of me to bring them along."

The Scot paced the length of the narrow room, then back again. "Likely she's upset to be going back. Being English, she has no great love for Scotland." Stopping at the window, he stood, hands clasped behind his back, feet braced to compensate for the sway of the ship. "As soon as we dock, I'll take her to London to see her publisher at the *Illustrated London News*. Perhaps if she sees the progress Chesterfield has made on the bound book he's making of her photographs, she'll come out of her melancholy. If not, I'll take her to a doctor."

He turned, his face grim. "Rafe, go on to Penrith as planned. I'll come as soon as we're finished in London. That will give you a chance to look over Cathcart's stock and decide if any are worth having. Thomas, I want you with me. I must attend other business while in London, and I canna leave the countess with only Tricks and that gowk, Pringle, for protection."

"There will be trouble?" Thomas's eyes brightened in anticipation.

"One never knows. The English are a treacherous lot, so they are."

Rafe frowned. "But aren't Scotland and England part of the same country?"

"No' in any way that matters."

The remainder of the voyage passed slowly for Rafe. Because of the countess's unsettled health, the Wallaces took their meals either in their stateroom or at a small, secluded table at the back of the first-class dining room. Since that left Rafe and Thomas on their own, they usually ate in their cabin, rather than go to the bother of changing into their fancy clothes just to eat dinner.

The one time they did dress up, Rafe saw Miss Cathcart seated at a prominent table with other wealthy travelers. That rigid expression was back on her face, although her eyes did light up for the moment their gazes met across the crowded room. At least, he thought they did. He saw no sign of her accoster, Calhoun.

Restless and bored, Rafe prowled the deck, hoping for another chance meeting with her, but never saw Miss Cathcart on the promenade again. He wasn't sure why he was so intent on seeing her. Perhaps her distress over the horses had touched him more than he'd thought. Or maybe he simply missed the company of a pretty woman. Whatever the reason, it created a restlessness within him that kept him awake long into the night.

On the last day of the crossing, they were all impatiently pacing the deck, desperate to reach solid ground again. Even Pringle braved the fresh air—assigned the task of walking Tricks—and was an amusing sight, being dragged helplessly along as the wolfhound raced along the railing, his nose to the wind.

But the countess showed less anticipation than resignation. And as the pale purple shadows of Ireland and England drew steadily nearer, Rafe noticed she seemed to withdraw into herself more and more. Remembering what Ash had said about her reluctance to return, Rafe hoped that was the cause of her melancholy, and not a return of her earlier illness.

"I explained to Cathcart that you'll be arriving in Penrith alone," Ash said to Rafe as they made another circuit. "And that the countess and I will follow after we conclude our business in London. When I told him you were traveling on horseback, he offered to take your trunk in his carriage. If that's acceptable, have the steward deliver it to their stateroom before we dock."

"Or I could send it with you." Rafe had planned on traveling light. Anything he couldn't do without he could roll in his duster and tie to the saddle.

"You'll be expected to wear your new suit at dinner," the countess reminded him with a look of sympathy.

"And talk," Thomas added with that smirk.

There went his plan to stay at the stable with the other wranglers.

"Come, lad." Ash gave his shoulder a friendly punch. "Will it be so bad dining with the lovely Miss Cathcart?"

"And talking."

*Hell.*

By the time the *Oceanic* docked and the mooring lines were secured, it was late afternoon, yet the port still teemed with sailors, travelers, and bustling stevedores unloading cargo from the many ships lined up at the wharves. Place smelled like a fish dump.

The earl had sent word of their arrival date on a fast mail steamer, asking his solicitor, Colin MacPherson, to meet the ship. Now, as they waited for the gangplank to be lowered, he scanned the faces onshore.

"There he is." The countess pointed to a robust man wearing a dark suit and bushy red muttonchops who stood beside two coaches at the front of the line of waiting carriages. "He hasn't changed at all in the four years I've been gone."

"Colin was at university with me," Ash explained to Rafe and Thomas. "MacPhersons have been the Kirkwell solicitors since my grandfather's time." Dropping his voice so that Pringle wouldn't hear, he added, "He is also one of the few outside of Heartbreak Creek who know of my affliction."

"It's not an affliction," his wife murmured, patting the thick arm she held. "It's a slight difficulty with reading. No more."

"Slight?" Ash grinned down at her. "'Tis like trying to decipher a plate full of wiggling worms."

The countess swallowed weakly.

"Sorry, love. Forget I said that."

As soon as they stepped off the gangplank, MacPherson approached, a big grin splitting his ruddy face. "Welcome home, Lord Kirkwell. Lady Kirkwell."

"I thank you for meeting us, Colin."

After introducing Thomas and Rafe and Pringle, Ash motioned them along as he steered his wife after MacPherson toward the two coaches. Men in fancy green livery were already loading their luggage onto the top of the plainer of the two carriages, while a coachman stood at attention beside the open door of the other—a black-lacquered, two-horse four-wheeler with a crest on the side.

"'Tis good to have ye home, milord," the coachman said, tipping his hat.

"Thank you, John. How go things at Northbridge?"

"Verra well, milord. Your sister and the McKenzie are planning a grand welcome, so they are."

"It may have to wait a few days. Do you mind if Tricks rides up front? He's smelling a bit strong, and the countess is feeling poorly."

"No' at all, milord. I've missed the lad, and the fresh air will do him good. When we stop for the night, I'll give him a good run."

As the coachman helped situate Lady Kirkwell and Tricks, Ash told the solicitor about their altered plans. Resting a hand on Rafe's shoulder, he added, "Since the lad, here, is traveling alone to Penrith, he'll need a horse and map."

"Of course. I'll make arrangements at the inn where we're staying tonight."

Rafe, Thomas, and Pringle moved on to the second coach. Thomas arrived first and insisted on riding topside with the coachman. Rafe would have joined him had there been room. But when he grudgingly took his place inside with the ever-dour Pringle, he consoled himself that he would be on horseback soon, while Thomas would be stuck on a coach for a long while yet.

As they began to move, Rafe looked out the window to see his trunk being lashed atop a carriage that was even more elaborate than the one carrying the Kirkwells. Yet despite Cathcart's show of wealth, men didn't doff their caps and step aside the way they did when the earl walked by. Rafe sensed that sign of respect had more to do with the man than with wealth or status.

Miss Cathcart stood at the carriage door, looking regal and unapproachable in deep blue, her narrow waist set off by the tight-fitting jacket, and a jaunty hat set atop her sleek deep brown hair. Yet the expression she wore wasn't that of a haughty miss leading a pampered life, but rather that of a woman who had suffered and now bore the scars of that hard experience like a coat of armor.

He curbed his curiosity to know why. She had wealth, position, beauty. Probably the greatest calamity she faced was a stain on her glove.

Another reminder to Rafe that he was an outsider in an unfamiliar world—one of privilege, rigid protocol, and a very different set of standards than those back home. A wrangler and battered ex-lawman had no place here, and wouldn't be welcomed into elite circles. He would have to watch his step.

And dress up for dinner.

*Hell.*

# *Four*

*R*ound shafts of sunlight shining through the bullet-pocked door. Voices calling in the street.

With a groan, Rafe leaned up on one elbow to peer over the sill of the shattered window. He couldn't see them, but he heard them. Inching closer.

He slumped back, willed away the spots circling behind his eyes. "Leave," he said to the woman huddled in the corner. "They're coming."

When she didn't move, he waved weakly toward the rear door. "Go, Miranda. Now."

Weeping. Terror in her honey brown eyes. "I didn't expect him to do this, Rafe. How was I to know?"

He didn't want to hear it. "Just go."

A last, lingering look, her eyes wide with fear, then she whirled and dashed through the door.

Boot heels thudding on the boardwalk. One set. Three. Maybe four.

Pressing his free hand over the seeping hole in his chest, he lifted the Colt. Aimed at the doorway. Fought to keep his hand steady.

The door burst open.

With a cry, he rose up, teeth clenched, his hand jerking as he squeezed the trigger again and again and—

The shouts stopped. The smell of blood and spent powder wafted through his mind, then faded. Silence.

Sensing a presence, Rafe twisted to see a man standing over him. He blinked in confusion. Thomas.

"Wh-What are you doing?" Rafe demanded in a wobbly voice, wondering why he was sitting upright in the bed, his hand raised.

"You called out."

"I did? I was . . . I thought . . ." He looked at his empty hand. At his chest. Around the unfamiliar room. No gun, no blood, no bodies twitching on the floor.

He sagged back, his mind in chaos, his heart drumming in his chest. Not Dirtwater, Texas. The inn in Liverpool.

Dreaming. That's all.

"What is wrong?" Thomas asked, stepping closer.

"N-Nothing." He took a deep breath, let it out. "A bad dream. That's all."

"It has happened before."

"It has? Why didn't you wake me?"

"I once suffered such dreams. This will help." He held up a strip of leather from which hung a twig bent in the shape of a hoop. Across the inside of the hoop was a web of fine threads, and attached along the outside were dangling feathers and beads and carved bits of antler.

It looked like something a big cat might have coughed up. "What is it?" Rafe asked, sitting up and swinging his feet to the floor.

"*Ianbla gmunka.* A dream snare." Thomas thrust it into Rafe's hand. "Good dreams move through the holes in the web, down the feathers, and into your sleep. Evil dreams are too big and stay trapped in the threads until the light of the rising sun kills them."

Rafe recognized some of the beads and carvings from Thomas's war shirt. "You made this?"

Thomas shrugged. "Hang it over your bed. It will protect you. And give better rest to those stuck in the room with you."

Seeing the Cheyenne's rare smile eased some of the tension. "Thanks."

A loud knock, then Ash's voice called, "Muster. Twenty minutes."

Thirty minutes later, they were all gathered outside the inn while the earl issued his final instructions. Commands, was more like it. The Scotsman might never again wear the uniform, but he would always be military. "Dismissed," he concluded, waving the others toward the coaches as a groom brought out a saddle horse for Rafe. "And Pringle, for the love of Saint Andrew, quit hovering. Go assist the countess if you lack something to do!"

"Thomas, wait," Rafe called, hurrying to catch the Cheyenne before he climbed into the driver's box of the second coach.

"Ho. Do you miss me already, white man?"

"When Ash takes Maddie to visit her publisher, go with them. Ask him if he has books about American Indians. Especially books dealing with tribal legends."

"What is 'legends'?"

"Stories passed down through the years that explain the beliefs of your people. Those that are shared around the campfire, or used to teach your children. Like the one about the dream snare. You have a lot of stories like that?"

Thomas nodded.

"See if Mr. Chesterfield has a book about them. If he doesn't, ask him if he wants one."

Excitement lit the Cheyenne's dark eyes. "There is such a book?"

"Not yet. I'm hoping he'll ask you to write one for him."

"Me? Write a book?"

"Why not? Just tell the stories as you know them. I'll help you write them down." When the Indian didn't respond, Rafe pressed harder. "You're not afraid to ask him, are you?"

Thomas snorted at the notion.

"And when you go see him," Rafe hurried on, seeing the coachman of the earl's carriage snap the whip over his matched bays, "be sure to look like a Cheyenne warrior."

"I am a Cheyenne warrior."

"Wear your war shirt. Take your axe and knife and anything else you have that marks you as a Dog Soldier. You cut quite a figure in your native clothing."

"I know."

The earl's carriage rolled out of the yard.

"Are you coming or not?" the driver of Thomas's coach called down.

The Indian gave him a glare that took the color from the coachman's face, then he turned back to Rafe. "I will think about what you have said, Rayford Jessup. Sleep well, *hovahe*."

Rafe had heard Thomas use that word in Heartbreak Creek and was pleased to see he'd moved from *ve'ho'e*—white man— to *hovahe*—friend. "Travel safe, Thomas."

Heavy gray clouds and a chill wind followed Rafe through boggy valleys and rocky hills on the three-day ride from Liverpool to the quaint little market town of Kendal. After another dreamless night—thanks to Thomas's snare—and a huge breakfast, he set out on the fourth morning for the small town of Penrith.

His nights might be dreamless, but his daytime thoughts kept circling back to Miss Cathcart. Which surprised him. They had little in common. Divided not only by an ocean, but also by station in life, their differences were vast. Yet her despair over losing her horses had moved him in an unexpected way. Still moved him—even to the extent that as he made his solitary way through the misty English countryside, his mind kept trying to devise ways to lessen that despair.

It was a habit from his marshal days when he'd thought every wrong could be righted and every lost soul could be saved. He had since learned that some things were never meant to be, no matter how strong his feelings were. And a deeper connection to Miss Cathcart was one of them.

His map indicated he was heading into the southern part of the Lake District, reputed to be one of the most beautiful areas of England—although it was hard to see much of it through the thick mist as he left Kendal the next morning. Following the River Kent, he rode past the ruins of old buildings and fallen castles toward the woodlands, mountains, and lakes of southern Cumberland.

Certainly not mountains on the scale of the Rockies, or as overpowering as the peaks and canyons around Heartbreak Creek, but impressive nonetheless. And green. Had the day been clearer, he might have had some inspiring views. Yet even mired in fog, it was interesting country—starkly barren on the rocky ridges, then dropping into tall forests and lush valleys riddled with emerald lakes. Good horse country if the sun ever came out.

Hunched against the soupy drizzle, he followed the waterways past small, neat farms and rolling green pastures bordered by stacked rock fences. Finally, on the afternoon of the fourth day after leaving Liverpool, he rode out of the Lake District and several miles past the town of Penrith to the pillared stone entrance of the Cathcart estate.

The house was a huge limestone monument to lavish spending, stretching five stories high, with a wing reaching out on one side, a portico on the other, and at least a half-dozen gables in the slate roof. A forest of chimneys poked into the low clouds, and there was even a peaked tower on one corner.

No wonder Miss Cathcart was melancholy, having to ramble around in such an oversized place. He guessed she hadn't been the one to design it.

But the stables were as fine as any Rafe had ever seen. Gratified that the animals lived as grandly as their owners, he angled toward the long, low building made of the same gray stone as the house and surrounded by grassy pastures and neatly fenced paddocks.

When he rode up, a barrel-chested man with more hair on his chin than his head came out of the open center aisle. Rafe dismounted and introduced himself, adding that he had come to look over the horses that Cathcart had for sale.

The man gave his name as Liam Hammersmith, head groom. He had an accent similar to Ash's, and a handshake that could crack a handful of Texas pecans. "Best run along, then, lad. They'll be looking for ye up at the house."

Rafe had hoped to bunk in the stable, but apparently that wasn't likely. "Front door or back?"

The groom frowned down at Rafe's mud-spattered boots and soggy duster. "Back would be best, I'm thinking."

Rafe agreed. He was hardly dressed in visiting attire. And certainly not in any condition to present himself to Miss Cathcart. But since all his clean clothes were in the trunk delivered here several days ago, there was no help for it.

"Back door it is then."

"Be sure to tell them who ye are," Hammersmith advised as Rafe untied his saddlebags from the skimpy pancake-sized saddle that had come with the gelding MacPherson had procured for him in Liverpool. "Cook is a scrapper and Shipley—he's the butler—can be summat harsh toward strangers."

Rafe nodded. Slinging his saddlebags over his shoulder, he left his weary horse in Hammersmith's care and trudged toward the imposing gray house perched like a giant Texas blue tick atop the hill.

Hopefully, he hadn't missed supper.

"Who's that?" Father asked, shifting his attention from the paperwork strewn across his desk to the tall window facing the side garden.

Setting her book aside, Josephine rose and went to look out. A man in a long coat was coming up the path from the stables. Even though his face was hidden by the wide brim of the Western-style hat he wore, she recognized the long legs and purposeful stride.

"It's Mr. Jessup," she said, ignoring a sudden flutter in her chest.

"Kirkwell's man? You're sure?"

"Quite." She would know the man anywhere, having thought of him far too often over the last days, anticipating his arrival with both excitement and dread.

Peering around the heavy velvet drape, she watched him walk past the rose beds and side veranda toward the back of the house. Where was he going?

Behind her, papers rustled. Father's desk drawer opened and closed. "Remember what I told you."

Face composed, she faced him. "Refresh my memory." She wanted to hear him say it again—needed the words to fuel her simmering resentment at being used so poorly. Hopefully, if she heard often enough how little he regarded her as anything other than a tool to be used to further his own purposes, this nagging sense of loyalty she still felt for her father would eventually fade.

A hardened heart felt no pain.

"You know what to do, daughter. Distract him. Play up to

him. Tease him a bit. I saw the way he watched you on board ship. Use that interest to win him over to our side, so he will convince the earl to meet our price."

"Shall I play the tart for him, Father? I am, after all, so very good at it."

His big fist slammed on the desktop, startling her. "Watch your mouth, girl! This is your future at stake, too. And Jamie's."

"Of course."

"You'll do as you're told," he went on. "And that's an end to it."

A knock on the door saved her from responding.

With a last glare aimed her way, her father smoothed back his thinning gray hair and shook off his anger like a dog shedding water. "Enter, Shipley."

The butler stepped into the room, his dour face more disapproving than usual. "There is a person at the rear entrance, sir. I tried to turn him away but he refuses to leave without a trunk he said you brought from Liverpool. He was quite adamant about it. And foreign. An American, I believe."

"Jessup." With a nod of satisfaction, Father rose.

"I'll take care of it, Father." Moving toward the door, Josephine smiled sweetly at the scowling butler. "Have one of the upstairs maids freshen the blue bedroom, would you please, Shipley? And send a footman up to prepare a bath. Oh, and be sure to inform Cook that we'll have another guest for dinner."

Shipley gave a ponderous sigh, making evident yet again his disappointment in his lowborn employers. "Yes, Miss Cathcart."

Mr. Jessup was munching on a muffin when Josephine walked into the kitchen. When he saw her, he passed the muffin plate back to Cook with a smile of thanks—which made the kitchen maids titter—dusted his hands, then removed his hat. "Miss Cathcart," he said, gazing down at her with that same unwavering intensity he had shown during their chat on the ship.

"Welcome, Mr. Jessup." She held out her hand.

His grip swallowed hers. Again without the protection of gloves, she felt anew the warmth of his skin, the roughness of calluses across his palm, the crushing strength in the fingers that held hers so gently. A workingman's hands. Well used and capable. Vastly different from those of the pampered gentlemen she knew. It made her feel almost demure, which was absurd considering her height.

"I apologize for the confusion." Pulling free of his grip, she motioned toward the butler hovering in the doorway. "I neglected to inform Shipley that you might arrive early. If you'll come with me, I'll show you to your room."

He followed without speaking. Yet she could sense his presence behind her. The sound of his boot heels against the tiled floor, the rustle of fabric as his coat brushed against his trousers, the faint smell of horses and damp wool.

She wondered if he was looking at her, assessing her figure from behind as they climbed the stairs. The thought unsettled her, drove her to fill the silence.

"Your ride from Liverpool went well, Mr. Jessup?"

"Yes."

"The rain didn't bother you?"

"Not much."

"What are your impressions of the Lake District?"

"It's green."

The absurdity of trying to carry on a conversation with a man who wouldn't talk finally got the better of her. Stopping on the second landing, she turned so abruptly he almost ran into her. "Is it me?"

"What?"

"Or are you this aloof with everyone?"

Confusion gave way to a frown. "I'm not aloof."

She bit back a laugh. "No?"

"I'm just not much of a talker."

"Yet you spoke eloquently enough on board ship."

"That was different." A reluctant tilt at one corner of his wide mouth. Not a full smile that showed teeth, or bunched his cheeks, or crinkled the corners of his dark blue eyes—he'd never given her one of those. But it was affecting, nonetheless, and made her feel she had won something to get even that. "We were talking about horses then."

This time she couldn't hold back a chuckle. They had that in common, at least. "Well, do try to be more talkative at dinner tonight," she said, continuing up the stairs. "Vicar Bohm and his wife, Agnes, will be joining us, and if you don't speak up, she will either regale us with the latest London gossip, or he will expound endlessly on the local forester's attempts to curb the overpopulation of carp in the area's fishing ponds. Personally, I would rather talk about horses. Here's your room."

She nodded to the maid fluffing the pillows on the large, canopied bed, and stepped aside so he could enter. "Shipley is sending up a footman to help you with your bath."

At his look of alarm, she added, "Or not, if you'd prefer. We dine promptly at eight. Drinks in the drawing room before, if you're interested. The items in your trunk have been pressed and are hanging in there." She pointed to the wardrobe. "If there's anything you require, have Mary, here, or the footman—"

"When can I see the horses?"

Despite his reticence, she could easily warm to this man. "Dawn comes shortly after seven." Which was about the time she usually showed up at the stable. But she'd never had a guest willing to join her there at such an early hour.

"Not tonight?"

She glanced at the window. The day was fading and dinner was less than an hour away. "It's late, Mr. Jessup. I'm not sure what you could see in the dark, but you are certainly welcome in the stables at any time."

He nodded.

She turned to the door, then stopped, unsure how to speak without offending him. "I don't know if you are aware, but we dress for dinner."

"I'd hope so. Especially in this climate."

She blinked, taken aback. Was he jesting? His chiseled face gave no clue. Clearing her throat, she tried again. "What I meant to say, Mr. Jessup, is that we dress more formally for dinner."

"More formally than what?"

"Than . . . well . . . what you're wearing."

"Ah."

The maid stifled a giggle.

His expression didn't change, but the amusement in his eyes told her he knew exactly what she had meant and was teasing her. She didn't know what to say to that, but was charmed nonetheless.

The footman's sudden appearance gave her an exit . . . and a way to tease him back. "There you are, Fredericks. Just in time to help our guest undress for his bath. As you can see, he's quite muddy. Scrub him well. Come along, Mary." With a parting smile at the apprehensive American, she ushered the maid into the hall, calling gaily back as she shut the door, "Enjoy your bath, Mr. Jessup."

She thought she heard raised voices behind her, but wasn't certain if they came from downstairs, or Mr. Jessup's room.

*The green or the lilac?* she wondered, moving with a light step toward her bedroom in the west wing. If one must play the tart, it was important to look one's best.

# Five

Rafe knew he shouldn't be staring at her so much, but he had never seen a woman look as beautiful as Miss Cathcart did that evening. She seemed in high spirits, smiling often, her sleek brown hair catching the light of the dozens of candles spaced along the table. A different woman from the one he had met two weeks ago, when she had sat so rigidly beside him at the captain's table.

What had changed? What had put that spark in her remarkable blue-brown eyes?

"What do you think?"

Startled, he glanced at Agnes Bohm, the vicar's wife, seated on his right. She blinked eagerly back at him like a tiny gray hen poised to pounce on a dung beetle. She seemed to be awaiting an answer from him, but he could barely remember the conversation. Something about mourning and widow's weeds.

"They're dark?"

"Exactly, Mr. Jessup! And far too somber, I think. It's simply not good for the country. After all, it's been almost ten years, hasn't it?"

Rafe nodded, still not sure what she was talking about.

"See, Mr. Bohm?" The elderly lady leveled her bright blinking eyes at her husband, who sat across the table beside Miss Cathcart. "Even an American agrees. Certainly her devotion to Albert's memory is commendable, but it's time for dear

Victoria to put aside her mourning. No one looks good in black. Especially at her age."

Apparently she had forgotten that she wore the next best thing—gray.

"Yes, dear," her husband said. "You're right. As always."

"But then," she went on with a dreamy look on her kindly face, "it's so gratifying to see a love that reaches beyond the grave, don't you think, Mr. Jessup?"

Actually he thought it sounded ghoulish. "I wouldn't know, ma'am."

"You're not married?"

Distrusting that avid gleam in her faded eyes, Rafe shook his head.

"Well." Reaching over, she patted his arm with a gnarled, blue-veined hand. "We'll have to fix that, won't we?"

"Oh, dear," her husband murmured.

Undeterred, the old lady went on, "We should introduce him to the Campbell twins. Lovely girls. And I doubt either of them would mind marrying an American." Leaning toward Rafe, she added, "They're quite tall, you see. And sturdy. Easily able to leave their mark in your Wild West, so to speak."

Their host, seated at the head of the table and as far away from the other four as he could get, belched quietly and signaled the footman for more wine.

Miss Cathcart hid behind her napkin, her shoulders shaking.

Laughing? At him? Rafe sent her a "what'd I do?" look.

Her shoulders shook harder.

Beautiful shoulders, with rounded curves and delicate collarbones that drew his eye to the hollow at the base of her graceful neck, and from there, down to the gentle swells rising above her low neckline—swells that were quivering with her efforts not to laugh. Jiggling, actually. Pressing so hard against the thin fabric of her purple dress he could almost see—

"Where exactly did you say you were from?" the vicar asked, jarring Rafe back to attention.

*The face. Focus on her face.* "Texas, mostly."

"He was a lawman there," Mr. Cathcart put in, his bleary gaze sliding from his daughter to Rafe. "A Texas Ranger."

"Deputy U.S. Marshal," Rafe corrected. "The Rangers were disbanded last year, although I suspect they'll be reinstated soon." The rampant corruption of their replacement, the newly formed State Patrol, was one of the several reasons he'd left Texas.

"What's the difference between Rangers and Marshals?" Mrs. Bohm asked.

"Jurisdiction." Rafe studied his empty plate, wondering if it would be rude to ask for seconds. "One is state, the other is federal."

"This is Mr. Jessup's first trip to our country," Miss Cathcart said, having finally gained control of her amusement.

"Is it?" Mrs. Bohm beamed. "And how do you find it, Mr. Jessup?"

"Wet."

Thankfully, the footmen stepped into the breach his comment caused, and began removing plates and serving dessert—another of those pudding things the English seemed to favor. Conversation wound through other topics and Rafe let his mind drift again, until he looked up from his admiration of Miss Cathcart's bosom to find her glaring at him.

He pretended innocence, but didn't think she bought it.

The remainder of the meal progressed with little conversation. Other than a nod or two when cornered, Rafe avoided further participation until their host stood and herded his guests into the drawing room for brandy or tea.

Rafe wanted neither. But it would be rude to refuse, and since he had already made enough mistakes for one night, he dutifully folded his long frame into a delicate, overly ornate settee he was half afraid would collapse beneath him. Sadly, it didn't, and for the next hour, he sat sipping tepid tea from a tiny china cup and feigning interest in gossip about people he didn't know and places he had never been.

It was apparent to him these people didn't have enough to do.

To pass the time, he mused on possible ways to avoid future dinner gatherings and take his meals with the grooms, then realized if he did so, he would miss the treat of seeing the beautiful Miss Cathcart and her alluring attributes across the table each evening.

Not something he was ready to forgo.

But even with her sitting so close that he could smell her

perfume—lilacs, maybe?—time dragged. Conversation moved from meaningless to inane and his efforts not to yawn grew desperate, until finally, the vicar asked for their buggy to be brought around.

Rafe bounded from the couch, thinking the evening was over at last and soon he would be free to visit the stables before he retired. Following the Cathcarts out onto the drive to see the elderly couple on their way, he saw that it had stopped raining and a light still showed in one of the stable windows.

His spirits rose.

Then the endless good-byes began.

His frustration must have shown. "Patience, Mr. Jessup," Josephine Cathcart whispered by his shoulder. "It's a virtue, you know."

"Not with me."

By the time the Bohms' buggy finally departed, the stable window was dark.

Mr. Cathcart said his goodnights and weaved back inside, leaving his daughter and Rafe standing on the drive. When Rafe gazed longingly at the dark stable, she chuckled. "Let them sleep, Mr. Jessup. They'll be there in the morning."

He masked his disappointment. "Dawn is at seven, you say?"

"Half past. Or thereabouts. Shall I see you then?"

"If you're up that early."

She wasn't. After a restless night, Josephine slept so late that by the time she arose, Jamie was already dressed and gone, and the sun was beginning to burn away the morning mist. Without waiting for her maid or a corset, she threw on her serviceable boots, a woolen work dress under her barn coat, tied a scarf around her unruly hair, and hurried down the path to the stables.

Halfway there, she came to a stop when she saw Rayford Jessup, hatless, his long open duster swaying at his heels, walking into one of the pastures below. A bag hung from his hand. Stopping several yards out in a grassy spot, he scattered the contents of the bag on the ground at his feet—from Josephine's vantage point, it looked like bites of carrot or apple—then he put the empty bag into the pocket of his coat and stood quietly, arms relaxed at his sides. After looking around for a moment, he began to speak. She wasn't near enough to hear his words, but the tone was slow and even. Every now and then, he gave a low, warbling whistle.

Speaking to whom? There was no one else in sight. Curious to see what he was about, she continued to stand on the path and watch.

He cut a striking figure—Heathcliff, wandering the moors around Wuthering Heights—mysterious, guarded, tortured. Although she suspected that Mr. Jessup's reasons to be wandering about had more to do with horses than lost love. Still, there was something romantic about him standing motionless in the mist, tall and lean, the sturdy length of back and breadth of shoulder showing strength as well as grace. She could imagine him equally comfortable on a horse as on a dance floor.

Did he dance? She loved to waltz. The whirling, fluid freedom of it was almost as exhilarating as riding a horse. Sadly, she rarely found suitable partners, being as tall as she was. All that panting on her breasts was quite distracting.

Down below, Mr. Jessup continued to speak to the trees at the back of the pasture. A gentle breeze ruffled his sun-bleached hair and sent mist swirling about his boots. She sensed he was waiting for something. Or someone. But she saw no one else and heard no other voices.

Then shadows moved through the trees. Big. Dark.

He whistled again.

Slowly the shadows emerged, taking on form and substance as they stepped hesitantly out of the mist and into the open.

The mares.

Heads up to test the air, they edged closer to this unknown intruder, their gangly foals close at their sides.

Mr. Jessup didn't move. His voice remained calm, his occasional whistle cutting through the still morning air like a bird's call.

Prissy, the bossy bay matriarch of the herd, snorted, then stepped hesitantly forward, ears pricked. The other mares and foals followed. She reached him first and for her courage received a scratching along her jaw and first chance at the treats on the ground. The other mares pushed in, crowding around him as they searched out every last morsel. Jessup gave each pats and scratches, murmuring all the time. After they had all sniffed his hands and gotten their praise and treats, he turned and walked away. The mares watched until he swung over the fence and disappeared into the stable, then dropped their heads to graze.

Bemused, Josephine continued down the path.

"Good morning, Mr. Hammersmith," she said when she saw the burly Scot coming out of the feed room in the center of the stable.

He tugged the brim of his cap. "Morning, miss. Looking for Jamie, are ye?"

"Have you seen him?"

"Aye." He tipped his head toward the other end of the stable. "He's yon with Mr. Jessup, feeding the barn cats. He keeps bringing them treats, they'll stop mousing, so they will."

"I'll remind him," she called back, hurrying along. The customary sense of welcome coursed through her as she moved past the long rows of split stall doors. Most of the top doors were open. In some, she saw horses nosing their feed boxes, hunting the last kernel of grain. Other stalls were empty, the occupants having been turned out into their paddocks so the grooms could clean up behind them.

The snuffle and stomp of horses, the muttered voices of men working in the loft overhead, the smell of manure and hay and leather oils, even the dusty taste of the air, all combined to give her a deep feeling of peace.

This was where she was happiest. Not in glittering ballrooms, or strolling the fashionable streets of London. Here, with Jamie and among her beloved horses, was where she belonged. How long before this joy was torn from her life forever?

Pushing that thought aside, she stepped around the rear opening, and saw Jamie talking earnestly to Mr. Jessup. The tall Texan stood at the paddock fence, one booted foot on the bottom rail, his arms folded along the top rail, and several rangy cats rubbing against the leg bearing his weight.

Jamie copied the pose—although being at least twenty-five years younger than his companion and a great deal shorter, his blond hair barely brushed the bottom of the third rail, and his interest was more on the man beside him than on the horse in the paddock.

Yet, for a moment, in the sudden glare as the sun broke

through the mist to crown their blond heads with golden light, they looked so alike they might have been father and son.

Ignoring the catch in her throat, Josephine stepped forward. "There you are."

Jamie whipped around with a welcoming grin. "About time, sleepyhead."

Without taking his foot from the bottom rail, Mr. Jessup pivoted, one forearm still stretched along the top rail, the other coming down to rest low on his belt. "Miss Cathcart," he said with a nod.

"Did you bring anything to eat?" Jamie asked, his hazel eyes bright with excitement. "I'm ever so hungry." At seven years old, he invariably was.

"Cook gave you nothing?"

"A muffin. But since Mr. Jessup looked hungry, I gave him some of it."

"That was kind of you to share." She glanced up to find Mr. Jessup studying her, his speculative gaze dropping down to Jamie then back. She had no idea what he was thinking. Or why it would matter.

"Have you breakfasted yet, Mr. Jessup?"

He shook his head.

"Then we'd be pleased to have you join us." She instructed Jamie to tell Cook that she and Mr. Jessup would be coming up shortly. "We'll eat on the side veranda, now that the fog is lifting. You may join us."

With a hoot, Jamie raced back through the barn.

In the awkward silence that followed, Josephine wondered why she felt the need to explain Jamie to this stranger. He would find out soon enough, since she had never kept Jamie's existence a secret. She adored her son. Took pride in him. And had long ago decided not to live under a cloud of evasions and innuendoes, or pretend a shame she didn't feel. Better he should hear that from her, rather than through the gossip mills.

Hiking her chin in challenge, she said, "Jamie is my son."

He nodded.

Both confused and somewhat deflated by so lacking a response to her momentous declaration, she made certain he understood the whole of her sordid situation. "His father decided to marry someone else."

This time he gave a shrug. "His loss."

That was it? Two words and a shrug? No shock? Disgust? No speculative gleam in his eyes or even a spark of sympathy?

She should have felt relieved. Instead, his utter indifference stung.

"So when can I see Pembroke's Pride?"

Rafe knew right off he'd made a mistake. He just didn't know what it was. One minute they were talking, the next, she was stomping away, muttering to herself. Was this about him asking to see the horse? Or what she'd told him about the boy? Had he failed some test he wasn't even aware had been put before him?

He had only said what he thought. Any man who walked away from his own child and a woman like Josephine Cathcart was either blind, a fool, or too stupid to appreciate his good fortune. So what was she mad about?

"Hold on," he said, coming up behind her in two strides.

She flung open the door to one of the empty stalls. "He's in his paddock." She pointed to an open door on the outside wall. "Through there."

Rafe didn't move. He knew now this wasn't about the horse, but about his reaction to what she'd said. Had she expected him to be shocked? "I knew Jamie was your son. He has your smile. And I meant what I said. Any man who would walk away from a woman like you is a fool."

"You know nothing about me."

"I know you're beautiful. And that you love your son and horses. And that you don't like steeplechasing, or eating fish with the heads on, and that you're beautiful."

She fought a smile. "You already said that."

"Bears repeating."

The smile won. "You're a confusing man, Mr. Jessup."

"So I've been told. Did I pass?"

"Pass?"

"The test."

He watched color rise up her long, graceful neck, and wondered if she would try to deny the obvious. Instead, she gave a grudging smile. "You're still here, so I suppose you did. Pems is through there." This time, she said it without rancor.

Figuring he'd gained back some of the ground he'd lost, Rafe let it go at that. Moving ahead of her, he went through the stall and ducked out the back door. Miss Cathcart followed as far as the open doorway.

The stallion stood by the fence on the far side of the small enclosure. Sleek and dark, with a proud headset, and a strong, deep chest. Good withers and croup. Straight legs. Nice slope in the pasterns and three white stockings.

A beautiful animal.

Since he was the intruder, Rafe remained by the doorway and let the horse come to him. After a moment, the stallion walked over, his big, dark eyes bright with curiosity.

He moved well. No outward signs of injury. Some weakness on the right side, and not as flexible as he might be, but that could be due to a lack of proper exercise. No menace. Confirmation square and solid, with good muscle and bone.

Attitude, style, and form. Perfectly balanced. No wonder Ash wanted him.

"How was he injured?" Rafe asked when the horse stopped in front of him, nostrils flaring as he took in his scent.

"A fall."

Rafe ran a hand over the stallion's right shoulder, then bent to stroke down to the white stocking of the lower leg. Nothing. He did the same with the left front leg without the stocking and found a lump below the knee that indicated an old splint injury. No heat or swelling, and the horse showed no tenderness or concern at Rafe's touch. But bending closer, Rafe saw the tell-tale line of white dots along the dark fur of the cannon bone. "Seems okay now," he said, masking his disgust.

"He is, physically. But he won't cross water."

Rafe looked back at her. "At all?"

"Not even a puddle."

"What does he do?"

"He shakes, sweats, backs away. If he's not on a lead, or you can't hold him, he turns and bolts."

Rafe rose, wondering what would send such a reasonable-appearing animal into blind terror. "I'm assuming he fell in water."

"Worse. He was trapped under it." She made a weary gesture and sighed. "Jamie's waiting. If you're through here, we'd best go on up. I'll tell you all about it over breakfast."

# *Six*

"Have you ever heard of the Grand National?" Josephine asked after the footman had cleared away their empty breakfast plates and Jamie had gone upstairs for his lessons. No use putting horrible images in a child's head.

"Grand national what?"

"Steeplechase. It's a hunt race run every April on the Aintree Racecourse in Liverpool. Over four miles—three-and-a-half furlongs. Two circuits, thirty fences. Many of the jumps are over five feet high and several have water hazards and ditches. It's a brutal course."

"Pembroke's Pride ran it?"

"Only once."

Smiling sadly, she traced a fingertip through a drop of spilled tea beside her cup. "Father started grooming him for the race when Pems turned four. He was fearless then. Stronger than any horse we'd ever had. Father was convinced if he could stay the course, Pems could win. In fact, he bet our futures on it." She gave a bitter laugh. "In a way, Pembroke's fall brought us all down. There's some justice in that, don't you think?"

When Jessup didn't respond, she glanced over to find his gaze fixed on her with the same intense regard she had noticed on the ship. He had turned his chair sideways so he could stretch out his long legs, and now sat slouched, one arm hooked over the back of his chair, the other resting on the tabletop. He didn't fidget, or drum his fingers, or jiggle his crossed foot, but seemed totally focused on each word, every nuance of expression, any movement within range of his sight. Relaxed, but intent. Always. It must be exhausting.

"Pems started out well," she continued. "He went into the first jump at a good pace, and had no problems with the second. The third has a wide ditch in front of it that throws some horses off stride so that when they approach the fourth fence, they're confused or out of balance. Each year several fall there or unseat their riders. But Pems handled both jumps beautifully. Others didn't, and began to bunch up after they cleared the fifth fence and started toward the sixth. Becher's Brook."

A familiar tightness coiled in her chest. Realizing she had twisted her napkin into a wrinkled wad, she smoothed it flat on the table. Images flashed through her mind and suddenly it grew more and more difficult to take a full breath.

A big, rough hand closed over hers.

Startled, she looked up to see Mr. Jessup studying her with a look of concern in his deep-set blue eyes. "Walk with me," he said.

*Walk where?*

But as soon as the question formed, she realized it didn't matter. A walk would be good. There was too much emotion running through her and a stroll might help settle her nerves.

Without waiting for her response, he rose and came around to pull back her chair. By mutual unspoken agreement, they started down the path toward the stables. But when they reached the bottom of the slope, instead of continuing on to the paddocks, he turned toward the long grassy field that stretched all the way to the front gates. She followed, the hem of her woolen skirt collecting dew as they left the path and walked through the meadow, scattering the small herd of sheep pastured there to keep the grass from growing too tall.

The last of the summer wildflowers bobbed as they passed by, heads tucked, petals already curled. Soon they would wither, and the beech leaves would turn, and dewdrops would give way to crackling frost. But today the breeze was just enough to keep the insects at bay, and the sun felt like a warm hand on her back.

They walked in companionable silence, Mr. Jessup kindly

adjusting his longer stride to match hers. There was at least a foot of distance between them, yet she was acutely aware of his sturdy presence beside her. He moved with a horseman's grace, his eyes scanning the path ahead, his hands clasped at his back. He had left his duster on the veranda, and without it, he seemed less bulky, his form more refined. But the strength was there in the heavy shoulders and width of chest, as well as the unyielding line of his stubbled jaw. Clearly a man more suited to a life of hard work in the outdoors than one spent hunched over a gaming table in a smoky gentlemen's club.

He didn't rush her, which she appreciated. And when she felt she could continue, she took a deep breath, and picked up the story where she had left off.

"The jump they call Becher's Brook is the most difficult obstacle on the course. It's only five feet high, but the landing side is quite a bit lower than the takeoff side—nearly a foot, in places—and a brook runs along the base of it. It isn't overly broad or deep, but it's hidden in the approach. Often, when horses clear the hedge and see the water moving below them, they panic, especially since the drop is farther than they expect. Many have fallen there, injuring themselves as well as their riders. Several have died."

They had reached the trees by then, and the burbling rush of the brook sent a chill through Josephine. She remembered that sound. Remembered the screams of the thrashing horses, the wild terror in their eyes.

Suddenly feeling a bit light-headed, she motioned toward a fallen log beside the water. "I think I'd like to sit for a moment."

She wasn't sure why she was dredging all this up. Perhaps she was hoping that if Mr. Jessup knew the entirety of what had happened, he might not take Pems away from her. Or maybe she hoped he could help. She'd seen the rapport he had with the mares. They trusted him. Perhaps Pems would, too.

He sat beside her, leaning forward, elbows resting on his thighs, his big hands clasped between his bent knees. He was near enough that their hips almost—but not quite—touched, and even seated, he seemed to loom over her. Yet despite his size, and being in this secluded place with a man she scarcely knew, she wasn't afraid.

Plucking a dried stalk from the grass at her feet, she began pinching off tiny bits of the long blade. "I'm not exactly sure what happened. From where we watched at the rail, everything seemed fine. Pems approached well. But as he gathered for the jump, the horse next to him shied and threw his rider into his shoulder. Pems faltered, yet collected himself and made it over the jump. But he landed poorly, half in the brook. As he struggled to climb out, the riderless horse came in on top of him. Both horses fell back into the water. Our race rider managed to leap clear even as more horses came over and piled on top of those already down. Suddenly there were several horses flailing in the water. With Pems on the bottom."

She didn't realize she had shredded the stalk until Mr. Jessup reached over and gently pulled it from her shaking hands. Then he took her hand in his and rested it on his knee.

He didn't speak. Asked no more of her than to sit quietly beside him in the dappled shade beside the babbling brook, while birds flitted through the branches overhead and the past unwound around them.

His shoulder brushed against hers. She smelled horses, sunwarmed cloth, the coffee he had taken with breakfast. "I don't need coddling," she said, desperate to maintain some distance.

"I know."

The vibration of his voice moved through his shoulder and into hers. She wanted to lean into it. Rest her head against his solid strength. Just for a while.

"Finish."

She took a deep breath and let it out. "I don't know how long he was under the water. Most of the horses scrambled up right away and ran off in wild disarray. But one had been kicked in the head and was slow to rise. Pems was under him.

"By the time we got him out, he was shaking, his sides heaving. I remember gulping at air along with him as if that might help him breathe easier. He could scarcely stand, yet he fought anyone who came near. Even me. I've never seen an animal's eyes show so much white." She shuddered at the memory. "It took five men on ropes to get him off the course. It was two months before he calmed down enough to accept a rider. Even then, he shied at the slightest noise. I fear he'll never be the same again."

"He will."

She looked up at him, a bit irritated by his calm assurance in the face of such a horrid tragedy. "How do you know that?" she challenged.

"I'll take away the fear."

Anger rolled through her. "You think we haven't tried to do that? We've done everything we could to get him to cross water, stand in water, let water run over his back. He becomes hysterical every time."

"So you stopped trying?"

"What else could we do? Nothing worked and everything we did seemed to make it worse."

"That must have upset you."

"Of course it did! I raised him. Tended him. Loved him." Horrified to realize she was starting to cry, she yanked her hand from his and swiped it across her eyes. "It broke my heart to see him fail time and time again."

He didn't respond.

Which only made her angrier. "What? You think that's why? That I was too close to him and let my emotions get in the way?"

He shrugged.

She wanted to strike him. Did he think it was easy watching an animal suffer that way? *Officious ass.* Crossing her arms over her chest, she watched water bugs dip and soar above the brook as memories played over again in her mind.

She knew that horses were herd animals. As part of their survival instinct, they were highly attuned to the emotions around them. Like fear. If one ran, they all ran, even if they didn't know what the danger was.

Slowly the anger faded. Could he be right?

She glanced over at the man beside her. He was staring off into the meadow, idly chewing on a long blade of grass. Had she done more harm than good in helping Pems? Had her worry only made the horse's fear worse?

"What would you have done differently?" she asked him.

He thought for a moment, then pulled the grass from his mouth and dropped it between his feet. "I wouldn't have stopped. I wouldn't have cared when he failed. I'd have kept at it until he accepted that my will was stronger than his. Then I would have rebuilt his trust."

"How?"

"With a lot of patience."

He seemed so sure. So resolved. "Could you do that for Pembroke?"

"He seems reasonable. Smart. Willing. If I can reach him, I can teach him."

"You mean that?" She wanted so desperately to believe. To hope.

He turned his head and looked directly at her. The impact of those eyes was almost a physical thing. "I always mean what I say, Miss Cathcart."

When she continued to stare at him, not sure what to make of his bold assertion, he reached over and tucked a loose curl back under her scarf. "And I meant what I said about you, too." Letting his hand fall back onto his knee, he gave that small, crooked half smile. "You really are beautiful."

"The post rider brought a note from Kirkwell today," Mr. Cathcart announced at dinner several days later.

Luckily there were no other guests in attendance, so Rafe was able to enjoy the meal without distractions other than the low neckline of Miss Cathcart's pink dress. The color suited her well, and seeing her pretty face across the table went a long way toward easing his aggravation at having to put on his fancy clothes just to eat a meal.

"Will they be arriving soon?" she asked her father. "I need to alert the staff."

"Near the end of the week."

Rafe frowned. He wasn't ready. Pembroke needed more work. If he left for Scotland now, who would continue his training? He looked up, met Miss Cathcart's gaze across the table, and realized he wasn't ready to leave her, either.

She looked away, a flush rising up her graceful neck. "How long will they be staying with us?"

"Only a few days. Then they'll continue on to the Kirkwell lands in Scotland. Quit fidgeting, boy. And sit up. You look like a sack of turnips lumped over that way."

This last was directed at Jamie, who quickly straightened, a red stain spreading across his cheeks. "Yes, sir."

If there were no guests of consequence present—which

apparently, Rafe wasn't—the boy was permitted to dine with the adults. Judging by Jamie's nervousness, eating in the formal dining room under his grandfather's critical eye wasn't as enjoyable as dining on the veranda with his mother. Rafe concurred. It was equally apparent that the boy feared his grandfather, which troubled Rafe.

"My daughter tells me you've been working with Pembroke's Pride," Cathcart said, turning his attention to Rafe. "How do you find him?"

"Unsettled."

"Oh?"

"But he's improving, Father," Miss Cathcart cut in with a look of exasperation at Rafe—for what, he had no idea. "Tomorrow, Mr. Jessup plans to put him under saddle."

"He's been ridden before."

"Not by me." Rafe forked a piece of potato into his mouth, and watched his host while he chewed. He didn't know why he disliked the man. They had hardly spoken. But he didn't much approve of the way he treated his daughter and grandson. Not that Cathcart did anything overt—or that it was any of Rafe's business how he treated his family. But Rafe was always suspicious of a man when his own kin feared him. Another holdover from his days as a marshal.

"What he means to say, Father, is that Pems is beginning to trust him."

"Let the man speak for himself," Cathcart snapped, motioning for more wine. After the footman poured, he downed half the contents, set down the glass with an unsteady hand, and fixed his gaze on Rafe. "A valuable animal, Pembroke's Pride. Best bloodlines in England. Goes back over forty years."

Rafe continued eating.

"Kirkwell would be lucky to have him. If I decide to sell."

"And if he's usable."

"Usable?" The older man gave a loud bark of laughter. "Hell, the randy bugger is a bloody humping machine."

"Are you finished with your dinner, Jamie?" his mother broke in, her mouth tight with disapproval. Or maybe embarrassment. Rafe couldn't tell which.

"Yes, Mother."

"Then you're excused."

"What about dessert?"

"You may take it in the nursery. Say good night, please."

The boy dutifully bade Rafe and his grandfather good night. "You'll come up to read a story with me, won't you, Mother? Before Nanny Holbrick puts out the lamp?"

"Of course, dearest. Off you go, now."

After the door closed behind him, Miss Cathcart turned sharply toward her father. "I'd rather you not speak that way in front of him, Father. He's only a boy."

Cathcart finished off his wine and belched. "You pamper him too much, girl. And he's far too old to have a nanny. When I was his age, I had to put food on the table for my mam and two sisters. Crawling through the mines, breathing black death, and getting kicked in the arse if I didn't move fast enough. No lullabies and nighttime kisses for me."

"I know, but—"

"No!" Her father's fist hit the table so hard his empty glass toppled. "You *don't* know! Sitting there in your fancy dress, eating fine food with a silver spoon—you have no notion, girl, what it cost me to make this rich life you're living today. You know nothing! Rogers, another bottle."

As the footman rushed off to get another bottle of wine, Rafe calmly set his napkin beside his plate and rose. "Miss Cathcart, would you care to take a stroll through the rose garden?"

She glanced up, her eyes overly bright, her face overly pale. That rigid, remote expression was back. "I would, Mr. Jessup. Thank you."

"You're not excused," her father slurred.

Rafe turned his head and looked at him.

The older man seemed to deflate. "All right. Go on, then," he muttered, waving them toward the door.

Motioning another footman aside, Rafe came around and pulled back Miss Cathcart's chair, then offered her his arm. Without a glance in the direction of the man slumped at the head of the table, he led her from the room.

"I'm sorry you had to witness that, Mr. Jessup," she said as he helped her into her coat in the entry. "He's usually not so . . . difficult."

Rafe didn't respond. His teeth were clenched so tight he doubted he would have been able to, even if he'd thought of something to say.

The night had turned cool, which helped take the edge off his anger. He reminded himself it wasn't his place to step into the middle of family arguments, but then an image of Josephine's stricken face flashed through his mind, and he knew he had been right to get her away before her drunken father went too far.

*Josephine.* He shouldn't think of her by her given name. They weren't familiars. They weren't equals. She lived in a palatial estate—he preferred the stables. She was bound by the rules of a society that had little meaning for him—he just wanted to be left alone.

Or did he?

The time he'd spent in Heartbreak Creek had put a crack in that resolve. The honorable people he'd met there had shown him that not every town was like Dirtwater, Texas.

Nor was every female like Miranda.

He looked over at the woman walking beside him, head down in thought, her arms crossed against the chill breeze. He wondered what she was thinking. If she resented his interference. She was a prickly one, Josephine Cathcart, and fiercely protective of her ability to take care of herself. He didn't want her thinking he had been coddling her again, even if that had been his intent.

"Thank you for getting me out of there," he said, breaking the long silence. "I was afraid I might do something."

"Do something?" Her head came up.

"I don't take kindly to bullies."

She continued to stare at him. In the dim starlight, he couldn't see her face that well, but he could sense her confusion.

"It's a weakness that's gotten me into trouble before," he explained. "I didn't mean to make an awkward situation worse."

She didn't respond. They came around to the side veranda, where they often took breakfast, then down the steps and onto the path that wound through the garden. They were more sheltered from the breeze on this side of the house, and the still air was thick with the smell of late-summer roses. All was quiet but for a distant whinny from the stable below, where a single light shone in the small room where Hammersmith stayed with the cats.

"He has a point," she admitted. "Jamie doesn't need a nanny anymore. But I hate the idea of him spending so much time alone up in the nursery." Bending, she plucked a weed from between the stones of the walkway and tossed it into the shrubbery. "Because of our situation, we rarely have callers. Other than Cook's grandson, or the stable boys, or the occasional visit from one of the servants' children, he has few playmates. Of course, Nanny Holbrick isn't much of a playmate, being almost in her dotage. But she loves Jamie, and her being there provides a caring and stabilizing presence in his lonely life." She gave a brittle smile. "Every child needs to be loved by someone other than his mother, don't you think?"

"He has his grandfather."

She didn't respond to that.

Somewhere in the trees at the back of the garden, a night bird called out. A lonely, solitary sound that reminded him of a bobwhite. He wondered who it was calling to, and why there was no answer.

"Do you have family, Mr. Jessup?"

He shook his head.

"They can be a trial sometimes." She paused to pinch a spent blossom from a long stalk, then continued walking, her fingers idly pulling the rose apart as she spoke. "My mother died soon after Father bought his first mine. I don't remember her, or those hard early years, so he was right when he said I have no notion what it cost him to climb out of those black holes and make a life for me and Mother. He could have turned me out after my disgrace, but he didn't. I'm grateful for that. And for all he's given me and Jamie. But sometimes . . ."

She slowed to a stop, let the petals fall at her feet, then brushed her hands on her coat. The scent of roses was so strong Rafe could smell nothing else.

"But sometimes," she went on, "I think he brought some of that darkness up with him. Or left the better part of himself down in those deep tunnels. It makes him cruel."

"He could do better."

She crossed her arms again and looked up at him, her head slightly tilted so that one dark curl fell across her cheek.

He wanted to brush it away. Feel the softness of her skin. Touch her in some small insignificant way. But if he did, he would only want more.

"We don't get to choose the life we're given, Mr. Jessup."

Miranda's face flitted through his mind—frozen smile on painted lips, empty eyes meeting his in the mirror over the saloon bar as a stranger ran his hand up her thigh. He forced the image away. "You're right, Miss Cathcart," he said more brusquely than he'd intended. "But we do get to choose whether we stay in that life or leave it."

"And if one is not strong or brave enough to break away?"

"Then find someone to help." How righteous he sounded. Like he had all the answers. Had he learned nothing from that fiasco in Texas?

Disgusted, he motioned toward the house. "Shall we go back inside? I can see you're chilled. And the boy is waiting for his bedtime story."

"Of course."

They spoke no more until they parted in the entry. But as Rafe watched her go up the stairs, he felt something move through him. A hollow feeling. Like the pang of an empty belly. But higher up, in his chest.

The numbness of the last year was thawing. He was starting to feel things again. Want things.

And he didn't like it.

# Seven

"What do you think of Mr. Jessup?" Josephine asked, watching in the vanity mirror as Henrietta brushed out curls she had pinned into her hair earlier.

"I like him better than Mr. Huddleston, if you don't mind me saying."

Josephine liked him better, too, and was heartily grateful their neighbor had given up his suit. Between the men she had met in America, Mr. Calhoun on the ship, and those Father had foisted on her here, she was becoming quite adept at repelling male advances. Too bad she had lacked that skill when she was sixteen.

"But Mr. Jessup . . ." Henny sighed. "Faith, and he's ever so handsome. And smart."

Josephine looked at her in the reflection. "Why do you say that?"

"One of the upstairs maids said he brought a whole trunkful of books all the way from America. Sure, and all the kitchen girls are half in love with him."

Josephine smiled at the cheerful young Irishwoman whose high spirits and love of gossip kept the loneliness at bay, even during Josephine's darkest days. "But not you, Henny?"

"Never say it." A bright laugh, then the pretty redhead leaned down to whisper, "To be sure, I don't mind passing my eyes over such a foine-looking fellow, but I've got me own beau, so I do."

"Do you? When did that happen?"

"While you were in America. But please, miss, don't tell Shipley."

"Why not?"

"Because, well . . ." Henny's rosy cheeks seemed to get rosier. "If he knew that we . . . what I mean is . . . consorting amongst the staff is not allowed."

Josephine turned on the vanity stool to frown up at her. "Consorting?" Did Henny mean what Josephine thought she meant?

"If he found out," the flustered maid said, the brush twisting in her grip, "we'd both lose our places. Then I'd have to go back to the farm and Gordon—"

"Gordon Stevens? The groom?"

The brush fell to the floor. Tears spilled over. "Oh, please, miss. Say you won't dismiss us."

"Hush, Henny. Of course I won't dismiss you. Nor will Shipley." Reaching into a vanity drawer, she pulled out a hanky and handed it to the weeping woman. "Now do stop crying and tell me why, if you're so in love, you and Gordon simply don't marry?"

"We can't. Shipley doesn't allow married couples on staff."

Josephine reminded herself to have a talk with the tyrannical butler. This wasn't the seventeen hundreds. Even servants had rights nowadays. "Then what do you plan to do?"

Henny dabbed her tears away, then let out a hitching breath. "Keep working until we can afford a livery somewhere. Gordon is ever so good with horses."

Josephine reminded her that Father was selling horses, not adding any.

"But surely he'll keep a few. For the carriage and such like."

"Hammersmith will be able to handle that without help."

"Then maybe Gordon could train as a footman?"

Josephine suspected Father would soon be letting footmen go, too. But rather than trigger another onslaught of tears, she broached a growing concern. "Are you being careful, Henny?" Seeing her maid's look of confusion, she elaborated. "If you're, em, consorting with Gordon . . . well, you wouldn't want to make the same mistake I did. Not that I think of Jamie as a mistake, but—"

"Oh, no, Miss Cathcart! Jamie is a perfect angel. Faith, if I ever had a son, I would want him to be just like our Jamie. But I won't be having a son anytime soon. Gordon makes certain of that."

"How?" Admittedly, she was ignorant of such matters, but if such a thing were possible, surely William would have thought of it back when they were consorting.

Henny leaned in to whisper. "French letters. Or some use Dutch cups."

Josephine vaguely remembered mention of such things in one of her romantic novels, but hadn't understood how a letter could stop the arrival of a baby. And she knew nothing about a Dutch cup.

The maid must have read her puzzlement. "They're preventatives. Baby preventatives."

"How do they work?"

A wave of color almost drowned out Henny's freckles. "The French letter is a thing . . . like a glove, but with only one finger, that fits over a man's . . . part."

"Part? You mean his . . ."

"Exactly. I have one in my cubby. I'll show you." She swept out the door.

By the time she returned, Josephine was in her gown and robe, warming herself beside the small coal stove set inside the marble fireplace.

"Sure, and Gordon's not fond of them." Henny pulled an odd flat thing out of a small box bearing the name *Dr. Power's French Preventatives*. "He says they're uncomfortable. Probably because they're made of vulcanized rubber, rather than gut. The Dutch cup fits over the opening into a woman's womb. I shudder to think how it gets there. You can have this one, if you'd like."

"My word." Loath to touch the thing, she opened the drawer for Henny to drop it in. Why hadn't William known of these preventatives? It would have saved them both from scandal and disgrace—although the latter was mostly on her part, not his. But then, if he put one on his . . . part, there would be no Jamie.

But still. How liberating. And how shocking to have such a

thing in her possession. She wondered if Rayford Jessup had ever heard of a preventative.

Over the next several days, Rafe rode Pembroke's Pride in the round training pen, working him at all gaits—in circles, figure eights, backing up, stops and starts. The horse responded well, changed leads when he was supposed to, and accepted Rafe's commands without pulling or fighting the bit.

Rafe praised him often and, after each session, rubbed him down for a long time, speaking to him constantly. The horse quickly became accustomed to his scent, his touch, the sound of his voice. The stallion was also beginning to lose some of his stiffness, and as he went through his gaits, his stride grew smooth and fluid as muscles strengthened and became more defined.

Rafe kept the sessions short. Knowing Pems was intelligent and would easily grow bored with the same monotonous routine, he varied his activity by having Hammersmith work the stallion on a longe line each afternoon while Rafe watched from the fence.

On the fifth morning, Rafe awoke to heavy gray clouds and an ache in his old shoulder injury that foretold rain. Knowing this was his chance to put Pems through his next test, he threw on his clothes, grabbed his hat and duster, and hurried to the stables.

"You're taking him out today?" Hammersmith questioned when Rafe came out of the tack room with the stallion's halter and lead rope and a carrot. "Looks like rain, so it does."

"I hope so." Plucking a curry brush from a peg, Rafe slid the bolt on Pembroke's stall door and stepped inside.

The horse whinnied in welcome. Having seen Rafe in his hat and duster several times, Pems wasn't as concerned by Rafe's altered appearance as he was the carrot in his hand. Rafe let him finish his snack, then buckled on the halter and led him out the rear stall door into his paddock. Stopping in the center of the open area, he took out the brush and began talking to the animal as he curried him.

Pems stood quietly, enjoying the attention as well as the brushing.

Until the rain began.

It started with a thick drizzle then progressed into regular rain. Not a Texas frog-strangler, but heavier than the misty soup Rafe had ridden through from Liverpool almost two weeks ago. He could feel the horse tense as water collected on his back and began to run down his sides. Stepping back to give him space, Rafe continued to talk calmly to him.

The stallion stomped, shook his head, snorted.

Because the paddock was mostly beaten-down dirt with a few patches of grass, the rain began to puddle here and there.

Taking a snug grip near the halter ring, Rafe took a step, keeping pressure on the lead until Pems moved forward. Praise, a pat, words of encouragement, then another step. And another.

The horse did well until they came to the first puddle, then he balked.

Rafe continued to urge him forward, speaking all the while.

The stallion snorted, eyes showing white, but Rafe talked him through it until eventually Pems stepped hesitantly over the puddle. Same with the next, and the next.

The puddles grew larger, running together into small pools. When they came to one that was too wide to step over, Pems refused to cross. Rafe backed him up and came at it again and again until, finally, the horse put one front hoof into the water. Then Rafe had him stand there.

The horse trembled, his nostrils flaring as his breathing accelerated.

Rafe spoke quietly, rubbing the crest of the stallion's muscular neck until the horse began to relax enough to drop his head. He snuffled at the puddle, tossed his head, and stepped back.

Again, Rafe massaged the horse's neck until he calmed, then brought him up to the puddle again. When the horse had both front hooves in the water, Rafe asked him to stand quietly while he stroked him and told him how well he was doing. Eventually the shaking stopped. The stallion's head dropped as he relaxed.

Rafe led him to the next puddle and did it all again. When the horse was able to stand quietly in an inch of water, Rafe figured he'd accomplished enough for one day, and led him back into his stall and out of the rain.

Miss Cathcart was waiting by the open doorway, grinning like a kid with new shoes. "You did it! I was watching. He did beautifully, didn't he? Can I give him a carrot?"

Rafe nodded, charmed by the sparkle in her blue-brown eyes. He had rarely seen her in such high spirits, and her smile made him smile. Stepping back so she could give the horse his treat, he noticed Hammersmith grinning over her shoulder.

"Good work, lad. Ye'll make him into a kelpie yet, so ye will."

Rafe wasn't sure what a "kelpie" was, but heard the praise in the Scotsman's voice and felt a surge of pride in the horse. "He did it himself, not me. Be sure to keep his paddock door open so he can go out if he wants. If it's still raining this afternoon, I'll take him out again."

"Aye. The rain will continue for a while, anyway." The groom rubbed his knuckles. "These auld hands tell me so."

"If he does well this afternoon, I'll take him to the training pen tomorrow."

"It'll be full of puddles, so it will."

"I'm counting on it."

Hammersmith left to scold the stable boys for being slow to muck out the stalls, but Josephine stayed, watching as Rafe rubbed down the wet horse with a piece of burlap. "He looks better every day. You've done wonders with him."

"He's a good horse."

"You're a good trainer."

Rafe kept his head down to hide how much her words pleased him. "Where's Jamie?"

"At his lessons. He's been badgering his tutor about Cheyenne Indians ever since he learned Mr. Redstone will be visiting. He's never met an Indian before, much less a Dog Soldier."

"Thomas is an interesting man."

"Do you think he'll mind if Jamie asks him questions?"

Rafe straightened, dropped his rag into a bucket holding brushes and combs and hoof picks, then searched out a dry spot on his trousers to wipe his hands. "Have Jamie take him on a walk. Thomas is a lot more approachable when he's outdoors."

She moved aside when he opened the stall door, then fell into step beside him as he carried the bucket of brushes back to the tack and feed room.

He thought she looked especially pretty today, although she was dressed in her usual brown dress and black boots. Maybe it was her smile, or the way curls were already sliding free of her scarf and showing bits of straw stuck in the dark strands. He almost reached over to brush the straw loose, but caught himself in time.

"Will Jamie be safe with him?" she asked as he scooped a tin of grain and headed back to the stallion's stall.

"Safer than he'd be with any other man, I suspect."

"Except you."

Another rush of heat into his face. "He'll always be safe with me. Both of you will."

"I know."

Leaning over the half door, he emptied the grain scoop into the wooden feed trough attached to the wall, grabbed the horse's water bucket, then straightened, almost bumping into her. "Thomas is patient with children. He can teach the boy a lot."

"About what?"

This time she dogged his heels to the feed room to return the scoop, then on to the water trough outside, where he rinsed the bucket, filled it, then carried it back to the stallion's stall.

"Living. Surviving. Understanding the world around him."

It rattled him the way she kept following him around. Reminded him of Jamie, except she was prettier and smelled better, and he never thought about kissing Jamie like he did the boy's mother. Irritated that he'd let that thought into his head, he set the bucket beside the horse's feed trough, then turned to face her. "Something I can help you with, Miss Cathcart?"

"What? Oh." She stepped back, that flush rising up her neck. "I'm bothering you."

Irritation faded. It wasn't her fault he let his mind wander where it shouldn't. "Not at all. But I'm getting hungry. I'd be pleased to treat you to one of Cook's muffins. They're really tasty."

The laugh that burst out of her took him completely off guard. He couldn't help but smile back. "I say something funny?"

She laughed harder. "I don't know when you're jesting or being serious, Mr. Jessup. You're a terrible tease."

"I don't mean to be."

"Of course you don't." The roll of her eyes belied the

statement. "Come along, then," she added, slipping her arm through his in a gesture so familiar and unexpected it left him at a loss for words. "I'm sure I can get you something more substantial for breakfast than a muffin. I know the cook personally, you see."

Docile as a spring lamb, he allowed himself to be towed along, that tiny rift in his resolve widening a fraction more.

Since the rain prevented them from dining on the veranda, and Mr. Jessup wouldn't go into the dining room dressed in his work clothes, Josephine reluctantly had a footman set up a table in the conservatory.

She hadn't entered the glass-domed hothouse since Mr. Huddleston's awkward advances. When she was an adolescent, the humid world of exotic plants had been her favorite place other than the stables. Here, the seasons never changed, and the perfume of thousands of blossoms scented the air, and she was the lonely princess awaiting her prince.

Then, at the lawn party on her sixteenth birthday, that prince had galloped into her life, as dashing as she had dreamed. The Honourable William Bristol, heir to Baron Adderly. Trim, elegant, perfect in dress and demeanor, he was everything she thought she would ever want.

The months following that first meeting had been a whirl-wind of parties and carriage rides and walks through the garden. And then one sultry evening, here among the ferns and ficus and dwarf tropical fruit trees, she had given her love and her body to the man who said it didn't matter that she was a coal miner's daughter and he was a baron's son. He loved her. He wanted to marry her, and would, no matter what his father said.

Foolish girl. Like Father, she hadn't understood the rules then. And when finally she did, and her prince walked away from her and their unborn child to marry the rich woman with a loftier bloodline that his father had chosen for him, it was here in this glass room where she had wept the bitter tears of a broken heart.

Hopefully, by bringing Mr. Jessup here—a man so different from William or Mr. Huddleston—she might supplant those unhappy memories with ones less hurtful, and the conservatory would once again become a place of reflection and relaxation.

As they entered the large glass room, Mr. Jessup slowed to look around. She guessed he had never been inside a cast iron and glass hothouse before, and enjoyed watching his reaction. Of course, being the restrained person he was, he didn't say anything, but she could see the spark of interest in his dark blue eyes.

"Do you grow things in here year-round?" he asked as he took his seat across from her at the small cloth-covered table that Rogers, the head footman, had set up directly under the peak of the dome.

She nodded. "Flowers, for the most part. But Cook has an herb bed and a few stock vegetable plantings in the back alongside the orange trees."

"How do you keep it warm?"

She indicated several small coal stoves along the outer walls, and the huge pots of water simmering on top of each. "In the summer, the sun heats it well enough. And if it becomes too hot, many of the higher panels can be opened."

Rogers came in with a tray of eggs, ham, an assorted fruit plate, toast points, and marmalade. As he served them, Josephine studied the man across the table. His shoulders far outspanned the narrow back of the delicate ironwork chair. He had removed his hat, and a long lock of sun-bright hair fell over his forehead, partially hiding the red mark left by the band of his Stetson.

He needed a good grooming. His hair was too long, and a dark stubble of beard shadowed his square jaw and stubborn chin. And although he had rinsed his hands in the washroom off the kitchen, there was still mud on his boots and horsehair on his cuffs.

Yet when she looked at him, she saw beyond the disarray to the soft-spoken man she had watched in the paddock with Pems. Big. Confident. Unhurried. She remembered how gently those strong hands had stroked Pembroke's neck, and found herself wondering what they would feel like on her own flesh.

Wanton thoughts. Such musings had gotten her into trouble before, and it would behoove her to put them aside now.

Still, despite good intentions, there was something about Rayford Jessup's aloof manner and crooked smile that made her want to break through that armored reserve to the man beneath. In so many ways, he was a mystery to her.

"Nice place," he said, pulling her from her troubling thoughts. "Thomas would like it." Amusement danced in his eyes when he added in warning, "Don't be surprised if you find him sleeping in here."

"I'll warn Shipley."

They ate without speaking. As she watched Mr. Jessup mow through his breakfast with single-minded determination, Josephine found herself wondering if he gave that same intense attention to other appetites in his life. More wanton thoughts. And why for this man?

Why not?

Here in this secluded setting, with the ping of raindrops on the glass panels overhead adding a sense of intimacy, it was easy to see Mr. Jessup as a heroic figure. Mysterious. Protective. Strong. A man who was incapable of dissembling and who always meant what he said, he was the antithesis of the other men she had brought here. What would her life have been like had she met him first?

"When was Pembroke's Pride injured?"

Chased once again from her errant thoughts, she saw that he had cleaned his plate, and now sat slouched back in his chair, hands folded over his belt buckle, watching her.

"I told you, last year at the—"

"No, before that," he cut in. "Probably several years before." She frowned. "I don't know what you mean."

"When he popped a splint."

"Popped a splint?" Now she was doubly confused. It had been several years since she had reluctantly relinquished Pembroke's care to Hammersmith. Once the stallion had reached maturity and they began using him for breeding, he had become too strong and unpredictable for her to handle. But surely she would have known if he were hurt.

"It's a common injury in young racing or jumping horses, especially if they're worked too hard, too early. Ever notice that knot by his left shin? That's where it healed." Apparently seeing she still had no idea what he was talking about, he explained that splint bones ran along the inside of the lower leg and were attached to the cannon bones by ligaments. If young horses were worked too hard, those ligaments often ruptured and became inflamed.

"Eventually," he went on, "the inflammation fuses the splints to the cannon bone, which strengthens the leg and helps prevent further injury. But it takes a long time, and it might be months before the horse healed well enough to be worked again."

"But I would have remembered if Pems had been laid up that long."

"Not if he was pin-fired."

"What's pin-fired?"

"A brutal practice." For the first time since she'd know him, Mr. Jessup showed agitation. Stretching a long arm from his slouched position, he began idly rolling his unused knife back and forth on the table beside his plate, his expression one of distaste. "Sharp pins are heated, then pushed into the horse's leg where the inflammation is."

Josephine drew back in disgust. "Why?"

"To make the inflammation worse. Some think that will cause the bones to fuse quicker, so the horse can be worked sooner."

"And you think someone did that to Pems?"

He looked up, those eyes boring into hers with an intensity that was almost intrusive. "I'm sure of it. I saw the white dots where the hot pins went in. When they heal, the hair grows back white."

She was horrified. As disgusted as Mr. Jessup seemed to be. "But who would have done such a thing?"

He didn't answer. The knife rolled back and forth.

"Surely not Mr. Hammersmith."

"Not unless he was ordered to do so."

Realizing what he was implying, she shook her head. "No. Not Father." Father would never harm Pems. The stallion was his hope and pride. Besides, Pems was hers, not Father's.

And yet . . .

Memories swirled in her head. There was that one time when Pems had pulled up lame after a hard workout. She remembered watching Hammersmith put cool compresses on the stallion's front leg. Father had assured her it was only a slight sprain and the horse would be fine after a few days of rest. She and Jamie had left soon after for a lengthy visit to London. When she'd returned, Pems had seemed fine, although

Father said he was giving him a break from his training for a while.

"I'm surprised you didn't know."

Just thinking about it sent a sour taste into her throat. "Had I been aware of the practice, Mr. Jessup, I assure you I would never have allowed it."

"I know you wouldn't. It's long healed, anyway. Luckily, horses are forgiving creatures."

Setting his knife aside, he sat up, signaling an end to the conversation. "Sounds like the rain has stopped. When will Jamie be finished with his lessons? I promised to take him for a ride. If that's acceptable with you, of course."

"It is if I'm allowed to accompany you. I haven't been out in ages." At his nod, she rose. "We'll meet you at the stable in an hour."

# Eight

Forty minutes later, Rafe was hurrying down the path to the stables under a patchy blue sky.

It was his second trip down since leaving the conservatory. He had gone down right after breakfast to ready the horses, but when Hammersmith learned they were taking an outing, he had advised him to change clothes.

"We're just going for a ride," Rafe had protested.

"Aye, lad. But going for a ride is verra different for society folk than for working men like us. And ye'd best shave, as well."

"Hell."

Other than his work clothes—he was only a wrangler, after all—Rafe had his regular Sunday suit, and the fancy dress suit Ash had insisted he needed. After a quick wash and shave, he donned the Sunday suit, a collared shirt, and a narrow tie. He had only his formal shoes and boots, so he wiped the mud off his boots and pulled them back on, decided to forgo the damp Stetson, but buckled on his gun belt. After slicking back his hair, he hurried to the stable.

"Will this do?" he asked Hammersmith, who was supervising the stable boys in saddling three horses and a pony tied in the aisle.

The Scotsman looked him over, then nodded. "Aye. But best leave the gun. This isna Ireland."

"No."

The groom sighed. "Then put it in here." He opened the flap

of a small bag tied to the English-style saddle on a leggy chestnut gelding.

"Stevens will accompany you." The older man nodded toward a groom dressed in a deep brown jacket similar to those worn by the Cathcart coachmen. Rafe wondered if he was accompanying them as protection, or a chaperone.

As Rafe began to lower the stirrups on the chestnut's saddle, Jamie ran into the stable, followed more sedately by his mother. They were both dressed in fine fashion—Jamie in a dark blue suit and his mother in a velvet riding habit with a long split maroon skirt and fitted black jacket. White lace spilled over the lapels and cuffs, and perched atop her tightly pinned hair was a small black hat with a narrow brim and a jaunty maroon feather. From the polished leather boots to her fine kid gloves, her clothes probably cost twice as much as all the clothes Rafe had brought with him from America.

Another reminder of the vast divide in their stations. Not in class. Social status meant nothing to him. But they were worlds apart in wealth and expectation and experience. He could no more picture her in a small cabin in Heartbreak Creek—no servants, no formal dinners, no place to wear all her fine gowns—than he could see himself suffering a lifetime of meals with the vicar.

While Hammersmith assisted Miss Cathcart, Rafe gave Jamie a leg up onto his pony—a stout roan with the drooping muzzle of an older horse—then swung up onto his big chestnut. With Jamie riding between his mother and Rafe, and Stevens following several yards behind, they started down the long drive to the front gates.

"We're going to Penrith." Jamie grinned with excitement. "And Mother says I may have a strawberry ice."

"I hope you don't mind stopping in town," his mother said. "I've a few items to purchase, and I thought we could take luncheon while we're there."

"Sounds fine, ma'am."

"You needn't call me 'ma'am,'" she admonished. "You're a guest, not a servant."

"Then what should I call you?"

"Miss Cathcart would be fine. But since I consider us friends, I would prefer Josephine."

An odd concession. Using first names might be common in Heartbreak Creek, but Rafe knew the English were more formal than that. Was she indicating she was open to other concessions, as well? Intrigued by the notion and willing to see where it led, he nodded. "Then call me Rafe."

"Can I call him that, too?" Jamie asked.

His mother smiled down at him. "No, you may not. He's your elder and should be addressed as Mr. Jessup."

"But he's your elder, too."

"That's different."

"But—"

Seeing this conversation was headed nowhere, Rafe broke in. "What's your horse's name, Jamie?"

Grinning, the boy reached down to pat the pony's neck. "Boots. Because of his black hooves. Yours is named Wellington because of his big nose. He likes to snatch bites of grass, so you'd best watch him."

Rafe matched his serious tone. "I will. Thank you. You're very knowledgeable about horses."

"Yes, I am." The boy straightened even more in the saddle. "I've been riding ever since I was little, you see."

"You're very good at it. Did Mr. Hammersmith teach you?"

"No, sir. Mother did."

"Did she?" Lifting his gaze over Jamie's blond head, Rafe met Miss Cathcart's—Josephine's—beautiful eyes. "She did a fine job."

"She says I'm a natural. But she's ever so good, too." The boy grinned proudly. "Mr. Hammersmith says had she been born a boy, she could have made a fine race rider."

"That would have been a shame." Still holding her gaze, Rafe smiled. "I like that she's a girl."

"Me, too."

Color bloomed on her cheeks, which made Rafe grin, and which for some odd reason, heightened her color even more.

"Hie to the gate," she called and, without waiting for an answer, nudged her gray into a canter.

Jamie and his pony tore after her, but Rafe hung back. While he waited for Stevens to catch up to him, he watched the two race ahead.

They were both good riders. Even though Josephine rode

sidesaddle, she seemed relaxed and well balanced, her back straight but supple, her hands light on the reins. Jamie rode in the same quiet manner, head up, reins in gentle contact with the snaffle, legs still. He definitely was a natural and should be graduating to a bigger horse soon.

The groom reined in beside him. "Sir?"

"Do you expect trouble in town, Stevens?" Rafe asked.

"No, sir. Penrith is usually fairly quiet."

"Usually?"

When Rafe continued to study him, the groom shifted in the saddle and looked away. "Well, sometimes things are said."

"Things?"

"About the boy."

Rafe tried to keep his expression pleasant. "*About* the boy? Or *to* the boy?"

"Both. But there's never any real trouble, sir. Not with me there."

"Good man. Thanks for the warning. I'll keep an eye out, too." Putting heels to Wellington's sides, Rafe galloped to catch up with the pair racing ahead.

He remembered Penrith from his earlier visit on his way to the Cathcart estate. A typical English market town, situated in a broad valley at the confluence of three small rivers, it had been cloaked in mist when he'd ridden through the first time. But today, the clouds were clearing off, and he could see most of the Eden Valley and the surrounding fells—the local term for the uncultivated stretches that were less mountain than rolling green hills—which were dotted here and there with Rough Fell sheep and upland ponies.

"That's Beacon Hill." Jamie pointed to a high round ridge. "If you go up there and squint your eyes real hard, you can see the peaks of the Pennines far away."

"Penrith flourished in the early coal mining days," Josephine said later as they rode down the main thoroughfare of small shops, pubs, and open market stalls. "But as the coal fields played out, it went into decline. It's only in the last few years that things have begun to flourish again. Tourists, for the most part. Penrith has many prehistoric sites and is home to several local castles and ruins."

"One of them is haunted!" Jamie's hazel eyes were round with animation. "Mother promised this year I might see it."

"Another day perhaps," his mother said, reining in outside a dry goods store. "Unless you gentlemen want to help me pick out ribbons, and needles, and threads for the housekeeper, I suggest you wait for me at Benderhoff's Tea Room. I shall only be a few minutes."

Before Rafe could offer to escort her, Stevens swung down and assisted her off her mare. "I'll keep an eye on her, sir," the groom said to Rafe in a low voice as he handed up the reins to his and Josephine's horses. "We'll be along shortly."

With a nod, Rafe led the horses after Jamie toward a tall, narrow building with several small tables and chairs on the stone terrace out front. "Why don't we take one of the outside tables," Rafe suggested as they dismounted. "So we can watch for your mother."

After tying the four horses to a rail on the side of the building, they returned to the terrace and took seats at one of the sunny tables out front.

Rafe looked around. Other than a few architectural differences, Penrith looked like many small American towns, especially those in the Northeast. Narrow lanes, crowded storefronts with painted signs hanging over the doors, and worn cobblestone streets, all stewing in the stink of too many people and animals crowded into too small an area. Rafe was definitely not a city person. He needed more sky and space, and a lot less noise. Still, for a town, Penrith wasn't that bad, especially on a sunny day. "Is this where you'll go to school, Jamie?"

"I'm not allowed."

"Oh?"

The boy shrugged and began bouncing the heel of his boot against the metal leg of his chair. "Mother says I'll be safer at home."

*Safer?* An odd choice of words.

Across the street, three boys a little older and larger than Jamie stopped rolling a hoop to stare at them. One said something to the others and they all laughed in that overly loud, forced way that boys use when being cruel.

Jamie looked away.

Rafe continued to watch them. "Those boys friends of yours?"

"No. Mother says to stay away from them."

"Good advice."

The boys gave up trying to get a reaction from Jamie and moved on to bedevil a three-legged dog darting down an alley.

Jamie continued to bounce his foot. "What's a bastard?" he asked after a long silence.

Rafe stiffened. "Where'd you hear that word?"

No response.

"A bastard is someone without a father," Rafe said. "Those boys call you that?"

Jamie nodded. "They said I was a whore's bastard."

*Hell.* Rafe looked after the boys and fought the urge to go knock some manners into them. "They're wrong." He thought for a moment, then added, "Sometimes people say mean things because of envy. You live in a grand house, wear fine clothes, and eat all the food you want. Plus, you have your own horse. They think belittling you will make them bigger. But it doesn't work that way."

"Mother says to pay them no mind."

"She's right."

Down the street, Josephine walked out of the dry goods store, Stevens close behind her, carrying her parcel. She walked with a jaunty step, the feather in her hat bobbing with each stride, head up, back straight. She stepped into the jewelry store, came back out a few minutes later, and continued toward them. No one spoke to her. Two women whispered behind their gloves and turned their backs as she passed by. A man leaning in the doorway of a tavern stared blatantly.

Rafe felt simmering anger build into a hot, hard knot in his belly. It took monumental effort to keep his expression from betraying the emotions surging through him when she walked up to their table. "Thank you for waiting," she said, ruffling her son's blond hair. "Hungry?"

"Famished."

"Then let's see what the fare is today, shall we?"

Lunch passed pleasantly, and they returned in early afternoon. After changing back into his work clothes, Rafe went down to work Pembroke's Pride. There were still a few puddles in the round pen, so he took the stallion there and put him through his paces on a longe line. At first, the horse resisted stepping into the puddles, but Rafe kept at it until the animal made it all the way around several times without balking.

Pleased with the progress the horse had made, Rafe took him back to his stall. He had almost finished brushing him when a voice said, "Ho," startling him so badly he dropped the brush, which in turn, startled the stallion.

Whipping around, Rafe glared at the man grinning in the doorway. "Damnit, Thomas, quit sneaking around that way. You almost got me stomped."

"I do not sneak."

"I should put bells on you." Rafe picked up the brush and dropped it into the bucket beside the door. "Ash here, too?"

Thomas nodded. "That is a handsome horse."

Rafe felt a swell of pride. "Yeah, he is."

"Is this the one the Scotsman wants?"

"One of the ones."

Hammersmith came down the aisleway, a slight falter in his step when he saw Thomas. "They be looking for ye up at the house, lad," he said to Rafe, giving the Cheyenne careful study.

Rafe introduced them, then motioned Thomas along as he headed up the path to the veranda. "There's a boy here named Jamie. He'll probably pester you with questions. Be nice to him."

"I am always nice."

"Then be extra nice. You kill Pringle yet?"

"No. But I think about it every day."

Rafe chuckled. "How was London?"

"It is a place with no sun, where white people speak a language I do not understand. It smells like a latrine."

"Did you get a chance to talk to Maddie's publisher?"

Thomas nodded. "It is as you said. He has no books that tell the story of the People. He wants me to make him one."

Grinning, Rafe clapped him on the back. "That's wonderful news, Thomas."

The Indian didn't smile back. "I am not sure. It took me a long time to read the book you gave me. I think to make a book would be harder than to read one."

"I'll help you. Others will, too. How is Maddie? Did Ash take her to the doctor?"

Thomas snorted. "White people. You complicate even the simplest things."

"What do you mean?"

"The Scotsman will tell you."

They were crossing the veranda when the door burst open and Jamie darted out, then came to a dead stop when he saw Thomas. "Is that him?"

Rafe nodded. "Thomas, meet Jamie Cathcart. Jamie this is Thomas Redstone, the Cheyenne Dog Soldier."

Jamie gaped, his eyes so wide white showed all around the hazel irises. Then he whirled and raced back inside. "Mother! He's here! I saw him!"

Thomas sighed.

"It'll be all right," Rafe consoled. "Just don't show him your scars."

They found the others gathered in one of the front parlors—the yellow salon?—the house had so many rooms Rafe couldn't keep all their names straight. The countess was looking better, he was relieved to see, and the earl seemed in high spirits. When he saw Rafe and Thomas, he crossed toward them.

"I'm pleased to see you well, Jessup," he said extending his hand. Dipping his head, he added in a lower voice, "As soon as I get the countess settled, I'll meet the two of you at the stable."

Since he wasn't dressed for visiting, Rafe paid his respects to the countess, nodded to Josephine, who sat beside her on the couch, then returned to the stable. A half hour later, Ash and Thomas came in, followed by a Kirkwell groom holding Tricks on a leash. "Give the lad a good run," Ash told the groom, then continued to where Rafe stood with Hammersmith.

Rafe introduced Hammersmith, then grabbed a bag of treats from the feed room and led Ash and Thomas out to the pasture, where they would have more privacy to talk.

"So what do you think, lad?" Ash asked.

"He's got some nice mares. A few nicer than others. Be interested to see what you think."

As the afternoon had lengthened, clouds had rolled in again and the air had that heavy, damp weight that foretold more rain.

Once through the gate, Rafe walked a few more yards, dumped his small bag of apple and carrot treats on the ground, then whistled.

An answering whinny, then the big bay mare trotted out of the trees, the other mares and foals close behind.

"That's Prissy. You'll need her to keep the others in line. She's ten, and has dropped three healthy foals over the years."

As the horses crowded around them, hunting their treats, Thomas and Ash moved quietly among them, murmuring softly, touching them here and there. After a moment, they returned to stand with Rafe. "Well?" he asked.

Thomas spoke first. "They are all good horses. But the big bay you call Prissy, the roan, that smaller bay, and the gray are the best."

"I agree." Ash nodded toward a dark chestnut, saying he liked that one, too, then pointed out the deficits of the others: one was too nervous, another too long in the back, and a couple of others with weaknesses in conformation. "We'll know more about the young fillies after they're weaned."

Rafe looked at him in surprise. "That won't be for a while. Are we staying that long?" It had been his understanding that Ash intended to take the horses back to Colorado before the deepest snows fell.

A huge grin spread across the Scotsman's face. "Maddie insists we stay until the wee bairn arrives."

Rafe drew back in surprise. "Bairn?"

"Aye. The lass wasna sick after all. She's known about the babe for a while, but dinna tell me until we reached London. She was afraid if I knew, I wouldna let her come. She wants it born at Northbridge, as is befitting the Kirkwell heir."

Rafe grinned at the Scotsman's exuberance. "And what if it's a daughter?"

"In Scotland, females can inherit, so long as there are no males before her. But I plan to have many sons."

Pleased that the countess was well, Rafe offered his congratulations and asked when the child was due.

"January. So we willna be going back to Colorado until early spring."

It was late October now. What was Rafe to do for the next five or six months? "If you purchase any of Cathcart's horses, will you be holding them on your land in Scotland until we sail?"

Ash shook his head. "No' unless Cathcart insists I move them out. I'll pay their keep, of course, but I see no sense in taking them up to the Highlands, only to bring them back down to Liverpool in a few months. 'Tis a long trip." He gave Rafe an innocent look. "But if they stay here, I'll need someone to watch over them, so I will. Do you think Mr. Cathcart and his daughter will mind having a bounder such as yourself under-foot for a while?"

Rafe busied himself stroking Prissy's neck. "You'll have to ask them." A half a year in Josephine's company. How would he manage that without doing something foolish?

"I will also need you in Scotland for a short while," Ash went on. "There's a warmblood stable near Edinburgh reputed to have verra good Hanoverian stock that will cross admirably with these thoroughbreds. I'd like for you to come with me to look them over, then bring any I purchase back here until we depart for America." That teasing grin again. "If it wouldna be a bother to spend so much time with the Cathcarts, of course."

Rafe felt heat rise up his neck.

Thomas gave his shoulder a friendly pat. "Do not worry, *nesene*. I will return to protect you."

"From what?"

"The Cathcart woman. I saw the way she smiled when you walked in."

Rafe shoved away from the fence.

"Now, lads." Stepping between the two, Ash looped an arm over each of their shoulders. "Let's go see these stallions Cath-cart has priced so high."

# *Nine*

Dinner was a full dress-up affair. Rafe was delighted to see that Thomas looked as uncomfortable as he did . . . but was less excited to see that the Vicar and Mrs. Bohm were in attendance again. He wondered if the Cathcarts had any other friends to invite, or if the circumstances of Jamie's birth had put the family outside acceptable society. Having a child without benefit of marriage was bad enough back home, but he suspected it was ruinous among the rule-bound English.

A sad thing. Jamie was a fine boy. And his mother . . .

He studied Josephine, seated at the opposite end of the table from her father, chatting with the countess. She was too beautiful and too openly proud of her son to be easily forgiven by her peers. Such a lack of remorse or repentance made her a prime target for those of lesser character, although she appeared to have accepted her banishment without the bitterness one might expect. He greatly admired her for that.

Dinner seemed to go on forever. Luckily, with Lord and Lady Kirkwell drawing most of the attention, Rafe was able to avoid conversation until the meal ended and Cathcart herded his guests into the drawing room for brandy or tea.

Agnes Bohm snagged his arm. "Will you be going to Scotland with Lord and Lady Kirkwell, Mr. Jessup?"

Unable to gracefully free himself, he allowed her to lead him to a couch in the drawing room. "For a while, ma'am."

"A lovely place, the Highlands," she said, waving him to the seat beside her. "Although not so beautiful as our Lake District. Have you had a chance to visit our local ruins?"

"No, ma'am."

"We have several." Turning to Josephine and Maddie, who had taken the settee across from them, she said, "You must take your guests to Brougham Hall while they're here. They say it's haunted, you know. In fact, we have several abodes that are rumored to host spirits."

While Josephine poured tea for the ladies and Vicar Bohm, Thomas wandered to the window, leaving Ash and Cathcart by the marble hearth.

Rafe barely attended the ladies' discussion of ruins and haunted castles, most of his attention fixed on the conversation between the earl and their host at the fireplace. It seemed to revolve around Pembroke's Pride, although he heard his name mentioned, too.

"I daresay we shall have another haunting soon," Mrs. Bohm went on with a labored sigh. "Especially after the tragic death of the baron's wife. Such a shame."

Cathcart turned sharply from the mantle. "Which baron?"

Mrs. Bohm looked up in surprise. "Why, Baron Adderly. Haven't you heard? His poor wife was so distraught over the loss of her third baby she leaped to her death at their house at Fell Ridge."

The vicar frowned at her over the rim of his teacup. "Now Mrs. Bohm. We don't know for certain that she leaped. She might have fallen."

"From the roof?"

At a sound, Rafe looked over to see Josephine staring fixedly at the cup shaking in her hand, her face almost as pale as the lace trim on her dress.

"How sad." Maddie Wallace's expressive brown eyes filled with tears. "Have they other children?"

"A son. Edward, I believe he's named. Although he's sickly, I heard."

Rafe continued to watch Josephine, concerned by the expression of panic in her blue-brown eyes. He was about to ask if she was all right, when Mrs. Bohm turned to her and said, "I'm surprised you didn't know, Josephine. Weren't you and the baron's . . ."

At a loud *harrumph* from her husband, her words trailed off. "Oh dear."

"Josephine," Cathcart said loudly. "Would you ask Shipley to bring a fresh pot of tea? And some of those chocolate confections Cook makes."

"Of c-course." Rising unsteadily, Josephine hurried to the door.

Even though he knew it would raise eyebrows, Rafe excused himself and went after her. He found her in the entry, one hand pressed to her stomach, the other clutching the newel post at the base of the staircase.

"Josephine?"

She looked up, her face slack with shock and distress.

The butler suddenly appeared. Rafe stepped forward. "Miss Cathcart isn't feeling well, Shipley. I'll see to her, but Mr. Cathcart wants you to bring more tea and some of Cook's chocolates to the drawing room."

The old man glanced from Rafe to the woman behind him.

"Now, Shipley."

"Of course, sir."

As soon as the butler turned away, Rafe took Josephine's arm and steered her past the staircase and down the hall toward the back of the house and the conservatory. A blast of warm, humid, flower-scented air rolled over him when he opened the door. The table where they had eaten earlier was gone and in its place was a grouping of metalwork furniture covered with thick cushions. He led her to a small couch.

She sank down and, slumping forward, dropped her head into her hands.

After a moment of indecision, Rafe took the chair nearby.

Neither spoke. He listened for sounds of crying. Heard none. But he could sense her pain.

Or was it relief?

He had guessed from what she had said the morning after he'd arrived, and by her reaction this evening in the salon, that this baron whose wife had fallen to her death was the same man who had deserted her and Jamie. And now her lover was free. Was she hoping he would come back to her?

The thought churned through his mind, raising more questions.

She took her hands away and sat back. No tears, but her distress was evident. He watched her gaze travel around the glass room. "This is where he told me he loved me." Her voice faltered. She shook her head, as if trying to shake off that memory. "Have you ever been in love, Rafe?"

It was the first time she'd called him by his given name, and hearing it spoken in her soft, accented voice moved him in an indefinable way. "I once thought I was."

"What happened?"

"I offered her a way out of a bad situation. She didn't trust me enough to take it." Some people couldn't be saved. Three bullets had taught him that.

"Still it must have hurt."

He shrugged. Miranda and Dirtwater, Texas, were a world away. He couldn't even put her and this woman in the same place in his mind.

"It took me years to get over William's abandonment. For a time I thought I would die of it—the shame—the way people stared and whispered. But as Jamie grew, I realized I wanted his father to have no part in his life. Not to punish him, but because he's so . . . weak." A frown puckered her brow. "Is that wrong of me?"

"Jamie deserves better. So do you."

A wobbly smile, then she looked away again, her eyes shiny and wet in the dim light of the hanging oil lamps. Silence, except for the sounds of their breathing and the gentle burble of water boiling in the pots on the coal stoves. "He brought me here," she said after a long while, "to the same place where he first said he loved me, to tell me he couldn't marry me or acknowledge our son."

Rafe looked down at his clenched hands, a slow burn of anger spreading through his chest.

"I was too naïve to see it coming." Her laugh was laced with sarcasm, but that didn't hide the pain behind the words. "Despite avowals of undying love for me and Jamie, the good baron's son decided it would be more advantageous for him to marry someone of higher rank. He could not, in good conscience, allow his family's title to be passed down to the son of a lowborn woman."

Her wandering gaze settled on him. "In fact, he sat right

where you sit now to offer his excuses. I remember feeling a sharp pain in my chest, as if something had shattered inside. I wondered if a heart could truly break."

"I'm sorry," he murmured through stiff lips.

"For what?"

"That you were hurt."

New tears. And what he saw in her mismatched eyes opened that fissure inside him a little more.

"You're the only person who has ever said that to me."

"Then I'm sorry for that, too." Realizing he was on the verge of doing or saying something he oughtn't, Rafe rose and wandered idly around the steamy room. Mist had collected on the glass panes overhead, and every now and then a drop landed on his head or shoulders. A gentle tap, like a nudge from his conscience, reminding him that this was not the place, or the time, or the woman for him. "I'll be leaving soon," he said.

When she didn't respond, he turned to find her studying him with a bleak expression. "Forever?"

"Only a short while."

"Oh. Good. I—"

He turned away again. "But I'm not sure how wise it would be to come back."

"Why not?"

"You. Me. This." Words failing, he raked a hand through his hair. "You belong here. I don't. But the thought of never seeing you again . . ." He took a deep breath and let it out in a rush. "I care about you, Josephine. But I see no future in it."

"I care about you, too, Rafe. You've become a dear friend."

He turned to face her. "You're not listening." Emotion was so thick in his throat his voice shook with it. "I *care* about you. As more than a friend. More than I should."

"It that wrong?"

"Not wrong. Hopeless. You're a rich man's daughter. I'm a wrangler. We're from different worlds. I could never—"

"There you are," a voice called.

Spinning around, Rafe saw the Kirkwells step through the doorway, followed by Thomas. For a moment he stood frozen, not sure if he was relieved or annoyed by the intrusion. Then tension bled out of him. Relieved. Saved from declaring something he shouldn't.

"What a marvelous room." The countess looked around with a bright smile. "It smells heavenly." Her gaze swung to Josephine, who stood beside the couch with a flustered look, and her expression changed to one of concern. "Are you recovered, Miss Cathcart? Your butler said you were unwell."

"A brief dizzy spell, but I—I'm much better now. Thank you."

"I'm so glad. Shall we sit and chat?"

As the women settled onto the couch, Thomas wandered among the pots and raised beds.

Ash crossed to where Rafe stood. "You should leave," the Scotsman advised in a low voice. "Cathcart is looking for her and it wouldna be good if he knew the two of you had been in here alone."

"We've done nothing wrong." *Yet.*

"'Tis no' me you have to convince."

Rafe struggled to slow his reeling mind. He owed Ash no explanations. But he did owe Josephine his discretion. "Did you and Cathcart reach an agreement on the horses?"

"For the most part. We'll talk tomorrow. Off you go now, lad. And take Thomas before he frightens the staff with his sneaking around."

The Cheyenne materialized at Ash's shoulder. "I do not sneak."

Ash startled. "Bollocks."

"Bells," Rafe advised.

"Aye. Maybe Hammersmith has some we could nail to the heathen's hide."

Josephine watched Rafe and his Indian companion depart through the side door and felt an immediate sense of loss. It was something that happened more and more of late whenever Rayford Jessup wasn't in sight.

What had he been trying to say to her? Good-bye?

The thought aroused a sense of panic that left her almost light-headed.

She rubbed trembling fingertips against her temple. How silly she was. A besotted schoolgirl. She was becoming entirely too dependent on his company.

But how could she not, when she had been so many years

without a comforting presence in her life? She hadn't realized how much she had missed that until Rafe stepped into the void. Having someone to talk to, a strong shoulder to lean on even for a moment, was a luxury she had dearly missed. And now, as she looked over at the gentle woman sitting across from her, she realized how much she had missed having female friends, too.

She was drowning. Sinking into a numb, empty space that terrified her. Why did everyone leave her?

Forcing her mind to her duties as hostess, she put on a smile and asked the countess if her rooms would do.

"They're perfect, I assure you. And have a lovely view of the gardens."

"I see you aren't traveling with a maid. Shall I loan you mine? Or assign one to you?"

"That's not necessary. Since moving to America, I've learned to do without. It's quite liberating, actually, to dress oneself. And if I find myself in difficulty, I always have Ash, bless his heart."

Josephine laughed with her. "I'm so glad you're here, Lady Kirkwell," she said on impulse. "This big house gets lonely with just the servants and the three of us rambling around in it."

"Three of us?"

Realizing her mistake, Josephine felt a momentary regret. But she quickly pushed it away, determined to be truthful with this lovely lady, even if it put an end to their budding friendship. Besides, she would know soon enough, anyway. "I have a son. Jamie. He's seven. His father is Adderly."

The countess blinked at her, her expression of interest changing to puzzlement. "Baron Adderly? The same baron whose wife—"

"Yes. We were involved before he married." She gave a bitter smile. "I was very young and thought we would marry someday. But when I told him about the child, he explained that commoners and aristocrats don't cross social boundaries."

She watched for signs of withdrawal, disgust. Braced for it.

Instead, Lady Kirkwell beamed, changing her attractive face into one of rare beauty. "Then I hope we shall be the exception. I need a friend. Especially now." Leaning forward, she whispered, "I'm in a family way, you see. And to have a friend by my side at this time would be a great comfort."

For a moment, Josephine couldn't respond. Then relief and joy coursed through her. "Congratulations, my lady. I'm so happy for you. It's a wonderful thing, having a child, and I would be honored to help in any way I can."

"Excellent!" The countess clasped her hands as if that was the best news she had heard in a long time. "I have many questions. And concerns. And the earl, bless his heart—that's an expression I learned from my Southern friend, who I hope you will meet someday—is no help at all. But then, one doesn't have to be brilliant to be an aristocrat, does one? Your foolish little baron is proof of that."

The next few days were such a whirlwind of activity Josephine had no time to dwell on how lonely she would be after her guests left. They toured ruins and fallen castles around Penrith, visited two ancient sites from much earlier times, and discussed with Henry Brougham the departed spirits that roamed his newly restored Brougham Hall. And on an especially warm, clear day, they rode to the top of Beacon Hill to take in the distant views of the Pennines and North Lakes.

The only thing to mar her happiness was the way Rafe seemed to avoid her. Was he regretting his impulsive words in the conservatory? She could feel him pulling away and didn't know how to stop it. But every day, the gap widened.

Lord and Lady Kirkwell were a treasure, not only because of the friendship they extended toward her, but also because of the kindness they showed Jamie. Never once did they indicate any concern over the circumstances of his birth, and always treated him as the innocent child that he was. Thomas Redstone was especially gentle and patient with her son's many questions, and whenever they went into town, Rafe made a point of standing by Jamie's side to scowl away any unkind remarks. For the first time in a long while, she felt protected enough to relax in public.

Father and the earl struck a sticky bargain over the horses . . . all except for Pembroke's Pride. Rafe had continued to work with the stallion, and his improvement was so notable Father was reluctant to part with the horse. Josephine didn't understand why until she walked into the stable one morning and

overheard him asking Hammersmith if he thought Pems would
ever be able to race again.

"He's retired from racing," she interrupted, walking up
behind them. "He's my horse, and I will never subject him to
that again."

Father turned in surprise. "Your horse? Since when?"

Even from several feet away, she could smell the whisky on
his breath, although it was scarcely ten o'clock. "Since you
gave Pems to me as a foal on my fifteenth birthday. Don't you
remember, Father, how we argued over the naming of him?"

"Perhaps so, but I have need of him now. And that's an end
to it."

Rafe and Thomas and Lord Kirkwell had been standing in
the opening at the other end of the stable by the mare's pasture,
and they all turned when they heard Father's raised voice.

He noticed their interest, and his face reddened with embarrassment. "We'll discuss it later, daughter."

But Josephine couldn't let it go. "It's clear the horse is still
having difficulties, Father. He may never fully recover. And
certainly not well enough to race again, even if I were to permit it."

"Permit it?" He stepped closer, his hands clenched.

For a moment she feared he would strike her. He never had
before, but with his increased drinking, and the debts piling
up, she knew his nerves were ragged. She stepped back, almost
bumping into a sturdy body behind her.

"Morning, Mr. Cathcart," Rafe said over her shoulder. "Here
to watch Pembroke's early workout?"

His deep voice carried no threat, but Josephine knew him
better now, and could sense the tension beneath the calm tone.

Father put on a tight smile. "Since you'll be leaving soon,
Jessup, I've turned his training over to Hammersmith. Stevens
will be riding him today."

Rafe didn't respond.

With a terse nod, Father whirled and walked away, calling
over his shoulder as he went, "Report to me later, Hammersmith."

"Yes, sir."

With an apologetic glance at Josephine, the groom walked
past her to where the stable boys were mucking out the stalls.

"Are you all right, Miss Cathcart?" Lord Kirkwell asked, his green eyes pinned on Father's retreating back.

"Yes, of course. It was nothing. A small disagreement."

"It didn't sound small." Rafe had that stubborn set to his strong jaw. "It looked like he was threatening you."

"He drinks too much." Shaking his head in disgust, Redstone walked away.

"My apologies, Miss Cathcart." The earl's glare shifted to the Cheyenne. "Thomas can be verra outspoken at times. Dinna wander off, heathen," he called, hurrying after the departing Indian. "We leave tomorrow, and if you're off on one of your scouting forays, I'll leave ye behind, so I will."

*Tomorrow.* Josephine felt that familiar panic grab at her throat. How dull her days would be without them. Without him.

"What were you and your father arguing about?" Rafe asked.

"He wants to race Pems again."

"It's too soon."

"I told him that. He didn't listen. Tomorrow? You're leaving tomorrow?"

He looked down at her, those deep blue eyes sliding over her face like a gentle touch. "You and Jamie could come with us."

Tempting. But Josephine knew that without her here, her father would get into even more mischief. "Just come back. You promised Jamie you'd help him pick out his new horse." *And I'm not yet ready to say good-bye to you forever.*

She scarcely slept that night, awakening several times, gasping for air and feeling suffocated. Toward dawn, she gave up trying to rest, and rose.

Sadly, it looked to be a beautiful day for traveling—she had hoped for an early snowstorm. After her wash, she debated what to wear, then decided she didn't want Rafe's last image to be of her dressed in plain barn clothing, so she donned a simple but flattering morning dress in the same deep blue as his eyes.

By the time she stepped out onto the side terrace, the sun was slanting through the trees by the brook. At the stable, grooms busily harnessed teams to the Kirkwell carriages, while

Shipley and the earl's man, Pringle, supervised the loading of the luggage for the short carriage ride to the train depot in Carlisle. The earl's huge dog waited nearby on a restraining leash, clearly excited by the bustle of preparations.

With that same breathless feeling that had plagued her through the night, Josephine lifted her hems out of the dew and hurried down the path.

She found Rafe standing at the open door of Pembroke's stall, talking quietly to the horse nuzzling his coat pockets for a treat. He looked big and alien in his long duster and Western attire, distinctly out of place among the earl's green-liveried coachmen with their tall hats, polished brass buttons, and white gloves.

And so unabashedly male.

She hadn't been the only one to notice. She had seen the way the kitchen and parlor maids looked at him, and knew that they, too, saw it. Strong, capable, protective. What woman wouldn't react to a man like that?

As she approached, he turned, and when that intense blue gaze met hers, she felt it all through her body. A shiver beneath her skin, a sudden weakness in her lungs, a warm tingle that spread down low, below her belly.

Desire. She had known it once. And now, with this guarded and enigmatic man, she felt it again. Only stronger. Much stronger.

She wondered if he felt it, too. If that's what he had been trying to convey to her in the conservatory several nights ago.

He closed the lower half of the stall door then, leaning a shoulder against the door frame, crossed his arms over his broad chest. His gaze traveled over her in an appreciative, but not blatant, way. "You look beautiful this morning."

She plucked a bit of straw from her skirt in a futile attempt to pretend the compliment didn't make her blush with pleasure. "I try."

"You succeed."

"Then the endless hours were worth it." Pembroke poked his head out the top opening of his stall door. Grateful for the distraction, she ran a hand down his white blaze. "How long do you think you'll be away?"

"Too long."

She gave him a look. "You're certainly being charming today."

"I try." He dipped his head to add in a soft voice, "I'll miss you, Josephine." Then he smiled—her first real smile—showing strong, white teeth, a dimple in his cheek, crinkles at the corners of his remarkable eyes.

It took her breath away.

"I—I'll miss you, too," she said, once she'd collected her thoughts. "Promise me you'll come back, Rafe. We—I—you're important to us."

"Josie . . ."

As she stared up into deep blue eyes, something primitive and undeniable and desperate gripped her. Fearing she might never see him again, she took his face in her hands and pulled his head down. "You come back," she whispered fiercely and, on impulse, pressed her lips to his. Then astonished by what she had done, and fearing his reaction to such boldness, she whirled and fled the stable.

# *Ten*

Before climbing into the carriage, Lady Kirkwell turned to Josephine with an expression of near panic. "Promise you will come for a visit soon. With train service now, the trip is not so long. I'm sure Jamie would enjoy exploring the castle and seeing all the armaments. And I would adore visiting with you again."

"I should like that, my lady. I hear the Highlands are quite beautiful."

"But lonely." The dainty auburn-haired woman glanced at her husband, who was saying his good-byes to Father. "Say you'll come," she murmured, giving Josephine a hard, fast hug. "I would so welcome a pretty English face amongst all those dour Scots. And I promise not to make you eat anything odd."

Josephine gave a wobbly smile. "Thank you, my lady, for your kindness to both me and my son."

"Mount up, lass," her husband interrupted, advancing in that military march Josephine found so amusing. "Tricks is loaded and we have a train to meet. Pringle," he shouted toward the second carriage as he helped his wife to her seat. "If you dinna put that flask away, I'll give you to Thomas, so I will."

Without waiting to see if his valet obeyed, he turned to Josephine with a smile that had doubtless melted many a heart. "'Twas good to see you again, Miss Cathcart. You have grown into a lovely lady since I last saw you." Lowering his voice so her father wouldn't hear, he added, "Dinna fret. I'll send the lad back soon. 'Tis clear he has his eye on you, and I wouldna want his wee heart to break."

She had to laugh. "I doubt that's a danger."

"Perhaps. But dinna let his rough ways fool you, lass. He's a good man."

"I know." Her gaze followed Rafe as he climbed into the second carriage behind Pringle. Had she shocked him with that kiss? Given him a reason to hurry back? The taste of him still lingered on her lips, the rough scrape of his whiskers still prickled her palms. Already, she longed to feel and taste him again.

"Plan to come for a visit," the earl said, breaking into her thoughts. He glanced back into the carriage, where his wife waited, then added softly, "The countess gets a bit lonely away from England."

"I shall try."

"Until then." With a mock salute and a sharp command to the coachman, he climbed into the carriage. A moment later they turned down the drive. The second carriage followed, and as it rolled past Josephine, Rafe's gaze met hers through the open window. What she saw in those intense blue eyes and that crooked smile told her he was remembering that kiss, too.

Because of the countess's condition, the travelers planned to take the carriages only as far as Carlisle, where they would board the train to Edinburgh, leaving Tricks and the coaches loaded with most of their belongings to continue on to Scotland.

The run to Carlisle was uneventful, except for Pringle's snoring. When Rafe boarded the train for Edinburgh, he made sure to pick a seat as far away from the old man as possible.

They reached the city late, and retired early to their rooms in the Wayfarer's Inn. Rafe slept fitfully, and was up the next morning before Ash. After a quick breakfast, leaving Thomas posted outside Lady Kirkwell's door, the earl and Rafe rode rented horses to the warmblood stable north of the city.

Rafe wasn't that familiar with Hanoverian warmbloods, but he realized immediately why Ash wanted to add them to his stable. Sturdy, well-tempered horses, they had strong backs and powerful, athletic frames, which, when tempered with the elegance, grace, and intelligence of the lighter thoroughbreds, would create a handsome strain of horses suitable for a variety of purposes.

At his suggestion, Ash selected one proven stud and one colt, along with three proven mares. After completing arrangements for Rafe and Thomas to collect them on their way back to Cathcart's from Scotland, they returned to the inn.

The next morning, they were back on the train, heading through the Ochil Hills, past Perth, and on toward Pitlochry at the base of the Grampian Mountains near the heart of the Highlands.

From what Rafe could tell as the train followed the River Tay through rising foothills, the Highlands were a lot like England, only rougher—although, considering the earl's love for one and contempt for the other, Rafe didn't mention that. A bit steeper and rockier than Cumberland or the lowlands, less cultivated, and certainly less populated. There was an untamed element to the wild terrain that captured Rafe's imagination. Bleak moorland covered with yellow gorse. Stark pinnacles and bare rocky ridges dipping down into misty valleys and deep, icy lakes—or lochs, as they were called in Scotland. After reading *Rob Roy*, Rafe could easily see why this land generated such devotion in its people, and produced such fierce warriors.

But he could never live here. Even in these wild Highland mountains. Not in any country where status of birth mattered more than character or accomplishment, or in a place with so much rain and so little sun. Surely, Josephine knew that.

Then why had she kissed him?

"This is a strange land," Thomas Redstone muttered, breaking into Rafe's thoughts. From his slouched position on the hard bench in the crowded railcar, the Indian waved a hand toward the streaked window at Rafe's shoulder. "There are not enough trees and too many mud holes."

"Peat bogs."

"I do not like them. And their little horses with too much fur. Paugh! I do not like them, either."

"Garrons."

"They could never catch a buffalo."

"Probably not."

Thomas wasn't a patient traveler. Being stuck on a train for several days seemed to grate on him even more than being stuck at sea. At least aboard ship he could move around.

"And these are not mountains," the Cheyenne went on in a sullen tone. "Mountains reach into the clouds and wear caps of snow. These are hills."

Rafe agreed. He remembered reading that the highest point in all of England—Ben Nevis—was less than four thousand five hundred feet high, while the peaks in Colorado Territory began at that height and continued upward for thousands more feet. Another thing he didn't tell Ash.

Hoping to distract the Indian from his complaints, he asked if he had thought any more about the book he would write for the countess's publisher.

Thomas gave him a disdainful look. "I will not write it. You will write it. But I will tell you what to say."

"What stories do you want to include?"

"There are many." Thomas thought for a moment. "One is about a Cheyenne girl who mated with a dog and birthed seven pups, who died and became stars in the sky."

"Yes . . . well . . . anything else?"

"Our children like the story of Sharpened-leg, a young brave who cut off his feet and sharpened his legs into points."

"Why the hell would he do that?"

"To play tricks on his friends. But when he tried to kick the tree where his friend hid, his pointed leg stuck in the wood and would not come free. So he hung there until he died. A reminder to be careful of the tricks we play on others."

"Jesus."

"For women, there is the lesson of the bad wife who left her husband. Her disloyalty brought such dishonor to her father that he killed her and cut her into pieces. Or maybe he cut her up first, then killed her. I do not remember."

"Hell, Thomas. Don't you know any happy stories?"

"Happy?" The Cheyenne's grin showed malice. "Like the one when Crazy Horse defeated a hundred bluecoats at Massacre Hill? That is a good story."

"You really are a savage, aren't you?"

The grin widened. "Yes, I am."

* * *

Two leisurely days later, they reached Pitlochry, where the Kirkwell carriages and Ash's wolfhound were waiting. It was only early afternoon and they hadn't far to go, so after the earl and the countess had changed into their great kilts and Ash had sent word ahead of their impending arrival, he herded them toward the carriages for the short ride to Northbridge.

Rafe had never seen the earl in his ceremonial garb. But as he watched him mount the magnificent black horse that had been brought from Northbridge for his triumphant ride home, he could see that donning his clan tartan changed him.

Despite the enveloping folds of plaid cloth that hung past his knees, he seemed freer than Rafe had ever seen him. Bigger. Taller. More given to sweeping gestures, rather than the tautly controlled mannerisms of a military officer. He was in his element.

In contrast, the countess seemed out of hers. There was pride in her posture and the lift of her head, but not the boisterous joy her husband displayed. Maybe because she was one of the barely tolerated English. Or because the years spent in this remote place while Ash was off soldiering hadn't been happy ones. The earl had told Rafe that he and his wife had been estranged for a time, and Maddie had gone to America to start a life without him. Perhaps coming back to Scotland had renewed all those unhappy memories.

Frowning, Rafe watched her climb into the carriage. The empathy that made him so attuned to horses now rose in concern for her. Was that fear he saw in her coffee-colored eyes? Did she think that because she carried the Kirkwell heir, she would be trapped in this bleakly beautiful place forever?

And it was definitely bleak. A broad, treeless valley, sandwiched between Loch Rannock and the boggy marshland of the Great Rannock Moor, it reminded Rafe of the stark grasslands of Oklahoma. But wetter. Especially with that roiling gray sky whipping the wind into an icy blast. At least here cyclones didn't spin down from the clouds, plucking man and beast from the earth without a trace.

The ride was a short one, led by Tricks and the earl on his prancing horse. A crowd of cheering people, all wearing the same plaid Ash and the countess wore, greeted him when they turned onto the long, rocky drive that led to an imposing stone structure perched on a slight rise near the loch.

Laughing, Ash leaned down to accept a ribbon-bound bouquet of heather from a child as he rode by, then he straightened to acknowledge shouts and well wishes with a grin and a wave. It was a rousing welcome that brought a smile to Thomas's stoic face, and a look of terror to Pringle's. Especially when they reached the house and the gray clouds parted in a slash to reveal a sunset of such violent hues, it was as if the jaws of hell had opened before them. A stirring sight.

Ash's ancestral home less so.

Wind-and-rain-scoured walls the same dark gray as the brooding sky rose at least sixty feet high. At one end sat a crenelated tower with several stones missing—at the other, a crumbling buttress in the process of either being repaired, or falling into decay. Tangled gardens, weed-choked walkways, what might have once been a moat, now a gully of tumbled stones. A proud, ancient castle waiting to become a ruin.

"Lord help us," Pringle muttered.

Battered doors crashed open as they rode through the outer wall and into an enclosed open area. "*Fàilte dhachaidh,*" a tall, plaid-draped woman cried, racing toward Ash. "Welcome home, my brother."

Behind her, a big, hairy fellow in a different plaid called out, "'Tis guid tae have ye hame, Kirkwell! *Failte gu Alba*—welcome to Scotland!"

Rafe guessed these two were the family caretakers left in charge of Northbridge during the earl's stay in America.

"Glynnis! Fain!" Ash rushed toward them, embraced them both in bear hugs, said something in Gaelic, then turned to assist his wife from the carriage. "Here's the countess . . . and our babe," he added proudly.

More welcomes. Hugs between the women—which Rafe was pleased to see erased that look of dread from Maddie's face. Then, with his arm still around his wife's shoulders, Ash, Lord Kirkwell and Laird of his clan, turned to the waiting crowd. "*Alba gu bràth,*" he shouted and raised a fist in triumph.

The crowd cheered wildly, their answering yells rising to a

crescendo when their earl tossed back his gray head and gave a savage war cry.

Rafe felt like he'd stepped into the pages of Sir Walter Scott's novel. He wished he'd brought the book with him to check the index for translations. Glancing over at the grinning Cheyenne, he hoped the Indian didn't join in with a war cry of his own, which would be less stirring than frightening.

Turning, Ash motioned to those waiting beside the second carriage. "Come, Rafe. Thomas. Pringle, ye may approach, as well, but dinna speak. Meet my sister, Glynnis, and her husband, Fain McKenzie."

After introductions were completed, the earl led them through the huge castle doors and into a place time had forgotten.

They walked over gritty stone floors scoured by thousands of feet over the years. From smoke-blackened beams hung huge chandeliers sprouting antlers and dozens of smoking candles. Above sooty fireplaces, ancient tapestries depicted bloody battle scenes. Instead of framed artworks, the walls were decorated with dented shields, battered swords, axes, and claymores. And in the place of honor in the Great Hall, above a fireplace that looked big enough to accommodate several stout men, hung the Kirkwell crest.

Rafe had to laugh. Northbridge so perfectly suited its master.

Awaiting them by the hearth were mugs of Scotch whisky—Rafe was becoming accustomed to the Scots' pronunciation and spelling—which brought a frown to Thomas's face and a smile to Pringle's. After several Gaelic toasts, washed down with the same smooth, smoky brew the earl kept in Heartbreak Creek, the doors were thrown open and the waiting crowd rushed in to fill the benches at the long, worn tables set up throughout the hall.

The noise and laughter bouncing off the stone walls grew to a deafening pitch. Even Tricks hid under a table to escape it. Or maybe he was hunting scraps.

Serving people bustled in and out, bearing trays laden with Scottish fare. Fish soup called cullen skink, turnips and potatoes called neeps and tatties, honey-coated fruits, poached fish, roasted meats and fowl, and a lumpy, congealed substance the countess said was a traditional Scottish dish called haggis.

Which was almost the exact sound Rafe made when she added that it was made of various sheep organs—or pluck—simmered in a sheep's stomach.

More whisky. Shouts and laughter. War cries. Heat rising from the giant fireplace further blackened the ancient beams overhead, while a smoky veil coiled around the vast array of armaments displayed along the walls.

It was stirring and primitive, and made Rafe want to rush out and fight something. But that might have been the whisky talking.

Once the meal ended, a more somber mood fell over the gathering. Ash and Maddie went to stand below the Kirkwell crest, and with great ceremony, the people of Northbridge lined up to pay homage to their new earl and countess and offer well wishes for their babe. It was an amazing homecoming and explained a great deal about Ash.

The next morning, Rafe awoke with a pounding head—then realized it was someone hammering on the door of the room he shared with Thomas. With a groan, he rose and opened it to find Fain McKenzie grinning in the hallway.

"Guid morn tae ye," he said, adding several extra *r*'s to the second word. "Kirkwell will be busy wi' the stewards today, and asked me tae show ye and the Indian aboot." Scratching his bearded chin, he looked past Rafe at Thomas's empty bed. "Do ye ken where the lad might be?"

"Anywhere." Rafe stifled a yawn. "Thomas has a habit of wandering off whenever the mood strikes him."

McKenzie gave a worried frown. "'Tis dangerous country, so it is."

"He'll be all right. Is there any food downstairs?" Maybe that would settle his rolling stomach.

"Aye. Bannocks and honey and *skalk*—a wee tot of whisky tae clear the sleep from yer head. Come along, lad. 'Tis well past dawn already."

Several minutes later, they were huddled against a heavy mist, riding rough-gaited Highland ponies along the loch. The wind cut through Rafe with bone-chilling malevolence, and he envied the fat sheep in their thick coats of wool that scrambled out of their way. Here and there, picturesque stone and thatch huts dotted the long slope that led down to the water's edge, their neatly walled gardens turned under for the winter and children waving from the porch.

It didn't seem to be an especially prosperous place. Yet Rafe saw contentment in the smiling faces, and the houses looked to be in good repair. "Are sheep the main source of income around here?" he asked, wondering how many sheep it would take to keep his workers fed and still provide Ash with enough money to buy pure-blooded horses and build a grand home in Heartbreak Creek.

The Scot smiled proudly, showing gaps in his strong white teeth. Rafe guessed he was a bit of a brawler, as most of these Highlanders seemed to be. Including Ash. "Our wool is the finest in the Highlands. Northbridge ships take it straight tae weavers in Ireland, where they spin it intae cloth sae fine 'tis like silk against yer skin."

"Kirkwell has his own ships?"

"Aye. Tew." McKenzie held up two fingers. "'Tis easier tae avoid the tariff collectors when ye have yer own docks and boats, so it is. Those bloodsucking English would starve us oot, if they could."

Judging by McKenzie's robust frame, the enterprise was doing well. "Does he smuggle anything else?"

"Smuggle?" The bearded man reared back to glare at him. "We dinna call it smuggling. We call it staying free. If the English had their way, they'd have us off our land and toiling in their sooty factories like slaves. We willna do it."

Rafe didn't respond. Being more partial to cattle, he didn't have much fondness for sheep and the harm they did to grass-lands. But here, in this wet climate, the grass probably recovered quickly enough to prevent lasting damage.

"And then there's the drink, o' course."

He looked over to see that sly look back on McKenzie's face. "Drink?"

"Scottish nectar." McKenzie gave a startling bark of laughter that made the horses sidestep and sent several fat ground birds into fluttering flight. "The Earls of Kirkwell have been making it for many years, so they have. And no' that auld stuff that rots yer gut. Northbridge Scotch Whisky is as smooth and gentle as a kelpie's kiss. And now that the earl is opening other markets in yer country, we're all sitting grand." His big grin faded into a scowl as he swung his bright blue gaze in all directions. "But ye dinna hear that from me, lad."

Ash and smuggling and whisky. Rafe wasn't surprised.

Pembroke's Pride's workouts continued. Josephine kept an eye on Hammersmith and Gordon Stevens, but the lessons in the round pen passed without incident and the stallion improved more every day.

Not so the relationship between Josephine and her father. Although there had been no additional discussion of her unmarried status after she told him about the incident with Mr. Calhoun and demanded he stop bandying it about that she was "available," the tension between them remained high.

They rarely saw each other except at meals, and those settled into a chilly reserve that robbed Josephine of what appetite she could muster. Because drinking made Father cruel and argumentative, she no longer risked having Jamie join them for dinner. She would have avoided those tense meals, herself, had her father not insisted she attend. In stilted silence, they sat at either end of the long table, Father staring at her as he drank more than he ate, while she ignored him and thought of Rafe.

Tonight was no exception.

He had called her "Josie." She'd not heard that name in a long time, not since they had left the tumbledown cottage in the village outside the mine where Father had toiled before fortune had lifted them into higher society. Back then, she had had friends, and neighbors, and other children with which to play. She had never felt as alone in that humble cottage as she did in this palatial home.

Then Rafe came into her life.

Did he think her too bold for kissing him?

He had seemed to respond, but it had been so long since she'd kissed a man she might have imagined it. Wishful thinking, perhaps.

Lining green beans in a row on her plate, she smiled at her own daring. That kiss had surprised her, too. Even before her

Great Indiscretion, she had never been an impulsive person.
And later, as her dreams had crumbled around her, she had
stayed in the shadows, terrified to attract more attention to
herself, draw more sneers and barbed comments—never spoken directly to her, but always within her hearing.

And then Rayford Jessup had come.

Uncomplicated. Incapable of guile or malice, he had seen
through her hard-built armor and the pall of criticism that had
shrouded her for so long. With him, she felt daring, and desir-
able, and worthy.

Without him, she could feel those old doubts creeping back
into her mind.

Lost in thought, she chewed a piece of roast pheasant. Such
a simple thing, a kiss. Such a commonplace act, to hold another's hand. But to one desperate for a touch, a kind word, a
caring smile, it was like the breath of life.

"Pembroke is doing well," her father said from the other
end of the dining table, startling her into a cough.

She cleared her throat. "He is." Even though her father
hadn't sold Pems out from under her, she still didn't trust him,
so she quickly added, "But he remains skittish around water.
I fear he always will."

"He could be the key to our salvation. I wish you would
understand that."

She did understand. She knew the prospect of sliding back
into poverty was intolerable to her father. Because she had
Jamie to protect, she was able to ignore the sly looks, innuendoes, and snide remarks that followed wherever she went.
However, Father had nothing to sustain him but his illusions
of wealth and the sense of importance they gave him. Without
them, he would perish. Or drag her and Jamie back into those
black holes of despair with him.

"What about the money the earl paid for the horses?" she
asked him.

"That bought us a bit of time. Nothing more."

A chill pressed against the walls of her heart. "So what are
you going to do, Father?" She knew, but needed to hear him
say the words.

His red-rimmed eyes slid away. "I have no choice, daughter.
If he wins, we stand to make a fortune."

"He won't win."

"He might."

Setting down her fork, she clasped her hands in her lap so he couldn't see that they were shaking. "He will never jump water, Father. Even after all the work we've put into him, he will barely step into it now."

He waved his free hand in dismissal. "He's got six months to learn. The Grand National isn't until April." Setting down his goblet with such force wine spilled like blood over his fingers, he glared at her down the long length of the table. "I'm entering Pembroke's Pride in the race. You'd best accept that. And when the time comes, girl, your horse will either make the jump or die trying."

# *Eleven*

Rafe eyed the aging valet slumped at a table in the kitchen, a greenish cast to his whiskered face and "a wee tot" of whisky in his trembling hand. "Do you cut hair, Pringle?"

Wincing, the old man pressed a hand over his ear. "Stop shouting."

"Will you cut my hair?" Rafe asked in a softer voice. "It's starting to curl over my collar. Before long, I'll look like one of these hairy Scotsmen." He shot a grin at the eavesdropping kitchen helpers and received a giggle in response.

"No."

Rafe bent down to look into the old man's bleary eyes. "No, you won't cut my hair? Or no, I won't look like a hairy Scotsman?"

"Both. Either. I don't care. Bad enough I'm banished to this wasteland of superstitious savages, I'll not whore out my skills like a common servant."

Across the room, the cook snorted.

Straightening, Rafe scratched his stubbled chin. "I could have Ash make you do it."

This time, it was Pringle who snorted.

"Or Thomas."

That got his attention. He frowned, then a crafty look came into his red-rimmed eyes. Lifting a shaking hand, he studied it for a moment, then smiled evilly at Rafe. "Certainly, sir. Do let me retrieve my sharpest scissors. And would you care for a shave with my straight razor, as well?"

"I would gladly cut it fer ye, sir," a breathless voice said behind Rafe.

Turning, he looked down into the hopeful face of one of the maids who giggled incessantly whenever he and Thomas came into the kitchen.

"Well, ah . . ."

"I've sheared many a sheep, so I have," she said, pressing her breast against his arm. "And hardly a nick, I'm proud to say. Shall we have a go?"

"Maybe later," Rafe said, and fled.

In the end, Thomas cut it, using his long-bladed hunting knife like a saw. A bit uneven around the edges, but Rafe had had worse.

That afternoon, the countess sent word for Rafe and Thomas to join her and Ash in the sitting area off their bedroom.

Like the rest of the castle, the earl's quarters were stark and cold and filled with masculine trappings left over from the previous earls, Ash's older brothers, both of whom had died in recent years. In her bright blue dress, Lady Kirkwell stood out like the first bluebell in a barren winter landscape. Here and there, small feminine touches had been added, but she had yet to make the room her own. Or any of Northbridge, for that matter. Perhaps she didn't want to do anything of a permanent nature lest she feel compelled to stay. Rafe hoped she wouldn't. He couldn't see a woman with such a gentle and vibrant spirit thriving in this austere place.

Curious as to why they'd been summoned, he and Thomas joined Ash and the countess in the chairs grouped around a crackling fire in the hearth.

"I'm so glad you came." The Englishwoman beamed, her face alight with that bright smile Rafe associated more with Maddie of Heartbreak Creek than the Countess of Kirkwell. "I have news—Heavens, Mr. Jessup! What happened to your hair?"

"Thomas cut it."

"With what? His hunting knife?" She said it with a smile, but when Rafe nodded, her expression changed to one of exasperation. "Honestly. It simply won't do. After we finish here,

I'll have one of the maids cut it. You look like you're wearing a thatched roof."

"Yes, ma'am."

Happiness restored, she pulled an envelope from her skirt pocket. "As I said, I have news. Lucinda has written, and I thought you might like to hear all the latest from Heartbreak Creek. Shall I?" Without waiting for assent, she pulled several sheets of stationery from an envelope and began to read:

" *'Dearest friends,*

" *'I received your letter and was happy to read that the crossing went well. I already miss you, and the town is so quiet it doesn't seem like home anymore. Now that the bridge line is complete, even the Chinese have deserted us. I almost wish Ash was here to rend the silence with a lively Scottish tune.'* "

"Aye." A wistful expression came into Ash's moss green eyes. "The pipes do have a way of lifting one's spirits. 'Tis sorry I am that I left them behind in Heartbreak Creek."

Maddie gave him a look, shuddered, then cleared her throat. "To continue . . .

" *'I'm delighted that you have recovered some of your energy, Maddie. My only disappointment is that you and I cannot go through our confinements together. Misery does love company, I hear. Do you have any idea how difficult it was for me to keep your secret? But I'm glad all is well.'* "

"What?" Ash bolted upright. "You told a stranger about our bairn before you told me?"

"Luce isn't a stranger," his wife argued. "She and Tait are family. And if I had told you, you wouldn't have let me come. Nor would you have made the trip without me. Now do hush, love, so I can finish the letter."

Muttering under his breath, the earl settled back.

" *'My guardian, Mrs. Throckmorton, was able to sell her Manhattan brownstone without difficulty, and is now happily ensconced in a suite at the hotel. She seems unbothered by Pringle's absence (but really, who would be?). I hope he has not been too big a trial for Ash, although Tait finds the notion of the old butler becoming Ash's valet vastly amusing. Mrs. T.'s retainers, Mrs. Bradshaw and Mr. Quinn, returned to Colorado with us, and Mrs. B. has graciously taken over management of the hotel. Mr. Quinn has taken a new position, as well. Making use of his background as a Pinkerton Detective, he is now Chief of Security for both the Denver & Santa Fe, as well as our own Pueblo Pacific Bridge Line. I only wish he would come up to snuff with Mrs. B. It's clear they care for each other but for some reason Mr. Q. won't commit. When you return, Maddie, we shall have to work on him.' "*

"Lord help the lad."

Ignoring her husband's muttered comment, the countess read on.

*" 'I'm also happy to report that Tait and Ethan Hardesty are in partnership to build a grand hotel near the site of the mineral spring in the canyon. Not at the spring, itself, since they're aware that area is sacred to Thomas's people. But lower down, where the spring empties into the creek. The plans look amazing.*

*" 'In sadder news, Audra Hardesty's father died in a tumble down the stairs several weeks ago. A dreadful blow, but she continues to keep the newspaper going and seems to have recovered from her father's death and the ordeal that vile murderer put her through. The new house Ethan designed for her is coming along well. As is yours, Maddie. I predict both will be ready for occupancy by the time you return.' "*

"Aye, and well they should be. A hotel isna the place to raise a bairn."

With a fond smile, the countess patted his hand. "You're interrupting again, dearest."

"Sorry, lass." He nodded for her to continue.

*" 'I am enclosing a letter from Pru. I sense she is growing homesick, despite becoming more and more involved with her school for freed men and women. She has also spent a great deal of time working on an education initiative with a local Negro preacher. I'm not sure what to make of it so I will say no more about it, and allow you to read her letter, yourself.' "*

Rafe glanced at Thomas, but the Cheyenne's face revealed nothing of his thoughts.

*" 'The Brodies are still out at the ranch, but come into town on a regular basis. All seem to be doing well, and you will not credit how big the children are now. I think R.D. is already shaving! And I actually saw Brin in a dress and it wasn't even*

*a Sunday. Baby Whit is growing so fast I'm sure Declan will
have him on a horse by his second birthday.*

" '*I must close for now. Nurse Tait is insisting I take a nap,
although I'm feeling much more energetic the more ungainly
I become. Odd, that.*'

"You know, it is odd," Maddie said, looking up from her
letter. "The bigger I get, the more . . ." When she saw the three
male faces staring blankly back at her, she smiled. "Yes, well,
never mind that. In closing, Lucinda writes, '*I hope you continue in good health, dearest, and please give my well wishes
to those in Scotland with you. Love, Lucinda.*' "

With a tremulous smile, Maddie folded the letter and slipped
it back into the envelope. "It seems so strange to be parted from
them."

"Now, lass." Reaching over, Ash brushed his big hand
against her cheek. "We still have time to go back, love, if that's
what you want."

Her small pointed chin came up. "Absolutely not. Northbridge is where all the Kirkwell heirs have been born. Our son
will be born here, as well."

"Or daughter." The smile Ash gave her was so charged with
emotion Rafe had to look away. Despite his brash ways, the
man was devoted to his wife.

"Shall I read Pru's letter?" she asked, pulling another missive
from the envelope on her lap. But her smile died when she looked
up and saw Thomas disappearing through the doorway.

"Perhaps later," Ash said, staring after his friend with a
troubled frown.

Time passed slowly for Rafe. After the first week, the raw,
misty beauty of the Highlands began to wear thin, and he found
himself longing for the dry, crackling heat of the American
Southwest just before a thunderstorm swept out of the sunbaked
sky. This constant half rain that kept everything soggy and
slick with moss gave him a chill he couldn't seem to shake, and
at night, his old wounds throbbed with a dull ache that left him
plagued with troubling dreams.

One morning after an especially restless night, when he and

Thomas left the room and went down the long stone staircase, the Cheyenne asked him where the dream snare was that he had made for him.

"I forgot and left it in my room at Cathcart's." He glanced over at the frowning Indian. "Have I been keeping you awake?"

Thomas shrugged. "Is she dead?"

"Miranda?"

"If she is dead, that is why she haunts your sleep. The People believe it awakens bad spirits to speak the name of one who has died."

"She's not dead. At least, I don't think she is."

Leaving the main structure, they crossed the bailey to the kitchen, located in a separate stone building. There, the usual oatcakes and honey awaited them, as well as several giggling maids. They ate, begged some suet from the cook, and left.

No rain for a change, Rafe was pleased to see, and the clouds were moving away to the east. Maybe they would finally have a sunny day. After saddling the ponies assigned to them, they stopped by a storage building against the inner curtain wall, gathered long poles and twine, then rode away from the castle.

"You will tell me what is wrong," Thomas said when they turned off the long drive toward the loch. "And I will decide if I must put my knife in your throat to release you." At Rafe's look of alarm, he flashed a broad grin. "I must do something. I am weary of hearing you call out in the night."

"Put a feather in your ear."

When they reached the loch, they tethered their horses to bushes by the shore, then walked out to sit on a flat outcrop hanging over the water.

After rigging his pole with a length of twine, Rafe tied on a hook baited with suet and let his line sink into the dark, icy depths. Overnight, the howling wind had died down. The surface of the loch was as glassy as the mirror behind the bar in the saloon where Rafe had seen Miranda for the first time.

"Speak now, *nesene*, of this woman who troubles your sleep."

Rafe wasn't sure where to begin. Drawing on memory, he pictured the dusty street, the warped boardwalk, the heat shimmers rising off the rooftops the day he rode into town. He had been full of hope back then, and flush with pride over the

Deputy U.S. Marshal badge pinned on his vest—even though his task in Dirtwater had been more mundane than heroic—to take the 1870 census.

But he soon learned that the rough Texas town wasn't one that welcomed scrutiny, especially from a representative of the federal government. And the powerful Amos Gault had much to hide. Although nothing had ever been proven, he was suspected of murder, robbery, importing foreign women for purposes of prostitution, and cattle rustling. The townspeople—from the local sheriff down to the newest offering in Gault's brothel—were terrified of him.

Miranda was no exception.

"The first time I saw her was in a saloon," Rafe finally began. "She was standing by the bar, studying her reflection in the tarnished mirror behind the liquor bottles, while a drunken cowboy pawed her like she was a lapdog."

"She allowed this?"

"She didn't stop him." Rafe flicked his wrist, felt a bump against the line, and flicked it again. Nothing. Surface ripples settled back into a mirror gloss. "She was beautiful. Eyes the color of clover honey. Had one of those innocent, wounded faces that made a man think she needed saving, and only he could do it." And like a trout chasing a mayfly, he had risen to his own destruction.

"You could not save her," Thomas guessed.

"I tried, but she went back to the man who put her in that life. Amos Gault. Ever heard of him?"

Thomas shook his head.

"No matter. He's dead now."

"You killed him?"

"Him and three others."

The Cheyenne thought for a moment. "That is how you got those bullet scars on your chest?"

Rafe nodded.

"Then you fought them well."

*But for what?* Nothing changed, except for four new graves in the town cemetery, and a weary disenchantment with his job, women, and his own judgment.

"What happened to the woman?"

"Never saw her after Gault died. I was laid up for a long time. When I got back on my feet, she was gone. Heard she went to San Francisco."

"If she is gone, why does she still trouble you?"

"She hasn't. Not for a long time. But lately . . ."

"Ho." Thomas nodded in understanding. "You have found another woman to save and do not know if you should."

Rafe reared back to glare at him. "You're loco."

Thomas smirked.

But Rafe couldn't deny the pull Josephine had on him. She was in a bad situation, too, but this was different. For one thing, he could do nothing to help her unless she left England and came back with him to Heartbreak Creek. He didn't see that happening. They were too different. Too far apart in too many ways. Plus, he had nothing to offer her compared to what she would be leaving behind. Oh, it might work for a while. But when reality took root, resentment would grow.

They sat for a long time without speaking. Or catching any fish. Rafe had hoped their quarry might seek the sun-warmed water near the surface, but the fish stayed in the murky depths. Probably afraid of that bright shiny thing in the sky.

A shadow drew his gaze up as a huge bird floated past on silent wings. An eagle, or maybe a vulture, or some large Scottish waterbird. He watched it glide just above the surface of the lake, then suddenly throw out its taloned feet and snatch a fish from the water. Its great wings pumping against the added weight, it carried its dripping prey toward the far side of the loch.

"I think I will not put my knife into your neck," Thomas decided. "Instead, I will make you another dream snare. But heed me, white man, it will be the last one."

They caught no fish that day. Or the next. And the morning after that, he and Thomas were back on the train, heading south.


"The post rider came today," Josephine's father informed her over dinner two weeks after their argument about entering Pems in next year's Grand National. "Brought a missive."

Rafe? Was he on his way back? Josephine looked down at her plate, lest her sudden interest give her away. "Oh? From whom?"

Father motioned the footmen from the room. Always a bad sign. More so when accompanied by that sly smile. "Your old swain, William Bristol—now Baron Adderly since his father's death these two years past."

The floor seemed to shift beneath Josephine's chair. Once she caught her balance, she looked up to find Father's smile had changed to a look of speculation. "What did he want?"

"To ask if he might come for a visit."

"A visit? Here?"

Her first thought was that Father had summoned him, perhaps hoping William would renew his pursuit of her now that he was free. But she quickly discarded the notion. It was too soon. Decency dictated a mourning period of at least six months. Besides, she was a ruined woman. And even though William had been the cause of it, she doubted his pride would allow him to align himself with a woman of her sordid reputation. "Why would he visit us?"

"Not *us*, girl. You."

An unseen hand closed around her throat. "But why?"

He shrugged. "He gave no explanation. Although he did ask if Jamie would be here. He wants to meet him. It's not unusual that a man would want to see his own son, is it?"

Fury took her breath away. She slapped her napkin beside her plate. "It is when he so vehemently denied him for all these years. I won't see him."

"You will."

"I will not!"

"You'll do as I tell you, girl!" He dragged a hand through his hair. His expression changed, softened into that cajoling smile he used whenever he sought to bend her to his will. "Now, love. What would it hurt to find out what he wants? Keep your enemies close—isn't that what they say?" He laughed without mirth, his lips and tongue stained red by the wine. "Besides, girl, aren't you the least bit curious about him?"

"No."

"They say he's lost that pretty face to hard drink and rich living. Yet you're more beautiful than ever. I'd think you would want to show him what he once spurned."

She rose. "Good night, Father," she said and swept from the room.

But the seed had been planted, and over the next few days it flourished in her mind.

How had William changed since she had last seen him? Had he truly grown stout and dissolute? Did he ever spare a thought for the heartbroken creature or the son he had left behind? She doubted it. But more worrisome was her fear that he would have the same effect on her he'd had eight years ago. Would she still feel that breathless anticipation when he looked at her in that special way?

She thought not. She was no longer the naïve ninny she had been when he'd seduced her. Disgrace and ostracism had hardened her, even as Jamie had opened her heart to a joy she had never known.

There was nothing to fear. In denying Jamie, William had relinquished all claims to her son. And in his abandonment of her, he had killed any lingering susceptibility to his charm. She had finally grown up.

"When is Adderly coming for his visit?" she asked Father at dinner two nights later.

"You've decided to see him?"

"I have. But I'm not yet certain I'll allow Jamie to do so."

"The boy is his son."

"The boy is *my* son. And I, alone, will decide if Adderly meets him." Seeing that mulish expression come over her father's face, she moderated her tone. "Let us see what he wants, Father, then go from there. Have you received word when he will arrive?"

"Thursday. In time for dinner. And I expect you to be there."

She smiled despite the twist in her chest. "Of course. I wouldn't miss it for the world."

Three days after leaving Northbridge, Rafe and Thomas arrived at the warmblood stable outside Edinburgh. By dawn, they were off again, herding Ash's Hanoverians, and an older gelding Rafe had bought, to the railway yards. There, they loaded them into stock cars, then boarded the drovers' car coupled behind it. Barring any delays, the train would arrive at Carlisle in midafternoon, which would leave them ample time to drive the horses on to the Cathcart stables before dark.

With each mile closer to their destination—to Josephine—Rafe's sense of anticipation and confusion built.

That kiss had changed things.

He wasn't sure what it meant or what he was supposed to do now. Hard experience had stolen most of Josephine's trust. Yet she seemed to trust him—with both her son and her wounded horse. Had that kiss been a simple thank-you? A good-bye kiss? Or something more?

He didn't lack experience with women. But because he'd never felt the urge to settle down, he had avoided ladies, relying on paid women to satisfy his needs. And since that one night with Miranda, which had almost cost him his life, he hadn't been with a woman at all.

But he didn't think his self-imposed celibacy was the sole reason he couldn't get Josephine out of his thoughts. What he felt was more complicated than that.

It was something he had never before experienced. This unfocused, undefined, restless *wanting*. Since meeting her, he felt as if something inside him had subtly shifted, and some inner stabilizing mechanism that usually kept him squarely balanced had slipped slightly off-kilter. It left him on the constant edge of confusion. And arousal. Just seeing Josephine walk into the stable awakened his body and warmed his heart.

He wanted her like he had never wanted anything in his life.

Logic told him he was wasting his time. But that deeper, more primitive voice in the back of his mind insisted he could have her in all the ways he imagined.

But first, he had to win her.

# *Twelve*

Thursday afternoon, Josephine was digging through her jewelry box to determine which of her paste replacements would look best with her blue muslin when Jamie burst through her bedroom door.

"He's back!" he cried, his face split by a wide grin that displayed the gap left by his first lost tooth. "And he brought hundreds of horses with him! And Mr. Redstone, too!"

Josephine tamped down an absurd rush of excitement. Composing her face into an expression of polite interest, she turned to her son. "Hundreds?"

"Well . . . ten. Perhaps eight. May I go see them? Please, Mother?"

"What about your lessons?"

"I'll finish them before bedtime. I promise. Please?"

How could she deny him when she felt the same impatience? "All right, you may go." And before she could remind him to change into his boots, he was racing from the room.

As soon as the door slammed behind him, she sank down onto the stool at her vanity, one hand pressed over her racing heart.

Fate. It was such a fickle thing. Other than Jamie, only three men had meaning in her life and they would all be gathered around the dining table that evening. How was she to enjoy the company of one, keep her guard up around the other, and prevent the third from dangling her before the other two like a baited hook? Realizing she couldn't let Rafe walk into an awkward situation without warning, she rose on wobbly legs and left the room.

Actually, there were only six new horses, she noted when she went down the path toward the stables—three mares, two studs, and a flaxen chestnut gelding, which the earl must have purchased for the countess. They were pacing the paddocks they'd been assigned, heads and tails up as they whinnied and snorted at the other horses watching from nearby pens and pastures.

They were beauties. The earl had chosen well.

But she was more interested in seeing Rafe.

When she entered the stable, she saw him standing by the feed room talking to Hammersmith, their silhouetted forms framed against the open doors at the other end of the center aisle. Rafe—tall, hatless, his hair flopped forward as he bent his head to attend to what the shorter, stouter man was saying. Even in repose, there was grace in his stance. That masculine sort of grace that spoke of confidence and strength, and which unerringly drew the feminine eye. She thought of their earlier kiss and felt again the surge of joy and desire that brought a tremble to her heart.

Then he lifted his head, saw her, and went completely still.

With his face in shadow, she couldn't read his expression. But the slow straightening of his long body, the squaring of his wide shoulders, the lift of his chin, all told her that the entirety of his attention was fixed on her.

A rush went through her. Hammersmith was forgotten. Sound faded. The world narrowed to the two of them, utterly focused on each other. Awareness of him tingled throughout her body, making nerves vibrate like the strings of a violin stroked by the master's bow.

A fanciful thought. Absurd. She had to stop reading those romantic novels.

"Miss Cathcart," he greeted her in his deep voice as she approached.

"Mr. Jessup." Her own voice sounded odd in her head—thin and reedy, as if her muscles hadn't the strength to push air out of her lungs. Another fanciful notion. Thrusting the thought aside, she took a deep breath and tried for a normal tone. "I see you've brought more horses."

"I have. How are you?" Then as if realizing the Scotsman stood watching, he quickly added, "And Pembroke's Pride?"

Josephine pasted on a smile. "I'm well. As for Pems, you must ask Mr. Hammersmith here. He's been overseeing his training during your absence."

"Aye, and he's doing well," the groom said, smiling through his beard. "Stevens has taken care to follow yer instructions. I ken ye'll be pleased."

"Glad to hear it, Liam." Even though he spoke to the older man, Rafe's dark blue gaze remained on her. "Would you care to see the Hanoverians the earl purchased, Miss Cathcart?"

"I would, Mr. Jessup."

Leaving Hammersmith staring curiously after them, Josephine followed Rafe toward one of the stalls that opened into the paddocks of the new arrivals.

"They'll produce excellent stock when crossed with the thoroughbreds." He swung open the stall door and motioned for her to precede him. "Stamina, size, and strength. Just what the army needs."

Josephine looked back at him in surprise. "You're selling their offspring to the army?"

"Only those not suitable for breeding." He closed the door securely then, without warning, turned and pulled her into his arms. "I've missed you, Josie," he whispered and brought his mouth down to hers.

Shock ballooned into a breathless feeling that left her weak and shivery. Rising on tiptoes, she leaned into him, hands clutching at the cloth over his arms.

Muscles quivered beneath her palms. She felt the urgency he held in check, and that made her own heart hammer in her chest.

She smelled horses and the faint sharpness of male sweat. Felt the prick of his whiskers against her chin. Tasted coffee when he slid his tongue along the seam of her lips. Awash in sensation, she opened her mouth to his and pressed harder against him, wanting to get past the thin layers of cloth that separated them.

"Rafe . . ."

He drew back, his chest pumping. "I'm sorry. Did I frighten—"

"No." Reaching up, she pulled his head down again. "You cut your hair," she murmured against his lips as she slid her fingers through the sun-bright curls at his nape.

"Several times."

"The bleached ends are gone."

"I'll grow more. Jesus, you feel good."

She lifted her face for another kiss, putting into it all the emotion he had awakened inside her. That sense of urgency built into something warm and liquid and undeniable.

This time, it was she who drew back, but only because she had run out of air. Bracing a hand against his chest for balance, she drew in a deep breath, blew it out, then gave him a shaky smile. "I missed you, too."

A crooked smile teased one corner of his wide mouth, slowly spreading his firm lips to reveal strong teeth and that elusive dimple. Blue fire sparked in his deep-set eyes. "I can tell."

Suddenly embarrassed by her forward behavior, she jerked her hand away and patted an errant strand of hair back into her bun. "Your trip went well?"

"It did. Why are you pulling away from me?"

"I—I'm not."

"Then come here." He opened his arms.

Helpless against his pull, she started forward, then lurched back when footfalls sounded in the aisleway. "Mother?"

*Oh Lord.* "In here," she called through the closed door. "Mr. Jessup is showing me the new horses."

The stall door swung open. Jamie looked in, Mr. Redstone at his shoulder.

The Cheyenne made a show of looking around. "What horses?"

"Don't," Rafe warned softly.

Jamie looked from one man to the other. "Don't what?"

"They're outside," Josephine broke in hastily, shoving open the paddock door. "We were just going out to see them."

"Ho. *Those* horses." Thomas moved to follow. "We will go with you."

"We can't," Jamie said. "Someone's here, Mother. I saw him ride up the drive beside a carriage. Grandfather came out to meet him, so he must be important."

*William.* She didn't realize she had spoken aloud until Rafe gave her a sharp look.

"William?"

"Baron Adderly."

He stiffened, his smile fading. "Here? Why?"

"Who is Baron Adderly?" Jamie asked.

"I . . . em . . . a dinner guest. Father invited him." Josephine was so flustered, she could scarcely form a thought, especially with Rafe glaring at her that way, and Jamie starting to look worried, and Thomas Redstone smirking.

She made an airy motion. "I'll explain it all later. Right now I must go see to our guest." She glanced down at her son, unsure what to do. She wasn't ready to explain to him about William. Wasn't certain she would ever be ready.

"The boy will help me feed the horses," Thomas Redstone said.

She met his knowing gaze and wondered how he knew. Had Rafe told him her sordid story? "Thank you, Mr. Redstone. Jamie, you'll dine in the nursery tonight. And Mr. Jessup—"

"I'll eat in the kitchen with Thomas."

Panic gripped her. "No! You have to be there." Then seeing the puzzled faces staring back at her, she added less stridently, "What I mean is that I would like for you to be there, Mr. Jessup. You're our guest, too, after all."

"Isn't Mr. Redstone a guest, as well, Mother?"

"Yes, of course he is. But—"

"I will not eat at the long table," the Cheyenne said flatly. "I do not like the foolish clothes I must wear."

Jamie grinned up at him. "Me, neither. Can he dine with me, Mother?"

"Certainly, if that's what he prefers. I'll have Cook send up an extra plate."

"Tell her to send two. I am hungry."

"Of course." Josephine let out a relieved breath. She gave the Indian a grateful smile. "That's kind of you to look after Jamie, Mr. Redstone. Thank you."

The Cheyenne shrugged. Turning his dark gaze to Rafe, who was still frowning at her, he said, "Now it is your turn to be nice, *nesene*."

An odd thing to say, she thought. But apparently the admonition meant something to Rafe. With a nod, he motioned her toward the house.

They didn't speak again until they were halfway up the path. "Your father invited him?" Rafe asked.

"Actually, the baron invited himself."

"Why?"

"I'm not certain. He wrote Father and said he wanted to see Jamie. But I've not yet decided if I'll allow him to do so."

"Does Jamie know about him?"

"That Adderly is his father?" She shook her head. "I haven't told him anything about that. Nor did I tell him the baron was coming for a visit." Tears clogged her throat. Why did this have to happen? Why now? *Curse you, William.*

Rafe put his hand on her arm, bringing her to a stop beside him. "You're worried. Why?"

The fear she'd held at bay for the last week finally burst forth. "What if he wants to take Jamie away, Rafe? What if he insists Jamie belongs with him?"

"He won't."

"But Father—"

"Jamie is *your* son, Josephine. If you don't want Adderly to see him, then he won't."

"This isn't America, Rafe. This is England and he's a peer. How could we stop him?"

He smiled—but it wasn't the teasing, lopsided half smile she loved, or the wide, dazzling grin that sent her thoughts into chaos. It was the smile of a man who had overcome adversity and welcomed the chance to do it again. She saw challenge in it. Resolve. And a hint of savagery. "Leave that to me."


Rafe dressed with care. Not because he felt a need to impress, but because he didn't want to embarrass Josephine. Appearance was everything in this stilted, rule-bound society. That, and being able to tout a fancy pedigree. And although he might not have the latter, he cleaned up as good as any man.

An hour after departing the stable, he left his room— bathed, shaved, combed, and brushed. Shipley met him at the bottom of the stairs, gave him a critical once-over, then with a sniff, directed him to the yellow salon. In the hallway by the double doors, Rafe tugged his collar away from his neck and smoothed back his hair one last time. Then he took a deep breath and opened the door.

Only Josephine and her father were present, engaged in a tense conversation by the hearth. They didn't seem aware that he had arrived, so he took a moment to enjoy the sight of Josephine.

She had on the same frothy blue dress she had worn earlier, but had added a ribbon at her neck and another in her upswept hair. He thought of those heated kisses earlier, and tugged at his collar again.

"Why aren't you wearing your sapphires?" Cathcart ask her as Rafe walked soundlessly toward them across the thick rug.

"I told you, Father, they're with the jeweler having the clasp repaired."

"The pearls, then."

"They aren't suitable with this neckline."

"I've provided you with a ransom in jewels, daughter. Surely you could have found something better to wear than a ribbon."

"Good evening," Rafe said.

Cathcart turned with a look of surprise. "Jessup, I hadn't realized you were back and would be joining us this evening."

And judging by his expression, he wasn't pleased at the prospect. "When I saw your daughter at the stable earlier, she kindly invited me." He gave her a slight bow. "You look especially beautiful tonight, Miss Cathcart. That ribbon perfectly matches your eyes. Half of the right one, anyway."

Color flooded her face. Rafe told himself it was because she was feeling the same rush of desire that had his nerves in an uproar.

"Good evening, Mr. Jessup. You look quite handsome yourself."

"Probably the haircut."

Her father's disgruntled look gave way to a relieved smile when the door opened behind Rafe. "Ah, there you are, Adderly."

"Am I late?"

"Not at all."

Rafe turned to see a pudgy man about his same age, with thinning brown hair, a goatee that unsuccessfully hid the slope of his weak chin, and brown eyes that were unremarkable except for the way they stared so intrusively at Josephine.

"Ah, Miss Cathcart, my dear." The newcomer's smile showed an overbite and too much gum. Reminded Rafe of a weasel. "As beautiful as ever, I see."

Josephine seemed incapable of a response. Or of accepting the hand the baron offered. In fact, she stood so still Rafe wondered if she had lost the ability to breathe, as well.

"Don't mind her," he cut in, covering for her lapse by

drawing the attention to himself. "I tell her that all the time. She's probably just tired of hearing it."

"Welcome, Adderly," Cathcart said with a strained smile. "Drink?" He waved a hand at a nearby table covered with glasses and bottles.

"Don't mind if I do."

Which was pretty obvious, Rafe thought, considering the broken veins in the man's cheeks and long nose. "Nothing for me," he called after Cathcart, even though he hadn't been included in the offer. And to make it doubly clear he wasn't about to be ignored all evening, he turned back to the newcomer with a broad smile and an extended hand. "Rayford Jessup. Don't believe we've met."

A flicker of disdain.

Were peers not allowed to touch commoners? Rafe would have to remind Ash of that the next time the earl punched him in the shoulder.

"Adderly. Baron Adderly." The shorter man gave Rafe's much larger hand a limp squeeze and quickly released it. Rafe had held livelier fish. "You're an American."

"I am. Sorry about the war." He refrained from wiping his palm on his jacket. "A baron, you say? Would that be higher or lower than an earl?"

The baron stiffened.

Josephine sighed.

"I only ask," Rafe went on, "because I know how important forms of address are to you English. I want to be certain I get it right."

"Lower," the good baron said through tight lips.

"Excellent. So I would address you as . . ."

"My lord."

"Adderly it is, then."

Before the weasel realized he'd been insulted—again—Cathcart arrived with his drink, which Adderly downed in two gulps.

"Jessup works for Kirkwell," Cathcart said with a glare at Rafe.

"Indeed?" The baron tried to look down his nose, but since Rafe was a foot taller, it wasn't that effective. "In what capacity?"

Rafe beamed proudly. "Horse advisor. *Head* horse advisor, in fact."

"Horse advisor? I've never heard of such a thing."

"I know. It's ridiculous. But then, he *is* an earl." Leaning down, Rafe added in a confidential tone, "Seems the higher they go, the dumber they get. Am I right?" Straightening, he gave a hearty laugh.

Which earned him another glare from their host, another eye roll from Josephine, and had the baron requesting a second drink.

For a reluctant talker, Rafe thought he was doing pretty damn well.

"What on earth is wrong with you?" Josephine demanded in an undertone a few minutes later when they followed Father and the baron toward the dining room.

"I was about to ask you the same thing," Rafe muttered. "How could you let that scrawny—"

"Stop." She tried to sound stern, but laughter made her voice wobble.

She studied the men walking several paces ahead of them. William was anything but scrawny. In fact, he had gained so much weight since she'd last seen him, she might not have recognized him.

And had he always had that overbite?

But the change she noticed most was the cruel twist of his mouth, especially when Rafe had toyed with him. Josephine sensed that if she and Father hadn't been witness to their sparring, the baron might have lashed out at the man he erroneously considered his inferior. William's overweening pride she remembered well. But that hint of cruelty was new . . . or perhaps at sixteen, she had been too besotted to notice.

"It's confusing," Rafe mused, breaking into her thoughts. "Everyone chides me for not talking more, and then when I do, I get into all sorts of trouble. Why is that, do you suppose?"

"Because you're incorrigible, that's why."

"Better than being a weasel."

"A weasel?"

"It's an insignificant, annoying pest. In America we consider them vermin. Apparently here, you make them into barons. Interesting."

"You sound jealous," she teased. "Are you intimidated by his grand title?"

"The one that's lower than an earl's? I think I might be. I'll need soothing, I suspect." He grinned down at her. "Perhaps later."

Fighting a smile, she looked away. This playful side of Rafe charmed her all over again. And terrified her, because she didn't know what outrageous thing he would say next. "Please try to be nice," she cajoled, echoing the sentiment Thomas Redstone had expressed earlier, which had confused her at the time, but now made perfect sense.

"I was nice."

"You were awful. You deliberately baited him."

"He's a pompous ass."

"He's our guest."

"He's still a—"

She put a finger to his lips to silence him, then quickly pulled it away when she saw that heated look come into his eyes. "Don't do that."

His brows rose in a show of innocence. "Do what?"

"I know you're only trying to show support for me, and I dearly appreciate that. But I fear if you push it too far, Father won't allow you to dine with us again. And I need you there, Rafe. I don't want to face him alone."

All amusement left his face. "You're not alone, Josie. I'm right here beside you."

Tears pricked her eyes. The man did know the perfect thing to say. "Just promise me you won't start something. In fact, don't speak at all."

"Really? Most women prefer I do the opposite. But . . ." The word trailed off on a deep sigh. "All right. I'll be quiet. Had I known my teasing would make this difficult situation more awkward for you, I wouldn't have spoken at all. I'm sorry I upset you." He tipped his head down. "Would a kiss make you feel better?"

"Hush!" She drew back, horrified Father or the baron might have heard.

"You're right." Laughing softly, he straightened. "We'd best wait until later for that, too."

# *Thirteen*

Dinner proceeded without incident. Rafe offered no more jibes, Father remained lucid, and William lived up to his recent reputation for heavy drinking, while Josephine toyed with her food and relived those kisses with Rafe.

What had come over him? He had always kept a proper distance—except for holding her hand those two times. Then suddenly he was corralling her in a stall and kissing her as if they had been parted for months rather than just over a fortnight. What had she unleashed with that one impulsive kiss?

With a sigh, she chased peas around her plate and stared dreamily at her carrots. Not that she was complaining, of course. She had enjoyed those kisses as much as he apparently had. Even now, the memory of them brought a warm rush that had her reaching for her wine goblet.

As she swallowed, she caught Rafe staring at her neck with such focused intensity her throat almost seized. Was he remembering, too?

She must have some dire weakness of character. What else would explain her lamentable susceptibility to inappropriate men? First William, who seduced and deserted her—and now Rafe, soon to leave her and return to America. When would she learn? Yet here she sat, calmly eating glazed carrots while the man who had debauched her sat on her left, the man who had allowed it sat at the other end of the table, and the man she wished would attempt it sat on her right. Although, she mused, poking at a piece of ham, for Rafe to properly debauch her, she must be chaste. And sadly, that horse had jumped the fence years ago.

Course after course came and went, until finally the dessert plates were cleared and Father rose, signaling an end to the interminable meal. Setting her napkin beside her plate, she prepared to bolt.

William had other plans.

Waving the footman aside, he came around to pull out her chair. "May I speak with you alone, my dear," he murmured in her ear as she rose.

"I—I'm not sure that would be appropriate. Father—"

"I've already spoken to him," William cut in smoothly. "He understands we have much to discuss and has graciously allowed us privacy to do so."

Betrayed by her father yet again. Why was she not surprised?

"Shall we go to the conservatory? I have such fond memories of it."

She almost lost her carrots. Panic building, she searched for a way to avoid the looming confrontation. If she refused to speak with him, what could he do? William's hand at her back sent a shiver of revulsion up her spine, and when she tried to twist away, she saw Rafe watching them intently.

His gaze narrowed on William, dropped to the hand by her hip, then rose to meet hers. That savage look was back.

And suddenly, the words he had spoken earlier flowed through her befuddled mind. *You're not alone. I'm right here beside you.*

A sense of calmness settled over her. The constriction in her throat eased and reason returned. With a smile of reassurance to Rafe, she let William steer her from the room.

She had no reason to be afraid. This wasn't eight years ago, and she wasn't the timid, lovesick creature she had been then. She was no longer awed by William's presence or his title, nor was she concerned about what effect he might have on her. The past was far behind her. There was nothing William could say or do that would equal the pain he had already given her, or weaken her resolve to put him from her life.

Alas, how wrong she was.

\* \* \*

Rafe watched the baron usher Josephine from the room and fought an almost overwhelming urge to go after them. Just seeing the weasel's hand on her back had awakened a level of anger he hadn't felt in a long time.

Go after her and do what? Confront Adderly for her?

Almost unconsciously, he rubbed a hand across his chest and the old wounds that still ached on cold, rainy nights. A reminder not to take on a fight that wasn't his, over a woman he couldn't have. He was a horse wrangler, not a hero. Best he remember that.

"Join me in my study for a drink, Jessup?"

Rafe looked over to find Cathcart watching him. "No, thank you."

"Join me anyway. I want to talk to you."

Wondering if his earlier weasel baiting was about to see him banished from future dinners, Rafe followed his host down the hall. He had been in Cathcart's study only one other time, when Ash had negotiated with him over the price of the horses. The earl might have difficulty with the written word, but his years procuring remounts for the Hussars had certainly honed his skills as a horse trader. In the end, he talked Cathcart down to a fair price. But the Englishman had hoped for more, and he had made up the difference by charging Ash a less than fair price for the horses' upkeep until they were shipped to America.

Ash paid it, just to be done with the man. He didn't suffer fools well.

Waving away another offer of a drink, Rafe settled into one of the leather chairs in front of the ornate desk. While Cathcart poured himself a drink from a decanter on a side table, Rafe studied the room.

Bookcases lined the walls. Collectibles and foreign oddities sat on shelves and tables, and a mounted tiger's head glared down from above the fireplace. Rafe suspected few of the books had ever been opened and most of the trophies had been purchased, rather than earned, by the owner. The dusty stuffed tiger over the mantle was probably the closest his host had ever come to a dangerous beast.

All flash and no lead. Rafe might have respected Cathcart

more if he had hung a painting of an old coal miner on his wall, instead of surrounding himself with the trappings of a life he had never led. He should have been proud of what he'd accomplished, rather than ashamed of his lowly beginnings. But then, this wasn't America, where almost everyone started low.

Cathcart sank into the throne-like chair behind the desk. "Jamie is Adderly's son." He watched Rafe over the rim of his glass as he sipped, then set his glass aside. "I can see by your lack of reaction that you knew."

Rafe shrugged.

"I can also see that you're taken with my daughter." When he got no response to that, he sat back, a look of irritation on his face, his fingers drumming on the arm of his chair. "I'm asking you to step away, son. Josephine is not for you."

Rafe knew that, but hearing another man say it aloud naturally brought up his hackles. It was an effort to keep them from showing.

Cathcart drained the glass, then shoved it away with a sigh. "The woman doesn't know a damned thing about hard work. Has a houseful of servants doing her bidding and a maid who tends her every need. Hell, she can hardly dress herself, much less cook." He smiled with contempt and shot Rafe a crafty look. "But she is beautiful."

Unable to deny that, Rafe nodded. "Yes, she is."

"Beautiful but ruined."

Anger flared. Seeking distraction before he took a swing at the man, Rafe looked away. Rain tapped gently at the windows that overlooked the rose garden and path down to the stable. Next week, he and Stevens should take Pems to the brook. Make the horse stand and listen to the water without asking him to cross it. Maybe Josie would go with them.

"She made a mistake with Adderly." Cathcart's voice drew Rafe's attention from the window. "There's no denying that. And the baron was a bastard to do what he did. They both acted foolishly. But now they've been given a chance to make it right. Especially for Jamie."

Rafe could guess where this was leading, but he didn't want to make Cathcart's betrayal of his own daughter easy, so he said nothing.

Leaning onto his elbows, Cathcart clasped his hands on the

desk in front of him and looked Rafe hard in the eye. "I'll not mince words with you, Jessup. The baron is interested in her. Interested enough to offer the title of baroness and all the wealth and privilege that goes with it. Which is something you can't do. But he's also interested in Jamie. His son. Maybe his *only* son before long."

A sick feeling twisted in Rafe's gut. Was Cathcart actually hoping to benefit from the death of Adderly's other son? Or was he simply repeating the baron's own words? Did either man have a conscience?

Probably not, since Adderly was already negotiating for a second wife when his first had been dead for only a few weeks. "He's young enough to have more children."

"Perhaps. But he's a heavy drinker, and not far from the age his father was when he died. He's thinking ahead. As am I. If his sickly son dies, and the baron can't sire more, what happens to the title?"

Rafe didn't know and didn't care.

"Jamie gets it." Eyes gleaming in triumph, Cathcart sat back. "Josephine is aware that because of her poor behavior, the boy will carry the taint of bastardy all his life. It sickens her. She would do anything to shield her son from that and give him the life he deserves. And now, thanks to the baron, she can."

"By marrying the man who ruined her?" Would Josie really do that?

"Why not? He's the boy's father, isn't he? And if she has a chance to elevate her son from bastard to baron, shouldn't she do it?"

A bitter taste rose on the back of Rafe's tongue. She probably should. At least she and Jamie would be out from under this man's thumb. But was the baron any better? Realizing he had clenched his fists so tight his fingers were going numb, he slowly straightened his fingers. "And how much will you get?"

"For what?"

"Selling your daughter to Adderly."

Cathcart blinked, then bounded to his feet, teeth bared, veins bulging on his forehead. "How dare you say that! Get out! Get out of my sight and off my land!"

Rising slowly from his chair, Rafe straightened to his full height, which was considerably more than Cathcart's. He didn't often use his size to intimidate a smaller man, but it felt good to look down on this pathetic sack of skin. "Should I take the earl's horses with me?" he asked calmly. He knew Cathcart needed the money Ash was paying for their keep, and was betting the man's greed would force him to overlook the insult.

"They can stay. But not you."

"Sorry." Rafe shook his head. "The contract states that I'm to oversee their care while they're here. They stay, I stay. I go, they go."

"Then, you can oversee them from the stable, you son of a bitch! I want you out of this house tonight!"

"Whenever I think of you," William said, looking around the glass hothouse, "I picture you here, among these fragrant blossoms, in our special place."

Rising from the chair she had taken to avoid sitting next to him on the couch, Josephine wandered over to pinch off a fading zinnia blossom. For nearly an hour she had sidestepped the man's busy hands and deflected his blatant references to their tawdry affair. She couldn't tolerate much more. "I don't know why you persist in referring to that lamentable time, William. Don't you think it would be best if we left the past behind us?"

He laughed in that intimate way that had once brought a blush to her cheeks, but now left her feeling faintly queasy. "I don't know if I can, love. Those hours with you were the finest in my life. I have never forgotten them or how much you meant to me."

"And yet you were able to so easily cast me aside." As soon as the words passed her lips, she wanted them back. They sounded petty and childish. Heartache had long since hardened to anger, then disappointment, and now disgust. She certainly didn't want him thinking she had pined for him all this time.

Still smiling, he rose and walked toward her, driving her back into the ficus leaves to escape him. "I didn't want to leave you, Josephine. You must know that. But Father insisted I marry Margaret. Our families had planned it since we were children. I couldn't go back on my word."

*Except with me.* "I wish you had remembered that before you seduced me."

Reaching out before she could sidle away, he gripped her

shoulders and looked into her eyes with a fierceness she hadn't seen in him before. This close, she could see gray hairs in his closely trimmed beard, signs of dissipation in the puffiness around his eyes and the sagging lines framing his mouth. A momentary sadness filled her for the loss of the handsome, careless young man he had been, and the innocence she had given him.

"I never loved Margaret. Not like I loved you, Josephine." His gaze dropped to her mouth. "God, I've missed you so much," he murmured, leaning in for a kiss.

She smelled alcohol, tobacco, the mustiness of his body. Repelled, twisted away. Did he expect her to be his mistress? The notion filled her with loathing, and the unreasoning fear that if she allowed him to kiss her even once, she would be tainted anew, sliding back into disgrace and self-loathing forever. "Don't."

His hands fell away. "What's wrong?"

"Did you think to sweep in after all this time and pick up where you left off? God, William. How arrogant are you?" Desperate to put space between them, she crossed to the door. With her hand on the latch, she faced him, her thoughts in turmoil, her emotions so battered she was scarcely aware of what she was saying.

"Perhaps you're lonely, William. Or still in shock over your wife's recent death. Or you think that because I succumbed to your advances once, I will again. I assure you, I will not. Whatever I felt for you is long dead. Now if you will excuse me, I bid you—"

"I want to see our son."

She froze, her hand still on the latch. "Why?"

He stepped toward her, saw her tense, and stopped. "Have you told him about me?"

"No. Nor am I inclined to do so."

"He's my son, Josephine."

"Is he? Since when?" Years of simmering resentment spilled out like acid. "And if so, why have you never acknowledged him? Or written to him? Or shown the slightest awareness that he was even alive? Why now, after years of pretending he doesn't exist, do you show up professing a fatherly interest?"

"Because now I'm free to do so."

"To do what? Acknowledge him? Give him the protection of your name?"

"Yes. If you'll have me."

She stared at him, uncertain she had heard correctly. *If you'll have me.* What did that mean? Was he proposing marriage? Again? Rain tapped on the glass overhead. The scent of so many blossoms swirled through her head, made her slightly dizzy. "I—I don't understand."

He opened his mouth, closed it, then let out a deep breath. "I've gone about this badly. Please, come sit down and let me explain."

She couldn't move. Couldn't think. She had put marriage out of her mind years ago. But if William was serious about marrying her and acknowledging his son, it would lift Jamie from shame of bastardy forever. Didn't she owe Jamie that?

He held out his hand. "Please, Josephine. Simply hear me out. Give me a chance to atone for the grievous wrong I have done to both you and Jamie."

Sitting on her vanity stool an hour later, Josephine stared at her reflection in the mirror and wondered what kind of person she had become. Marriage to William would certainly protect her son and restore her reputation, but at what cost? And didn't William realize that by dangling the lure of putting Jamie in line for the barony, he was anticipating the death of his son, Edward? *God.* How could she even contemplate such a thing?

Clapping a hand over her mouth before a wail of despair escaped her lips, she bent over her knees. Driven to mindless motion to counter the emotions churning inside, she began to rock, tears spilling in hot streaks down her face.

It was a hellish bargain. One based on the death of a child and her own desperation to provide a secure future for her son. And to sweeten the offer, William had even offered to pay off Father's debts.

A laugh bubbled up her throat and broke free in a sob. All she had to do to save her father from bankruptcy and her son from a life of scorn and humiliation was to cast aside any hope of personal fulfillment, and enter into a loveless marriage with a man she despised and could neither trust nor respect.

Of course, she had to consider it. A high price to pay for a foolish, youthful mistake, but she would do it if there was no other alternative. It was her debt, not Jamie's, and he deserved his chance at a better life. But how could she bear it?

Behind her, the door creaked open. Swiping the tears from her face, she straightened as Henny slipped in.

"I'm sorry to be so late, miss, but Shipley—Oh dear! What's wrong?" Rushing over, she pulled a hanky from the vanity drawer, pressed it into Josephine's shaking hand, then knelt beside the stool. "Whatever has happened, miss? Why are you crying? Is it because of Mr. Jessup?"

Josephine yanked the handkerchief from her face. "What about Mr. Jessup?"

"It's wretchedly unfair, is what it is." Rising to her feet, Henny began taking the pins out of Josephine's hair. "Faith, and everyone below stairs is talking about it. Mr. Jessup is quite a favorite."

Josephine ducked away from the Irish maid's busy hands. "Henny! What happened to Mr. Jessup?"

Light green eyes blinked down at her in surprise. "Sure, and he's been banished, Miss Josephine. Your father ordered him out of the house. It was quite a row, so it was. Rogers heard your father yelling, although Mr. Jessup never once raised his voice. He's a steady one, our Mr. Jessup. Steady as a rock, he is."

*Banished?* The prospect of losing Rafe was intolerable. She knew he would leave her life at some point, but it was too soon. She still needed him. Just knowing he was nearby gave her strength, a happy reason to rise each day. "Banished where?"

"Why, to the stables, miss. Shipley has already sent his belongings down to that little room in the loft where that Indian stays. Mr. Jessup deserves better, I think, him being a gentleman and all, even though he's not a sir. Mr. Hammersmith offered him his own quarters by the tack room, but Mr. Jessup said no. Gordon would have given up his bunk in the room he shares with the stable boys, but Mr. Jessup told him to keep his bed. Sure, and he's a lovely man, he is."

Josephine didn't know whether to be outraged or relieved. At least Rafe remained on the premises. She would still be able to see him. Talk to him. She dabbed away the last of her tears and wondered what Rafe had done to cause Father to send him from the house. Was it something that involved William?

As Henny helped her out of her dress and into her night-clothes, Josephine played back through her mind those awkward moments in the yellow salon when Rafe had baited William. He knew how she felt about the baron. He'd seen her revulsion when William had touched her. And after those kisses in the stable, he must know what was in her heart.

*What will he say when he hears of William's proposal?*

The thought brought new tears, but she blinked them away. She couldn't dwell on that now. Or on what lay ahead. The future, no matter the planning, was never certain, and to survive it, she had to prepare for any contingency.

Resolved, she tied the sash on her robe and went to the bureau. From her jewelry case, she pulled out her remaining item of value—the garnet necklace Father had given her on her sixteenth birthday—the same day William had come into her life. How fitting that she should save them for last. She dropped the necklace into a velvet pouch, and handed it to her maid. "Henny, I need you to take these to the jeweler's shop tomorrow. Tell Mr. Graves I don't want copies made this time, but to sell the necklace outright. I don't care what he offers, take it. Can you do that without anyone finding out?"

"Yes, miss. I know what to do. Same as before." Slipping the pouch into her pocket, she gave a saucy grin. "Sure, and it'll give me a chance to spend a bit of time with Gordon, so it will."

After Henny left, Josephine retrieved a small box from the wardrobe and dumped the contents on the bed. Banknotes and coins spilled across the counterpane. All that remained of her jewelry. She ran her fingers through the plunder. This was her safety. Her chance for escape from the unbearable. Even a married woman deserved a nest egg of her own.

# *Fourteen*

Rafe didn't see Josephine the next day. Nor the day after that. Even Jamie stayed away from the stable, which was unusual. He missed having the boy shadow him all day, pestering him with endless questions. He missed them both.

He teased himself with the possibility that Cathcart had locked them in their rooms to prevent them from seeing him. But when there was a break in the rain on the third day, and he saw her and the weasel walking in the rose garden, he knew she was avoiding him by choice. Just as well. Like Cathcart said, he had little to offer them, and with the baron, she had a chance to make Jamie's life a lot easier.

Still, it rankled, and put him in such a foul mood Thomas defected, too, heading off onto another of his scouting forays. Rafe hoped the Indian had enough sense to keep himself out of trouble.

Later that afternoon, Adderly left. Rafe stayed close, in case Josephine came to the stable. She didn't. Nor did Jamie. When morning came and they still didn't come, he knew they wouldn't. Which told him the baron had made his offer, and Josephine had probably accepted it.

The thought of that disturbed him more than it should have, considering he had no hold on her. He told himself she had made the wise decision—she had her son to consider, as well as her own future. And with her father foolishly risking everything they had on a damaged horse, she had better prospects with the weasel than if she ended up on the street.

He knew all that. And he knew he had no right to expect her to do differently. He was well aware of the insurmountable differences between the two of them, and the advantages Adderly could give her that he couldn't. But the realization that she was lost to him forever cut so deep he could hardly deal with it. It was a whole different kind of pain than he had ever suffered before.

Then he reminded himself that she was a woman. And he'd learned the hard way how fickle women could be. But horses weren't. So he turned to them—the only creatures he fully trusted.

Over the next few days, Hammersmith weaned the foals and moved the mares Ash had bought in with the warmbloods bound for America. Rafe worked with them every day to get them accustomed to his handling. He took extra time with the three stallions—unpredictable creatures by nature and often difficult to control—to make sure they would be as manageable as possible during the long trip to Colorado. Knowing that even in separate pens, they would have to travel in close proximity to the mares, which could prove a problem if any of the mares came into season—and knowing the mares would be less fractious if they were in foal, he started the breeding program he and Ash had decided upon.

It was a risk, taking pregnant horses on such an arduous trip. But if they could ship them on a fast steamer, and give them a lengthy break before boarding the train for Colorado, they might not suffer too much stress. Assuming all the mares settled and survived the trip without aborting, the earl would be adding eight new crossbred foals to his herd next year.

Meanwhile, since he was no longer in charge of Pembroke's training, Rafe worked with him through Stevens. Gordon took his instructions well and had a gentle way with horses, so the troubled animal adapted quickly to the change in handlers. But Rafe still gave him his rubdowns and muscle massages.

The rainy morning they took Pems to visit the brook was a difficult one. But with time and patience, the frightened horse finally trusted them enough to stand beside the rushing water without trying to bolt. After a while, even the shaking stopped and the stallion relaxed enough to drop his head and graze.

A small step, but still a step.

The next three days they took him to the brook every morning, then put him through puddle training in the round pen in the afternoons. Luckily, in this soggy place there were always plenty of puddles available. By the end of the week, the horse was able to stand hock-deep in still water without shaking.

"Think he'll ever jump water again?" Gordon asked, washing mud off the horse's legs after one of his afternoon sessions.

"Maybe." Rafe leaned a shoulder against the wall beside the stall door and crossed his arms. "Given time. And if he has enough faith in his rider."

"He barely accepts me," Gordon said. "But with you, I bet he'd do it." Rising, he dropped the rag into the bucket, then gave Pems a pat and rubbed behind his ears. "Do you think the master might change his mind about racing him?"

Rafe shrugged. "Not unless he finds another way to make quick money." Like selling his daughter and grandson to a weasel.

"Cor, I wish someone would take the poor beast away from here." Gordon shot Rafe a hopeful look.

"I'm not a horse thief."

"You could buy him. I don't have much, but I'd pitch in what I can."

"The earl already offered and Cathcart said no. Besides," Rafe added, smiling at the young man he was growing to like more every day, "isn't there a pretty lady up at the house you could share those savings with?"

The Englishman blushed. "Miss Cathcart's maid, Henny." Picking up the bucket, he stepped into the aisleway.

Rafe secured the stall door behind him, then followed as Gordon carried the bucket out the back of the stable. "Haven't seen her around lately." In fact, other than the stable hands, Rafe hadn't seen much of anyone. "How's Jamie? I thought he'd be in a lather to see the horses we brought back. Usually, the boy is always underfoot, but he hasn't been to the stable in over a week." Since the baron came, in fact. A troubling thought arose. Surely Josephine hadn't let him take the boy.

"He's sick."

Rafe frowned. "Bad?"

"Chest cold. Henny says his mother is a bit of a worrier and won't let him go out until he stops coughing." After emptying the bucket of dirty water into the pasture, the groom carried it to the pump to refill it.

"Any other news from up at the house?" Rafe tried to sound offhand.

Gordon's grin told him it hadn't worked. Fortunately, the groom had sense enough not to remark on it. "Henny says since Baron Highpockets left, Miss Josephine has been in quite a state. Fights with her father all day and cries herself to sleep at night. Scarcely leaves her room."

Rafe felt that protective streak quiver along his back. "Maybe her father locks her in."

Gordon shook his head. "Henny would have told me if he had." Picking up the bucket of fresh water, he went back to Pembroke's stall.

Rafe followed.

After setting the bucket in the corner, Gordon closed both doors and turned to Rafe with a look of concern. "But one thing is certain. Something's amiss." Lowering his voice, he leaned closer to add, "First, shopkeepers are complaining they're not being paid. Then the master sells most of his horses. Henny says Miss Josephine is pawning her jewelry. And now, since the baron left, the whole house is in a bloody uproar." He straightened and shook his head. "I hope we're not all out looking for work before month's end. It doesn't bode well."

Rafe looked out the double front doors at a line of heavy clouds coming in from the west. He felt it, too. Like that edginess before a sudden weather change. Or that prickly feeling on the back of his neck when he sensed something was off.

It was coming up a storm, for sure.


"Can I? Please, Mother? I've scarcely coughed all day. And I never got a chance to see the new horses Mr. Jessup brought back."

"Are your lessons complete?"

"Yes, ma'am."

Josephine knew how hard it was for Jamie to stay inside this long, especially when the sun was out. "All right, but you'll walk with me, rather than running down there at breakneck speed. I don't want you becoming overheated. And if you start coughing, we return without argument. Understood?"

"Yes, ma'am."

"Then collect your coat and boots. I'll meet you at the veranda door."

A bright morning sun greeted them when they stepped outside a few minutes later. The air was so clear that distant hills usually shrouded in mist rose in purple silhouette against the crystal sky. After a week of rain, finally, a beautiful day. Possibly their last for a long while.

As they headed down the path to the stables, Josephine saw signs of the changing season all around them. Geese honking overhead—sheep and horses already growing thick coats— trees by the brook almost bare of leaves. Winter was on the way. "Watch your step," she warned, seeing the rime of frost on the rocks along the path. "Here, hold my hand."

"I'm not a baby."

"No, but I am. I don't want to slip."

Pleased to help, he took her hand.

"We should have worn our gloves. Your fingers are like ice."

He grinned up at her. "You girls truly are babies."

"Yes, we are. Luckily, we have brave fellows like you to look out for us."

And this morning, Josephine wasn't feeling brave at all. After avoiding Rafe for so long, she was apprehensive about seeing him, afraid he would press her about what had happened with William. But until she made her decision, she didn't want to discuss the baron's proposal and Father's insistence that she accept it. It was all so sordid and demeaning. Granted, after several days in William's company, she no longer despised him as much as she once had. In truth, her heated resentment had cooled to bored indifference. He was tolerable, she supposed, but for a lifetime?

Would Rafe think less of her for even considering William's offer?

She kicked a rock off the path and sighed. Of course he would. A man couldn't kiss a woman the way he had and not have feelings for her.

She had feelings, too. Feelings that kept her tossing most of the night. Desire. Guilt. A terrible sadness she couldn't seem to shake. But she also had responsibilities to Jamie, and even Father. Rafe would understand that.

*If only.*

How many times had she tortured herself with those two words? If only Father hadn't thrown all his money away. If only William were a better man. If only Rafe hadn't come into her life and shown her what love could be.

She faltered. *Love?*

A few stolen kisses didn't signify love. Just because she admired and respected Rafe—and yes, desired him—didn't mean she was in love with him.

Did it?

"Can't you walk any faster?"

Jarred out of her thoughts, she looked down into Jamie's impatient face. "You'll catch me if I fall?"

"I could roll you down. That would be faster. Look, there's Mr. Jessup!" Jamie pointed at the man standing beside the gate into the back pasture. "I wonder if Mr. Redstone is with him." And before she could stop him, he pulled out of her grasp and raced down the slope, shouting and waving.

Rafe waved back and continued to stand by the fence, watching. Even from this distance, she could feel the power of his gaze. Like a whisper in her ear. The brush of fingertips along her neck. A sigh against her lips.

Whimsical thoughts. As far-fetched as those in Mrs. Radcliff's salacious novels. Yet they brightened her mood and brought happy anticipation where dread had been. Whether she was in love with Rafe or not, just seeing him brought a smile to her face. And until she had to tell him good-bye, she would enjoy what time with him she had. Lifting a hand, she waved and, with a lighter step, hurried down the slope.

Rafe watched them, his lips pressed against a smile. He tried to stay angry, but couldn't. The sight of her and the boy coming toward him was so welcome his disappointment at being ignored faded away.

"Heard you were sick," he said when Jamie ran up to the fence, panting. "Feeling better?"

"I wasn't that sick. Mother treats me like a baby, but she's the baby. She was afraid to walk down the path by herself."

"Was she?" Rafe watched Josie move through the front

stable doors and felt that knot of tension in his chest begin to loosen. "I wonder why."

"She said she was afraid she'd slip on the path. But I don't believe her."

"I don't, either."

"You don't, either, what?" she asked, squinting against the brightness as she moved out of the shaded interior. Sunlight swept her face, bringing out strands of red and gold in the soft brown wisps that framed her cheeks and making the blue in her right eye glisten like a shard of polished blue topaz.

Rafe winked at Jamie. "Man talk."

"Ah."

"Is Gordon grooming the new horses?" Jamie asked. "Can I brush them?"

Rafe nodded and, without thinking, reached out to ruffle the boy's blond hair. "He's fixing to feed them. I bet he could use your help."

Jamie needed no other encouragement. Dashing back inside, he raced past the horses peering anxiously out the top doors of their stalls, the thud of their pawing hooves reminding Gordon to hurry with their breakfast.

Rafe smiled down at Josie. "It's good to see you."

Color bloomed on her cheeks. "I meant to come earlier, but—"

"I know," he cut in. "Jamie's been sick." He didn't need an explanation. He knew why she hadn't come to see him; she didn't want to talk about the weasel. Not wanting to, either, he changed the subject. "I was about to take Pembroke for his morning session at the brook. Come with me."

"I thought you weren't training Pembroke anymore."

"I'm not training him. I'm just taking him for a walk." He saw her glance after Jamie, and added, "Don't worry. Stevens will keep an eye on him."

She let out a deep breath, then smiled, all awkwardness forgotten. "I'll tell them where we're going while you get Pems."

He watched her walk away, enjoying the way her long back put an extra swing in her hips and made her skirts sway with each step. The woman could move.

Smiling, he opened Pembroke's stall door. The stallion was growing stronger and more confident every day, and as a precaution in case the stallion became unruly, and not wanting to endanger Josie, he snapped a stud chain onto the halter, crossed it over the noseband and out the left cheek ring, then attached it to the lead rope. Applying as little pressure as possible, he led the horse out of the stall.

In the aisleway, he stopped by Gordon. With an eye on Jamie and his mother by the front stable doors, he said in a low voice, "When you finish feeding, see if the boy wants to brush that gelding I brought from Edinburgh."

The groom grinned and nodded.

Rafe continued on to where Josie waited.

Releasing Jamie to his feeding chores, she gave the stallion's neck a pat, then fell into step on Rafe's other side. "He's doing so much better since you arrived. That wary look is gone, and his confidence is greatly improved."

"He's come a long way."

"But he still shouldn't race again."

He wondered who she was trying to convince. Or if she was using her reluctance to allow the horse to be raced again as her justification to accept Adderly. Rafe cared for Pems, too. But he would sacrifice the stallion for Josie without a qualm.

Leaving the path, they cut across the sheep field toward the brook. A week of rain had beaten down the grass since he'd first walked this way with her. Shedding trees had added a slick layer of leaves on top of it that clung to his boots and made footing slippery. With every step, the ground *squished* and water rose to fill the depressions his boots made in the soggy earth.

How could people live in such constant dampness? He'd need fins if he stayed much longer.

"I'm trying to talk Father out of racing him," Josie said.

Rafe bit back a sharp retort. He knew what the alternative was, but he didn't want to spend what time they had arguing about it.

Pembroke started to hang back when they neared the brook. Rafe talked to him and worked his neck until the nervous horse dropped his head, then he urged him closer, repeating the process whenever the horse balked, until finally, the animal was within ten feet of the water. Satisfied, Rafe asked no more of him, and stood quietly beside him until Pems relaxed enough to graze.

"That's amazing." She smiled, despite the tears glistening

in her eyes. "I never thought to see him this calm around running water."

"His doing, not mine." Rafe motioned to the log beside the bank where they had rested before. "Care to sit awhile?"

With a nod, she tucked her coat tightly around her knees and sat.

Rafe settled beside her, legs outstretched and crossed at the ankles, his left hand resting on his thigh, his right loosely holding Pembroke's lead.

Unspoken words hung between them, but Rafe didn't push it. If she had something to say, she'd say it. And what woman didn't have something to say?

After a while, she surprised him by reaching over and taking his left hand in hers. Neither of them wore gloves, and when she twined her fingers through his, the cool softness of her palm felt satiny smooth against his rough skin. Images burst into his mind of other places her skin would be smooth—that dip at the base of her spine—the pulse point where her neck met her shoulder—the undercurve of her breast. Aware that his body was reacting to his imaginings, he shifted and recrossed his legs.

Josie tipped her head against his shoulder and gave a small sigh—a soft exhalation barely heard, but felt all through his body.

He sat motionless, afraid to scare her off, awash in her flowery scent and the sound of her breathing, weakened by the need building within him. And for that one perfect moment as they sat peacefully beside the brook, everything he wanted and would ever want was in the palm of his hand.

"Adderly has offered marriage," she said and sent him plummeting.

Dreading what was to come, Rafe watched Pems attack the grass with short, choppy movements, and thought how uncomplicated a horse's life was. No regrets, no hopes or disappointments, no concerns about the past or the future . . . just this moment, his hungry belly, and the patch of grass at his feet.

"He says he'll acknowledge Jamie as his son," she went on. "Even put him second in line for the title."

He didn't want to hear this. Every word was another brick in the wall rising between them, another reminder of what he couldn't give her. Yet walking away would be even worse. "Your father told me."

She made a derisive sound. "Did he also tell you that if I agree, Adderly will pay off his creditors?"

"I figured." By what measure did a man set the price for his own daughter?

"I don't know what I should do, Rafe."

Anger jangled along his frayed nerves. Did she expect him to make her decision for her? Give her permission to walk away from him? "What do you want to do?" he asked, unable to keep an edge from his voice.

She lifted her head and looked at him, stripping him bare with that blue-brown gaze. "You know what I want."

He did. And the impossibility of being able to give it to her fed the simmering resentment he had battled all week. "What? You want me to take you away from all this?" Taking his hand from hers, he waved it in a sudden gesture that startled Pembroke. "Your grand house and servants? Save Jamie from a fine education, and you from a life of luxury as a baroness? Christ, Josie. Haven't you heard anything I've said?"

She shrank away from him, her eyes showing the same startled expression Pems wore. "Why are you so cross with me?"

*Cross?* He stared at her, unable to find the words. He wasn't cross. He was disgusted. Frustrated. So howling mad his jaw ached. He rubbed his forehead, trying to dispel the anger that gripped him so tightly he could hardly draw in air.

"It's not you, Josie. It's me. I'm angry with myself. Humiliated, in fact." Letting his hand drop, he leaned forward, elbows braced on his bent knees.

The stallion returned to grazing. Birds continued to flit overhead, and the sun stayed in the sky. Life went on, despite the fact that he'd been so wrong about his selfish, solitary existence, and everything he thought he knew about himself was turning to dust in his hands. It was a wonder he didn't crumble with it.

"Until recently," he said, "I was content with the freedom to go where and when I wanted. No encumbrances. No expectations. It's easy to drift when you don't care. Then I met you."

He made himself look at her, saw the hurt in her eyes, and it hit him like a bullet through his chest. "And now when I have a reason to put down roots," he went on in a gentler tone, "it's too late. After years of trying to protect people and fix things, I find I can't take care of the one woman who needs me."

"How can you say that? You've taken excellent care of me. Don't you remember how you saved me from a nasty confrontation with Father at dinner that night? And how ready you were to step in against William last week? And aren't you always there to protect Jamie from those bullies when we go to town? Don't think I don't notice that. And appreciate it."

"Watching over you isn't the problem, Josie. I can protect you. With my life, if need be. I just can't provide for you." Seeing she still didn't understand, he said it as plainly as he could. "I have no home. Probably no employment once I deliver the horses to Colorado. No future prospects of anything but drifting from one place to another, scraping by until maybe, someday, I have enough to buy a little patch of land somewhere. That's no kind of life for you and your son."

Anger flared in her eyes. "Isn't that for me to decide?"

It sickened him to hurt her. To fail so miserably. To watch all hope of a future with her and Jamie slip through his hands. But if he made no offers, she would have no decisions. He might not be able to save her from Adderly, but he could save her from making a worse mistake with him.

"Maybe. But good choices are based on what's best, Josie, not on what we want. That's what I'm trying to do. Much as I want you and Jamie, I'm telling you to go with Adderly."

"You won't even fight for us?"

"With what? Good intentions? Someday promises? I have nothing, Josie. And no way to take care of you. You need to understand that."

Unable to bear that look of disappointment in her eyes, he rose and held out his hand. "We'd better get back. I see Jamie waving at us."

# Fifteen

Josephine walked silently beside Rafe, her mind reeling. Would he truly stand aside and let them go to Adderly? Even though he knew she would rather stay with him? Had they no hope at all?

Or was he simply offering excuses for not wanting to take on the burden she and Jamie would impose on his solitary life? Perhaps he didn't care about them as much as she had hoped.

"Come see," Jamie shouted excitedly when they approached. Once he was certain they were following, he raced into the stable, calling back as he went. "It's the most wonderful horse ever. Gordon says I can name him myself. I think I'll call him Thor." Stopping outside the stall where Gordon waited, he waved impatiently. "Hurry, Mother. I brushed him all by myself. Do you think Thor is a good name? Perhaps Lightning. He looks very fast. No, wait! Blaze! That's what I'll call him."

Josephine stepped ahead of Rafe and Pems to look into the stall.

A glossy flaxen chestnut gelding stared curiously back. He was on the small side, but sturdily built, and judging by the droop in his bottom lip, well seasoned. But he had kind eyes, and a perky set to his ears, and a blaze that stretched from his forelock to his pink nose.

She smiled in approval. "He's a handsome fellow for certain."

Jamie beamed. "He is, isn't he?"

Rafe reached out to gently push the curious stallion's head away from the stall door. "So you like him, then?"

Josephine watched his broad, strong hand idly stroke Pembroke's neck and felt an answering quiver beneath her own skin.

"I do. Ever so much. And I think he likes me, too. Doesn't he, Stevens?"

"He does, Master Jamie. He took to you right off, he did."

Rafe smiled. "Would you like to try him out in the round pen?"

"Truly? Could I?"

"If your mother approves."

Josephine saw the way Rafe smiled at her son, and felt a stab of disappointment. He was so perfect with him. He could enrich Jamie's life more than all of William's wealth could. Couldn't Rafe see that that was more important to her than luxury or position?

"Well, Mother?" Jamie prodded.

"Do you think it'll be safe?" she asked Rafe.

For the first time since they'd left the brook, he looked directly at her. She expected to see at least a trace of her own turmoil in those guarded eyes—a show of regret on his face, perhaps. Sadness. But other than a slight tightening of his lips, there was nothing. Perhaps he didn't care as much as she thought.

His gaze flicked away. "The boy's a good rider. And the horse is well trained. I'll stay in the pen and keep an eye on him."

"Please, Mother, can I?"

"*May* I," she corrected. Masking her hurt behind a practiced smile, she looked at Rafe. "The countess won't mind?" She didn't want Lady Kirkwell thinking they had appropriated the horse her husband had purchased for her.

"I don't know why she would."

"Then, you may, Jamie. But listen to Mr. Jessup's instructions. And when he says the ride is over, don't argue."

"I won't. I promise."

After asking the groom to help Jamie saddle the gelding, Rafe took Pembroke on to his own stall.

Always observant around strange horses, especially with her son underfoot, Josephine watched the proceedings. She was impressed with how calmly the horse stood, even with

Jamie darting back and forth under his neck to supervise the saddling. "The countess will be pleased."

Stevens buckled the cinch, then ran a finger under the leather to test the tightness. "The horse ain't for the countess, miss. He bought him with someone else in mind." Catching her eye across the saddle, he tipped his head toward Jamie, who was busy with the buckles on the breast collar.

Josephine was surprised. "Why would Kirkwell purchase a horse for . . . someone else?"

"The earl didn't buy him. Mr. Rafe did."

"For . . ." She glanced at Jamie.

"Yes, miss. He thought it was time for something bigger."

She didn't know what to say. If Rafe had so little, why was he spending his hard-earned coin on a horse he could never use?

She knew why. Because that was the kind of man he was. The exact kind of man that her son needed. That she needed.

And at that moment, as she stood in that dusty stable, watching her son master the simple task of caring for a horse, everything fell into place. If Rafe offered marriage, she would accept. No matter his circumstance or prospects, no matter what hardships might loom ahead, no matter what fine offers William made or how hard her father pushed . . . she would have Rayford Jessup as her husband.

But how could she convince the stubborn man to ask?

By the time Jamie and Stevens had finished saddling the horse, Rafe returned from Pembroke's stall. Untying the halter rope, he handed it to Jamie, allowing him to lead the gelding through the stable toward the training pen.

Josephine followed, smiling as she watched them—Jamie stiff with pride to be handling the horse all by himself—Rafe striding silently beside him, head bent to attend her son's ramblings.

What a magnificent man.

He walked with a rolling gait—almost, but not quite, a swagger. Confident. Controlled. He had taken off his jacket, and she found her gaze drawn to the drape of his work shirt over his broad shoulders and the way it rippled against the long curve of his back with each step. And—*oh, my*—he did have the finest legs. Muscled, yet lean, with a slight bow at the knees. A horseman's legs. She imagined them gripping his mount's flanks, and felt the inner muscles of her own thighs contract in response.

"They're a nice pair."

Startled from her wayward thoughts, she glanced at Stevens, walking beside her. "Pair?"

"Master Jamie and the horse. Mr. Jessup chose well."

She brushed a hand over her heated brow and put on a smile. "Yes. It was very kind of him."

"He cares about the boy." Stopping outside the pen Rafe and Jamie had entered, the groom rested his arms along the top fence rail. "We all do."

Her mother's heart swelled with gratitude. The world beyond might look askance at her son, but within these gates, he was safe and dearly loved.

"I appreciate that, Stevens."

A blush spread over his cheeks.

In the pen, Rafe gave her son a leg up, waited for him to slip his boots into the metal stirrups, then put the reins in his hands. He spoke quietly for a moment—adjusting Jamie's grip on the leathers, and reminding him to keep his heels down, his back straight and tilted slightly forward. Then he stepped back. Crossing his arms over his chest, he gave a low-voiced command.

Jamie put his heels to the gelding's sides and the horse began to move at a walk along the rail.

A sense of melancholy moved through Josephine. The bond between the tall, reticent man and her lonely son was already so strong she feared what would happen if Rafe went back to America without them. She knew the pain of abandonment. But Jamie was only a child and had suffered so much already.

After several trips around at the slow pace, Rafe gave another command.

The horse moved into a trot. Jamie began to post, every motion controlled and balanced.

Rafe was correct; the horse was so beautifully trained and had such a gentle disposition, all of her lingering concerns quickly faded. They were a joy to watch—the horse, head tucked, flaxen tail swinging side to side—Jamie, sitting so tall and confident, a huge grin on his lightly freckled face—and Rafe, standing quietly in the center of it all, arms folded, feet spaced, mixing soft-spoken instructions with generous praise.

Her eyes stinging with unabashed pride, she turned to Stevens. "They're doing well, don't you think?"

"I do, miss. Our Jamie is a right fine horseman."

"Do you think we could take him for a short ride beyond the gates this afternoon?"

"I'm sure Jamie would like that. I couldn't accompany you, but maybe one of the younger grooms might. Or Mr. Rafe." A worried frown creased his brow. "I'd gladly change places with him, rather than take Pembroke out for the first time."

"Out where?"

"The brook. Mr. Rafe has held off putting a rider on him outside the pen until we're sure he can handle puddles better. Your father thinks it's time, but I have to admit I'm a bit nervous about it."

"You should be. It's far too soon." Angrily, Josephine shoved away from the fence rail. "I'll talk to him. Does Mr. Jessup know?"

"No, miss. Your father sent word after the two of you left to take Pems to the brook."

"Don't saddle him until you hear from me." Muttering, Josephine started back through the stable.

"Begging your pardon, miss."

She turned back to the red-faced groom.

"Mr. Cathcart said you might try to talk me out of it, and I shouldn't listen. I'm sorry, miss."

With a nod, Josephine whirled and continued out of the stable. What was Father thinking? Did he want to kill Pembroke?

"Father," she said a few minutes later when she found him in his office, poring over a column of figures. Working numbers had always been a struggle for him, and she could tell by his beetled brow that things weren't going well. Not wanting to get his ire up right away, she softened her tone. "I need to speak to you, if I may."

Without looking up, he licked the tip of his pencil and scribbled something on the paper in front of him. "I won't change my mind."

"About what?"

"Sending Pembroke's Pride to the brook today."

"But why, Father? He's not ready. What's the hurry?"

"This is the hurry!" In sudden anger, he slapped a hand on a stack of letters and glared up at her. "Overdue bills. More come in every day. Yet you continue to buy fripperies, and eat fine food, and delay making a decision on the baron's offer. You leave me no choice in the matter."

A familiar feeling of dread moved through her. "Choice about what?"

"It's either Adderly or the horse."

"I don't understand. How will Pems shore up our finances?"

Setting the pencil aside, he sat back and studied her, his mouth pursed, his fingertips drumming on the arm of his chair. "There's a hunt race south of Liverpool next month. A private course. The field won't be large—maybe a half-dozen entries—but it carries a heavy purse. I intend to enter the stallion in it."

Shocked, Josephine sank down in the chair at the front of his desk. His plan to enter Pems in the Grand National was foolish enough; at least with that race, they had six months to prepare. But now he wanted to try him in a month? "He's not ready, Father. He won't win."

"Perhaps not. If he doesn't, we're only out the entry fee. But if he does, being a long shot, he could win us a fortune."

She was aghast. "You're betting on him? You say we're in dire straits, yet you're squandering money we don't have on an injured horse that probably won't even finish the race?"

"That remains to be seen. If your wrangler is as good as he thinks he is, and he's done his work well, the stallion could win."

She repeated the words he had spoken earlier. "Or die trying."

"Maybe." Her father's callous shrug showed his indifference. "But if he can't run, he's useless to me, anyway."

Josephine clenched her jaw to keep from shouting in his face. How could he be so foolish? If circumstances were as bad as he said, why didn't he sell the house? The rest of the horses? Whatever assets he had left?

Then understanding came, and she almost laughed. He was already attempting to barter his last assets: her and Jamie. Swallowing back her disgust, she struggled to keep her voice even. "Who will be riding him?"

"The groom."

"Stevens? He's too big."

"Not as big as Jessup. Besides, Pems is strong. Stronger than any horse I've seen. He can carry the added weight."

"I'll ride him," she offered on impulse. "I know him as well as anyone. He trusts me. And you know I'm a good rider."

The notion took hold, bringing with it a surge of excitement. She would have to ride astride, which would raise eyebrows, but she was already a pariah, so that was of little concern. If youthful memory served, astride was easier than sidesaddle, and with a month to practice, she was certain she could become proficient. At least with her on his back, Pems had a chance.

"Let *you* ride him?" Father's mocking laugh slowed her racing thoughts. "And make a laughingstock of me?" With a snort, he waved the suggestion aside. "Rumors already abound. I'll not add to them by putting you on vulgar display. Besides, if something untoward happened, and he fell or balked, I wouldn't want you hurt."

Fine words, but Josephine didn't flatter herself that his concern was out of care for her. He simply didn't want to jeopardize his last means of escaping this wretched financial debacle.

She thought hard, but could come up with no way out of this situation, other than to accept William's proposal or risk her beloved horse. But if Rafe's hard work paid off, and Pems actually won . . . that would change everything.

"If you're serious about racing him, Father, at least allow Mr. Jessup to continue his training. He's better than Stevens."

"Perhaps. We'll see how the groom does this afternoon. Now, go. I have work to do."

As she walked out of Father's office, she saw Rafe marching toward it with Shipley in his wake. By the thunderous expression on his face, she guessed Stevens had told him about Father's plans. Stepping forward, she dismissed Shipley with a nod, and put a hand on Rafe's arm to keep him from barging through the office door.

"It won't do any good," she said once the butler had disappeared down the hall. "I've already talked to Father. He'll not budge."

Rafe muttered something and dragged a hand through his wind-tousled hair. "Pems won't cross water. Maybe in a few months, but not now. What's the rush?"

"Debts. Come." Taking his hand, she led him to the veranda overlooking the rose garden and the slope down to the stable. Once outside and assured of privacy, she told him Father was determined to enter Pems in a race next month. "He's even betting on him to win. Worse, he wants Stevens to ride him."

"Gordon?" Rafe's blue eyes went wide with surprise. "He's too inexperienced."

"I know. But Father didn't seem to care. I think perhaps he doesn't have the extra funds to hire a qualified race rider."

"Hell. None of this makes sense. If he pushes the horse too soon, it might endanger his chances to race in the Grand National next April."

A half-formed thought arose, but before Josephine could think it through, movement down at the bottom of the slope drew her attention.

A groom raced into the stable, shouting. Although they were too far away to hear his words, it was obvious that something was wrong.

She stiffened, alarm prickling her neck.

Several stable boys ran out. Two raced into the sheep pasture; a third started up the slope to the house.

Sudden terror almost stopped her heart.

*Jamie!*

Wondering what had happened, Rafe watched the two grooms run across the field, sending sheep into bleating flight. Then he saw the riderless stallion lurching in a tight circle in the trees by the brook, trying to free himself from the reins tangled around his front leg. Nearby, Hammersmith knelt beside a prone figure half-concealed in the tall weeds. Not Jamie. Gordon.

"It's Stevens," he called to Josie as he charged down the slope at a full run.

Fearing the frantic stallion would injure one of the boys trying to approach him, he waved them away as he ran across the field. "Leave him! Get the dray!"

The boys ran back to the stable.

Rafe slowed to catch his breath, then speaking in a calm monotone, approached the thrashing horse. "It's all right, boy. You're all right."

When his voice finally cut through the fear, the stallion stopped fighting and stood trembling, his sides heaving, his neck twisted at a sharp angle against his shoulder. The bridle held his mouth open, the bit pulling his lower jaw to the side. Blood dripped from his mouth where the bit had cut his tongue. Foam ran from his neck and chest. White ringed his dark eyes and his nostrils showed red as he struggled to breathe.

Rafe took out his penknife, opened it, and stepped closer. "Easy, boy. You're all right. It's just me."

He quickly sliced through the leather. As soon as the pressure gave, Pembroke's head flew up, but Rafe grabbed the loose end of the reins and held him fast. When he was sure the horse wouldn't bolt, he glanced over to see Hammersmith and the two stable boys trying to slide Gordon onto a blanket.

He saw no blood, and the groom was awake. Rafe guessed by the way they handled him, that it was Gordon's leg that had been injured.

The cart arrived, pulled by the stable workhorse. They quickly loaded Gordon into the back, then Hammersmith climbed into the driver's box and drove toward the house.

The immediate crisis over, Rafe let out a deep breath. He saw Josie standing at the stable door with Jamie, and the last of his crippling fear began to fade.

The saddle had twisted sideways, so Rafe removed it and set it in the grass. Then he checked Pems for injury. Other than the cut in his mouth, minor scrapes on his front legs where his back hooves had clipped them, and a raw place under his foreleg where the reins had rubbed, the horse wasn't hurt. But he would definitely be sore for the next few days. Relieved, Rafe picked up the saddle and saddle pad, and led the stallion back toward the stable.

*Damn Cathcart.* Gordon could have been killed. In addition, with this setback, weeks of hard work with Pems might be undone. *Christ.* At least now, if the bastard wanted to prevent further injuries, Cathcart would have to let Rafe take over the training.

"He's all right?" Josie asked when he approached.

"Nothing serious. I'll longe him in the pen later to see how he goes. Did you get the gelding brushed and put away?" he asked Jamie, hoping a change in subject would take that worried frown off the boy's face.

"Yes, sir. I gave him a carrot, too."

"Good." They walked together into the stable, Josephine

following well behind Pems. Rafe left the saddle and blanket in the tack room, then continued with Jamie to Pembroke's stall.

"Will Gordon be all right?" the boy asked, a quaver in his voice.

"He will. A busted leg is all."

"Will it hurt terribly?"

Fearing a gush of tears, he tried to keep his voice light. "Maybe a little. But Gordon is tough. He'll be up in no time. You decide on a name for the gelding?"

"Blaze." Jamie swiped a sleeve under his nose and looked up. "Do you think that's a good name?"

"I think it's a perfect name." Opening the stall door, he unhooked the stallion's lead and sent him inside. After securing the latch, he hunkered in front of Jamie, who stood beside his mother in the aisle. "So you like Blaze?"

Another swipe at his nose. "I think he's the best horse in the whole world."

"Then he's yours."

It was almost comical the way the boy's jaw dropped. "Mine?"

"If you promise to take care of him and treat him well—and your mother agrees"—he shot a glance at Josie and was alarmed to see tears gathering in her eyes, too—"then he's yours."

"You're *giving* Blaze to me?"

"I'm giving *you* to Blaze. The horse needs a boy like you."

"Truly?" His voice rose to a near squeak. "Mother, can I keep him? Please? Please?"

"Ssh, you'll scare the horses," she warned, still fighting tears, even though now she was smiling. Rafe would never understand women. "Yes, you may keep him." Her eyes met Rafe's, and her wobbly smile warmed into something else, something that made him forget his resolve to stay detached, and made a mockery of everything he'd said down by the brook. "I think he's perfect for you."

# *Sixteen*

Before Rafe could think of a suitable response, a carriage came through the front gates. Wondering if it was Adderly again, he followed Josie and Jamie to the front stable doors and saw a well-dressed man with a black bag step down from the carriage and walk hurriedly toward the house. Too skinny for the weasel.

"That's the doctor. I'd best go." Josie glanced hesitantly at her son. "Would you mind—"

"Let the boy stay here." Rafe smiled down into Jamie's worried face. "I'll need help tending the stallion's scrapes and repairing his bridle."

She knelt in front of her son. "I will send word about Stevens as soon as the doctor finishes with him."

Jamie nodded.

"Shall I have Cook send down a picnic lunch? You could share it with Mr. Jessup."

A more enthusiastic nod this time.

"Mind Mr. Jessup, then." She rose, sent Rafe a smile of gratitude, then hurried up the slope to the house.

Rafe and Jamie went back into the stable.

"Hope those aren't your favorite clothes," Rafe said, opening the door into the small room where Hammersmith stored feed and medicinal items.

"No, sir."

"Good." Rafe retrieved a tall brown bottle off the shelf, checked the white label, then went back into the aisle. "Because this is going to stink."

A short while later, they left Pembroke's stall, reeking of the horse liniment they had rubbed into the stallion's stiff muscles.

Wrinkling his nose, Jamie wiped his hands on his trousers. "That truly does smell dreadful. Will it help, do you think?"

"It should." Rafe looked up to see Hammersmith coming down the aisle with a basket in his hand. His mouth was pressed into such a thin line it almost disappeared into his beard.

Fearing bad news and wanting to spare the boy, Rafe stepped forward to meet him. "How bad?"

"By the blood of Saint Andrew," the Scotsman began, then saw Jamie watching, and altered his tone. "Both bones broken in his shin. Bruises. The bones stayed in place, so the lad's leg should heal well. Ye are to resume the stallion's training. The master wants him jumping the creek by the end of the week. If he willna do it," he added in a lower voice, "he says he'll put a bullet in him."

"He better not!" Jamie cried from behind Rafe.

Hammersmith groaned. Forcing a smile, he said, "I dinna think he meant it, Master Jamie. Speaking from temper, is all."

"I'll check Pems this afternoon," Rafe said. "See if any injuries appear that I didn't find earlier." And if they did, he would buy the horse himself, rather than allow him to be destroyed. Or have Thomas steal him if he ever came back. Indians were good at that.

"Cook sent this." The groom held out the basket. "Aye, and it smells better than you, I warrant."

Rafe waited for Jamie to offer to share their meal with Hammersmith, and was proud when he did. But the Scot said he and the other grooms had already taken lunch at the house, as they usually did, and advised them to eat outside so they wouldn't stink up his stable. After washing their hands at the pump, they took the basket to the brook and sat on the same log where he and Josie had suffered through that awkward conversation several hours earlier.

Another time when he should have kept his damn mouth shut. He could still see the hurt in her eyes. At the time, he had thought putting his cards on the table might help her see the hopelessness of the situation.

Instead, he had made it worse.

*Won't you even fight for us?* she had asked, as if doubting his feelings for her and her son.

*God,* if she only knew. When he saw her wounded look, and realized that something rare and precious had slipped through his hands, he was filled with a desperation to get it back.

But why, if nothing had changed?

He looked beyond the pasture at the stone mansion on the hill. He could never compete with that. But maybe, if he could offer something more . . . *be* something more . . .

It came to him then, as he sat beside Jamie, wolfing down a cold lunch of baked chicken, biscuits, roasted potatoes, and an entire tin of peaches, that he wanted to change. To be better than he was. To take the risk of opening his heart again. All because he was falling in love with Josie.

*Falling.* His chewing slowed. The perfect word for how he felt. Spinning out of control. Flailing in midair, tumbling headlong into a place he had never been.

Strangely, he wasn't afraid. In fact, he felt energized, more hopeful than he had in a long time. Everything seemed sharper, more defined. His senses were more acute. This chicken leg tasted better—although he suspected it was pigeon, not chicken—birdsong sounded sweeter, the clouds hovering overhead felt less depressing.

If that wasn't due to the fumes from the liniment, then it must be love.

He grinned, the word rolling through his mind, kicking up hopes and ideas along the way. He would fix this. He would make it work. He wouldn't live a life without Josie and her son.

"Jamie, what do you know about America?" he asked on impulse.

"It's where cowboys and Indians and buffalos live."

"Ever thought of moving there?"

He looked up, squinting against the struggling sunlight. "Is it far away?"

"Across the ocean."

"By France?"

"The other way."

The boy thought for a moment, then sighed. "Mother wouldn't let me."

"What if she came, too?" Rafe smiled, thinking about it. A nice little cabin—nothing too big or elaborate—nestled in a field of columbine, ringed by tall pines and aspen, and bordering a clear mountain stream.

And live on what? Juniper berries and balsam root?

"Could I bring Blaze?"

Rafe studied the boy, realizing from the question how lonely he must be, isolated by his wealth, his birth, his mother's worry. But in America, Rafe could claim him as his own and no one would even care. "Sure."

"When can we leave?"

*When, indeed.* Seeing a reflection of his own impatience in the boy's hazel eyes, Rafe grinned and ruffled his thatch of blond hair. "I'm thinking on it." If he intended to make this happen, he needed a plan. Something that would give him a way to build a life for the three of them in America.

And it all started with Pems.

Now that he was back in charge of the stallion's training, he would have to make some revisions. Work him a little harder. If they hadn't lost too much ground with the mishap this morning, and there were no other problems, the stallion might— *might*—be able to run in a month.

And if he won . . . hell . . . that could change everything.

That afternoon, Hammersmith brought Gordon back to the stable in the cart.

"How is he?" Rafe asked as they loaded the droop-eyed groom out of the back.

"They should have kept him at yon house," the Scot complained, bowed under Gordon's weight as he and Rafe carried him to his bunk in the room he shared with the other grooms. "I've no time fer nursemaiding."

"Bugger that, you sheep-humping Scot," Gordon slurred between gasps of pain. "As cheap with your help as you are with your coin—mind that rail!—bloody hell!"

"Dinna pay him any heed," Hammersmith muttered, pulling

the sheet over Stevens's slack form. "The laudanum is wearing off." Bending close to Gordon's ear, he shouted, "And I'll no' be giving ye more, ye worthless cur, if ye dinna watch your tongue. There's a bairn present." He punctuated that with a thump on the injured man's head.

"Ow." Gordon's eyes blinked open, wandered for a moment, then settled on the boy watching wide-eyed at the door. "Hallo, Master James. A word of advice. Don't break your leg. It hurts like a bloody, buggerin'—"

"Best come along, Jamie," Rafe cut in, steering the boy away from the door before he heard too much. "Your mother will be looking for you."

"Gordon used bad words."

"He didn't mean to. It's just the medicine talking."

"How can medicine talk?"

"Never mind. And it would be best if you didn't tell your mother."

"Yes, sir."

After pointing the boy up the path to the house, Rafe walked back into the stable just as Hammersmith came out of the room where Gordon was. "Can I talk to him?" Rafe asked. "I'd like to know what happened at the brook."

"Aye. I canna give him more laudanum for a while yet, so he's still awake."

Rafe pulled a stool near Gordon's bed, sat down, and asked him what happened when he took Pems to the brook.

"He refused the jump, like I figured he would. Took him around again. Same thing. Third time, the bloody bastard dug in his heels and sent me flying. Guess I pushed him too hard. Is the Scot bringing more laudanum?"

"Soon. And don't fret about Pems. He fared better than you."

Gordon tried to move his leg, then winced. "He's well then? I saw he was caught up in the reins."

"He's sore, but fine. How about you?"

A weak grin split the groom's pale, weary face. "Cook is sending Henny down with my meals, so it's not too terrible." He motioned Rafe closer. "She's glad to get away," he whispered. "The miss and her father are fighting again. Even heard your name mentioned a couple of times."

Rafe wasn't surprised. His feelings for Josie put him squarely in Cathcart's sights. "Don't worry about that. Just get yourself healed."

"The doctor is bringing a crutch so I can get around. I suspect I'll be back on my feet well before you return to the colonies."

"We haven't been colonies for nearly a century," Rafe reminded him.

"Bugger that." The injured man motioned him closer again. "Any chance the earl might need another wrangler for the trip?"

Rafe straightened in surprise. "You want to emigrate?"

Gordon nodded.

"What about Henny?"

"Her, too. She figures if Miss Josephine marries the baron, she'll be looking for another position, anyway. Not hoity-toity enough for a frigging baroness." Gordon frowned. "Did I say 'frigging'?"

"You did."

"But not in front of Jamie."

"No, only 'sheep-humping,' 'buggering,' and 'bloody hell.' But don't worry. He said he wouldn't tell his mother. You're serious about emigrating?" Rafe would help Gordon toward that goal, but wanted to make sure it wasn't just the laudanum talking.

"We don't want to be servants all our lives. But it would help if we had employment and a place to go. We can pay our way, if we must. Where's Hammersmith? He said he'd be back soon."

"If the earl doesn't need you, someone will. There's always room for hard workers." And if things work out as Rafe hoped, he might even be able to hire Gordon, himself.

Clouds were sinking down to meet the mist rising off the fields when Rafe took Pembroke out to the round pen for his afternoon workout. He started him at a walk, and gradually moved him through his gaits. The stallion was definitely stiff, but seemed sound, so Rafe worked him just long enough to limber him up, then brought him back inside. More liniment and a good massage, then he fed and watered him, and called it a day.

Henny brought Gordon's dinner. Rafe was pleased to see that Josie came, too, carrying a plate piled high with food.

Since he had been banished from the house, he usually had to go get his own plate from the kitchen then bring it back here to eat. Apparently, even the house help had been warned away from him.

"I hope you're hungry," she said, handing the plate to him.

"We can share. Unless my stink chases you off."

She laughed. "Don't you know liniment is perfume to a horse lover? Let's hope it helps. Pems wasn't looking that spry when I checked on him just now."

"He's mostly sore. He'll be fine."

They settled on overturned buckets in the tack room—stables weren't usually dressed out for callers—and he asked how Jamie was handling all the doings up at the house.

"He's worried." She forked a bite of potato in her mouth, then slowly chewed. He had never seen anything quite so arousing. "He overheard that Father planned to shoot Pems if he can't jump. I told him you wouldn't allow that."

"I won't."

"How will you stop him?"

"I'll think of something." He wasn't ready yet to talk about the ideas bouncing around in his head. They were too new. Too impossible. He needed more time to think them through and come up with a workable plan.

They sat in silence for a time. There was something intimate about eating off the same plate. Hearing her chew and swallow. Sitting close enough that her arm rubbed against his as she ate. Intimate and arousing. *Hell,* everything about her aroused him. It was damned distracting. But nice.

"He's also planning his move to America," she said after a while.

Rafe gave her a sheepish look. "Jamie told you about that?"

"He's quite excited about it. Apparently I'm invited, too." She looked at the green bean impaled on her fork. "I know you mean well, Rafe, and were simply trying to distract him, but I'd rather you didn't put wild ideas in his head."

Rafe studied her for a moment. "What if it's not a wild idea?"

She froze, the bean halfway to her mouth.

"What if I figured out a way to provide for you and Jamie?"

She returned a green bean to her plate, wiped her fingertips on the napkin, then fixed her gaze on his with a directness that made his skin tingle. "How?"

"I'm not sure yet. But if I can work it out, would you go to America with me?"

"Go with you to America."

He nodded.

"Permanently. Forever."

He nodded.

She thought for a moment. Then she tipped her head to the side in that teasing way she had that told him she was fighting a smile. "Is this a proposal of marriage, Mr. Jessup?"

Heat rushed up his neck. "Not yet. But maybe soon. You'll be the first to know, I promise."

Her smile faltered. "Then ask me when you're certain, and I'll give you my answer then."

He hid his disappointment. He'd botched it. "Fair enough."

After they finished eating, he set the empty plate on the floor by his boot. "Have you told Jamie about Adderly yet?"

She shook her head. "If Pems takes the race, and Father wins the money he needs, perhaps I won't have to."

"That's wishful thinking, Josie. He won't win. I doubt he'll even finish."

"He might. He could surprise everybody." She gave him a smile that reminded him too much of her crafty father. "Especially with you riding him."

"Me?"

"Stevens won't be able to. And who else can manage him?"

"But I'm even heavier than Gordon—at least eighty pounds more than most race riders and over a foot taller. That's too big a handicap for any horse, no matter how strong he is."

"Perhaps not in this race. Since it's a private course and not sanctioned by any of the hunt organizations, there are no weight or height restrictions. It has its own set of rules." Leaning forward, she rested her folded arms on her knees. "Which is why Father is so anxious to enter Pems in it. It's his last hope of avoiding his creditors, even if it ends up costing Pems his life." She turned her head and looked at him. "But I think he might pull it off, Rafe. I think Pems could win this."

He refrained from snorting.

"This isn't the usual hunt course," she went on, her enthusiasm rising with every word. "Father told me all about it. It's not a fenced track, but across country, through fields, and bracken, over stone fences, and down into rocky dells. The obstacles are more random and natural. For that reason, they can be more dangerous. But there are fewer of them, spaced widely apart. Which plays into Pembroke's speed."

"No water?"

"Certainly there are water crossings. Brooks, ponds, bridges."

This time he couldn't mask his doubt. "You saw what happened today with Gordon. You truly think Pems could handle all that?"

She shrugged. "There would be no screaming crowds. No banners waving. No artificial barriers or hidden water. And no having to face a jump he's already refused. Point A to point B. However you can do it. If your horse falls and is able to get his legs back under him, he can continue. If you fall, or are intentionally knocked off by another rider, you can remount and ride on."

Rafe pictured it. Horses crowding each other, tripping over rocks and downed limbs, riders whipping their mounts and each other. "It sounds like a brawl."

"It is. For that reason, only the strongest horses even attempt it. And only the strongest riders cross the line. Plus, there will be few other horses entered. Perhaps only six or so." She put her hand on his forearm, her eyes bright with excitement. "The key is to hold Pems back. Let the other horses go ahead so he can see what's coming. The harsh nature of the course would eliminate several horses right off. By the end there might be only a few remaining, so when you reach the final sprint, you can send Pembroke on and let him run like we know he can."

Rafe smiled, admiring the sparkle in her amazing eyes and that flush of passion in her cheeks. "You've thought this out."

"I have. I even offered to ride Pems, but Father won't permit it."

Thank God the man had *some* sense.

"Pems can do this, Rafe. I'm sure of it. It's not a matter of how fast a horse can run the course, but if he's strong enough to finish it. And you know how strong Pems is. And how much he trusts you."

He shook his head. "I'm too heavy. Besides, your father would never agree to let me ride him."

"We'll see." Josie collected their empty plate and rose to leave. "All I ask is that you think about it."

Rafe did. While he tended his chores and Ash's other horses, he thought of little else. By the time he finished his duties, the idea had taken hold and he knew what he had to do.

After collecting clean clothing from the loft, he hauled three buckets of water to the feed room and washed off as much of the liniment stink as he could. Then he dressed and left the stable.

It was raining again. Not actual rain, but a mist so thick it lay like a fallen cloud and swirled around his legs as he trudged up the path to the house. Even wearing his hat and a jacket, he felt wet and chilled by the time he stepped onto the front porch and lifted the ornate brass knocker.

Shipley answered. When he saw who it was, his look of surprise gave way to one of confusion. Before he could question why a wrangler had come to the front door rather than the back, Rafe stepped inside, handed the befuddled butler his hat, and asked if Mr. Cathcart was in his office.

Shipley gaped at him.

"Office it is, then. I know the way." Without waiting for the bemused butler to recover from his surprise, Rafe headed down the hall.

The house was quiet, the lights dim. He wondered where Josie was. Maybe curled in her bed somewhere overhead, her hair tumbling loose, a book braced against her raised knees. Was she a reader? He hoped so. The idea of lying in bed beside her, just reading, was unbelievably arousing.

*Hell.* He was getting himself worked up again. He had to curb these randy thoughts.

But his imagination had already caught fire, adding details that sent a surge of desire through him. Maybe her nightdress was lacy and delicate—or thin and clinging, like silk—or maybe she wore nothing at all.

Realizing he shouldn't be dwelling on such things moments before he spoke to her father, Rafe filled his mind with images of nuns and kittens and greasy gray balls of haggis. By the time he reached Cathcart's study, he had regained control. He was also slightly queasy.

Since the door was partially open, he gave a courtesy knock, then entered. "Good evening, Mr. Cathcart. Might I have a word?"

With a start, the Englishman looked up from his papers, saw who it was, and frowned. Before he could ask what Rafe was doing back in the house he had been thrown out of a week ago, Shipley arrived, red-faced and panting.

"My apologies, sir. He barged—"

"Good night, Shipley." Rafe closed the door in the astonished butler's face, then turned back to the man behind the desk.

"What do you want?" Cathcart snapped, his fingers gripping the edge of the desk, his eyes wary.

Wondering if the man had a loaded gun in the drawer by his hand, Rafe smiled to show he had no evil intent.

"I have a proposition for you. One that will get each of us exactly what we want."

# *Seventeen*

"May I sit?"

Cathcart scowled, his jaw clamped tight.

Taking that as a "yes," Rafe settled into the chair facing the desk, his right ankle resting atop his left knee, his hands hanging off the ends of the armrests. "I understand you intend to enter Pembroke's Pride in a race next month."

Cathcart's eyes narrowed.

"With Stevens laid up," Rafe went on, when it was apparent he wouldn't get a response, "I'm guessing you'll need a trainer."

"I already told Hammersmith that with Stevens injured, you would be handling Pembroke."

"I'd like to hear it from you."

Cathcart considered that for a moment. Tension easing, he leaned back in his huge chair, the ink-stained fingers of his right hand tapping a rhythm on the wooden arm. "Think you can get the stallion ready in time?"

"As ready as he'll ever be."

More thinking. Tapping. "Can he win?"

"Doubtful. But possible."

Greed sparked in Cathcart's eyes. He leaned forward. "How possible?"

"Depends on who his trainer is, and who rides him in the race."

"What if I asked you to do both?"

"Are you offering me the position of trainer and rider?"

"I am."

Rafe flicked a gob of mud off the boot resting on his knee, watched it thump against the desk, then slide to the carpet. "Ordinarily I'd say I was too big to race him. But since we haven't the time to accustom the horse to an unfamiliar rider, I'd say yes to both." He looked up with a smile. "But it would cost you."

"How much?"

"The horse. Win or lose."

Silence. Then a harsh laugh burst out of Cathcart. Shaking his head, he sat back again. "You must think I'm a fool. I'll not part with my best horse. And anyway, why would I give him up now? You might decide not to enter him. Or if you let him run and he wins, the purse would go to you, not me."

Rafe pretended to give that some consideration. "Then how about this? You give me a signed Bill of Sale today, but date it the day of the race. That way, you still have full ownership until he runs."

A sly expression came over Cathcart's ruddy face. "Dated the day *after* the race. That way you won't try to pull him out at the last minute."

"If your main concerns are the winner's purse, or me pulling him out before the race," Rafe said thoughtfully, "then date the bill for later that afternoon. Hammersmith said the race starts at ten o'clock. So date the bill for later . . . say, noon. And you still pay the entry fee."

Cathcart studied him for so long, Rafe started to sweat. Then finally, the Englishman nodded. "Deal."

Rafe mentally raised a fist in triumph. "Then draw up the papers. As soon as they're signed and witnessed, I'll begin the stallion's training." He rose and started for the door.

"That's it?"

Rafe turned.

"You expect me to just *give* you the horse? He's a valuable animal. Worth a lot of money."

"You're right," Rafe agreed. "But then, so is my training. With my help, you have a chance—a slim one, but still a chance—of making back what he's worth plus a great deal more. Without it, you have a damaged horse that won't even bring a decent stud fee considering all the problems in his past." Rafe let that sink in, then added, "However, I concede your point. So in exchange for the horse—win or lose—I won't charge you for the training. That way you're only out the entry fee, but you have a chance of winning more than the horse is worth, both in the purse and any side bets. Would that be fair?"

"You should pay the entry fee."

"Perhaps," Rafe said with a smile. "But I won't. You've heard my terms. Take it or leave it."

"Damn you."

Reading that as another "yes," Rafe nodded. "Have the papers ready tomorrow. I'd like to get started as soon as they're signed and in my hands." He started for the door, then hesitated. "One other thing," he said, facing Cathcart again. This time, he didn't smile.

"Until the race is over, I'd rather you didn't send your daughter and grandson to Adderly. Unless that's what she wishes, of course."

Cathcart blinked. Color rose in his cheeks. "The hell you say, Jessup! You don't come in here and dictate to me about my own daughter! Get out! Now!"

Rafe hated all this posturing. It brought out the meanness in him. "Does this mean our deal is off?"

Cathcart's bullish neck seemed to swell over the top of his tight collar.

"If so," Rafe went on calmly, "then of course, I'll do as you ask and leave tonight. I'll also wire the earl that you're canceling your contract with him for the care of his horses. When should I tell him you'll send reimbursement for the advance payment he made?"

"You bloody bastard!"

Realizing he might have pushed the man too far, Rafe softened his tone. "I'm not trying to be unreasonable, Mr. Cathcart. You know I care about your daughter. And you know she doesn't want to marry a man who has abused her trust once already. Give me time to see if I can best Adderly's offer. That's all. Just until after the race. Besides, even if she was willing to accept the baron, he couldn't marry her before then, anyway."

Cathcart glared at him, lips pursed so tight his mouth looked like a pale pink scar slicing across his face. Rafe could almost see the calculations spinning behind his eyes as he tried to determine what would work best to his advantage. Greed was so predictable.

"Just until the race," Rafe pressed, impatient to be gone before he did or said something he might regret. "That's all. Then let her choose."

"You actually think she'll pick you?" Cathcart's laugh sounded forced and unsure—a coward's attempt at bravado. "She might not care much for Adderly, but she'll never pick a penniless horse wrangler over a wealthy baron. She's not foolish."

"You're probably right, so it's not much of a risk, is it?"

Silence, except for the drumming of Cathcart's fingertips against the arm of his chair. "You'll not move back into the house," he finally said.

Rafe didn't respond.

"And you'll stay away from my daughter."

"That's up to her."

Cathcart's fist slammed on the armrest. "No! It's up to me!"

Rafe shrugged, neither agreeing nor disagreeing.

For a moment, they glared at each other, then the older man let out an explosive breath that seemed to deflate half his bulk. "You're a bloody bastard, Jessup. But since I don't think she'll stoop to align herself with a man like you, I'll give you until the race. One month." He picked up his papers, already dismissing the issue from his mind. "I'll send the postdated Bill of Sale down in the morning. As soon as the race is over, win or lose, the stallion is yours, then I want you gone from my daughter's life forever. Get out." He waved a hand like he was shooing a fly. "And don't come again unless you're summoned."

Relieved to have the battle over, Rafe left. As he closed the door behind him, he saw Josephine coming from the direction of the conservatory. He stopped in the hallway to watch her approach, admiring the bounce in her step, the way curls bobbed against her shoulders with every stride, the lift in her stubborn chin. A woman of purpose. Beautiful, intelligent, strong enough to stand alone if she had to. With a woman like her by his side, a man could accomplish anything.

"What are you doing here?" she asked when she caught sight of him in the shadows.

"Talking to your father."

"About what?"

"Training Pems. Walk me out."

As soon as they crossed through the front door, he closed it behind them and pulled her into his arms.

She didn't resist.

Her lips were cool, her breath warm. She tasted of apples and cinnamon. Smelled like the flowers in the hothouse. Fit so perfectly against him, he couldn't imagine holding any other woman in his arms. Gentling his kiss so that they barely touched, he learned again the contour of her mouth, traced the softness of her lips with his tongue.

She was manna to him. All his hopes and desires brought together in this one beautiful, fearless woman. Everything and anything he would ever want.

The kiss grew more urgent. He stroked his hand up to cup her breast. Felt her warm softness, the beat of her heart against his palm. Heard the catch in her breath when he drew the pad of his thumb across the hardened tip.

"Josie . . ." he whispered, his body shaking, his mind thrown into chaos by emotions so powerful he didn't know what to do with them.

She leaned into him, pressed her soft breast into his hand. "Come to my room."

Reluctantly ending the kiss, he dropped his forehead against hers and struggled to contain the heat arcing through him. This wasn't supposed to happen. Not yet. Not until he had something to offer and a way to take care of her and Jamie. "I'm not allowed in the house."

"Then I'll come to the stable."

Something in his chest twisted. Had he reduced her to this? Furtive couplings in a dusty loft? She deserved so much more. They both did.

Taking his hand from her breast, he stepped back. "No."

She went still. In the faint light cast by the oil lamp beside the door, he watched tears rise in her beautiful eyes and knew he had hurt her. Again.

"Josie . . . honey . . ."

"You don't want me?"

He would have laughed had he been able. Instead, he pulled

her body tight against his, let her feel the effect she had on him and how much he wanted her. "Can you doubt it?"

Color darkened her face. But she didn't pull away. "Then why? I don't understand."

"You will."

"When?"

"After the race." Fearing if he stayed longer, he wouldn't be able to leave her at all, he gave her a hard, quick kiss, then released her and opened the door. "Go to bed and dream of me."

With a deep sigh, she stepped inside.

Reaching past her to grab his Stetson off the rack, he leaned in for one last kiss, then straightened. "By the way, your father said that he won't send you and Jamie to the weasel. Not for a while, anyway."

"*Send* me?" One dark brow rose. "I should hope he wouldn't try."

He grinned, liking this feisty side of her. "And he wants me to stay away from you."

"Then I fear he'll be disappointed, since it's not his decision, one way or the other."

"That's what I told him."

"And what did he say to that?"

" 'Get out.' "

She laughed. Which he liked even more.

"I'll see you in my dreams tonight," he told her with a grin. "Wear something pretty. Or not."

*A month*, he thought as he stepped out into the mist and headed down the hill. That was all the time he had to retrain a frightened horse, collect what advance pay he could from Ash, and lose as much weight as possible without making himself sick.

With Josie as the prize, he'd find a way to do it.

The next morning, he awoke with a start from a lusty dream about Josie to find a figure sitting cross-legged in the dawn shadows, watching him.

"Ho," a familiar voice said.

"Jesus!" Rafe lurched up onto his elbows, his heart kicking against his ribs. "Thomas, what are you doing?"

"Waiting for your eyes to open."

"Hell." Rafe fell back with a groan. "You've got to stop that."

"Stop what?"

Bells. Maybe shackles. Clappers on his heels.

Once his pulse slowed, he sat up and swung his feet to the plank floor. A chill swept over him even though he wore unions and wool socks. He had thought Colorado was cold, but this constant dampness was worse. Reaching back for the thin wool blanket, he pulled it over his shoulders, then glared at the Indian in the corner.

The Cheyenne had reverted back to his warrior ways, it seemed. Fresh feathers dangled from his temple braids, and new bits of carved antler were sewn onto his war shirt. Rafe could only imagine how he'd gotten them. "Well, now I'm awake. What do you want?"

Thomas smirked. "If the woman knew this is how you greet the day, she would not look at you the way she does."

"Go to hell." Rafe rubbed a hand over his face in an effort to clear the fog of sleep from his mind. He had already spent half the night fretting over, dreaming about, and wondering what he should do about that woman. He didn't want to talk about her now. "Why are you here?"

"I am ready to begin our book."

"Now?" Rafe yawned and scratched his head.

"But I have decided it will not be about the legends of the People. It will be the story of a Cheyenne warrior's journey."

"Journey where?"

"From boyhood in the mountains, through a trail of broken treaties, to death at the hands of your George Armstrong Custer at the Battle of Washita River."

"Doesn't sound like a very happy book."

"It was not a happy journey."

Rafe struggled to bring his thoughts into focus so he could understand what Thomas was trying to accomplish. "That isn't what Chesterfield talked to you about. He may not like this new idea."

Thomas shrugged. "It is a story that must be told. Every day I hear things about the People that are not true. We are not noble, or savage, or uncivilized, or mystical, or red devils. We are different from the white man, but still the same. Yet we are told that unless we become more white, we will die. But if we discard our ancient beliefs, will that not be the end of the People anyway?"

Rafe didn't know how to answer that, so he said nothing.

"I will tell the struggle of Chief Black Kettle. You will write it down. Then we will have on paper the true story of the People before it is lost forever in time."

"I thought you couldn't speak the names of those who have died."

Thomas lifted his chin in challenge. "The Great Spirit knows what is in my heart. He will protect me."

"If he forgets, you can always borrow my dream snare."

Thomas wasn't amused.

So Rafe let it drop. "Since it's not the story he asked for, Chesterfield may not publish it."

"I do not write it for him. I write it for the People. For me." A smile warmed his dark eyes. "And for you, as well, *nesene*. So that you will understand the man who walks beside you."

Rafe suspected that, in a small way, he was writing it for Prudence Lincoln, too. "All right," he said, stifling another yawn. "We'll start on it tonight. But first, we're going to have another talk about what happens to poachers in England."

As ordered, Josephine dreamed of Rafe that night. Restless, troubling dreams that had her kicking off the counterpane and awakening to the night chill, her mind and body filled with feverish longings and nameless fears.

America. So very far away. And so dangerous. She had heard about the hazards of the Wild West. Indian attacks, snakes, wildfires, scorpions, hairy spiders, and even poisonous lizards there that grew as long as Jamie was tall.

But Lady Kirkwell was also an Englishwoman, and she seemed completely enamored with America, especially the small town in Colorado where the earl was building his thoroughbred stable. In their brief conversations before they left for Scotland, the countess had spoken often of the beauty and vastness of the mountains, the forward-thinking people who lived practical, useful lives and didn't frown upon a woman for pursuing her own dreams.

"The freedom of it!" the countess had added with that beaming smile. "I didn't wear a corset for *months*, and lace gloves only to church. And I learned to shoot a gun, and traveled about in a gypsy wagon with only a dear old man as a chaperone." Her smile faded. "Of course there were difficult times, as well. I had a terrifying night alone in the woods, battling wolves over the remains of my chaperone, and I had to shoot a man in Denver. But"—she brushed aside those astonishing revelations with a wave of one dainty hand—"of course he deserved it. I was only protecting my husband, after all." A look of nostalgia came into her lovely brown eyes. "My time in America was most liberating. I do hope you have a chance to visit someday."

It now seemed she might . . . *if* all of Rafe's plans bore fruit, and *if* she was willing to uproot her son and walk away from everything they had ever known and loved.

Aware that Rafe would be spending as much time as possible with Pems, she didn't distract him by going down to the stables except when she came with Henny each day to bring lunch. He looked weary, and she wondered if he had as much trouble sleeping as she did. He seemed distracted, too, and his appetite had lessened.

"I'm worried about Mr. Jessup," she told Henny one afternoon as they left the stable with the empty luncheon plates. "He seems to be losing weight."

"It's because of the race, miss. He fears he's too heavy."

"That's ridiculous." After handing Rafe's empty plate to her maid, Josephine marched back down the slope. She had learned more about the race from Hammersmith, and knew that strength was more important in this race than weight.

She found him talking to Mr. Redstone outside Pembroke's stall. "Might I have a word, Mr. Jessup," she said, advancing on them.

Mr. Redstone faded out the back of the stable in that astonishing habit he had of disappearing without a sound.

Rafe's crooked smile lifted the weary planes of his chiseled face. "We're back to Mr. Jessup, now?"

"You don't have to lose weight," she said without preamble. "Talk to Hammersmith."

"I have."

"Then he doubtless explained that this race is less about

speed, than the ability to withstand punishment. Do you know what a melee is?"

"A medieval brawl."

"Just so. Think of a melee on horseback with a race thrown in. You'll be whipped, bumped, kicked by other riders, knocked off in any way possible." She allowed her utter disgust to show. "It's brutal, for both the horses and their riders. The only reason there has not been a public outcry against it is because most of the bettors and participants are from the highest level of society and only those invited even know when and where the race is to be held each year." She frowned, her blue-brown eyes narrowed in confusion. "Why are you smiling?"

"Because now I know how Pems can win."

# *Eighteen*

Rafe set a rigorous routine for Pembroke that included endurance exercises, sprints, jumps, and of course, water training. Thomas was a huge help, accompanying them on their daily rides, astride Barney, a calm gelding Pems knew well. Luckily, the stallion had been thoroughly trained the year preceding his entrance in the Grand National hunt race, so he already knew his pacing.

Other than getting him over his fear of water, it was a matter of building up his endurance and wind with increasingly longer runs up and downhill, then using short full gallops to enhance muscle strength. He was already an experienced jumper, so those exercises were as much to reinforce his previous training as to train Rafe, since he had never entered in a steeplechase race.

The rest of the time was spent in water training. Their daily trips to the brook went from standing and grazing, to stepping into the water, and finally, hopping over the brook at Rafe's command while on a lead. From there, Rafe progressed to hurdles in the pen on a lead, then hurdles in the pasture under saddle, to hopping the brook under saddle.

It was a long and arduous process, characterized by almost as many steps backward as forward. But Rafe persisted, and Pems slowly made progress. In fact, he seemed to enjoy having a task to perform, and grew more confident with each small achievement.

And all the while, a vision of the future grew in Rafe's mind.

After making his bargain with Cathcart, Rafe had written to Ash, explaining about the race and why he needed an advance on his pay. He ended with the hope that the earl might come for a visit to see how the warmbloods had settled in and advise him on training Pembroke. "And be sure to bring the countess," he had written in closing. "I know Miss Cathcart would be happy to see her. She so seldom has visitors, and greatly values your wife's friendship."

Actually, he was hoping for an ally. He had seen the alarm in Josie's eyes when he'd mentioned America, and knew she needed reassurance. And who better to dispel her concerns than a gentle, warmhearted woman who had not only survived the Wild West, but seemed to have thrived in it?

After completing the stallion's training in the pen and pasture, Rafe and Thomas rode out one crisp afternoon for their first cross-country run over fences, hedges, rock walls, and bridges, as well as three jumps across the brook. Because Rafe would be using Josie's strategy of holding Pems back until the final sprint, he let Thomas go over the jumps first, relying on Pembroke's herd instinct to keep him moving after Barney. But when they went into a full gallop, he let Pems go. And he was as fast as any horse Rafe had ever ridden.

To avoid souring the stallion, Rafe kept all the routines as varied and short as possible, then spent a lot of time talking to and massaging the horse during the cooldown period. Now that he knew Pems would belong to him in a few weeks, he allowed himself to become more attached to the stallion, and was grateful the horse responded with increasing trust.

Rafe was learning, too. Hammersmith helped him with jumping techniques, and Thomas taught him how to fight and defend himself on horseback. Mostly, it was fun, although he suspected Thomas put a bit more into it than necessary. But Pems took to it with enthusiasm, sending more than one horse limping back to the stable until Rafe learned to curb the stallion's inbred fighting tendencies. He would have made a grand warhorse.

Every evening, Rafe climbed to the loft, so exhausted and sore he could hardly think. Then for an hour, he sat on his cot and wrote down Thomas's words as he detailed the struggle of a well-meaning, but stubborn, Indian who fought to keep his family and his tribe safe under an onslaught of white intruders, false promises, and bloody skirmishes.

Thomas was right. It was a story that needed to be told.

And little by little, as the days slipped by, Rafe began to believe . . . in both Pembroke's Pride, and his dream of the future.

"Where are you two going?" Father asked a week-and-a-half before the race.

Turning from the front door, Josephine said over Jamie's blond head, "For a ride."

"Don't be gone long. We have company coming."

"Lord and Lady Kirkwell?" she asked hopefully. Rafe had told her that he had written to Scotland and she longed to see the countess again.

"They'll arrive in a day or two. Adderly is coming this afternoon." He smiled down at Jamie in a way that put Josephine on guard. "He's bringing a gift for the boy."

"A gift? Why would he do that?"

"Can't a man give his own—"

"No!" she blurted out. "It—it wouldn't be proper."

"I don't mind," Jamie offered.

Josephine leveled her gaze at her father. "We will discuss it in your study. Jamie, wait for me at the stable." Then without checking to see if her father followed, she marched down the hall. As soon as she heard the door close behind him, she whirled. "I thought you agreed not to push an alliance with Adderly until after the race."

He walked calmly past her to his desk. "Agreed with whom?" he asked, sinking into his overlarge chair.

"Mr. Jessup."

He frowned up at her, his blunt fingers tapping a drumbeat on the wooden armrest. "You openly discuss such things?"

Knowing he was trying to change the subject, she didn't respond.

"I'm not pushing an alliance, Josephine. Adderly contacted me, saying he wanted to meet his son and he had a gift for him."

"I haven't yet told Jamie about the baron."

"Then it's time you did. It's apparent the boy is forming an attachment to that wrangler. Have you thought about what will happen to him when Jessup leaves?"

"*The boy* is named Jamie. And whether Jessup stays or leaves has no bearing on my decisions about Adderly and any gifts he might bring."

"The boy—Jamie—should know who his father is. A gift is simply the baron's way of introducing himself and letting his son know he cares about him. That's all."

"All of seven years too late, you mean."

"Think, daughter! If you refuse his gift, or refuse to let him see his son, he might take legal action. And how do you think that will end—a toff against a commoner? He won't be the loser, I can guarantee you that."

"I'm Jamie's mother," Josephine insisted. "No court would take him away from me." And if anyone tried, she could always deny that William was his father. Such an admission would hardly damage her already ruined reputation.

"Perhaps. Perhaps not. But is that something you're willing to risk?" When she didn't respond, he slapped his hand down on his desk. "Damnation, girl! You know how dire our financial situation is. If the worst happens and we lose everything, wouldn't you rather live as a baroness than a scullery maid? And what of Jamie then?"

She wanted to scream. Shake her fist at him for putting her in this horrid position. Instead, she whirled and tried to pace off the fury twisting in her stomach. She felt like she was being pulled apart. Jamie, Rafe, Father, Adderly—they all wanted something from her. But she had wants, too. Was she to live her entire life in shame because of one foolish mistake? Or be forced into a loveless marriage to protect her son?

She could almost feel her hopes for the future slide from her grasp.

"This is no time to think with your heart, girl," Father warned. "Use your head for once."

She would rather use the back of her hand across his smug face.

But he was right. This wasn't only about her. It was Jamie's future, too. And he deserved to know who his father was, and what he would be leaving behind if they went with Rafe to America.

And if he chose to stay here instead?

Then she would stay, as well, since she could never leave without him.

And once Rafe left, if—*when*—Father lost everything, she would have no choice but to accept Adderly's offer. She almost doubled over with the pain of it. But beneath all the despair was the conviction that she *must* keep that option open. For Jamie's sake, she couldn't afford to burn the bridge back to Adderly.

The idea made her stomach turn. "As you wish," she finally said. "I'll talk to Jamie." Spinning on her heel, she left the room.

It would be best to tell him during their ride, she decided. But they rode for several miles before she gathered enough courage to broach the subject. No mother wanted to tell her child she had been indiscreet, and because of it, he had been born a bastard. What could a child understand of love and lust and foolish dreams? All she could give him was honesty, and hope he would forgive her someday.

"Jamie," she began, "a man came to visit us a few weeks ago. Do you remember him?"

He plucked a leaf from Blaze's mane and tossed it aside. "Was it while I was sick and you wouldn't let me go to the stable?"

She nodded.

"I saw him from the window. He seemed rather round. And not as tall as Mr. Jessup. Is he the one coming today with a gift for me?"

"Yes. He is Baron Adderly. And he—he's your father."

Jamie looked over at her, his hazel eyes wide with surprise. "I thought my father was dead."

"I allowed you to believe that he was. But I know now I was wrong."

He pulled his horse to a stop. "He's alive?"

"Very much so," she said, reining in beside him.

"Why didn't you tell me?"

Inside her gloves, her hands felt damp. "I only wanted to protect you. I thought it would be easier for you to understand if I waited until you were older to tell you."

"That's the same thing as a lie, and you said we were never

to lie to each other." The quaver in his voice told her he was as near to tears as she was.

"I know, dearest. I'm sorry. I was wrong in so many ways."

Seeing the hurt and confusion in his face made her desperate to put her arms around him and reassure him that he was still her Jamie and she was still his mother, and nothing had changed.

But of course, it had.

"I'm sorry I didn't tell you the truth, Jamie. But I'm not sorry I have you."

He looked away, his small chin quivering. "If he's my father, why doesn't he live with us?"

"Because he has another family somewhere else."

He wound his small fingers in Blaze's mane. "Another son?"

"Yes. His name is Edward. He would be your half brother. I've never met him, but I hear he's quite nice, although rather sickly."

He digested that, then nodded. "So I'm not a bastard, after all."

A stab of anger pierced her. "Where did you hear that word?"

"In town." A flush turned the tips of his ears red. "Mr. Jessup said it means someone who doesn't have a father. But you say I do have a father, so that means I'm not a bastard. Isn't that so?" He gave her a hopeful look.

Emotion clogged her throat. "It—it's more complicated than that, I'm afraid. A bastard is a child born to two people who aren't married to each other."

"Oh."

Another long silence.

"Why didn't he marry you?"

"He said he wanted to, but his parents had already arranged for him to marry someone else."

"That doesn't seem fair."

"No, it doesn't."

"Well, I would have married you, no matter what you said." Gathering the reins, he nudged Blaze into a walk.

Tears filled her eyes. The unassailable logic of a child. Catching up to him on her mare, she tried to smile, even though his loyal defense of her almost broke her heart.

"Has he known about me for long?" he asked after they had ridden a ways.

"All of your life."

"Then why didn't he ever come to see me? Didn't he want me?"

Under the hurt, she heard anger in his tone, and oddly, that reassured her. He had a right to be angry at the way William had ignored him. They both did.

"He had other responsibilities," she hedged. "Then recently, his wife died. Now that he's free, he wants to marry me and acknowledge you as his son."

"So I wouldn't be a bastard anymore?"

"That's part of it."

He thought for a moment. "If you married him, would we go live with him and his other son?"

"Probably."

"What about America?"

Josephine pressed her gloved fingertips to her forehead where a throbbing had begun. The questions were endless. And so hard to answer. "That's another issue, dearest," she said, letting her hand fall back to the reins. "And something we'll decide later. For now, I simply want you to know who the baron is and that he's coming to meet you."

They had reached the turn to Penrith. Jamie reined in. She stopped her mare beside Blaze, and looked at her son expectantly. She could almost see him sorting it out in his head. What could a seven-year-old understand of this mess? And how would she fare in the final arrangement? Would he ever forgive her?

"Do we have to go into town today?" he asked, breaking the long silence.

"Not if you don't want to."

"I'd rather not."

"Of course." Seeing that he was wrestling with questions and doubts and fears about where he fit now, she wanted to reassure him that the most important things in their lives hadn't changed and never would. "Jamie, I need for you to understand something." She waited until he looked at her before continuing.

"You're my son. I love you more than the breath in my body." Sudden emotion constricted her throat and she had to wait for it to ease before continuing. "Even when you're a grown man with a family of your own, you will still be my son, and I will still love you with all my heart. Whether I marry the baron, or go to America, or move to the Highlands of Scotland to raise sheep, that will never change. Ever."

She was gratified to see some of those worry lines relax into a wobbly smile. "If we go to America, will I still be a bastard?"

How often had that word been used to hurt him? It had certainly left a scar. "Perhaps not." *If* Rafe was truly hinting at marriage, and *if* he decided to adopt Jamie. So many uncertainties. But she couldn't burden Jamie with those now. "Such things aren't as important there as they are here." Or so she hoped.

He looked over at her, that childish innocence tarnished a bit, and a hint of sadness in his hazel eyes. "I don't like it when you lie to me."

"I know. I sh-shouldn't have. I promise I will never do so again."

"Then stop crying. I don't like that, either."

She gave a broken laugh and wiped her eyes. "All right. No more tears."

He stared past Blaze's ears, his lips pursed in thought. "Do you want to marry the baron?"

"I haven't decided. Nor will I, until you and I have discussed it fully. But today, you needn't worry about anything but meeting him."

"Very well. I shall meet him. But I still think I would rather go to America with Mr. Jessup." And with a belligerent thrust of his chin, he sent his horse into a trot.

Rafe was finishing with Pems when Jamie and Josie led their horses into the stable. When he had seen them leave earlier, he had noticed Josie had the same fretful, panicky look she had worn that first night on the ship. But now she just looked weary, and Jamie was the one who looked worried.

"That was a short ride," he said, stepping out of Pembroke's stall into the aisle, where they were rubbing down their horses. He admired Josie for tending her own mount and for teaching her son to do it, too. He considered it the mark of a true horseman. He also admired the way her long skirt draped her pear-shaped butt when she bent to run the brush down her mare's leg.

She straightened. "We have a guest coming this afternoon and couldn't be gone long," she said listlessly. "How is Pems doing?"

"Better every day. He jumped the brook twice this morning without having to go at it a second time."

She dropped the brush into the bucket and faced him with a strained smile. "I never thought he'd be comfortable around water again."

"He's still not comfortable, but he's doing better. How did Blaze go for you today, Jamie?"

"Very well, sir." Jamie untied the gelding's lead from a ring in the support post. "When we turned for home, I watched him like you told me, but he didn't speed up even a step. I don't think he's barn sour in the least."

Rafe nodded, curious why the boy wouldn't look him in the eye.

"After you put Blaze away," Josie called after him as he led the gelding to his stall, "run up to the house and wash. Adderly should be arriving soon."

*The weasel?* Rafe frowned at that unwelcome news, but when he started to ask why the baron was visiting again, she shot a look toward Jamie and motioned him to silence.

As soon as the boy left the stable, he rounded on her.

She spoke first. "Before you ask, neither Father nor I invited him. He's bringing a gift for Jamie. And he wants to meet him."

*Hell.* Rafe rested his hands low on his hips and glared out the double doors, half expecting to see the weasel's carriage rattling through the front gate.

"I talked to Jamie."

Seeing her face crumple, Rafe felt a moment of panic. Crying women always rattled him. "About what?"

"Adderly. I told Jamie he's his father."

He glanced toward the room where the grooms slept, heard low voices, and knew Hammersmith was still talking to Gordon. Taking Josie's arm, he led her into the feed room, where they would have more privacy.

"How'd he take it?"

"Better than I expected." More tears, falling in glistening streaks down her cheeks. "Oh, Rafe. He's such a good, kind boy. He never once blamed me, or became cross with me, or looked at me the way others do. H-He still loves me."

Rafe pulled her into his arms, his own eyes stinging. "Of course he does, Josie. Why wouldn't he?" She fit so perfectly against him. Soft and warm, tall enough that he didn't have to bow his back to hold her. Yet as he felt the beat of her heart against his chest and the dampness of her tears on his neck, a deep sense of hopelessness crept into his mind. How was he to do all that she needed him to do? Protect her from the manipulations of Adderly and her father. Shield her and her son from the viciousness directed toward them because of Jamie's birth. Convince them to come with him to America, and find a way to support them if they did.

The obstacles seemed insurmountable, his hopes as substantial as puffs of smoke. Especially since everything—his dreams, her happiness, any chance of a future for Jamie—all hinged on a damaged horse winning a brutal race.

It would be easier to light a candle from a star.

With a sigh, Josie pulled out of his arms. "I must go." She swiped a gloved hand over her damp cheeks and patted a few strands of dark hair back under her tiny hat. She looked resigned, defeated, her shoulders slumped and a sea of despair swirling in her mismatched eyes.

"Josie, we can leave here today," he blurted out in blind desperation. "Ash will give me an advance on my pay. We could go up to Scotland and take a ship from there to—"

Her hand on his chest made him forget what he was saying. A sad, shaky smile creased her tear-streaked face. "Is this another almost-proposal, Mr. Jessup?"

Heat rushed into his face. "It's an idea." And not a great one, if he read her look of disappointment right.

*Hell.* He was a bumbling fool. Rushing his fences. Making promises he didn't know if he could keep. But when he thought of the weasel getting his hands on her and Jamie, and when she looked at him like that . . .

"I'm trying to protect you and Jamie. I only want to keep you safe. But . . ." He spread his hands in a helpless gesture, then let them fall back to his sides. "But I don't know what to do, Josie." He had never felt so inadequate in his life. And he didn't like it.

Her hand moved from his chest to his cheek. Even through the soft leather of her glove, he could feel the warmth of her palm. "You don't have to do anything, Rafe. This is for me to do. I've avoided the issue of Jamie's parentage for too long, and it's time I dealt with it. Knowing you care enough to want to help gives me the strength to do that."

"But I—"

She stopped him with a kiss. A salty kiss. A kiss so filled with tenderness it almost undid him. "You give me courage, Rafe," she whispered against his lips. "And I adore you for that." Another kiss, then she drew away. Before he could pull her back into his arms and give voice to the tempest of emotions roiling inside him, she turned and walk from the room.

He followed her into the aisle, wanting to do something, say something to bring her back. But the words stuck in his throat. In silence, he watched her walk away, his body taut with frustration and indecision, a hundred unspoken words and questions rattling around in his head.

He wasn't sure what had just happened, or what Adderly's return meant, or what his hesitation might have cost him.

But he knew something had changed.

# Nineteen

Adderly arrived just before luncheon. Josephine was in the yellow salon, trying to read a book, when she heard his carriage on the drive. Filled with apprehension, she rose and went to the window.

Father was already stepping off the porch to greet him; two jovial fellows well met, their faces wreathed in smiles—the cads—while Shipley sent footmen forward to retrieve the baron's luggage. By the number of cases they carried inside, it was apparent he planned to stay for several days.

Footsteps in the hall. Composing her face into a bland expression, she turned from the window just as Jamie rushed in.

"Is it him?"

"He. And yes, it is."

"Oh." He looked terrified and excited at the same time.

Still a child, and faced with issues beyond his control or understanding. The awareness that she had done this to him was like a tear in her heart. "You look quite handsome," she said, filled with pride, despite a building dread.

"What do I call him?"

"Sir, or my lord, or Lord Adderly. You can decide later if you wish to address him as Father." Seeing the worry on his wan face, she forced a smile. "Come stand beside me, so I won't be nervous."

With a look of relief, he scampered into place just as the door opened again and Father ushered the baron into the room.

Josephine stood frozen, her gaze fixed on William's face. But when she saw the way he looked at Jamie and the emotion behind his tentative smile, some of her fear drained away. "Welcome, Lord Adderly," she said, extending a hand as he approached, and hoping he didn't see the tremble in her fingers.

"Miss Cathcart. You're looking beautiful as always." A dip of his head, then he released her hand and stepped back.

She was pleased to see a reflection of her own panic in his brown eyes. Resting a hand on Jamie's shoulder, she felt tension ripple through his small frame, and gave a squeeze of reassurance. "Adderly, may I present James Cathcart, my son. Jamie, this is Baron Adderly."

Jamie gave a slight bow. "Good day, sir."

"Delighted, I'm sure." Hands clasped at his back, William rocked on his heels, the buttons on his waistcoat straining over his girth. "May I call you Jamie?"

A quick look at Josephine, then Jamie nodded. "Yes, sir."

"Do you know who I am, Jamie?"

"Mother says you're my father."

"She is correct. I am your father. And I've been far too long in coming to see you. I regret that. To make amends, I have brought you a gift."

"Thank you, sir."

A pause. "Would you care to see it?"

Another glance at Josephine, another nod. "Yes, sir."

"Excellent. It's outside." William's smile seemed more relaxed as he extended a hand toward the door. "Shall we?"

Josephine followed them into the entry, where Father fell in beside her. "That wasn't so bad, was it?"

Good manners prevented her from striking him, though she was sorely tempted.

Bright afternoon sunlight greeted them when they stepped outside. It was a moment before Josephine's eyes adjusted to the glare. When they did, she saw Adderly speaking to one of his blue-liveried grooms. The man walked to the back of the carriage and untied a horse tethered to the boot. A glossy gray gelding, with dapples on his shoulders and haunches, and a paler gray hue in his mane and tail. After handing the lead to Adderly, the groom stepped back beside the coach.

Smiling, William ran a hand along the horse's neck. "This is Thunder, Jamie. A fine thoroughbred with impeccable bloodlines. I would like for you to have him as a gift from me, your father."

*Impeccable bloodlines.* How ironic. And how thoughtless of William to use such a phrase in front of the woman he had cast aside for lacking an acceptable pedigree, and the boy he had ignored because of his common blood. But then, William had never given much attention to the feelings of others.

"B-But I already have a horse," Jamie said.

"Since when?" his grandfather barked.

Seeing that telltale throb in Father's temple, Josephine stepped in, hoping to defuse a situation that was already awkward enough. "It's most kind of you to give Jamie such a fine animal, Baron Adderly. Isn't he a beauty, Jamie?"

"Yes, ma'am." Jamie scrambled out of the way when the nervous gelding shied at the sudden clatter when a coachman dropped the mounting step into the boot at the back of the coach. "Th-Thank you, sir."

Smiles all around, even though the tension was thick enough to cut with a blade, and anyone who had ever been around horses could see that the young thoroughbred was too green, too high-strung, and too big for a boy of Jamie's size and age. But rather than make an issue of it, Josephine nodded to the butler hovering near the front door. "Have one of the grooms take Thunder to the stable, will you, Shipley? And tell Cook we will take luncheon now."

But Father couldn't let it go. "Don't brush this off, daughter. I want to know where the boy got this other horse he mentions and why I wasn't informed."

"Mr. Jessup gave him to me," Jamie said.

"Jessup?" Adderly frowned, his gaze flicking from Jamie to Josephine to Father. "Isn't that the man who calls himself a wrangler?"

"Yes, it is." Josephine smiled at the two men staring at her; one in confusion, the other in fury. "Mr. Jessup was kind enough to bring the horse back for Jamie when he returned from Scotland."

"Without asking me?"

"I saw no need to involve you, Father, since—as Jamie's mother—it was my decision to accept or reject the gift on my son's behalf."

"Well, now that Adderly is here," Father ground out, "he can decide which horse his son will keep."

Jamie looked at Josephine in panic. "But I love Blaze. I don't want to give him up."

"You'll do as you're told, boy!"

"Father," Josephine murmured in warning.

"No!" He rounded on her, fists clenched at his sides. "This lack of gratitude is precisely what comes of coddling the boy too much. I'll not be talked back to in my own home, nor will I allow a guest to be treated in such a disrespectful manner! Boy, go to your room!"

Josephine met Jamie's stricken look with a weak smile. Better he should be absent while they sorted this out. He was confused enough as it was. "It's all right, dearest. Off you go now."

As soon as Jamie raced inside, Josephine whirled on her father. "That was completely uncalled for!"

"Please," William cut in, his face flushed—with embarrassment or anger, Josephine couldn't tell which. "This is entirely my fault. I should have checked with each of you first. Let's allow the boy time to think it over, then I'm certain he'll make the proper decision."

Still glaring at her father, Josephine nodded. How humiliating.

"Of course," Father said, his own face ruddy with anger. "After you, sir," he added, waving them inside.

Josephine's stomach was tied into such a tight knot she didn't know how she could sit through a meal in the company of these two men, much less swallow a single bite of food.


At noon, Henny brought lunch down to the stable.

Although Gordon had been out of bed for over a week, he still couldn't manage the slope, even with the crutches the doctor had brought, so he continued to take his meals in the bunk room with Rafe. By his smile when Henny walked into the room, he didn't seem to mind.

"Faith, and you wouldn't believe the shouting!" Fueled by righteous anger, the pretty Irishwoman fluttered about, settling

Gordon in a chair with his injured leg propped on his cot, then passing out their plates and mugs—tea for Gordon, coffee for Rafe. "And right in front of the house where God and all the staff could hear. It's a scandal, is what it is!"

Rafe frowned, food forgotten. "What happened?"

"Miss Josephine gave back as good as she got, that's what happened! And I don't blame her for it. The master should have kept quiet, rather than tearing into her and Master Jamie in front of the baron. It was a disgrace, so it was."

"Henny, what happened!"

She reared back in surprise. "There's no need to shout, Mr. Jessup."

If Josie was in trouble, he needed to know now, before he went charging up there. Striving for patience, he set his mug on the floor by his foot, and the plate on the end of the bed. "Then, please, Henny, tell me what happened."

She let out a deep sigh. "It's all because of that horse the baron gave Jamie."

"The gray gelding the groom brought down?" Gordon asked.

Henny nodded. "Thunder, he's called."

Rafe was astounded. "Adderly gave that horse to Jamie?" No wonder Josie was upset. The animal was entirely unsuitable for a boy Jamie's age.

"He did. And when Master Jamie said he already had the horse you had brought him and he didn't want to give him up, his grandfather started shouting about disrespect to the baron and such like, then sent the lad to his room. Sure, and Miss Josephine was chewing nails, so she was, and I don't blame her. To his credit, the baron tried to smooth things over, but when they went in to lunch, they were all three scowling like vicars on race day. Faith, and it's a mess."

It sounded like it. But Rafe trusted Josie to send word if she needed him.

*This is for me to do*, she'd said. A gentle way of telling him this was a part of her past and didn't include him. If he went up there now, uninvited and rushing to the rescue, it would be the same as telling her he didn't believe she was capable or strong enough to handle it.

*Hell.* She was stronger than he would ever be. Bullets and bluster might be his weapons, but they were no match for Josie's endurance and strength of character. She had withstood sneers and barbed comments for years now. She could certainly handle a weasel and a drunkard.

But just in case, he'd be here—waiting and watching and hoping she would come to him if she needed him. And even if she didn't.

Instead, it was Jamie who came. And Rafe soon learned that if a woman's tears rattled him, those of a child were like a knife in his chest.

The boy ran into the stable just as Henny was going out. Seeing the look of terror and despair on his tear-streaked face, Rafe dropped the halter he was carrying, and stepped forward. "What's wrong?"

Jamie kept running, almost knocking Rafe off balance when he plowed into him, his arms going around his waist in a tight hold.

"I don't want him! They can't make me take him!"

Startled and not sure what to do, Rafe glanced at Henny, watching from the doorway.

But she was crying, too, one hand pressed over her mouth.

Realizing he was on his own, Rafe tentatively rested a hand on the boy's shoulder. "Jamie, talk to me."

Tears. Muffled words. Sobs.

Gently pulling the arms from around his waist, Rafe dropped to one knee, and was further surprised when Jamie threw himself against his chest, his thin arms going around his neck this time.

"I won't give him up!"

It felt odd. The shaking body pressed against his felt odd. Too small and fragile to be causing such a ruckus in his heart. "Jamie. Son, what's wrong?"

*Son.* It just slipped out. But it felt right. Holding him felt right.

Motioning to Henny to go on, Rafe continued to hold the boy and stroke his back like he did with Pems when the stallion was afraid. After a few minutes, the hitching sobs dwindled to wet sniffles. "Talk to me, son. Tell me what's wrong."

The dam broke under a rush of angry words. "I won't give up Blaze. He's my horse and I won't give him up. Ever!"

"All right."

The boy drew back, nose and eyes running, but defiance

flashing in his reddened eyes. "And I don't want Adderly for a father, either! I don't want to go live with him. I want to go to America with you."

Unsure how to respond, Rafe bought time by brushing a lock of blond hair off the boy's sticky brow.

"We could take Mother and Blaze and Pems with us," Jamie added, warming to his plan. "And I shall never come back to see Grandfather or the baron ever again."

"What about the gray? Thunder, I believe he's called."

"I won't see him, either. And I won't bring him to America with us."

Rafe wondered what he'd unleashed with his earlier ill-advised remark about going to America. Who knew kids were so literal?

"Here." He pulled out a faded neckerchief and pressed it into Jamie's hand. "Wipe up." He hid his distaste while the boy smeared snot all over his face, then shook his head when Jamie tried to hand the kerchief back. "No, you can keep it."

"Truly?"

"Sure."

Grinning, the boy stuffed the damp, wadded kerchief into his pocket like it was a rare treasure.

"The gray is a fine horse, Jamie."

"I still don't want him."

Rafe thought for a moment, then tried a different tack. "A fellow can have more than one horse, you know. More than one father, too."

Jamie blinked at him, hope and confusion reflected in his hazel eyes.

"In fact, I have several horses, myself."

"Several boys, too?"

"No. No boys. Or girls." Not yet, anyway. But the prospect of another towheaded boy and a pretty, dark-haired daughter moved him in an unexpected way.

"I could be your boy. If you wanted."

"I'd like that. Very much."

"And perhaps Mother could be your wife. That way, she wouldn't have to marry the baron."

"I'd like that, too." Rising, Rafe rested a hand on Jamie's shoulder. "How about we take another look at Thunder." He gently steered the boy toward the gray's stall. "Even if you decided not to ride him, I think he's too fine a horse to let go. In fact, he might be a good companion for Blaze. What do you think?"

"I had another reason for visiting today," Adderly said, carefully cutting his chilled breast of duckling into tiny, precise pieces before moving on to begin slicing his glazed carrots.

Josephine remembered that about him. Having had the rules of the dining table drilled into her by her dragon of an etiquette tutor, she recalled how surprised she had been at her first dinner with William when she had seen him cut all of his food into tiny portions before he took his first bite. She had been so fearful of making a mistake in front of a baron's son she hadn't expected him to be the one to disregard the rules.

*Cut. Set the knife across the top of your plate. Take a bite. Set down the fork. Chew at least ten times. Sip from your goblet. Gently press the napkin to your lips, return it to your lap, and begin again.* She could still remember Mrs. Capshaw barking those words in her ear. No wonder she had such a delicate digestion.

Not so Rafe. He ate like a man who enjoyed his food—and needed a lot of it to fuel that big body. A man with an appetite. When he chewed, it did the most fascinating things to his cheeks and jaw, and when he swallowed . . . She smiled, remembering how it seemed to involve every muscle and tendon in his throat, all the way down to that small hollow at the base of his neck, where sometimes a few dark, curling hairs—

"Daughter?"

Startled, she looked up to find both men staring expectantly at her.

"What do you think of the baron's invitation?" Father prodded.

"Invitation?"

"To visit his home at Fell Ridge. Weren't you listening?"

*Fell Ridge? The scene of his wife's recent death?*

Misreading her hesitancy, William sought to reassure her. "It would be entirely proper. My maiden aunt is visiting and will act as chaperone. And of course, you may bring your maid, or my aunt will be happy to provide one. As for traveling arrangements, I will accompany you on horseback, rather than ride inside the carriage."

Too bad he hadn't considered propriety eight years ago. But what Josephine found even more disturbing was that within weeks of his wife's passing, Adderly sought to parade her replacement before his bereaved son. "Isn't it a bit soon to be entertaining? Edward must still be in distress after his mother's recent passing."

"That's precisely why I've invited you and Jamie to visit." William seemed to wrestle with himself then come to a decision. "Edward isn't well. An incurable weakness of the heart, the doctors say. That and his mother's death have pushed him into a deep state of melancholy. It is my hope that if he has someone to play with—a brother—he might revive somewhat."

Josephine felt a swell of sympathy. She couldn't imagine a parent's despair at having a child so gravely ill. "I'm sorry. Is there no chance of recovery?"

"The doctors are not hopeful. And I would like for Neddy to meet his brother before . . . well . . ."

"Of course we shall come." How could she deny his heartfelt request? Her own fears seemed petty in the face of such a tragedy. Although, she did have to wonder why, if his son was so terribly ill, had William taken the time away from him to visit here? "When did you propose this visit to take place, and for how long?"

"A couple of days, if you could spare them. I'm not sure Neddy would be up to a longer visit at this time. If it's convenient, I could escort you and Jamie to Fell Ridge when I return home tomorrow."

Pushing aside her reservations, Josephine smiled. "It sounds lovely," she said, trying to inject enthusiasm into her voice.

Hopefully, Jamie wouldn't prove difficult. But she wasn't certain how Rafe would react. He had low regard for the baron and took few pains to hide it.

However, it was clear, judging by his satisfied smile, that Father fully approved of the visit. Doubtless, he thought it would bring her closer to accepting William's suit, and himself one step nearer to solvency.

How irritating that everyone seemed to have plans for her future—William, Father, even Rafe. Perhaps it was time she made plans of her own.

# *Twenty*

J amie took the news that they would be going to the baron's
home the following day with the expected scowl of resistance. But he did seem calmer about the horse debacle. She
understood why when she let slip that he had sneaked down to
the stable to visit Mr. Jessup.

"He said I didn't have to give up Blaze. That I could have
lots of horses if I wanted. And more than one father, too."

She was a little disquieted that Jamie had gone to Rafe rather
than his own mother, but she understood why. The Texan's
quiet steadiness brought a sense of stability and balance to
those around him. She had seen it in horses. Had felt it within
herself. So it shouldn't surprise her that her troubled son would
be drawn to that calm strength, as well.

"So you're content to visit Adderly's home?"

He gave the listless shrug of a child faced with an irksome
chore. "I wouldn't mind meeting my half brother, I suppose.
How old is he?"

"I'm not certain. I know Neddy is younger than you. And
sickly. You must take special care not to play too rough with him."

"How long will we be away? Mr. Jessup said the earl and
countess are coming, and I shouldn't want to miss them."

Josephine smiled, having forgotten that happy news. "Two
days. What would you like to bring? Perhaps some toys to share

with Neddy?" As she spoke, she motioned to Nanny Holbrick, standing just outside the door. "Nanny will help you pack."

After explaining to the elderly woman what he would need to bring for the short visit to Fell Ridge, Josephine excused herself and went down to the stable, hoping Rafe would take the news of their visit to Fell Ridge as well as Jamie had.

He didn't. Although being the reticent man that he was, he said nothing, but listened in scowling silence, feet braced, arms crossed over his chest. "When?" he asked in a clipped tone.

"Tomorrow."

"How long?"

"Two days, not counting the two mornings of travel. We should return near the time the Kirkwells arrive."

"We?" His head came up, disapproval evident in the tightening of his lips and the muscle clenching in his beard-shadowed jaw. "Jamie's going, too?"

It rankled, having to balance everyone's wants against her own. Everywhere she turned, she came up against a wall of expectations, and every decision she made disappointed someone, it seemed. "I think it's important that he meet his half brother." *And know the life awaiting him if I marry Adderly.*

She didn't say that, of course. To speak those words aloud would awaken doubts she hadn't the strength to face right then.

"I'll miss you," he said simply.

Irritation dissolved. How did he always know the perfect thing to say?

They spoke of inconsequential things for a moment more, then she left before Father or William came looking for her. He made no move to delay her. Yet all the way back up the slope to the house, she was aware of him watching from the doorway of the stable as if loath to see her leave.

But if that was so, and he truly thought he would miss her, why hadn't he given her a kiss as he often did when they parted?

The next morning, Rafe left Pems tied in the aisleway near where Thomas was saddling Barney for their daily cross-country run, and walked past the silent Indian toward the tack room.

They had had sharp words the night before over something insignificant—Rafe couldn't even remember what—and the Cheyenne was still stewing in silence.

Which was fine with Rafe. After a sleepless night worrying over Josie and Jamie and what their visit to Adderly's might mean, he wasn't in the mood for chitchat.

Apparently, Thomas was. Regarding him with an expression of disgust, he cocked his head toward the Adderly carriage heading down the drive. "Why do you let him take her?"

He didn't have to ask who the Cheyenne was referring to. Pretending disinterest, he positioned the pad and English saddle on the stallion's back, then lifted the flap and buckled the leather girth strap. "Not my call."

A derisive snort, followed by the usual "white people" remark.

Rafe ignored both.

Thomas reached between Barney's front legs to secure the breast collar strap to the cinch. "I would not let any man take *my* woman from me."

Rafe couldn't ignore that, and the implication of cowardice sent his temper to a flash point. "No, you'd walk away first, wouldn't you?" Thomas had never said why he'd left Prudence Lincoln in Indiana so abruptly, but with the Cheyenne's habit of disappearing when things got tense, he could guess.

Thomas straightened.

Rafe could tell by the Cheyenne's furious expression that he had crossed a line, but he didn't care. He could also see that their heated exchange had drawn curious faces to the doorway of the bunk room. He didn't care about that, either.

"I think I will enjoy knocking you from your horse today," the Indian said in a cold, flat voice.

"You always do. But hell, why wait?" Beyond conciliation, and too stubborn to back down, Rafe waved a hand toward the back of the stable. "What say we step outside and get it over with right now?"

He wasn't much of a brawler, but today he was in the mood to give it a go. Not just to punish Thomas for his caustic remark, but because he needed an outlet for all the emotions he had held in check for so long.

Thomas gave a wicked smile. "I will hurt you, white man."

"You're welcome to try." Whirling, Rafe stalked past the gawking stable hands and out the back of the stable.

Trailing grooms, Gordon on his crutches, and a frowning Hammersmith, Thomas followed.

Committed and anxious to get started, Rafe stepped through the rails of the round pen, pulled off his shirt, and tossed it over a post. Ignoring the murmurs when the watchers saw the bullet scars on his chest and back, he said to Thomas, "No knives or guns."

"I will not need them." More murmurs when Thomas pulled off his shirt, exposing the thick ridges of scar tissue across his chest from the brutal ordeal of the Sun Dance ceremony.

"No biting, eye gouging, hair pulling, or kicks to the groin," Rafe continued as they walked side by side into the ring.

"I am a Cheyenne warrior. Not a little white girl."

"We'll see."

Stopping in the center of the pen, they turned and faced each other from a distance of six feet.

Rafe was ready and primed for battle. Frustration had been burning in his gut and he welcomed a chance to vent it. He shook out his arms and legs. Flexed his shoulders. Rolled his head to loosen his neck. Then balancing his weight on the balls of his feet, he bent slightly forward, hands up and ready. "I'll try not to hurt you too bad, redskin," he taunted.

A snarling lunge from Thomas, and the fight began.

Rafe had size and height. Thomas had quickness and agility. Both could give and take a lot of punishment.

Within minutes, blood was flowing.

Rafe's world shrank to the reach of his arms, the sound of their grunts as fists struck hard. Pain became secondary to the ferocity of physical exertion and the elation of pitting his strength against Thomas's.

He called on all the rage that had festered inside of him since that hot, dusty afternoon in Dirtwater—his disappointment when the woman he thought he'd loved ran away—his disgust when the townspeople he fought to save left him to live or die on his own. He fought with savage determination to win back all he'd lost that day, and all he stood to lose now if Josie walked away, too.

But the wounds he'd suffered a year ago began to take their

toll on him and he finally began to tire. The fifth time he hit the ground, Thomas sank onto his knees beside him, his chest heaving, blood dripping from a cut over his eye. "Are you done yet?"

Fighting for breath, Rafe rolled onto his back and stared up into the cloudy sky. He hurt so bad he figured he'd have to die to feel better. "For now."

With a groan, the Cheyenne slumped down beside him. "You are a good fighter," he said between breaths. "For a white man."

"For an Indian," Rafe countered, his own lungs pumping, "you do okay, too." Once he caught his breath, he pushed himself into a seated position, wincing at the pull of sore muscles.

The watchers had left. The dust had settled, mostly on him and Thomas. And Josie and Jamie were still gone. Nothing had changed, other than the bruises he'd be sporting tomorrow. Still, he figured it was worth it.

More groans as Thomas sat up, one arm clamped across his middle. He wore his usual smirk behind a split lip and a rapidly swelling eye. "Do you feel better now, Rayford Jessup?"

Rafe spit blood into the dirt, then gave Thomas a weary grin. "By God, I do. Nothing clears a man's mind like a good brawl, and that's a fact."

Thomas held out a battered, blood-smeared hand. "We are friends again?"

"We are." Ignoring the pinch of his cracked knuckles, Rafe shook the Indian's hand, then struggled to his feet. "Come along, then. Pems is waiting for his run." And time was running out.

The following afternoon, as Rafe and Thomas led their winded horses into the stable, a carriage rolled through the gate. Anticipation faded into a momentary disappointment when Rafe saw the gold crest emblazoned on the black lacquered door. Not Josie.

"Ash is here," he said to Thomas. "He must have brought the countess, or he would have ridden rather than come by carriage."

Hopefully, Josie and Jamie would arrive soon, too.

Knowing Ash would come to them when he could, he and Thomas tended their horses, then washed at the pump at the back of the stable. Rafe was debating whether he should change clothes in case Josie came early, when the earl walked into the stable.

"Hallo, lads. I've come to invite you to join the countess and me for an early tea in the conservatory."

"Cathcart doesn't allow me in the house," Rafe told him.

"I'll convince him to make an exception." Handshakes all around, then the Scotsman clasped his hands behind his back and regarded the two men before him with a stern expression. "Did your banishment have aught to do with fighting, I'm wondering?"

"More to do with Miss Cathcart. And a bargain I forced her father into."

"Ah." The Scot looked from one to the other. "And who won?"

"I did," Thomas and Rafe said at the same time.

Seeing Hammersmith coming toward them, Ash requested they go make themselves presentable, then turned to the Scottish groom with a jovial smile. Babbling to each other in such thick Scottish accents Rafe could scarcely make out a word, they went out to view the warmblood mares, while Rafe and Thomas went up to the loft to change.

A few minutes later, the three of them headed up the slope. "So what is this bargain you made with Cathcart?" Ash asked.

Rafe explained about the private steeplechase race, and the high-stakes wagers, adding that Pems was making such amazing progress he might actually have a chance of winning. "And whether he does or not, the stallion is mine once he's finished the run. I already hold a signed postdated Bill of Sale."

"Clever lad. Is that why you asked for an advance in pay? To bet on the horse?"

"That's part of it." Rafe didn't want to discuss his hopes of bringing Josie and Jamie back with him to America, so he changed the subject. "Do you have need of another wrangler? There's a groom here who was injured when Cathcart insisted he ride Pembroke before he was ready. He'd like to emigrate with his woman. They're both good people."

"Aye. I can always use help. The countess and I are agreed that if we have a son, we might need to spend more time in

Scotland, since he'll be heir to the lands and title. But we dinna want to give up our home in Heartbreak Creek, so we'll need a dependable man to oversee the house and manage the stable in our absence. If he had a wife, that would be even better." He glanced at Rafe. "We were hoping you might consider the position."

Rafe stopped in the path, his mind spinning. "Me?"

Thomas and Ash stopped beside him. "Aye. You could stay in the house. Or if you'd rather something smaller, we could see to it, although houses left vacant dinna hold up over time. I'd pay you well."

Rafe was stunned. It was too good to be true. A home. A steady position. A place for Josie and Jamie. And he'd be paid to do something he loved.

There had to be a drawback. "What if you have a daughter?"

Ash thought for a moment. "Even if that's the case and we spend most of our time in Colorado, the countess willna give up her photography. And I canna let her travel about making her tintypes and such without proper protection. So we'll be needing someone whether we're in Scotland or off on a photography expedition." He grinned at Thomas. "I'd ask the savage here, but he would probably cure buffalo hides in the parlor and wander off whenever the mood struck him. In addition, he's no' as good with horses as you are."

"I am good with horses," the Cheyenne protested.

"Aye, and you've probably eaten one or two, I'll warrant."

Thomas shrugged. "Winters can be hard in the mountains."

The Scotsman gave him a look of disgust, then turned back to Rafe. "No need to decide now, lad. But think about it."

Rafe didn't have to think about it. His mind was already racing ahead to all the tasks awaiting him. Convincing Josie and Jamie to go with him. Winning enough money to cover passage for all of them, plus Pems and Blaze and the new thoroughbred if Jamie decided to take him, too. Making a real proposal to her.

Something shifted inside him, as if, after all these years and all his struggles, everything was finally falling into place.

This could really happen.

It was astonishing . . . and a bit terrifying.

A wife. A son. A home. His lonely, wandering life over. Forever.

Ash's hand on his shoulder started him up the path again. "Come along, lads. The countess is waiting in the conservatory. Oh, and a word of caution. Dinna comment on her size. She's sensitive about her expanding girth, so she is. And she has a special surprise," he added, grinning at Thomas. "A letter. All the way from Indiana. And addressed only to the heathen."

Rafe was glad the earl had warned him. His wife had certainly ballooned in the few weeks since they'd last seen her. Still, she looked more beautiful than ever. Looking at her, sitting there with that pleased look on her face, made him conjure in his mind an image of Josie, her body ripe with his child, smiling at him the way the countess was smiling at her Scotsman.

Thomas didn't stay for tea. As soon as Maddie handed him his letter, he disappeared out the back door. Cathcart didn't join them, either, for which Rafe was grateful, and Ash only stayed long enough to gobble half the cakes and tiny sandwiches, before rising from the wrought iron settee he was sharing with his wife. "I offered Rafe the position of overseer and stable manager in Heartbreak Creek," he told her. "Convince him to accept it. Meanwhile, I'll change out of my traveling clothes and make certain Pringle isna prancing about in your corset or passed out drunk on our bed." A quick kiss on her forehead then he was walking toward the door, already pulling his cravat loose.

It was hot in the steamy room. The countess didn't seem bothered, so Rafe didn't suggest they go elsewhere. In fact, he was glad to have a few moments alone with her. He had questions only she could answer.

"Pringle isn't truly so bad," she said as soon as the door closed behind her husband. "In fact, I daresay Ash is beginning to warm to him, although he would hardly admit to such a thing. He's never met with the kind of resistance Pringle displays, and I think he sees it as a challenge. Whip him into shape, as it were. Now what can I do to convince you to take the position Ash offered? It would be such a relief to both of us if you would."

"You don't have to convince me, my lady."

"Excellent." She clapped her hands together at that wondrous news. "But when we're not in company, do please call me Maddie. I consider you a dear friend. More so now that you'll be permanently joining our Heartbreak Creek family."

"About Heartbreak Creek, ma'am. Being an Englishwoman, did you find it difficult to adjust to the harsh conditions there?"

"Not at all. I found the entire Western experience exhilarating. In truth, after spending time in your country, I feel torn between this island and America. But now—with your help—we've hit upon the perfect compromise."

"No regrets?"

"Not a one." Tipping her head to one side, she studied him, one auburn curl resting against her freckled cheek. Rafe guessed few English ladies ever exposed themselves to enough sun to bring on a case of freckles. But Maddie was an exception in many ways. To her, every day was an adventure. Every change, a challenge. Freckles seemed of little consequence in the grand scheme of her busy life.

He wondered if Josie would be so open-minded.

"I sense your concerns are not so much pertaining to yourself," she said thoughtfully, "but to bring assurance to someone else."

Ash had once told him to beware of his wife—her artist's eye saw everything and it was fruitless to lie to her. So he didn't try. "Yes, ma'am."

"Josephine Cathcart?"

"Yes, ma'am."

Another clap of her hands. Another beaming smile. "What wonderful news! I like Miss Cathcart so very much."

Rafe held up a hand. "Whoa now, ma'am. I haven't asked her yet. I just thought that maybe if she talked to you about it, you could put in a good word about your impressions of America. Especially Heartbreak Creek. Let her know the Wild West isn't as wild as she might think."

Smiling brightly, the countess sat back, one hand resting on her rounded stomach. An interesting pose. One that made Rafe feel vaguely uncomfortable, a little awed, and oddly protective, all at the same time.

"First of all," the Countess of Kirkwell said, "you must get her a gun and teach her to shoot. A scattergun, as well as a pistol.

Once she's mastered that, it's simply a matter of fending off vicious animals, discouraging untoward advances from desperately lonely men, and becoming accustomed to the shocking variations in temperature. And Indians. Not all are as noble as Thomas. Some, in fact, can be quite hostile. As are the wolves and bears and mountain lions. She needs to be aware of the dangers. Oh, and how to prevent frostbite and avoid forest fires."

And on and on. Rafe was questioning the wisdom of involving her when she surprised him by reaching over and resting her hand on his arm.

"You mustn't worry, Rayford. Josephine is a courageous woman. She and Jamie will do well in your country. And as soon as I tell her about the glorious sunsets, the astonishing beauty of the mountains, and the wonderful people waiting to welcome her to Heartbreak Creek, she will be—as you Westerners say—hell-bent for leather to get there. Although I never quite understood that one. What is 'hell-bent for leather,' do you think? Is it even an actual term?"

"I think it means determined, ma'am."

With a sigh, she sat back. "I suppose I should caution her about those, as well—all those colorful, and not always intelligible, sayings you Westerners use. Until then," she added, sending him a repressive look, "I shall caution *you* about brawling. Avoid it. Women don't approve."

# Twenty-one

After a quick wash in the trough after Pembroke's last work-out, Rafe went up to the loft, where he found Thomas frowning at the letter Maddie had given him earlier.

He assumed it had come from Prudence Lincoln. But he couldn't tell by the Cheyenne's expression whether he was having difficulty deciphering it, or the news it contained was bad. Or maybe that was the bruises left from their tussle.

"Need help?" he asked, wincing as he pulled off his dirty shirt.

"I can read." Thomas squinted up at him through his swollen eye. "But I will need help to answer it."

"Sure. Get the tablet."

While Rafe slipped on a clean shirt—surely Josie would return late this afternoon—it had already been two-and-a-half days—Thomas retrieved the pencil and tablet they'd been using to write his book, then sat on his cot, watching him.

"You white people have too many clothes."

Ignoring that, Rafe sat across from him. "What do you want to spell?"

"*Eho'nehevehohtse.*" Thomas handed him the tablet and motioned for Rafe to write that down.

"What? No." Rafe shoved the tablet back at him. "You have to write it, yourself." He wasn't getting involved in something that personal.

"But I am not good at spelling."

"I'll help. But it has to be in your own handwriting. She'll know if it isn't."

"How?"

"If she's the one who taught you, she'll recognize your writing by the way you form the letters."

The Cheyenne thought for a moment. "Then you will mark down my words, and I will copy them onto another paper."

Still uncomfortable with the notion, Rafe positioned the pad on his knee and held the pencil ready. "It better not be too long. I've got horses waiting."

"*Eho'nehevehohtse,*" Thomas said again.

"What's that? Cheyenne?"

"It means 'one who walks in wolf tracks.'"

*Of course it does.* "How do you spell it?"

Thomas thought for a moment, then shrugged.

*Hell.* Rafe licked the tip of the pencil. "Say it again. But slow."

Thomas did and Rafe wrote the word by how it sounded. When he finished, he studied it. Seemed long and overrun with *e*'s and *h*'s, but hopefully, Miss Lincoln would recognize the word. "Next."

"Look for me, Prudence Lincoln," Thomas dictated. "When the wind blows cold and the Long Nights Moon rides in the sky, I will come to you. Listen for my voice in the shadows. Then rise from your dreams, *Voaxaa'e,* and together we will fly away."

Another word with too many vowels. Rafe did his best. "What else?"

"*Nemehotatse, Eho'nehevehohtse.*"

Jesus. Thomas had to repeat it three times before Rafe was able to get it all down. "What does that mean?"

"It is not for you to know." Thomas held out his hand. "I will copy your letters now."

"That's it? That's all you're going to say?"

"It is all that is important."

Glad to be done with it, Rafe handed the tablet to Thomas. "After you're finished, fold it up and copy this address across the front of it." He pointed to the Indiana return address on Prudence Lincoln's letter. "Ask Miss Cathcart or the countess to post it for you." Rising, he grabbed his hat off a peg. "Don't take too long. Ash wants to look over the studs, and you know how impatient he is."

Early the following day, Josephine stared pensively out the carriage window, grateful William had chosen to ride horseback rather than inside the coach. She wasn't in the mood for conversation—Jamie's constant chatter was distraction enough.

She needed to think.

The visit to Fell Ridge had been a disturbing experience. Not because it had been awkward, and uncomfortable, and terrible . . . but because it hadn't.

William had been charming. Neddy, although a bit spoiled—no doubt because of his condition—had been kind to Jamie. Fell Ridge, itself, while not as overblown as the monstrosity her father had built, was luxurious and comfortable and in good repair, probably because of the late baroness's generous dowry. The staff seemed content, the stable well managed, the grounds manicured. A lovely place to live.

If one didn't mind a marriage based on expediency, rather than love.

She could do it, she supposed. William wasn't intolerable. But whatever amorous feelings she had harbored for him years ago had long since faded into benign disinterest. Marriage to him would strictly be a way to protect Jamie and avoid a life of penury. Good reasons, to be sure. But . . .

"I don't think I would like it," Jamie said, breaking into her depressing thoughts.

"Like what?"

"Neddy said when he dies, I shall be the heir. But I don't think I would like being a baron."

How awful for a child to be so aware of his own mortality. And how heartbreaking for him to visualize a future in which he had no part. "Why wouldn't you want to be a baron?"

"A baron must be very proper. Neddy isn't even allowed in the garden without a footman following him about. And he has to dress in his fine clothes every day, even if he only sits in his room. And since there are no other noble children nearby to visit him, he has no friends. Not even among the servants. Not like me and Stevens, or Cook's grandson. Did you know he has tutors all day long? Plus," he added, clearly shocked by this more than all the rest, "he has to eat in the dining room *every* night. It all sounds rather horrid." With an elaborate sigh, he slumped back against the padded seat. "I think I should like going to America ever so much better."

When put that way, who wouldn't?

But if one thought it through . . . a life of security and privilege, versus having to adapt to a strange country, harsher surroundings, and certainly less luxury.

Jamie would undoubtedly be safer at Fell Ridge. But would he be happier?

Would she?

"What did you think of the baron?" she asked.

Jamie bounced his heel against the front of the velvet-covered bench and thought it over. "He seemed nice enough, I suppose. But strict. If Neddy makes the slightest misstep, he's called down for it. He says that barons have a great many rules they must follow."

William had always been a slave to his position. Was that what she wanted for her son?

The trip from Fell Ridge was a short one, and they arrived home well before tea. As Rogers came forward to open their door and set the mounting step, Josephine was delighted to see the Kirkwell carriage parked down by the stable.

"So our other guests have arrived?" she asked Father when she and Jamie came up the front steps.

"They have. The earl is out riding with that wrangler of his. The countess is in the conservatory. Welcome back, Adderly," he called, hurrying down to greet the baron as he swung off his horse. "You'll stay the night, I hope."

"I would be happy to."

"May I go to the stable, Mother?" Jamie asked. "I shan't get dirty, I promise. I only want to tell Blaze I'm back."

"After you change your shoes."

As Jamie ran off, she turned to the butler waiting by the door. "Please have the gold bedroom prepared for the baron, Shipley. And ask Cook to send a fresh pot of tea to the conservatory straightaway." Slipping off her gloves, hat, and cloak, she handed them over with a nod of dismissal.

As Father and William headed to his office for drinks, she hurried toward the back of the house, anxious to have a few moments alone with Lady Kirkwell.

The countess looked radiant. And noticeably larger. "I'm so happy to see you, my lady," Josephine said, taking a seat beside the countess on the settee. "You must be faring well. You look beautiful!"

"Thank you. And it's Maddie. I thought we dispensed with the title."

They chatted amiably for several minutes. The maid brought in a steaming pot of tea and a plate of scones. As soon as she left, Josephine said, "I so enjoyed our chat about the American West, my lady—Maddie. It sounds most exciting. I doubt I would be as brave as you in the face of so many dangers."

"Oh, I'm certain you would do admirably."

"Truly? I confess I've thought a great deal about it of late."

Lady Kirkwell smiled at her over the rim of her cup. "Since Rayford Jessup arrived perhaps?"

Josephine felt heat rise into her cheeks but didn't look away. "Just so. In fact . . ." She hesitated, wondering if she was revealing too much. But the joy of having another woman with whom to share confidences proved too enticing. "In fact, he has hinted that he would like Jamie and me to return to America with him."

The countess beamed. "I know. And I must say I'm thrilled! Simply thrilled."

Josephine blinked. "You know?"

"Rayford told me. In fact, he asked me to put in a good word. He's worried that you have concerns about living in the Wild West. He thought perhaps I could lessen your worries."

"My worries are not only about where we would live, but *how* we would live. Rafe has not been encouraging about his employment prospects."

"You poor dear." Reaching over, the countess rested her hand over Josephine's. "Tell me everything. Perhaps I can help."

And suddenly, it all came pouring out. Adderly's proposal and what it would mean for Jamie. Rafe's offer and what it would mean for her. Her father's financial straits, the race, and Rafe's determination to find a way to support them. It was as if a dam, weakened by years of loneliness, had burst within her, loosening a rush of secret hopes and barely formed dreams never before voiced. It was a flood she couldn't seem to stop. And yet through it all, the countess simply smiled and held her hand and listened.

It was a gift. Acceptance and friendship . . . two things Josephine had been lacking for so long. And now that she had someone to listen, she felt almost desperate to get out all the thoughts and worries and aspirations she had built up over the years.

When she finally ran out of words, she slumped against the cushions, feeling drained and embarrassed. She must have talked without pause for a quarter hour or more. "I—I apologize for rambling on this way. You must think I'm—"

"Amazing. The bravest woman I know." Maddie gave Josephine's hand a squeeze, then sat back. "Except perhaps for Lucinda," she added thoughtfully. "After all, she did live for a while in a brothel. And then there's Pru, and what that murderous Arapaho Indian did to her—although she never did say precisely what that was." A dismissive wave brought a return of her bright smile. "But never mind all that. The point is that you're an amazing, courageous woman, and it's no wonder Rayford Jessup is so taken with you. I cannot *wait* to introduce you to the ladies of Heartbreak Creek. They'll adore you. I'm certain of it."

Josephine pressed a hand to her temple, trying to slow the whirlwind of emotions spinning through her head. Hadn't Maddie heard a word she'd said? "But I don't know if we will ever make it to Heartbreak Creek. There are so many obstacles, and if the race doesn't go well—"

"Rubbish. It will all work out." Smiling like a cat with cream on its whiskers, Maddie picked up her cup and sipped. "Talk to Rayford. You'll see."

As Pembroke cleared the rock wall by the front gate late that afternoon, Rafe saw the weasel's carriage parked at the stable beside the Kirkwell coach.

Josie was back.

Laughing, he sent Pems into a full gallop, racing past Ash as if his horse were standing still.

A few minutes later, anxious to see Josie and tell her about the position Ash had offered, he handed the reins to a groom outside the stable, telling him to loosen the girth and walk the stallion until he was cool before unsaddling him. "And no water for half an hour," he added, just as Jamie came out of the bunk room, followed by Gordon on his crutches.

"You're back," the boy called, running up. "We are, too."

"I can see that. Did you have a good time?"

"Yes, sir. But I missed Blaze. And you," he added shyly.

"I missed you, too."

Ash came in, handed off his horse to a groom, and said his hellos to Jamie. Then turning to Gordon, whom he hadn't seen when he'd arrived the previous day, he extended a hand and introduced himself. Mindful of Hammersmith instructing the grooms where to walk the horses, and Jamie nearby, he added in a lower voice, "Rafe says you wish to emigrate to America?"

"Yes, my lord. Henny, too. We plan to marry as soon as we can find positions."

"Henny is Miss Cathcart's maid," Rafe clarified.

Leaning closer, Gordon explained, "We're not allowed to work here if we're wed."

"I see." Clasping his hands behind his back, the earl frowned at Gordon's leg. "How much longer on the crutches?"

"The doctor says only a few more days. A week maybe."

"Good. I'll talk to Cathcart and see if he's willing to release you."

"Thank you, my lord."

Ash looked around, a scowl forming between his green eyes. "I dinna see the heathen."

"Mr. Redstone?" Gordon shook his head. "He left shortly after you and Mr. Jessup rode out and hasn't yet returned."

"Barney's gone, too," Jamie offered.

"Bollocks."

"He'll show up." Rafe was impatient to get cleaned up in case Josie came down to the stable. "You know how he is."

"Aye. That's why I'm worried. Best go look for him."

"Now?" Rafe had given up trying to keep the elusive Cheyenne in his sights. Short of locking the Indian in a stall, there was little chance of curtailing his tendency to roam. "Maybe he's out looking for us."

Ash shook his head. "I've a bad feeling about this, lad. If

he went looking for us, he would have found us. Naught escapes those sharp eyes. Best saddle another horse and go now, while there's light yet."

"Can I go with you, Mr. Jessup?" Jamie asked, catching the end of the conversation.

"Not this time, Jamie. I won't be back until after dark." Noting the boy's disappointment, he tried to soften it with a bribe. "But I promise to go riding with you tomorrow. All right?"

Happiness restored, Jamie grinned. "Yes sir."

"Maybe your mother will want to come, too," Rafe added, then regretted doing so when he saw the studied glance Ash sent his way.

Josephine was so enjoying her chat with Maddie she didn't realize how late it was until Shipley came to inform them that Lord Kirkwell, Baron Adderly, and Mr. Cathcart awaited them in the yellow salon for drinks before dinner.

"Heavens," Josephine exclaimed. "And I'm still in my traveling clothes." After telling Shipley to show the countess to the salon, she hurried to her room. There, she found Henny waiting with her rose-colored silk and an excited expression on her face.

"Oh, Miss Cathcart," she gushed as she helped Josephine out of her heavy bombazine. "I know this isn't the best time to bring it up, but Gordon has spoken to the earl and he said 'yes.' Quickly now, step into your dress. Faith, and the color is lovely with your dark hair."

"Spoken to him about what?" Josephine asked, turning so the maid could do up the buttons in back.

"Gordon says if your father releases him, the earl has a position for him. In America! Isn't that wonderful?"

"Gordon wants to emigrate?" Turning, Josephine looked at Henny in surprise. "What about you? Do you want to emigrate, as well?"

"Sure and I don't want to leave you, miss, but if Gordon and I go together, we can marry. And he's always dreamed of going to America."

Josephine wasn't sure what to think. "When would you go?"

"Not for a while, I'm thinking. Not until the Kirkwell babe is born. Sure, and you should have plenty of time to find a replacement. There now," she added, stepping back. "You look as beautiful as a summer rose in that rich color. Off you go. They're waiting."

Pushing to the back of her mind Henny's disturbing news, Josephine rushed down to the yellow salon, hoping Father might have lifted Rafe's banishment in deference to the earl's visit.

He hadn't. And she understood why when she overheard the earl tell his wife that Thomas had wandered off and he'd sent Rafe to find him. Hiding her disappointment at not being able to see him until tomorrow—even though they had only been parted for a few days, she missed him terribly—she accepted a glass of Madeira wine from Adderly and settled on the settee beside the countess.

Despite the pleasant company, she felt an underlying tension in the air. Perhaps because William hovered in such a proprietary manner, as if her visit to Fell Ridge had established them as a couple in some permanent way. Or perhaps it was the distraction she noted in the earl. Surely, he wasn't worried about Thomas Redstone's disappearance. From what Rafe had told her, it was a common occurrence with the Indian.

However, Lady Kirkwell—Maddie—was in her usual good spirits, and Father . . . well, as was his habit, he worked too hard to fit in with his lofty guests, and drank too much in the process. She was relieved when Shipley came in a few minutes after her arrival to announce dinner.

Rafe wasn't sure how to find Thomas, or where to start looking. The Cheyenne was hard enough to track in daylight, but with night coming on, Rafe's best hope was to let the Indian find him.

Hunched against the cold wind cutting through his duster with relentless insistence, he reined Thunder across the brook that separated the Cathcart estate from its neighbor, and rode into a deep forest of lindens, yews, and ancient oaks.

Silence closed around him. Other than the occasional scurry of a night creature, and the rustle of withered leaves overhead as the wind cut through the high branches, he heard nothing.

He debated calling out, but not knowing who owned these woods, or who else might be in the vicinity, he decided against it.

The deeper he rode, the darker it grew. He wished he'd chosen a mount other than the horse Adderly had given Jamie. He had hoped to put some miles on the gray to help settle him down, but the flighty gelding was so spooked by the gloomy surroundings he shied at every shadow and sound.

Luckily, Thomas found them before they'd ridden too far.

"Are you looking for me, white man?" he said, appearing so suddenly out of the darkness that Thunder jumped three feet sideways.

"Damnit, Thomas! You trying to get me killed?" Rafe demanded once he brought his frightened horse under control.

The Indian motioned him to silence. He swung his gaze in a wide circle.

Rafe did, too, but neither saw nor heard anything unusual.

After a moment, Thomas edged Barney closer to the trembling gray. "There are others in the wood tonight," he whispered. "Be silent. Wait here while I see what they are doing."

"You're not riding off alone—"

But he was already gone.

*Damn.* Pulling his coat closer, Rafe waited. Minutes passed. A distant sound that Rafe couldn't identify, then a groan. But it could have been one branch rubbing against another in the wind. He watched Thunder's ears, but they were swiveling every which way and pinpointed no specific direction that might signal the approach of something or someone.

He was glad he'd worn his gun. Not that he expected trouble, but—

Furtive rustlings to his right. The crack of a twig behind him.

Then suddenly men burst out of the trees.

Hands grabbed at the reins as Thunder reared and crow-hopped. Before Rafe could bring him under control and pull the six-shooter from the holster on his hip, other hands dragged him from the saddle.

"We got him!" a man yelled as Rafe slammed to the ground. A barrage of kicks and fists rained down on him. He struggled to protect his head as someone started on him with a short club.

"Enough!" a voice barked. "The magistrate doesn't want the blighter killed! Get his gun and tie him with the other one."

Dizzy and half-blinded by pain and blood from where the club had opened a gash by his temple, Rafe felt himself dragged to his feet and his hands tied behind him. Swaying unsteadily for balance, he looked around.

Thomas lay draped over Barney, his hands and feet tied, blood dripping from his nose and a cut on his cheek. Two men stood beside him with drawn guns.

"You know this person?"

Rafe looked up at a man on horseback who seemed to be the leader of the group. *Magistrate*, someone had said. If these men were working for a judge, they must be with the law. "Who are you?" Rafe countered.

"Constable Harris." The man pointed at Thomas. "Do you know this man?"

*Constable*. Rafe felt a surge of relief. "You're making a mistake. I was a Deputy United States Marshal. We're from the Cathcart place. We work for the Earl of Kirkwell."

"Americans," someone muttered then spit in disgust. "Bugger that."

"Well, you'll be working for the crown now," a voice jeered. "For seven long, hard years."

"Unless you're transported to Australia," another added over the laughter.

"Or hanged."

Guffaws all around.

"What are you talking about?" Alarmed, Rafe looked from one to the other.

"You're not in America now," Constable Harris said. "And we don't suffer poachers in England."

# *Twenty-two*

F ather had just invited the earl and Adderly into the salon
for after dinner drinks when Shipley appeared at the dining
room door to announce visitors. "I put them in the drawing
room." He looked flustered . . . an unusual state for the stone-
faced butler.

"Who would be calling at this hour?" Father asked, clearly
perplexed.

"Your neighbor, Mr. Worthington, and a Constable Harris,
sir. He brought Mr. Jessup and Mr. Redstone with him. In
custody."

"In custody?" Josephine gaped at the butler.

Maddie clutched her arm. "There must be some mistake."

Muttering under his breath, the earl shoved past Shipley.
Father and Adderly followed, Josephine and Maddie on their
heels.

Their neighbor, Mr. Worthington, a dour man with a pes-
simistic outlook and warts on his chin, stood talking to a man
Josephine didn't know but assumed was Constable Harris. Two
other unfamiliar men stood guard over Rafe and Mr. Redstone,
their hands resting on the butts of pistols stuck in their belts.

Josephine gasped when she saw Rafe's battered appearance.
His clothing was mussed and torn, dried blood covered the side of
his face, and more blood slowly seeped from a cut at his temple.
One cheekbone was swollen and an old bruise darkened his jaw.

Thomas Redstone looked no better, bleeding from several places at once, and showing a large lump on the side of his head.

They were both in manacles.

"Good heavens!" she cried rushing toward them "What happened?"

The earl blocked her approach. "Attend my wife," he ordered quietly.

"But—I—he's hurt. I should—"

"You should attend my wife," he repeated, his green eyes boring into her. "I will see to this." His expression brooked no argument, and Josephine read the underlying message. *Do as ordered and let me handle this.*

Reluctantly, she led the countess to a pair of wingback chairs flanking the window overlooking the garden. They both sat. Or rather, Maddie sat; Josephine perched on the edge of her chair, ready to leap to her feet if needed. Hands twisting in her lap, she strained to hear the low-voiced argument across the room, but was able to pick up only a word here and there.

Mr. Worthington seemed quite agitated, frequently punctuating his angry words by pointing an accusatory finger at Rafe and Thomas. She heard the word "poaching" and felt a shock of fear. Poaching was a dire offense in Cumberland, punishable by heavy fines, prison, deportation, or in extreme cases, hanging.

"You mustn't worry," Maddie whispered. "Ash can be quite persuasive. It's the Scot in him, I think. Kirkwells have always been volatile. One never quite knows what they'll do."

Watching him, Josephine believed it. Feet braced, hands clasped tightly behind his back, he loomed over Worthington in a most intimidating manner, seeming to grow larger as he argued his points. Or perhaps the old man was shrinking under that forceful tirade.

Rafe and Mr. Redstone stood silent, the Cheyenne staring stoically at the far wall, Rafe listening intently, his gaze moving from one speaker to the other.

Father seemed incensed, his face blotchy with temper. It impressed her that he was so ardent in his defense of Rafe and Mr. Redstone, then realized what drove him when his voice rose above the others. "But he has a race to run in a week!"

Kirkwell shot him a quelling look, then resumed speaking

in a calm, but forceful way to both Worthington and Constable Harris. Adderly said nothing, listening to the others with keen interest, his gaze going often to Rafe.

Poor Rafe. He looked ghastly, his handsome face a mass of bruises, dried blood, and swollen lumps. What had they done to him?

The countess must have read her thoughts. "It's not as bad as it looks. Half of those bruises are due to a set-to he and Thomas had earlier."

Josephine blinked at her in surprise. "Set-to? Over what?"

Maddie fluttered her fingers in dismissal. "Nothing of import, I'm sure, since they were quite cordial to one another when we arrived."

Puzzled, Josephine turned back to the men, trying to read by their gestures how it was going. Worthington was scowling. Father was nodding vigorously at some point the earl was making to the constable. Adderly stepped in with a comment, which led to more discussion, until finally, the constable held up his hands in surrender. Worthington shook a warning finger at Father, then stomped from the room.

Relieved that it was over, Josephine rose.

But then the Constable motioned for the two guards to take Rafe and Thomas Redstone away. Rafe paused to say something to the earl, before being shoved roughly after Thomas.

Frantic, Josephine ran to the three men still left in the room. "What's happened? Where are they taking them?"

"Where they belong," Father snapped, crossing to the decanters and glasses on a side table. "I knew there was something underhanded about that wrangler."

"He wasna night poaching," the earl argued. "He was trying to find Redstone and got caught in the cross fire."

"Makes little difference. They were both trespassing. Drinks anyone?"

William nodded and walked over as Father poured from a bottle of Northbridge Whisky the earl had brought.

Still in shock and not sure what was happening, Josephine rushed to the window. When she saw Rafe and Thomas being loaded roughly into a cart, panic sent her charging for the door.

The earl caught her arm. "Let them go, lass. 'Tis only temporary. Rafe will be allowed to race."

"Then he and Thomas will return here?"

A regretful look came over his chiseled face. "No, lass. As part of our arrangement with Worthington and the constable, they must leave England and never return."

*Ever?* Josephine gaped at him, her lungs unable to draw in air. Over the buzzing in her ears, she heard Maddie ask where they were being sent.

"Penrith for the night, then on to jail in Liverpool."

"Jail? But you said Rafe would be able to race." How else could he win enough money to take them to America?

"He will," Kirkwell assured her. "Although he'll still be in custody, he'll be allowed to ride Pems in the race. Then as soon as it's over, he and Thomas will be escorted directly to the ship taking them to America." He gave her a look of sympathy. "'Tis better than an English prison or transportation to a penal colony, lass. We must be grateful for that."

Grateful? That everything was falling apart? That finally, after years of being shunned, she had lost her one chance at happiness? She couldn't bear to think of it. "What about Pems? How will he get to the race without Rafe?"

"Stevens will take him by rail."

*And the training he'll miss?*

Numbly, she turned back to the window to see the wagon roll down the drive, flanked by Worthington and the constable, one of the guards driving the wagon, the other watching the prisoners in back. *How can this be happening?*

Her mind reeling, she sank into a chair.

She wanted to weep. Scream. Pretend none of this had happened. All Rafe's hard work for naught. All her hopes of a new start, gone in the blink of an eye.

Talk continued around her. Part of her listened, part of her didn't care.

"If Rafe and Thomas are sent back to America now," Maddie argued, "who will take our mares and stallions to Colorado?"

"They will." Ash explained that Hammersmith and several grooms would have to help him drive the mares and stallions to the docks in Liverpool, so they could be loaded and ready to leave when Rafe and Thomas arrived after the race.

"But what about their things?" Josephine roused herself to ask. "And Jamie? Is he not even allowed to say good-bye to them?"

"Bring the lad to the race. He can say good-bye then."

*Good-bye.*

The word clamored through her head. Was it truly to end this way? What about his plans for a piece of land somewhere? What about her?

"Did he say anything else? Leave a message for me?"

"Only that you must come to the race. He was verra insistent on that."

Moving on leaden legs, she left the room. But in the entry, she stopped, not sure she had the strength to tell her son that Rafe had been arrested and taken away. Unwilling to face him in her emotional state, she went out the side door and down the slope to the stable.

Gone. Without a good-bye. Without a chance to tell him . . . what? That she didn't care about status or luxury or a fine title? That all she cared about was . . .

Him. The thought swept over her like a breath of cleansing air. She more than cared about Rayford Jessup. She loved him. Loved him enough to bet every penny she had on a horse race. Enough to leave the country of her birth and follow him to America. All he had to do was commit—give her a true proposal—tell her that he loved her.

But he never had.

A lamp still burned in the aisleway of the stables. Low voices from the bunk room at the far end told her several of the grooms were still awake. Unwilling to answer their questions about this latest catastrophe, she went quietly up the ladder into the loft. At the top she stopped to get her bearings.

It was dark and musty in the cavernous space. Swallows, startled from sleep, flitted through the rafters. Mice scurried through the piles of dried grass. Most of the loft was open storage for hay, but at the other end was a small storeroom Hammersmith had converted into sleeping quarters for Rafe and the Cheyenne. Because of fire danger, there were no lanterns where the hay was stored, and it took a moment for her eyes to adjust. Then shutting her mind to the rustlings and scurryings around her, she moved cautiously through the dimness to the storage room. On a shelf inside the door sat a lantern and matches. She lit the wick, then looked around.

Spartan, at best. Crude shelves here and there. Two rope-strung cots covered with faded blankets, a trunk full of books, clothing draped over nails and bedposts. An odd, delicately woven hoop, decorated with feathers and beads, hanging above the cot where a plaid shirt had been carelessly thrown.

Rafe's shirt. Rafe's cot.

She moved toward it.

The air smelled strongly of the horses resting in their stalls below. Hay dust covered everything. Even though its occupants had been gone only a few hours, the room already had an abandoned feel to it.

She picked up the shirt, pressed it to her face, and drew in the scents trapped in the worn cloth. Horses, coffee, the mustiness of a hardworking male.

Rafe.

Eyes brimming with tears, she sank onto the foot of the cot.

"Oh, Rafe," she whispered to the empty room. The awareness that he was gone, perhaps forever, was like a blow to her chest. Clasping the shirt against her body, she bent over, eyes clamped tight against the press of tears.

For a brief moment, she had found hope again. Because of Rafe, after so many years of being a pariah, she had begun to see herself as someone of value, someone worthy of love.

Now he was gone, taking that fragile hope with him. All she saw stretching ahead was a bleak future of empty, lonely years. Jamie, being molded into a proper little baron. Herself, the fallen woman risen to baroness. Accepted, perhaps, but still without friends, love, or joy.

Was the security William offered enough to counter all that?

She wanted to rail at the unfairness of it. Yes, she had been foolish. Yes, she had done wrong. But how long must she pay for that?

Hot fury slowly faded into cold resolve. In the eyes of society, she could never atone for her lapse in morality. She might be shielded by position if she became the wife of a titled man she didn't love, but she would always be tainted by scandal. She couldn't—wouldn't—live that way. Whether she could make a life with Rafe, or not, she wanted more than the future William offered. She deserved more.

Rising, she dropped the shirt onto the bed and went to a cluttered shelf, seeking some small memento of her brief time with Rafe. A book perhaps. A shaving mug. Something to cling to in the lonely years ahead.

On top of a stack of books, she found a dog-eared tablet. Opening it, she saw the words "Thomas's Story" written in bold script. Sticking out beneath the last page was a folded paper. She pulled it out and opened it.

A Bill of Sale, conferring ownership of the stallion named Pembroke's Pride to Rayford Jessup, signed by her father and dated noon, the day of the race.

Josephine blinked in surprise. When had her father sold Pembroke to Rafe? Was this part of Rafe's plan to build a life for them? It made little sense, but it occurred to her that she held in her hands the most valuable thing Rafe owned. This was *his* hope. *His* dream. And if he couldn't be here to guard it, she would.

Slipping the bill into her skirt pocket, she turned and left the room.

In the dark, dank cell in the prison north of Liverpool, Rafe stared out of the single barred window at the few stars showing through the wispy clouds.

A long way until dawn, he figured. He glanced at the figure slumped against the far wall, arms crossed, head drooping. If he hadn't seen Thomas breathe, he might have wondered if he'd willed himself to death. This was only the second night since their capture, but he could see that Thomas's spirits were already in decline.

The previous night in the Penrith jail without food or water had been fairly unpleasant, especially considering how beat-up they were. But today's train ride to Liverpool hadn't been too bad, even though they had been manacled and chained to their seats, which—along with their battered faces—had drawn stares and whispers from the other passengers.

At least, when they'd arrived at this cell—their home until the race—the manacles had been removed and they'd been given water and a waste bucket. And a few minutes ago, plates of food had been shoved through the gap under the door.

Rafe studied the slop on his plate, not sure what it was, or if he could eat with the stink of sewage wafting through the small barred window. Still, knowing he had to keep up his strength, he managed to gag it down.

Thomas didn't even try. Nor had he spoken a single word since he'd awakened after their capture.

"You've got to eat." Rafe shoved the other plate toward the Cheyenne.

Thomas didn't move.

The clatter of a baton against the bars in the doors announced the changing of the guard and awakened a chorus of shouts, curses, and pleas from the other prisoners. It promised to be a long night. Closing his eyes, Rafe tipped his head back against the wall and let his mind drift until it settled on Josie . . . the way she smelled like the roses in the garden . . . the warm softness of her breast in his hand. What was she thinking? Had she given up on him? Would he ever see her again?

"I was wrong, Rayford Jessup," Thomas said, finally breaking his long silence. "I should have heeded your words."

Rafe let it pass. He had regrets, too. But they mostly centered on Josie. "I can't believe you let them sneak up on you."

"They did not sneak. They dropped ropes down over me from the trees."

That would do it. "Eat," he said again.

With obvious reluctance, the Cheyenne reached for his plate. "How long will we be in this place?"

"Not long. Day after tomorrow they'll take us to where the race is being held. Ash will meet us there." Hopefully Josie and Jamie would be there, too.

Thomas finished eating and set his plate aside. "I was in jail once before."

His tone was weary and flat, which Rafe suspected came less from his injuries than from a lowering of morale. For a man as restless as the Cheyenne, being locked in a cell was probably worse than being confined to a ship.

"Declan Brodie was sheriff then. He put me there."

Brodie was a local rancher and sometime sheriff in

Heartbreak Creek. He was also a longtime friend of Thomas's. "What for?"

"I was drunk and angry and almost killed a man in a fight."

Rafe guessed that was the reason Thomas didn't drink alcohol now. "Angry, why?"

"Because I could not find the trapper who had killed my wife and son."

Rafe thought of the pouch containing the bullet Thomas had vowed to return to the murderer. "You must have found him at some point, since you don't wear the pouch anymore."

"I buried it. I knew it was time for me to put the past behind me and seek a better way."

"With Prudence Lincoln?"

Thomas didn't respond to that. "Now that the Scotsman has offered a place for you at his home in Colorado, will you put the past behind you and take a new woman?"

"Like Josephine Cathcart?"

"I see no other woman showing interest in you, white man."

Rafe heard the smirk in the Cheyenne's voice. The jail food must have perked him up. "I put the past away a long time ago."

"Ho. Then your bad dreams are about the days you have yet to live?"

Rafe pressed the heel of his hand against the ache in his forehead. "I was going to talk to her the day you disappeared. But then Ash sent me to find you."

"Blame the Indian. The white man's favorite pastime."

"You are a troublesome lot."

"You will see her at the race. Ask her to be your woman then."

He planned to. He just hoped he wasn't already too late. He still didn't know what had happened on her visit with the weasel. She might have already accepted Adderly's offer. The thought stole what strength he had left. With a groan, he stretched out on the rank, straw-filled pad on the stone floor.

Two nights and a day in this stink hole. Four days until the race. Would she be there? Would he have a chance to talk to her, tell her about the job Ash had given him? Or after the mess he'd gotten himself into, had she washed her hands of him altogether?

Women. He'd known crazed horses that were easier to figure out.

"Did you finish your letter to Prudence Lincoln?" he asked around a yawn.

"Yes."

"Did you give it to Josie or the countess to mail?"

"I have not seen either since I wrote it."

Another yawn. "I hope it's not too late." For either of them.

"When will you be leaving for Liverpool?" Josephine asked Maddie over breakfast the morning after the Constable took Rafe and Thomas away.

"Tomorrow at dawn."

"So soon?" Josephine had hoped for more time before she sprung her plan on the earl and the countess. She had been up most of the night trying to figure out what to do. She wasn't certain yet where she and Jamie would go, but knew they could no longer stay here. Even if Father won enough money to avoid bankruptcy, she couldn't continue this sterile, isolated existence.

"I agree it's absurd," Maddie said, spooning jam on a toast point. "But Ash insists. The man plans everything like a military campaign, and apparently, a soldier's day begins with first light. Which no doubt accounts for why we're always at war. No one is reasonable at that hour."

"But the race is still several days away."

"It's because of the horses. Ash says we must go slowly, although I think he's more concerned about me." Maddie smiled indulgently and patted her rounded midsection. "For such a capable man, he can be quite the worrier."

"Are you still going to the race?"

"We wouldn't miss it. I think Ash wants to make certain Thomas and Rafe arrive at the ship safely. Like most Scots, he holds scant trust in English law. With reason, I fear. Will you be going by train or carriage?"

"By train, for the most part. Since the trip by rail will be a matter of hours rather than days, we won't leave for a while yet. I'm surprised the earl didn't send his horses by train."

"He would have, if he'd had time to make proper arrangements for so many animals. At least this way, by the time they board the ship, they'll be weary enough to behave on the crossing."

"You'll be returning straight to Scotland from Liverpool?"

"Yes." Maddie nodded to Rogers for more tea. She waited for him to pour, then said, "Ash is sending down one of his channel freighters to fetch us. He feels it would be easier for me to travel by water than rail. I hope he's right. The crossing from America was most unpleasant, although that might have been due to my condition, rather than the motion of the ship."

Josephine hesitated, then realized she had no choice but to forge ahead with her contingency plan in case Rafe wasn't able to take them to America. "Might you have room for Jamie and me? I should so love to visit your Highlands, and Jamie has never been to Scotland."

"Of course!" Maddie brought her hands together with an exclamation of delight. "I can think of nothing I would like more. As I said on my earlier visit, I would adore having you at Northbridge. Do please come!"

"Come where?" Father asked, walking into the room.

Wondering how much of their conversation he had overheard, Josephine watched him cross to the covered dishes on the sideboard. "The countess has kindly invited Jamie and me for a visit to Northbridge. I have long wanted to see the Highlands, and Jamie would be enthralled with all the old castles and ruins."

A startled look came over Father's face and he moved so sharply he knocked a spoon from the serving dish—a reaction that proved she was correct in her suspicions that he had been up to something. When she had returned from the barn the night of Rafe's arrest, she had heard him talking with William behind the closed door of his study. Then when the baron left the following morning, she had expected him to press her about his proposal, but neither he nor Father had mentioned it. Instead, William had promised to see her and Jamie again soon, adding that he would be coming to the race, too.

She hadn't expected that. It didn't alter her plans, but it did mean she would have one more person to keep an eye on.

After filling his plate, Father carried it to the table, sat, and shook out his napkin. "I should think the best time to visit the

Highlands would be in spring or summer," he said as Rogers poured his tea. "Rather than now, with winter upon us."

"Not at all, Mr. Cathcart," Maddie said cheerfully. "Late fall is quite beautiful, too, with the changing colors and snow-caps on the peaks. And if we do have an early cold spell, we shall have a grand time skating on the ponds, and taking out the sleigh, and building bonfires to welcome the change in seasons."

Father tapped against the shell of his egg with more vigor than necessary. Frowning at the mess he'd made, he pushed the eggcup aside. "When would you leave, daughter, and how long would you be gone?"

"I shouldn't think we would be away for more than a couple of weeks. There are things here that require my attention." She hoped he would interpret that as a reference to Adderly's suit. By his relieved expression, he did.

"As to when we would leave," she went on, "Lady Kirkwell says the earl is sending one of his ships down to Liverpool, so we would depart immediately after the race. It should be a wonderful adventure for Jamie to travel to Scotland by sea, don't you agree?" Before he could respond, she turned to the countess. "I shall have my maid pack an extra trunk of warm clothing, as well as a box of toys to keep Jamie amused on the trip." Hopefully, that would keep anyone from questioning why they were bringing so many trunks for a two-week visit.

"I cannot wait to tell him about the trip," she continued. "He'll be thrilled. He was a bit down when I explained that Mr. Jessup and Mr. Redstone would be leaving England after the race, and I think a trip to the Highlands will be just the thing to lift his spirits."

At the head of the table, Father cut into his slab of ham and smiled.

# Twenty-three

Josephine and Jamie were up in time to see Lord and Lady Kirkwell away. In fact, she had been awake most of the night, battling doubts and breathless hopes, and finally, toward dawn, disturbingly erotic dreams.

"Are you certain this will work?" Jamie whispered, holding Maddie's hand in a tight grip as they hurried down the stairs.

"Of course it will," she whispered back, praying she spoke the truth.

Out on the drive, the travelers stood at attention as Lord Kirkwell strode down the line in his military way, barking instructions. "Mount up," he ordered when he finished, then turned to his wife, to add less brusquely, "You, too, love."

Another round of hugs and well wishes. Before Maddie climbed into the carriage, Josephine blurted out, "If you see Rafe, tell him good luck."

Maddie gave a sly smile. "Of course. Perhaps you'll have a chance to speak to him, yourself. I'll see if Ash can arrange it."

"That would be wonderful." Josephine looked around to make sure they were not being overheard before adding, "And please thank the earl for attending to that matter we discussed."

"He was happy to do it. Take care of your mother, Jamie. We shall see you soon." A last hug, then they were away.

Kirkwell's three stallions stepped out first—the earl on their Mercury, and two other grooms riding the warmbloods. They were an impressive sight, trotting down the drive with their heads and tails high.

The carriage came next, followed by Prissy, the dominant mare, ridden by Hammersmith. The other mares, both thoroughbred and warmblood, followed as a herd behind Prissy, kept in line by two of the Kirkwell grooms.

And finally, at the end of the procession, Gordon Stevens drove a cart carrying the stallion's tack, enough grain and water to get him to Liverpool, and Rafe's and Thomas's belongings. Henny sat beside him—dismissed after her marriage to Gordon the previous day—waving madly to the servants gathered on the steps to see them off. Unaware of the trial awaiting him, Pems trotted along behind, tied to the back of the cart, under the watchful eye of the groom who would bring the cart back to the stable after Gordon and Henny and the stallion boarded the train.

As the caravan rolled away, Father and the servants went back inside. But Josephine and Jamie watched anxiously until the procession reached the front gates, when a rider came out of the trees to join the march—a young groom on a handsome chestnut gelding with a flaxen mane and tail and a white blaze running from his forelock to his nose.

"There he is," Jamie whispered, bouncing on his toes in excitement.

Unwilling to risk his letting something slip, or getting his hopes up in case something went wrong, Josephine had only told her son that they were visiting Scotland for a short while, and that the earl would be taking Blaze with him so Jamie would have a horse to ride while he was there.

"But you mustn't say anything to Grandfather," she had warned him. "He might be angry that you didn't take Thunder instead." Fortunately, Father had never gone to the stables to see Blaze, so he would never know he was gone.

Now, as the travelers disappeared out the gate, she smiled down at her son. "I told you it would work. He'll be waiting for you on the ship. Now run help Nanny finish your packing. And remember, love, not a word."

"I remember."

As he scampered off, she let out a breath of relief. The first part of her plan was in motion. Hurrying up to her room, she felt a sense of anticipation, as well as regret. She was happy to start a new life, either in America or Scotland, but sad that she wouldn't be able to say good-bye to all the people here who had treated her kindly, despite her disgrace. She did, however, leave a note for Nanny Holbrick that included a pension to ease her old age, and consoled herself that if she and Jamie went to America, at least they would have Henny and Gordon there with them.

The following days passed with agonizing slowness.

Jamie was still deeply troubled about Rafe's and Thomas Redstone's arrests and when she'd told him the two men were being sent away from England, he had been stricken. "But what about us? Isn't Mr. Jessup taking us with him to America?"

"I don't know what his plans are," she had hedged. "Perhaps at the race, we'll have a chance to speak to him."

But as the day of departure neared, she worried that she was doing the right thing, taking her son away from all he had ever known. "Are you certain you don't want to live at Fell Ridge with your father and Neddy?" she finally forced herself to ask over breakfast the day they were to take the carriage to the train depot.

"I should hate to disappoint them, but . . ." Jamie looked down at his plate, the tips of his ears turning red. "Would you be terribly upset if I said I would rather go to America with Mr. Jessup?"

Leaning over, she put her arm around his shoulders. "Not disappointed in the least," she whispered, "since that is what I would prefer, too." Fearing she had said too much, she drew back to look him sternly in the eye. "But you mustn't speak of this to anyone, Jamie. It might not come to pass. And if Grandfather knew, he might not allow us to go to Scotland."

Smiling bravely, he drew an *X* over his heart. "I shall never tell. I swear it."

Later that morning, after a short carriage ride to the Penrith depot, she and Jamie followed Father aboard the train bound for Liverpool. In a few hours—if the earl was able to arrange it—she would see Rafe again. And tomorrow, once the race was run, she and Jamie would know in which direction their future lay—north, to Scotland—or west, to America.

She was almost dithering she was so excited.

\* \* \*

"Where are we staying tonight?" she asked her father several hours later when the train pulled into the Liverpool station.

"Edgewood Hall. The host of the race, Lord Brantley, has set aside rooms for us. You and Jamie will be sharing one on the third floor near the nursery."

"And where will you be?"

"Playing cards. And hopefully," he added with a wink, "driving up the wagers on the race. I've touted it about that Pembroke's Pride is stronger than ever. Many thought he could have won the Grand National had he not been injured and pulled from the race. They're anxious to recover their losses."

"Is it wise to wager everything on him?"

"I know what I'm doing, daughter. You'll see."

When they stepped onto the platform, a groom in gray livery came forward to greet them. After seeing that their luggage was loaded onto a heavy wagon, he directed them to a two-wheeled buggy pulled by a high-stepping bay. Obviously their host had an eye for horseflesh.

It was a lovely afternoon, and as the breeze tugged at her hair, Josephine felt a wild urge to lift her face to the sky and laugh with pure joy. Soon she would see Rafe. Soon she would be free and her new life would begin. Soon . . .

After a short ride, they turned onto a long drive that led to an imposing mansion surrounded by tall yews and lindens. As they circled to a stop by the front entrance, she noticed a sprawling stable to the left of the house, half-obscured by a stand of chestnuts and wild cherry trees. A number of well-dressed men and women moved along the paddock fences, studying the horses that would race the following day.

Rafe was down there. She could almost feel a change in the air because he was so near.

Lord Brantley's butler, Kendricks, an older man with white hair, a hawkish nose, and such presence Josephine felt like curtsying when he introduced himself, escorted them to their rooms.

The one Josephine was to share with Jamie was spacious and well appointed, but not overly ostentatious. Obviously reserved for guests of the second tier. Before Kendricks left to see to their luggage, she asked him to inform Lady Kirkwell that Miss Cathcart would very much like to see her whenever it was convenient.

A short while later, he returned with Henny and a train of footmen bearing far too many trunks for a one-night stay. "We're traveling on to Scotland," she offered in explanation, then regretted doing so when Kendricks gave a condescending smile. Since her fall from grace, she felt nervous around unfamiliar servants, especially ones as haughty as Kendricks. But at least he couldn't look down his nose at her, since she was several inches taller than he was.

"Lady Kirkwell," he enunciated in funereal tones, "will be delighted to meet you in the back gardens in a quarter hour. One of the footmen will direct you. I am also to inform you that Baron Adderly has arrived and hopes to sit with you at dinner this evening."

"Thank you, Kendricks." She refrained from bowing.

As the door closed behind him, Henny rushed over to help her out of her traveling cloak and bonnet. "Faith, Miss Josephine, is this not a grand place? There are so many rooms, I fear I shall get lost."

"How was the train ride?" Josephine asked, slipping behind a screen to change. "Was Pems any trouble for Gordon?"

"None at all, miss. And since Mr. Jessup arrived, he's as happy as a lark."

Josephine felt a bump in her chest. "Mr. Jessup is already here, then?"

"His Cheyenne friend, too."

Glancing over the top of the screen, Josephine saw Jamie sitting on the broad windowsill, watching carriages come up the drive. "Is Mr. Jessup doing well?" she asked Henny in a lower voice.

"I think so, miss," Henny whispered back. "With them under guard and such, I haven't been able to speak to him, but he seems to be doing fine." A final fluff of Josephine's skirt, then she stepped back. "Blue suits you, miss. You look quite grand. Shall I stay with Jamie while you visit Lady Kirkwell?"

At Josephine's grateful nod, the Irishwoman turned to Jamie. "Would you like to see the nursery, Master Jamie? Faith, and I've never seen so many toys all in one place."

"May I, Mother?"

Josephine nodded and blew him a kiss. "Mind Henny, dearest. I shall be back to see you before dinner. Be sure to lock the door behind you, Henny. There's an extra key on the bureau." Grabbing a shawl from her trunk, she hurried from the room.

A few minutes later, she stepped off the rear terrace into a lovely rose garden with pebble-covered paths bordering two large ponds. Maddie stood by the nearest one, tossing bits of bread to two stately swans.

"Have you been waiting long?" Josephine said, rushing up.

"Not at all." After tossing the last of the bread into the water, Maddie looped her arm through Josephine's and together they strolled down the path.

"How was your trip?" Josephine asked. "Any difficulty with the horses?"

"They were angels. Rayford did a fine job preparing them for travel." Tipping her head to the side, she regarded Josephine with a coy smile. "He's here, in case you were wondering. He's taken over the stallion's training since he arrived, and they both seem in fine form."

Josephine couldn't hide her excitement. "You've talked to him?"

"No, but Ash has. He says both he and Thomas look much better than they did when last we saw them, although the cuts and bruises might have brought an unexpected benefit."

"In what way?"

"It proves they can take punishment. Ash says this race is as hard on the riders as the horses, and Rayford's size and battered face are having an intimidating effect on the other riders." Reaching into an inside pocket on her fur-trimmed pelisse, she pulled out a folded paper. "Rayford asked Ash to see that this reached you."

Josephine almost snatched it from Maddie's gloved hand. She quickly opened it and saw the same bold handwriting she had seen on the tablet in the loft.

*I need to see you. Rafe.*

She almost laughed aloud. The man was as stingy with words on paper as he was in speaking. Folding the paper, she slipped it down the neckline of her dress since she was wearing a shawl and her dress had no pockets. "Where are he and Thomas staying?"

"At the stable. As they are still in custody, they are sharing a room with one of the constable's men."

"How is that going?"

"Swimmingly . . . for everyone but the poor guard." Between chuckles, Maddie explained. "With Rafe needing to take Pems out for exercise runs, and Thomas wandering off at every turn, the poor man is run ragged. However, once Ash assured him that he wouldn't let Rafe escape, the guard agreed to stay behind to watch Thomas. Which is fruitless, of course. The Cheyenne can disappear in the blink of an eye. It's amusing, really."

"So Pems has been able to continue his training?"

"Just so. In fact," Maddie added with that coy smile, "they should be taking a second run even as we speak. Toward those trees over there, if one were inclined to watch them ride by." Grinning, she pointed to a thick stand of beeches.

"Truly?" Grabbing the countess's gloved hands, Josephine gave them a quick squeeze. "Oh, thank you, my lady. Thank—"

"It's Maddie. Now go." Laughing, Maddie gave her a push. "You mustn't keep them waiting. Ash is an impatient sort, you know."

Josephine almost flew down the path. Just as she rushed into the trees, strong arms grabbed her and lifted her off the ground.

"Josie," Rafe said, pulling her hard against his chest. Before she could catch her breath, his mouth found hers, and in an instant all her fear and worry and doubt dissolved in his kiss. She couldn't keep her hands from wandering over him, touching his beard-roughened cheeks, his silky hair, the muscles across his shoulders. She was falling, sinking into him, and couldn't get close enough.

"I've missed you," he murmured against her lips, after that initial hunger gave way to a gentler assault. "I need you. These last days . . ." Words gave way to deeper kisses. His grip tightened until she could scarcely breathe.

She could feel the beat of his heart against her breasts. Hear the urgency in his voice as he murmured how sweet she felt, how perfectly she fit against him, how much he'd been wanting to hold her like this. When finally they ran out of air, he pulled back as far as his hands on her shoulders would allow and looked into her face. He no longer smiled, and the laughter was gone from his beautiful eyes. "I'm sorry, Josie. I've made such a mess of things."

At the finality in his tone, a chill wrapped around her heart. She had hoped for a true proposal, but this sounded more like good-bye.

Releasing her shoulders, he dragged a hand through his sun-streaked hair. "I wanted to talk to you after you came back from the weasel's, but then Ash sent me to find Thomas, and . . . well . . ."

*Just say it*, she begged silently, tears burning behind her eyes. *Say you love me or say good-bye.*

He stared off into the distance for a moment, then blurted out, "Don't marry Adderly, Josie. I may not have a title or a fancy house, but I can give you more than he ever could. I can love you like you deserve. I can be there for you and Jamie. I can—Jesus, why are you crying?"

"Are you finally proposing to me, Mr. Jessup?"

A great sigh escaped his chest. The crooked smile she loved spread across his weathered face. "I am, Miss Cathcart."

"Then say it."

Something raw and hungry built in his eyes.

She felt the heat of it low in her belly. Then lower. A shivery, tingly sensation racing along the nerves under her skin.

"I'm not much of a talker." Eyes locked on hers, he reached out and brushed his fingertips across her cheek, along her lace collar, then down the buttons of her short jacket to her waist. "Wouldn't you rather I show you?" His thumb brushed over the puckered nub pressing against the cloth of her dress.

Her legs went weak. Her lungs faltered. Trembling and breathless, she leaned into his hand. *Yes . . . show me. No. Ask me, then show me. Now.*

Frowning, he drew back. "What's that?" He poked a finger at her chest. "Is that paper?"

"It's your note. Continue with—"

"You kept it? That's sweet."

"You were saying . . ."

Grinning, he dropped his hands to her waist and pulled

her closer. "Ash has offered me a position at his ranch in Colorado." He grinned and gave her a hard, fast kiss. "We'll have a home." Another kiss. "Enough money to send Jamie to a good school." A slow lick along her bottom lip. "Maybe even a—"

"Stop." She pushed him away while she still could. "You're proposing to me because you have employment?"

"Well . . . partly."

"Not because you love me."

"That, too."

"Or because you can't bear to live without me?"

He let out a deep breath. "Hell. I did something wrong, didn't I? Tell me what it is and I'll fix it."

"Ask me properly, that's how you can fix it. Tell me that you love me. That you need me. That I'm as necessary to you as the air you breathe. I've never been proposed to before, and I want it done properly."

A smile broke over his face. One that dazzled her anew and brought more tears to her eyes. "Marry me, Josephine Cathcart, and I'll love you 'til I die."

Near enough. "I would be honored, Rayford Jessup."

"About time," Lord Kirkwell said, stepping out from behind a tree.

Josephine almost fainted.

"Evening, Miss Cathcart. Congratulations, Rafe."

"Jesus, Ash. Can't a fellow have some privacy when he's proposing?"

"Not when his jailer is headed this way. He looks mad, so he does. Give her a kiss, lad, then let's head him off. Apparently Thomas has escaped again."

Spirits were high at dinner that night. Lord Brantley, an older man with an overabundance of energy and a timid wife, was a gracious and jovial host, and his guests were as excited as he seemed to be about the race the next day.

Josephine could scarcely eat and passed most of the meal in a daze.

She was marrying Rayford Jessup.

She and Jamie were going to America.

Not even Adderly's officious attentions could dim her joy. If it hadn't been for Maddie's effusive well wishes earlier, and Lord Kirkwell's insistence that it was all his doing, she might have thought she'd dreamed it up. Although she was anxious to share the news, she wanted to wait until Rafe could be by her side before she told Jamie. Nor had she told Father. Anticipating an unpleasant scene, she thought it best to tell him after the race.

As for the baron, although she wouldn't mention Rafe's proposal unless necessary, she couldn't, in good conscience, allow William to continue in his misconceptions about their relationship. Toward that end, and with some trepidation, she asked him to walk with her after dinner.

Lanterns on the balustrade lit their way as they strolled along the terrace. Down below, evenly spaced along the garden paths, flaming torches cast dancing reflections on the still water of the ponds.

The night was cool but clear, which boded well for the race. Although now, with his employment in Heartbreak Creek secure, it wasn't as imperative for Rafe that Pems do well. Still, she wanted the two of them to win, not only for the prize that would bear their names, but to show the world the miracle Rafe had wrought.

"There was something you wished to say to me?"

Startled from her reverie, she glanced at the man walking beside her. She guessed by his complacent smile that William expected her to say she was accepting his proposal. The thought of how closely she had come to doing just that sent a chill through her.

When they reached the far end of the deserted terrace, she stopped and faced him. "I am honored that you asked me to be your wife, William, but I cannot marry you. Not even to give Jamie your name, and certainly not to save my father from his creditors. I don't know what I'll do or where I'll go. Perhaps to Scotland. Perhaps to America. But I will not stay here in a loveless marriage. I'm sorry."

She braced herself, not knowing how he would take her refusal. Disappointment. A few harsh words. An argument perhaps. But nothing could have prepared her for the startling reaction he gave.

# Twenty-four

"America!" The word burst out of him with a fervor that took her aback. "You can't go to America!" He stepped toward her, his face twisting in fury. "I will not allow you to take my son away from me!"

"He was never your son, William. By your choice, not mine." She'd done her best to be civil, but if he was determined to be difficult, she wouldn't stay to be browbeaten. "Good night." Whirling, she started for the terrace door.

"Wait!" His hand caught her shoulder, whipped her back around. She stared into a face she scarcely recognized. "Leave if you must, Josephine, but don't take Jamie from me."

"*Take* him from you? You never had him. Nor will you."

"No, you're not listening!" He shook her roughly, his fingers digging into her arm. "You mustn't do this! I need him!"

His vehemence shocked her. William had never before been violent with her. "Release me," she ordered in an unsteady voice.

He seemed not to hear. "The barony needs him." His voice wheedled, but his grip remained tight on her arm.

"You're hurting me, William."

"You're young. You can have more children."

"So can you. Stop or—"

"No, I can't! Would I be begging you like this if I could?" With a curse, he abruptly let her go and stalked away, fists at his sides.

She stared after him, held motionless by shock. "What are you saying?"

"Oh, Christ." Stopping by the balustrade, he pressed a hand over his eyes. "Just . . . don't. Don't take him away. Please. I'm begging you."

She heard the tremor in his voice, and knew something was terribly wrong. "Why can't you have more children, William?"

Jerking his hand away, he rounded on her. "For God's sake, Josephine! Why are you pushing me like this? Can't you simply believe me when I say Jamie is my last hope?"

"Last hope of what? What's wrong?"

"Bloody hell." He gave a broken laugh. "I forgot how persistent you can be." Blinking hard, he lifted his face to the starlit sky. He looked defeated. Beaten. A shadow of the prideful man she had once known. After a moment, he took a deep breath and faced her again, his expression bleak. "I'm diseased."

Diseased? What did that mean? "Are you dying?"

"Better that I were." He looked away. "I have a venereal disease."

The words churned in her mind. *Venereal disease.* She was ignorant, but not that ignorant. She knew such infections were common among prostitutes. But she had never thought William dissolute enough to make use of such a creature.

"It's called gonorrhea," he went on when she continued to gape in mute disbelief. "I've had bouts of it on and off for years. The doctors have dosed me with turpentine, extract of cubebs, copaiva, even solution of mercury. It helps for a while, but never seems to cure it completely. They say I will never sire children again." He laughed bitterly. "I'm not sure if that's because of the disease or the cure."

"Wait." She lifted a shaking hand. "You've had it for *years*? Am I . . . because of our involvement, will I . . . am I at risk?"

"No. Absolutely not." He took a step toward her then stopped when she drew back, unable to hide her aversion. "You're quite safe. I contracted it after Neddy was born."

After? Thoughts jumbled in her mind. "Does that mean your wife . . ."

"Yes." That look of shame again. "I passed it on to her before I knew."

Horror gripped her. "Is that why she lost her babies?"

"Yes."

"Why she took her own life?"

"Yes. But she overreacted—"

"Overreacted!" Rage exploded inside her, drove the air from her lungs. Rage for his innocent wife. For the poor lost babies. For herself for ever considering this man worthy of her love. "And now . . . after causing your wife's death . . . you propose to cause mine?"

"No!" He moved toward her. "It's not like that! I would never—"

"Stop! Stay away from me!"

He stepped back, his mouth twisting into bitter lines. "Don't worry. Gonorrhea isn't like leprosy. You can't catch it through casual . . . touching."

She wanted to run from him, from this terrible revelation, but didn't think her legs would carry her.

"Josephine, please . . ." He lifted a hand, saw her flinch, and with a look of regret, let his arm drop back to his side. "I would never infect you. I couldn't. I'm . . . impotent. Incapable of . . . of sexual congress."

Then why marry her at all? She knew he didn't love her, despite his pursuit. And if not for love, or children, then why . . .

The answer almost buckled her knees. Jamie. The proposal, the sudden attention after so many years, all his grand promises, were simply to get Jamie.

*Dear God.* She clutched at the balustrade, fearing her legs would give way.

Numbly, she heard him speaking in that wheedling tone again. "I know you don't love me, Josephine. And after the way I treated you, I don't blame you. But we can make this work. I'm a rich man. I can cover your father's debts. Protect you. Give Jamie all the advantages due him as heir to a barony. I could never consummate the marriage, so you wouldn't be at risk. And if you were discreet, I would even allow you to take lovers if that's what—"

"William, stop!" She couldn't bear to hear more. "Listen to what you're saying. How can you speak of Jamie as the heir while Neddy is still living? How unfeeling are you?"

He stiffened. "I am simply trying to do my duty, Josephine. To you. To Jamie. To the barony. Try to understand."

"I cannot. And I never will." She could scarcely even look at him. Yet in the midst of the chaos in her mind, one thought rose to the surface. One that was every bit as horrifying as his revelation. "Does my father know?"

"I . . . he . . . may have heard things. But we never . . ."

Clapping a hand over her mouth, she fled from him into the house. Seeing a footman in the entry, she had him show her to an unused salon, then told him to find Horatio Cathcart and send him to her immediately.

As he hurried away, she clasped her arms around her trembling body and struggled for calmness, wondering to what depths her father had sunk. Her lips felt numb. Her heart seemed incased in ice. Bad enough that he would offer her to the highest bidder, but to knowingly push her into a sham marriage that would be no marriage at all?

*Father . . . how could you?*

The door opened and her father walked in, scowling in impatience. "What is it, girl, that you must pull me away from a winning hand?"

"Did you know?"

Something in her tone must have alerted him. He turned to close the door, then faced her again, his expression guarded. "I have no idea what you're talking about."

"When you fostered this unholy alliance with Adderly, did you know?"

"Know what?"

"That he's diseased!" She shrieked the word, not caring who heard.

"Lower your voice! Do you want the servants to hear?"

"Answer me! Did you know he has a venereal disease?"

He didn't have to speak. She saw the telltale flush, the sidewise slide of his gaze. She knew all his signals when he lied. She had seen them endless times.

It left her breathless. She didn't know whether to scream or weep. She didn't know how her heart continued to beat. Her own father. The man who was supposed to be her protector. Who was supposed to love her.

She shook her head, still reeling from the blow. "I know I brought shame to you. I know I wasn't the daughter you wanted. But, Father . . . to do this? Why?"

"Josephine—"

"No! I don't want to hear your excuses. I've heard them too many times, and your actions speak loudly enough." Drawing on the remnants of her tattered pride, she hiked her chin. "It is clear to me that I am only a pawn in your endless quest to further your own interests. I understand and accept that. Perhaps, I even deserve it for the embarrassment I have caused you. But Jamie is innocent in all this. And I will not allow you to use him as callously as you've used me."

"You're being overly dramatic."

"Am I?" She hated that she couldn't keep her voice from shaking, that this man still had the power to disappoint and hurt her. Even now, he looked at her with that bored, condescending expression he reserved for women behaving in what he considered an unreasonable, overly emotional, irrational manner.

She would tolerate it no more. She would tell him everything and be done with it. The lies, the secrets, the hidden purposes were over.

"I have refused Baron Adderly's offer of marriage, Father, and have, instead, accepted Rayford Jessup's. Jamie and I will leave with him for America immediately after the race tomorrow. We will not return."

His expression shifted from shock to fury, that vein in his temple pulsing like a parasitic worm moving beneath his skin. "The wrangler? You would turn down a title—legitimacy for your son—wealth and position—for a *horse wrangler*?"

"I already have."

"What about our debts? The baron could save us from bankruptcy. Does that mean nothing to you?"

She shrugged. "I am sad for it, but they're your debts, Father. Not mine."

"You benefited, too."

"I did. And I thank you for that. But I'm weary of being dragged into your delusions, and serving as a lure to bring wealthy investors into your latest scheme. I am done with it." She started to move past him, then stopped and looked him hard in the eye. "I suggest you bet wisely tomorrow, so at least you might gain the means to flee your creditors."

"You're a selfish fool."

"Good-bye, Father." Head high, she walked from the room.

But once in the hall, bravado deserted her. She felt adrift, suffocating in a sea of emotion. She didn't know where to go. What to do. She needed Rafe, but he was under guard in the stable.

Then a new thought burst into her mind, and fear closed like a fist around her heart. Surely neither Father nor William would try to take Jamie from her. Would they?

Breathless with terror, she raced up the stairs.

Flinging open the door of the bedroom she and her son shared, she saw Henny pulling the curtains closed and Jamie already asleep. Thank goodness he was such a heavy sleeper or her abrupt arrival might have awakened him.

"Henny, we have to get Jamie away," she whispered.

After briefly explaining Rafe's proposal and how Father and the baron had reacted to it, she bundled her sleeping son and lifted him from the bed. Motioning to the maid to grab the reticule containing the money from her pawned jewels, she followed Henny into the hall, hovering beside her as she locked the door. "I'm probably being overly cautious," she whispered as they hurried down the servants' stair. "But if you had seen the baron's face when I said I wouldn't marry him . . ."

"Faith, miss," the maid whispered back. "I'm just happy you're marrying Mr. Jessup instead of Adderly. He was never right for you, if you don't mind me saying. And what an adventure the four of us will have in America. Come along now, our Jamie will be safe in Gordon's and my room."

Josephine's arms were aching from Jamie's dead weight by the time Henny stopped before a closed door. Knocking softly, she opened it just enough to peer inside. "Are ye decent, love? I've brought the miss and Jamie."

Luckily, Gordon was as happy as Henny about Josephine's news, and just as ready to help hide Jamie in case Father or the baron tried to prevent her from taking him to America. "I doubt they will do anything," she told them as she laid her son down on a pallet of blankets Henny had hastily spread in the corner behind a screen—thank God he was still asleep—"but until I can talk to Lord Kirkwell about what to do, I want him in a safe place."

"'Tis no trouble, miss," Henny assured her. "Sure, and Master Jamie is like one of our own. He'll be safe here for the night."

Gordon nodded in agreement. "We'll watch over him until you come in the morning before the race."

"Bless you both. I'll tell you if there's a change in plans."

Several minutes later, she knocked gently on another door, this one with gilt trim and located on the top floor of the wing reserved for the loftier guests.

Maddie opened the door. One look at Josephine, and she pulled her into the room. "What's wrong?"

"Hopefully, nothing. Is the earl here?"

"He's down in the billiards room, entering Rafe's wager in the book."

"I need a bet placed, as well." She set her reticule on a table beside the door. "But that's not why I'm here. I need your advice."

"Certainly. Come sit by the fire and tell me how I can help."

Out of a last lingering loyalty to her son's father and the man she had once loved, she didn't mention William's disease, but did tell Maddie about his and Father's strong reactions to her decision to marry Rafe instead of Adderly. "I worry that they might try to prevent me from taking Jamie to America."

"Surely not."

"Truthfully, I don't know what they might do." Too agitated to sit, Josephine rose and paced before the marble fireplace, her hands clasped tightly at her waist. "He's safe with Henny and Gordon Stevens for now. But I wonder if it would be better if he were away from here altogether. Perhaps Gordon could hide him on the ship we'll be taking to America. Or on the earl's freighter. No one would dare search that. I would go with him, but it might arouse suspicion if I went missing, too, don't you think? Oh, I do wish I could talk to Rafe. He's so calm and levelheaded." She stopped before Maddie. "What do you think Lord Kirkwell would advise me to do?"

"Let's send for him and see, shall we?" Rising from her chair, Maddie crossed to the bellpull beside the door, gave it a tug, then stood waiting. "Before he joined the Hussars, Ash was a forward rider with the green-jacketed Riflemen, and this is precisely the sort of intrigue he adores. I'm sure he'll have a solution."

After an interminably long few minutes, Lord Kirkwell's man, Pringle, knocked on the door then entered, his necktie askew, his white hair in disarray, and pillow creases on the side of his face. "Yes, my lady," he said with a ponderous sigh.

Maddie told him to fetch Lord Kirkwell from the billiards room straightaway, adding, "He might be upset at the interruption, but tell him I insist."

Cheered by the prospect of putting a twist in his employer's plans for the evening, Pringle bowed graciously and, with a happy glint in his bleary eyes, shuffled from the room.

"Those two," Maddie muttered, returning to her chair. "It's as if they were still in the nursery, the way they go at one another."

A few minutes later, the door burst open and the earl rushed in, his face ashen with fear. "Is it the babe? Are ye well? Pringle said it was an emergency."

"He exaggerated. But Jamie and Josephine need our help." The countess waved him to the chair Josephine was too nervous to use. "Do stop blustering and sit down. She's upset enough as it is."

After a series of muttered threats relating to his valet, the earl finally settled enough to listen as Josephine went over it yet again. With this, her third recitation, the situation had lost much of its urgency and she wondered if perhaps she had overreacted. But unwilling to risk Jamie, she plowed on.

The earl listened without interrupting. She could almost see the plans and strategies forming behind his intense green eyes. When she finally finished, he nodded once then rose.

"You've done well, lass. The bairn should be safe with Stevens. But just in case, I'll have my men watch their door and yours. I will also post a lookout for Adderly and your father."

Josephine nodded, not sure she trusted that grin on the earl's rugged face.

Whistling through his teeth, he started toward the door.

"Oh, and Lord Kirkwell." She hurried to the table beside the door. "Could I prevail upon you to place a wager in my name?" Opening her reticule, she pulled out all the money she had and put it into his large hand. "On Pembroke's Pride, please. To win."

The Scotsman frowned at the sheaf of bills bound with a blue ribbon. "'Tis a great deal of money, lass. Are you that certain the horse will win?"

"I am."

"Then I pray 'tis so." He slipped the money into his coat pocket, then flashed that brilliant smile. "Now return to your room, and dinna worry. Our battle plan is sound." As he stepped into the hall, he turned back to his wife and in a carrying voice said, "Dinna wait up for me, love. It will take a while for Thomas to skin a man as fat as Pringle." Laughing softly, he shut the door.

"Well," Maddie said with a troubled look. "A battle plan. That sounds rather . . . ominous, don't you think? Let's pray it doesn't come to that."

Josephine smiled weakly. "Yes, let's." But she was more worried about Pringle.

Rafe slouched on his cot, wondering how long it took a man to drink himself senseless. He had never tried it, himself. But Ash had been working at it for well over an hour—pouring glass after glass of Northbridge Whisky—offering up endless toasts to big-breasted women of negotiable morals, the queen, their fallen brothers, and any other excuse he could come up with to raise a glass.

Yet their guard, Henry Hicks, remained conscious.

Thirty years ago, before a musket ball through his knee had ended a promising career, Hicks had been in the infantry—which was probably where he'd learned to hold his liquor so well. Now, instead of drinking and killing men in foreign places for the crown, he drank and hunted men at home for the magistrate. But even Ash, a veteran of many a skirmish, was showing red in his eyes, and he'd swallowed less than half of what ex-Private Hicks had consumed.

Rafe was becoming impatient. Earlier, when Hicks had stepped out to relieve himself, Ash had relayed what Josie had told him and explained her concerns for Jamie. Seeing Rafe's determination to go to her, the earl had quickly warned him to patience, saying he had a plan. That was over an hour-and-a-half ago, yet here they still sat, watching a man down enough whisky to level a regiment, while they did nothing.

"It were hot enough to melt the hinges off the door to Satan's lair," the guard slurred. "A march across the sands of Araby at high noon would have been like a traipse in the park compared to the cursed heat o' that blighted day. All around me, men were dropping like singed flies, poor buggers." A deep swallow, a wet belch, and a heartfelt sigh. "War is a hellish thing."

"Aye, so it is." While Hicks stared morosely into his cup, Ash turned his head and spit a mouthful of expensive alcohol into the corner.

Across the room, Thomas snorted, and Rafe knew he'd be in for more snide "white people" remarks when this was done. Not that it wouldn't be warranted this time. Unlike Ash, Hicks knew nothing of war. He'd been injured in a training exercise two weeks after he'd enlisted, when the man beside him had fainted and accidentally discharged his musket when he fell. But it made a good drinking story, which fit neatly with their goal of getting Hicks so drunk he wouldn't remember that Thomas had been gone all afternoon and would be leaving again soon, or that Rafe would be absent until dawn.

Finally, after another half hour, a gentle thud announced the brave warrior's slide from his chair to the floor, where he lay like a heap of dirty laundry, his whiffling snore rising to the rafters.

"Aboot time," Ash muttered.

Rafe had noticed that with each swallow of whisky, the Scotsman's accent had grown stronger. Another glass, and he'd be speaking gibberish.

Muttering, Ash dug through the guard's pockets. Pulling out a key, he stumbled over Hicks and unlocked the manacles chaining the runaway Indian to his bed, then returned the key to the guard's pocket. Being the more trustworthy of the two prisoners, Rafe hadn't been consigned to chains.

"Tae yer post, ye bluidy savage. And stay alert. If Cathcart or that buggerin' baron go nosing aboot, come tell me. And no killing, ye ken? Rafe, go in through the servants' entrance. Tell Gordon and Henny I'll come fer the bairn 'afore the race. Now off ye go, lads. And Rafe," he added as Thomas slipped out the door. "Best get some sleep tonight. The lass has risked a great deal on yer winning the race tomorrow. Ye'd no' want tae disappoint her."

Rafe grinned. "I don't intend to."

# Twenty-five

As ordered by the earl, Josephine went back to her room and prepared for bed. But after changing into her gown and brushing out her hair, she was still too agitated to sleep. Pulling on her heavy robe, she paced the small bedchamber as best she could with all the trunks and valises stacked against the walls.

Perhaps she should have traded rooms with Gordon and Henny, in case William or Father came here. Or she and Jamie could have stayed in the dressing room of the Kirkwells' suite. Or maybe she was worrying over nothing, and neither Father nor William had any intention of spiriting away her son.

But she couldn't deny that they both posed a threat. Father, because if he could force her to marry Adderly, his debts would be paid. William, because he wanted Jamie as a spare heir for his title. But if she could get through this one night and the race tomorrow, she and Jamie would be safe.

An hour later, worn ragged by the turmoil and emotional stress of the day, she finally took off her robe, turned down the lamp, and climbed into bed.

Perhaps she never truly fell asleep. Or perhaps she did, and was awakened by a dream, or a noise different from those usually heard in a sprawling structure filled with a number of people. But at some point as she lay in darkness, she became aware that she wasn't alone.

A thump. Whispered mutterings. A muffled crash.

Bolting upright, she reached for the lamp, then gasped when a hand closed over her wrist.

Frozen in fear, she stared at the shadow looming over her. Big, male, breathing softly as he released her wrist and fumbled to find her shoulder.

"This better be you, Josie. Or I'm in big trouble."

Air left her in a rush. "R-Rafe?"

"What's all that stacked beside the door? I damn near killed myself."

"My trunks." Alarm exploded in a rush of words. "Is something wrong? Is Jamie all right?"

"Shh. All's well." His hand brushed over her cheek. The solid roughness of it reassured her. The mattress sagged under his weight as he sat beside her. It was so dark she could feel him more than she could see him.

"How did you get in? I thought I locked the door."

"Henny gave me her key." He leaned closer, startling her with featherlight kisses along her neck. "I wanted to make sure you were all right."

Warm breath fanned her cheek. The frantic drumming of her heart subtly changed as anticipation overcame fear. "I could have shot you."

"You don't have a gun."

"I'll get one." Shameless in her relief, she leaned into him, seeking his touch, his warmth, his calmness. "I've been frantic with worry, Rafe. Father and William are so upset that I'm taking Jamie to America, I was afraid they might—"

His mouth stopped her words, and by the time he ended the kiss, she was too befuddled to remember what she'd been saying.

"Gordon and Henny told me what happened. Jamie is safe and sound asleep and one of Ash's grooms is watching their door. Thomas is watching for the weasel and your father, and I'm here to watch over you. Everything is fine. Now kiss me."

Instead, she drew back and tried to see his face, but he was only a big, darker shadow among the other shadows in the unlit room. "I thought you and Thomas were still in custody. How did you escape your guard?"

"Ash got him drunk. Your hair smells like flowers." He

loosened the thick braid hanging past her shoulder blades, then combed his fingers across her scalp and down through the heavy waves. "I've been wanting to do this."

Her eyes drifted closed. She almost purred. "I'm glad you're here, Rafe. I want this race over and the three of us safely on the ship. I'm so afraid they will try to take Jamie."

"Not while I'm here. Are we going to talk all night? I was hoping . . ." His voice trailed off as his hands moved along her waist then up across her ribs to the underside of her breast and then finally . . .

*Yes.* She let out a shuddering breath when he cupped her breast and his thumb brushed across the taut peak pressing against the thin fabric of her gown. Thoughts scattered. Resistance died. Primed for his touch these few weeks, her body reacted instantly.

"You're so soft."

"You sh-shouldn't be in here."

"You want me to leave?"

When she couldn't dredge up an answer, he continued to caress her with slow, delicious, deliberate strokes. A shiver ran through her. Breathing became difficult. Tipping her forehead against his chest, all of her senses focused on what his fingers were doing. Circling. Tweaking. Soothing. Gentle tugs that sent desire pulsing all through her body.

The man had magic in his hands.

Needing to move, to do something to release the tension coiling inside her, she lifted her head and pressed her mouth to his neck. The earthy, male scent of him blended with the faint saltiness of his skin. Whiskers pricked her lips as she traced the quickening pulse in his throat with the tip of her tongue.

"Lay with me, Josie."

His deep voice vibrated through her. The call to lust. To carnal delight.

To trust.

William had said almost the same thing years ago. He had told her he loved her, needed her, wanted her for his wife. Believing him, she had given up all that she was—her heart, her body, the sum of her hopes and dreams—her trust.

And then he had walked away.

If it happened again—with Rafe—it would be the end of her.

The mattress shifted. His hands dropped away and cool air filled the space where he had been. As she struggled to gather her thoughts, she heard a scraping noise, then the hiss of a match flaring to life. She watched him light the wick of the lamp on the bedside table, lower the glass shade, then sit back.

He studied her, his hands relaxed on his thighs, a fall of blond hair shading his eyes. "What's wrong, Josie?"

He said it without accusation. Or impatience. Or even disappointment. As if her answer was of utmost importance to him. As if *she* was of utmost importance to him, and he was here to protect her and make her worries go away.

She didn't know how to answer. Rafe wasn't like William. He wouldn't use her then abandon her. He could never be so weak in character, and she was wrong even to let that doubt into her head. "Nothing," she said with a shaky smile. "Nerves, I suppose."

He took her hand in his. "It's just us, Josie. You and me." He looked down at their clasped hands. "But you're right. I was wrong to rush you. I only want to watch over you. Well . . . not only that," he added with a wry smile, "but I'm content to wait if you want."

"Hold me."

His arms came around her and pulled her against his strong body. She felt the steady, strong beat of his heart against her cheek, and some of the doubt drained away.

*Safe. Loved.* That's how she felt with Rafe. *Protected.* That sense of calmness that always surrounded him enveloped her, too, and closing her eyes, she allowed herself to relax against his solid strength.

It was scandalous to be sitting here in her nightclothes, clinging to a man like a wanton. But she didn't feel scandalized. She didn't feel wanton. She felt at peace. Because Rafe didn't push, she had no reason to pull away. Because he didn't demand, there was nothing to resist. He simply waited to see what she wanted and needed, then he provided it.

She had seen it work on the horses. Had felt it ease her own pain down at the brook that day she had rested her head against his shoulder. Could feel that same soothing power move through her now.

She didn't feel rushed. She felt loved. Pulling away, she looked up into his chiseled face and smiled. "Wait here. I must get something."

Rafe watched her dig through pouches and pockets in one of the valises stacked against the wall. He wasn't sure what had just happened, but sensed something was different. She was no longer afraid.

He didn't know why she had suddenly shied away from him, or what had brought her back. It confused him. She confused him. Being around her sometimes made him feel like a kite on a string, jerked in one direction then another by unpredictable winds.

But he didn't mind. That was Josie: a strong, beautiful, complicated, sometimes prickly, and often unpredictable woman. And he loved her dearly for the challenge she gave him.

"Found it." Straightening, she turned and walked toward him. His breath caught.

Lamplight spilled over her, highlighting every rounded curve beneath the thin cloth of her gown and drawing his eye to each puckered peak and dark shadow.

How could she sleep in such a ridiculous amount of fabric? From the high, lacy collar, to the gathered ruffles at her wrists, and down to the fluttering hem that reached her toes, it completely covered her tall form. Yet she looked magnificent in it. Seductive, but chaste at the same time. And that shy smile . . .

"Found what?" he asked, hardly recognizing his own voice.

"This." Sitting beside him on the mattress, she held up her open hand to show him the object in her palm.

Words deserted him.

"Do you know what this is?" she asked.

He cleared his throat. "I do."

"Gordon says they're not very comfortable. But apparently they work."

"You discussed preventatives with Gordon Stevens?"

"Of course not. With Henny."

He hid his relief. "Is that where you got that?"

"Yes. She had a whole box of them."

Good for Gordon. "Why did she give one to you?"

"I asked for it. I thought that perhaps . . . you and I . . . well . . ." Holding the preventative between her thumb and forefinger like it was some nearly dead thing that might leap back to life at any moment, she carefully placed it on the night table. Then hiking her chin, she looked him straight in the eye. "I think you should wear it when we consort."

"Consort?"

"It means—"

"I know what it means."

This couldn't be happening. He wasn't truly sitting here, with a substantial and growing motivation to make love to this woman as soon as possible, while she discussed what they were going to do and what he should be wearing when they did it. As seductions went, this wasn't his best. Then why was he struggling not to laugh?

"Don't you want more children?" he asked, curbing his amusement, and a little bothered by the notion that she might not ever carry his child. She was a good mother. In his endless fantasies of her, his fifth or sixth favorite was of her holding their babe.

"Of course I do. Especially yours. But we're not married yet."

*Ah.* Considering her history, he could understand her hesitation. "Would you rather wait until we marry before we . . . consort?"

She gave it some thought. A disturbing amount of thought.

Fighting down a sense of panic, he forced a smile. "You know I'll never abandon you, don't you, Josie? I wouldn't—couldn't—do to you what the baron did."

"No, of course you couldn't." She lifted her head, and when he looked into those magnificent mismatched eyes and saw the faith reflected there, it humbled him. After all she had gone through and suffered, she still had trust. He let out a deep breath and some of his frustration.

"Maybe it would be best if we waited," he offered. "Ash said the ship's captain can perform a marriage ceremony. Or we can have a fancier wedding in Heartbreak Creek. Or we can do both. Whatever you want."

That seemed to make up her mind. "This is what I want. You. Now. Making love to me."

Gratified, and hoping to get things moving along again, he stood and unbuckled his belt.

She watched, her blue-brown eyes as round as a kid's in a candy store. Until he took off his shirt.

"My word!" She stared in horror at the scars on his chest. "What happened to you?"

*Damn.* He should have been more careful. Now he'd have to prime her all over again . . . not an altogether unhappy prospect, now that he thought about it. "A gunfight. Back when I was a Deputy Marshal." As he continued to undress, he was careful not to turn around, since the scarring was more extensive on his back where the bullets had exited. "Don't worry. They look much worse than they feel. Want me to help you take off your gown?"

She blinked at him.

Taking that as a "no," he balanced on one foot, then the other, to pull off his boots and socks. "You don't have to remove it, if you don't want. But I'll feel pretty foolish being buck naked while you're covered from neck to toe."

More blinking.

He must be out of practice. It had been a year, after all. Still hopeful, he set to work unbuttoning his trousers.

"You're taking off *everything*?" she asked when his trousers hit the floor.

Her shocked reaction didn't say much for the weasel's expertise. "Down to bare skin. Otherwise, that thing"—he nodded in distaste at the preventative—"won't work very well."

"Oh. Of course."

Strong, complicated, unpredictable, *and* modest. Once he added naked to that list, she'd be perfect. He reiterated his offer on the gown. No use him being the only one putting on a show.

"No, that's all right. I'll just go over there and . . . em, tend to it."

She left the bed and hurried toward a vanity and bureau against the far wall. Keeping her back to him—although he could see her every move in the vanity mirror she faced—she loosened the bows down the front of her gown.

Hardly daring to breathe, he watched her pull the gown over her head and drop it to the floor. And there she was—everything he'd dreamed her to be—only better—reflected back at him in the oval mirror.

She was so beautiful it made his chest ache. Tall. Slim.

High, round breasts. Narrow waist. Two dimples at the base of her spine he ached to explore with his tongue. And the long, lean legs of a lifelong rider. The thought of those legs wrapping around him made his throat clench.

Unaware of him watching, she fiddled with her loosened hair, pulling long, dark curls forward so that they covered her breasts. That modesty again. It made him smile. He quickly stripped off the rest of his clothes, tossed them aside, and walked over to slip his arms around her waist from behind.

She startled, but allowed him to pull her closer so that she rested against him from his chest to his thighs. Being tall for a woman, she fit perfectly.

The vanity was low and they were both taller than the mirror, so their faces weren't reflected in the glass. But their bodies were, and his sun-darkened arms looked alien against the paleness of her soft skin. Lifting a hand, he brushed one of the long curls back over her shoulder, then ran his lips along that vulnerable tendon that joined her shoulder to her neck.

"You're so beautiful," he whispered into her ear.

She shivered.

He felt it all through his body. Heard surrender in her sigh.

Watching in the mirror, he ran his hands over her, gentling her to his touch . . . drawing out her fear . . . learning what made her sigh and tremble in his arms. He stroked her breasts, watched her nipples grow tight, then moved his hand lower. With one callused fingertip, he gently traced the faint white lines where her body had stretched to accommodate Jamie. He hoped someday it would stretch again to accommodate his child.

She put her hand over his, stopping his exploration.

He started to take his hand away, but she held him fast. "I didn't want what he did to change me. Make me different, or less than I was. I wanted it not to matter. But when I see these marks, I know it did. I'm sorry you have to see them."

He thought of his own scars—ugly, reddened dents where the bullets had gone through, tearing out flesh and muscle and chips of bone. A brutal, meaningless maiming.

But her scars . . . they meant life.

He turned her in his arms. Cupping her face in his hands, he kissed her, putting into that one point of contact all the love and pride and wonder he felt for this fearless, forceful woman.

"You're perfect," he murmured and kissed her right cheek. "The only woman I've ever truly loved." He kissed her left cheek. "The only woman I will ever love." A last kiss, square on her mouth. "For all of my life."

A tear slipped down her cheek as her arms went up and around his neck. Her breasts flattened against his chest, hot and soft, centered by two small, hard points pushing into his skin. "Show me," she whispered into his ear.

That was all he needed. Sweeping her up into his arms, he carried her to the bed, laid her across the coverlet, and climbed up beside her. Resting on one elbow, he smiled down at her as he stroked her again, his hand sliding lower until she opened her legs in invitation.

Soon she was squirming beneath his fingers, her hands tangling in his hair as he dipped his head to kiss her breasts.

"Aren't you going to put on the preventative?" she asked in a breathy voice.

*Hell.* He'd forgotten. He rolled onto his back. "Let's hope it still fits."

She looked over at his face, then her eyes drifted down. Her expression of alarm was both gratifying and a clear indication of how miserably the weasel had failed to measure up. He couldn't help but be pleased.

"That's a joke," he said. "Although if we don't get started soon, it might not be." Sitting up, he reached for the preventative on the night table.

She caught his arm and pulled him back down. Smiling, she slid her arms around his neck. "Never mind."

Relieved and grateful, he settled in to kiss his way from one end of her long, beautiful body to the other.

He tried to go slow, wanting it to be perfect, as good for her as he knew it would be for him. But she wouldn't let him, driving him on with restless touches and gasps of pleasure. She came alive under his hands, all taut curves and hot, smooth skin, and her quivering responses added fuel to the fire that raged inside him.

"Yes," she cried, rising up beneath him.

He couldn't breathe, couldn't think. He became a tool for her pleasure, a trembling shell in her eager hands. And when he moved inside her and her strong legs gripped him tight, pulling him even deeper, the feeling was so intense he had to close his eyes so nothing would distract him from the heat of her, the sweet, salty taste of her on his tongue, the sound of her cry when she soared into bliss.

It was a wonder. More than he had ever imagined. And as he shuddered above her in a final pulse of pleasure, he knew in that one searing moment his life and everything in it had finally become all he had ever dreamed it could be.

Josephine awoke, disoriented and groggy. Shivering, she sat up, the sheet clutched to her naked body. The room was cold. The air smelled faintly of their lovemaking and burned coal oil. Although the lamp on the bedside table had run out of fuel long ago, there was enough light coming through the window for her to study the man sprawled on his back beside her, snoring softly.

Most of his bruises had faded, except for one at the corner of his eye. Asleep, he looked younger. Less determined. Still handsome, but in a softer, more boyish way. She loved this Rafe, too. Vulnerable in sleep, his strong limbs relaxed . . . hers to touch, and admire.

He wasn't a true blond, judging by the dark brown hair that covered his chest . . . except for the three shiny dents where the bullets had gone in. They saddened her. But the scars were part of him now. A signpost pointing back to a troubled time in his past. A reminder of how fragile life could be.

"You fixing to buy, ma'am, or just take a gander?" a drowsy voice said in an exaggerated accent.

Laughing, she looked up from her perusal of his chest to his beautiful deep blue eyes. "You're an amazing man, Rayford Jessup."

"I'm pleased you think so. But I'd be happy to prove it again, if you'd like."

Her smile faded. "You will be careful today, won't you?"

He studied her in that quiet, calm way he had.

"I doubt Father or William would—"

"William? Oh, you mean the weasel."

She thumped his shoulder. "Don't laugh, Rafe. These men could hurt you."

He smiled and reached over to cup her breast.

"Or hire someone to hurt you."

Idly stroking her, he continued to smile.

Which frightened her even more. Big, capable men like Rafe thought they couldn't be hurt, but he had scars to prove that wasn't always so. Realizing that admonitions to be careful would fall on deaf ears, she tried a different approach. "In fact, why don't you simply hang back, let someone else take the lead and the punishment. Now that the earl has offered you a position, you don't have to win."

"And lose the big bet I placed on Pems? Did I mention how much I love your breasts?" He started that circling, tugging, massaging thing again, making it difficult for her to follow what he was saying. He looked up at her, his jaw stubbled with dark whiskers, his blue eyes alight with desire. "Stop worrying, sweetheart. Pems will do all the work. I'm just along for the ride. And speaking of rides . . ." He lifted her thigh over his hip, opening her to his touch. "Are you sore?"

The intimacy of the question shocked her. She was still not accustomed to how natural and at ease he was with his body and hers. "A little."

One finger slipped inside. "Shall I soothe you?"

"We don't have time." *Oh, my.*

"I'll make it quick." Another finger joined the first.

She gasped. "You'll turn my head with such lofty promises."

But she didn't stop him. And he did soothe her, without a thought to his own needs. And when she sank trembling onto his chest, she felt as boneless as a rag doll.

Kissing the top of her head, he slid from beneath her. "I better go. I can hear the servants moving in the hall." He made sure she was all tucked in, patted her bottom, and told her to go back to sleep.

She watched the play of muscles from his shoulders to his buttocks as he pulled on his trousers. "I'm too worried to sleep."

"You needn't be. You know I won't endanger Pems." He bent to pull on his boots. "Or myself. But I intend to win. Pems has earned this chance, and I won't hold him back."

She sat up, the sheet tucked under her arms. "Promise you'll be careful."

He buttoned the placket on his shirt, tucked it into his denim trousers, then faced her, hands low on his hips, his weight resting on one muscular leg. "You're not going to lose either of us, Josie," he said with quiet conviction. "The race is barely four miles long. Less than half an hour. Then we'll leave this soggy island behind and be on our way to America."

Not wanting to burden him with her fears, she gave him as brilliant a smile as she could muster. Still wrapped in the sheet, she rose and crossed to a trunk. Pulling out a blue satin sash, she held it toward him. "Take this as a good luck charm. It perfectly matches your eyes." Seeing his dubious look, she laughed. Using her free hand, she draped the scarf around his neck and pulled him down for a kiss. One kiss led to another, then a third. After the fourth, she finally released him and walked with him to open the door. "I love you, Rafe."

"I love you, too. And I won't let you down, Josie. I swear it." A last kiss, then he stepped into the hall.

"Rafe?"

He looked back.

She dropped the sheet. "I'll be thinking of you." And smiling, she closed the door in his surprised face.

# Twenty-six

Rafe crossed to the stable, still so rattled by the vision of Josie standing nude in the early dawn light he didn't see Thomas until he plowed into him.

The Cheyenne shoved him aside. "See? I do not have to sneak. You white people could step on a diamondback before you heard the first rattle."

"I was thinking."

"You cannot think and watch where you step at the same time?" Shaking his head, he fell in beside Rafe. "How did we let you people defeat us?"

"So you admit defeat?"

"The war is not yet over."

Rafe doubted it ever would be, but didn't allow himself to be drawn into a discussion of it. The morning was mostly clear, he was pleased to note. But clouds were building in the west over the Irish Sea. He hoped the rain would hold off a few more hours.

Even though the horses weren't allowed to test the course before the race, he and Ash had walked the area several times. In addition to a dozen other jumps, there were three water obstacles—two brooks, and a river deep enough in one spot to require the horse to swim a short way. That would be a trial for Pems. But the stallion did have one big advantage—a long final sprint. If he got that far.

Thomas studied him. "You look tired, *nesene*. Bad dreams? Or did something else keep you awake?"

"Actually, I slept very well, and without a single troubling dream." In fact, rather than keeping him awake, Josie had curled against his side, insisting that he sleep so he would be well rested for the race. Sated and blissfully relaxed, he hadn't argued. But tonight . . .

"Did you see any sign of Cathcart or the weasel during the night?" he asked the Cheyenne.

"No. And the man the Scotsman put outside the room of Gordon Stevens saw no one, either."

"Good." When they entered the stable, Rafe saw Ash standing outside the room he and Thomas shared with the guard. He looked impatient. But then, he frequently looked impatient; he didn't handle idleness well. "Is he awake yet?" Rafe asked as they approached.

Motioning them to silence, Ash led them inside. Hicks still lay sprawled on the floor. "It willna be long," the Scot whispered. "He's starting to groan. Heathen, put the chains back on before he awakens and sees you're loose." He gave him the key he'd retrieved from the guard's pocket.

Muttering in his native language, Thomas locked the manacles over his wrists and handed back the key. Ash slipped it into Hicks's pocket a moment before the ex-private rolled to a sitting position, one hand clamped to his brow.

Bending down, Ash spoke loudly into the bleary-eyed face. "Your duties are done now, Mr. Hicks. Release the savage so he can relieve himself and help Jessup prepare for the race. I'll keep a watch on them."

Hicks swept a coated tongue over his dry lips. "But I have to escort them to the docks," he said on the heels of a rumbling belch.

With a look of disgust, Ash backed away. "So you will. After the race."

Mumbling, the guard fished out the key and unlocked the manacles.

As soon as he was free, Thomas and Rafe left to ready Pems.

To deter mischief, Lord Brantley had posted a man in the aisle of the stable overnight to watch over the seven horses entered in the race. Not trusting an Englishman to do the job right, Ash had posted one of his own clansmen outside Pembroke's stall as a further deterrent.

Neither man reported trouble during the night.

While Thomas ducked into the tack room to finish the modifications he was making on Pembroke's saddle, Rafe went in to attend the stallion.

"Morning, fella," he said in answer to the horse's soft whicker when he stepped into the stall. "Sleep well? Me, too."

Speaking quietly, he told Pems about his night with Josie while he went through the motions of currying the glossy bay coat, but using his hands, instead of a brush. "I slept like a log. Not a single evil dream." Making small circles with his fingertips, he moved down one side of the stallion's spine, then the other. "But then, it's hard for Satan to find you," he went on, "when you're sleeping in an angel's arms." After working his way down the horse's legs, he started a deeper massage on the slabs of muscle along the animal's shoulders and rump. "Do you still have bad dreams, Pems?"

The stallion answered with a deep sigh and let his head droop, his eyes half-closed.

"She's a wonder is what she is." Rafe pressed, then released, his fingers digging deep into the dark fur until he felt the tension in the muscles begin to give. "But you know what I'm talking about, don't you, boy? I've seen the way you look at that new little warmblood mare."

The stallion was almost asleep now, resting on three legs, partially leaning into Rafe's hands. Pems loved his massages. And in return for taking the time to give them, Rafe earned a little more of the animal's trust with each session.

"You're a good horse," Rafe told him. "With a strong, brave heart."

Pems had gone through his retraining as well as any horse Rafe had ever known, and had approached his fears with the strength of a champion. Hopefully, he would prove his courage in the race today. But more important, Rafe prayed nothing would happen to damage the trust he had worked so hard to rebuild in this magnificent animal.

"You'll do well today. There will be no finer horse on the course."

After an hour of deep kneading, Rafe gentled his touch,

stroking the stallion as he had at the beginning of the massage, slowly bringing the horse back out of his doze.

Josie had responded well to his touch, too. He smiled, remembering how she'd trembled beneath his hands. He found himself mentally devising new techniques he might try once they were safely on the ship and headed home.

*Home.* A word he hadn't used in a long time. But it felt right. No matter where he rested his head, when he was with Josie and Jamie, he felt like he had finally found a home.

"The saddle is ready," Thomas said in a quiet voice so he wouldn't disturb the drowsy stallion. "I have tested the extra straps. They are strong."

With the modifications Thomas had made to the saddle—giving him an extra hand- and foothold in case he was shoved or bumped—and the tricks the Indian had taught him, Rafe felt better prepared to handle whatever punishment the other riders might send his way. But he was more concerned about Pembroke's safety than his own. Horses were a lot more delicate than they looked.

"Has he eaten?" Thomas asked.

"I was just fixing to get it."

"Then I will wait to weave the loop into his mane."

Rafe had continued the same diet he'd put Pembroke on during his training—several scoops of sweet feed morning and night, along with twenty-five pounds of hay. But since he'd arrived, he'd been supplementing with an oats and molasses mash, thinking it might give the stallion an extra boost during the race.

After Pems ate and Thomas had finished braiding the loop in the mane near the stallion's withers—another handhold to replace the raised horn that was missing in English saddles—Rafe checked the horse's hooves and shoes. Then he turned him out into his paddock to become accustomed to all the comings and goings, and the scent of the other horses. The race wasn't for a couple of hours yet, and Rafe wanted the stallion as relaxed and rested as possible.

When he came out of Pembroke's stall, he saw Ash leaning against the wall, talking to one of his grooms and tapping a short, stout whip against his leg.

Masking his distaste, Rafe asked if he had entered his wager in the book.

"Aye. Right now, Brantley's own Phantom is the favorite. The odds turned heavily against Pembroke's Pride after Cathcart bet on Brantley's gray, rather than his own horse."

Rafe was surprised. "He bet on another man's horse?"

Ash nodded. "Which will make it that much sweeter when you win."

Rafe hoped so. Even though Josie was correct that he didn't need the extra funds now that he'd accepted the position Ash had offered, winning a big bet would allow him to set up his own stable sooner than he had anticipated.

"You will need this." The Scotsman held out the leather bat.

"I don't hit horses."

"'Tis no' for Pems, ye numptie, 'tis for defense against the other riders." He shoved the whip into Rafe's hand, then murmured, "Look sharp, lad. Company."

Rafe turned to see Josie and Jamie entering the stable.

When the boy caught sight of him, he ran forward. Rafe hadn't seen him since his arrest, and was pleased to see the commotion hadn't affected him. "Mother said I could watch at the finish line. She said Pems would be the very first horse across."

Rafe smiled and ruffled the boy's blond hair. He hadn't yet married Jamie's mother, but he already felt like the lad's father. "I hope so."

Looking up, he watched Josie continue toward them and felt a hot rush of desire, tinged with an almost overwhelming drive to protect her. He had felt that way once before, but this time, it brought peace, not pain.

His woman. His son.

She moved with a natural grace, fully feminine, yet forceful at the same time. A woman of confidence and purpose, one any man would be lucky to have in his life. As she stopped before him, he studied her face for lingering regrets about the previous night. But all he saw was a warm smile, an answering heat in her unusual eyes, and a faint blush tinting her cheeks.

"You're looking well, Miss Cathcart."

"I am well, Mr. Jessup. Quite well, in fact. And you?"

"Never better."

"I'm delighted to hear it." Darting a glance at the Cheyenne and the Scotsman blatantly watching their exchange, she gave a small nod. "Gentlemen."

"Miss Cathcart," they said as one.

"We're well, too," Ash added with a wickedly innocent smile. "In case you were wondering."

"Me, too, Mother," Jamie piped in, not wanting to be left out.

"I'm delighted to hear it." The blush deepened, even though a smile teased the corners of her lips. Turning back to Rafe, she asked if she might have a word. "I wish to say something to Jamie and would like for you to be there when I do."

"Am I in trouble?" her son asked in alarm.

Rafe mentally speculated on what the boy might have done to put that guilty look on his face.

"Not at all," his mother said.

"Am I?" Rafe asked, shifting her attention away from Jamie.

"Not yet."

"What a relief. Shall we walk along the drive?"

"Excellent." With a nod to the watchers, the three of them strolled out of the stable and onto the pebbled drive that circled past the house and on to the massive entry gates. Jamie lagged behind, apparently still concerned about the upcoming talk. Picking up a stick, he whacked at rocks along the way.

After a short distance, they left the drive and crossed a freshly scythed field toward a tall chestnut tree. Jamie followed, this time beheading weeds.

A comfortable feeling moved through Rafe. He pictured the three of them walking together in Heartbreak Creek, maybe returning from a boisterous sermon at the Come All You Sinners Church of Heartbreak Creek and heading toward the hotel for Sunday dinner. A family. Smiling and happy, with a rich future stretching ahead of them.

Amused, he glanced at the woman and boy walking beside him and wondered if they knew what awaited them. The ladies of Heartbreak Creek weren't known for their restraint—nor was sometime sheriff Declan Brodie's brood. For a boy who had grown up with few friends, Jamie might be overwhelmed by the three older Brodie boys. Especially the mischievous Joe Bill. Rafe would keep an eye on them.

"Jamie," his mother said when they stopped in the sparse shade cast by the few remaining leaves on the tree. "Would you mind terribly if we didn't go to Scotland?"

He looked up at her, his worried expression changing to puzzlement when he saw her smile. "Why wouldn't we?"

"Because Mr. Jessup has asked us to go with him to America, and I would rather do that, I think."

"You *think*?" Rafe murmured.

Jamie glanced from his mother to Rafe. He looked like he wanted to believe, but wasn't sure if he dared. "Forever?"

"We might come back for a visit someday, but yes . . . forever. Mr. Jessup has asked me to marry him, you see."

The hazel eyes went wide.

Thinking the boy might need reassurance, Rafe went down on one knee so his eyes were almost at the same level as Jamie's. "But as pretty as she is," he said in a solemn tone, "and as much as I love her—and you—I won't marry her unless you approve and say you'll come to America with us."

That wasn't entirely true. No matter what the boy said, Rafe had no intention of letting Josie get away from him, or of leaving either of them behind. He'd prefer Jamie's cooperation, of course. But if he didn't get it . . . well, he had already been accused of poaching; kidnapping wasn't much worse.

He needn't have worried. With a shouted *"Yes!"* the boy threw himself against his chest as he had in the Cathcart stable when he'd been worried about losing Blaze. Only this time, Rafe was the one with tears in his eyes.

After a moment, Jamie pulled back to look into his face. "If you marry her, will I be your son?"

"Yes."

"Will I still be called a bastard?"

Unable to answer for the knot in his throat, Rafe shook his head. He would make sure that word was never spoken to the boy again.

"Can Blaze come with us?"

"He's already on the ship." Another choking hug. Before he let the boy go, Rafe whispered in his ear, "But you have to promise me that you'll never bet on horse races again. Gambling can ruin a man." Feeling the boy stiffen, he added, "I won't tell your mother about it. But I'm curious. What did you wager?"

"Your cowboy kerchief against a chipped knife that Lord

Brantley's grandson has," Jamie whispered. "But you mustn't worry. Pems will win your kerchief back."

By nine o'clock, people were coming down from the house. Hours before, an early breakfast had been served in tents set up on the front lawn near the starting point, and now the guests were coming to the stable for a last look at the horses on which they had bet so heavily.

As tradition dictated, each rider wore the colors of his horse's stable. Cathcart had sent down an altered jacket for Rafe in the deep brown worn by his grooms, a pair of buckskin trousers that were a bit snug, a crisp white shirt, a necktie, and a hat, which Rafe didn't even try on. The other riders wore jackets in green, blue, gold, scarlet, black, and a gold-trimmed gray for Brantley's man that looked disturbing similar to a Confederate uniform.

Leaning against the aisle wall beside the stall where Pems waited, Rafe studied the horses that had already been brought out of their stalls, and the riders standing with them, receiving last-minute instructions from their employers. He hoped Cathcart wouldn't try to offer any advice to him. The man knew as much about horses as Rafe knew about coal mining.

The owners seemed an amiable bunch, their high spirits heightened by several glasses of champagne at breakfast. Rafe could almost smell the greed in the air.

The riders seemed capable and friendly enough, except for the man wearing the gold jacket. Several times, Rafe had caught him staring his way as he quietly conversed with his horse's owner. Both men had hard, cruel faces—the rider, even more so. His horse was a tall, long-legged sorrel with a nervous eye. Rafe noted the horse didn't like anyone approaching from behind, a sure sign of a kicker. He would take care to keep Pems well out of range of those back hooves.

The rider in green was very young, and carried a hint of desperation in his eyes. Probably his first race. His bay was equally green and restive, although Rafe couldn't tell whether the nervousness originated in the horse or the boy. They wouldn't be a threat unless they inadvertently got in the way.

Brantley's gray—the favorite—was a fine, sturdy gelding

with a relaxed demeanor and the look of experience about him. Rafe guessed he was a bit past his prime, but in a race like this, experience would account for more than speed, except in the final sprint. Ash told him the gray had won the last two races here, so he was doubtless familiar with the countryside. A huge advantage over the other horses. Rafe decided he would position the stallion close behind him, figuring the gray would approach the jumps and hazards in a calm manner, which might help keep Pembroke calm, too.

The rest of the riders seemed confident and experienced. Good horsemen, with respect for their mounts. Competitors, yet not destructive about it.

But he would have to keep an eye on the nervous sorrel with the hard-eyed rider. Especially after he saw the horse's owner slip a long thin object that looked more like a cane than a whip under the stirrup flap of his saddle.

"That isna good." Ash stepped to Rafe's side, his gaze narrowed on the rider in gold. "That's no' a normal whip. 'Tis more like a cane with a blade hidden inside. In rough terrain like this, a knife slash might no' look so verra different from a cut caused by a protruding rock or tree limb."

"I doubt he would dare such a thing. Nor would Brantley allow it." From what Rafe had seen of their host, Lord Brantley seemed a fair-minded, honorable man, not a fellow easily drawn into underhanded dealings. Rafe liked him.

"Perhaps he doesna know. I should tell him."

Rafe shook his head. "We could be wrong. Don't worry. I'll watch him."

"So you should. Where's Pems?"

"In his stall. Thomas is saddling him. I saw no need to get him agitated by all the gawkers wandering about."

"Good lad." The Scotsman looked around, then added in a lower voice, "The wager book is closed. By the look of it, you'll win a great deal when Pems finishes first. The lass, as well."

Rafe was surprised. "Josie placed a bet?"

"Aye. On Pems to win."

Rafe smiled, touched by her faith in him. Now, he was even more determined to win. "When will the payout be?"

"Soon after the race. Assuming you win, I'll put yours and the lass's earnings in one of the trunks in the Kirkwell carriage, and post extra guards for the ride to the docks. Since you and the heathen will be going with Hicks, and I'll be on horseback, the lass and bairn can ride in the carriage with the countess. Stevens and his wife, as well. Your baggage will go on the constable's cart with Pembroke's tack."

"How far to the port?" Rafe wanted to be out of this place as soon as he could. He had an odd, itchy feeling that until they were on the ship sailing out of the harbor, something could still go wrong.

"About eight miles. They'll be loading my horses soon. If we arrive before the tide turns, you can be away by late afternoon."

"I hope so." After a lifetime of wandering, Rafe was ready to settle down.

Pushing away from the wall, he followed Ash out the back door of the stable to check the sky one last time. Clouds were moving in, but weren't threatening rain yet. The breeze was calm, the ground moist but not muddy. Good conditions for a run.

"Because the freighter taking you and the horses is an older design," Ash went on, finalizing the plans they had discussed earlier about the trip to America, "it will travel slower than the *Oceanic* did. But you should still arrive in Boston within two weeks. My American banker will meet you at the docks with railroad vouchers and extra men to help unload the horses and take them to the stable, where they can rest for several days before boarding the train."

"How long will the rail part of the trip take?" Rafe wanted the horses let out for exercise at least once every day, even if they had to take a later train. Earlier, Ash had provided a list of rail yards that included holding pens.

"With frequent stops, it might take several weeks to reach Heartbreak Creek. Longer, if you think the horses need more rest. I leave that to your discretion. The vouchers are open-ended, so you'll be able to load on and off whenever you feel the need. Thomas and Gordon and two more lads will ride in the drovers' car behind the stock car to assist with that. You and your bride will have a private compartment."

Rafe stopped and looked at him. "Bride?"

Ash's grin spoke of mischief. "The captain of the freighter is a canny Scot and a friend. At my request, he'll be marrying the two of you the night you board. With the bairn there, you'll want to set a proper tone, so you will." His grin broadened. "Unless, of course, you'd rather wait until you reach Colorado?"

After the previous night, Rafe had no intention of waiting another six weeks to make love to Josie again. "Will it be legal?"

Ash grinned and clapped his back. "Are you doubting me, lad?"

Not an answer, but Rafe didn't care. "Okay. We'll wed on the ship."

"Aye. I thought so. That's why I've arranged for a private berth on board both the ship and the train. The lad can share accommodations with Thomas."

"Thomas agreed to that?" Although the Cheyenne seemed to like Jamie, he was probably looking forward to time on his own for a change.

"Aye, after I promised him the foal of his choice out of the first birthing next spring. Think of it as my wedding gift to you."

Hearing the blast of a trumpet, they both turned to see people moving out of the stable toward the tents in front of the house.

"Time to get Pems, lad. The race starts in fifteen minutes."

And if everything went well, an hour from now, he and Josie would be collecting their winnings and heading with Jamie to the docks.

Josie and Jamie, the countess, Gordon and Henny crowded the stable aisleway, offering smiles and well wishes. Luckily, neither Cathcart nor the baron were there to dampen the festive atmosphere.

When Thomas led Pembroke out of his stall, Rafe smiled to see an eagle feather stuck in the stallion's dark mane. The Cheyenne had also woven half of Josie's blue sash into the braided loop. Apparently, Rafe was supposed to wear the other half around his neck and tucked beneath his brown jacket. Josie was happy to tie it for him.

"You both look magnificent," the countess said with a beaming smile, her hands resting on her rounded midriff.

Josie smiled, too, but Rafe could see the worry in her unusual eyes. "I'll be careful," he whispered in her ear. "I have grand plans for when we reach the ship."

That pretty blush tinted her cheeks. "So do I."

His imagination sparked, sending heat rushing through him.

"Mr. Rafe," Gordon called, limping into the stable.

Sending the others on to join the crowd by the starting ribbon in front of the house, he waited for the groom, Thomas standing nearby with Pems.

"I've already loaded Redstone's and your belongings onto the constable's cart," Stevens said, stopping beside him. His leg was healing well, but was obviously still painful.

"What about Josie and Jamie's luggage?" Rafe asked.

"They're tying it onto the Kirkwell carriage even now." Gordon hesitated, then added, "I think we should post a guard. Earlier, after I loaded the cart, I went back to add my and Henny's valises, and it looked as if someone had gone through your things."

"Only mine?"

"It seemed so."

Puzzled, Rafe nodded, wondering why anyone would search his trunk. It was probably nothing, but just to be safe, he suggested Gordon have Hicks move the cart close to the Kirkwell carriage. "Ask Ash's men to keep an eye on it."

"I will."

"Good man." Rafe appreciated Gordon's attitude. They would work well together. And it would mean a lot to Josie to have Henny nearby.

The groom left. He and Thomas and Pems continued toward the house. As they approached the horses waiting nervously by the ribbon, another trumpet call announced five minutes until the start.

Thomas gave Rafe a leg up onto the flat racing saddle, then showed him the straps. "Slip your boots into these if you start to slide." He pointed to the braid in Pembroke's mane. "This will allow you to hang off to one side if you need to."

Hoping it wouldn't come to that, Rafe nodded his thanks.

Thomas stepped back. "You will do well, *nesene*. You ride almost as good as a Cheyenne."

"Hell, who doesn't?" Grinning, Rafe put two fingers to the brim of the Stetson he wore despite English tradition, then nudged the stallion toward the other horses lining up at the ribbon.

The time had come to put all that training to the test.

# *Twenty-seven*

Rafe took a position on the outside, two horses down from Brantley's gray. The young rider in green was in the center, flanked by two experienced riders, and the nervous sorrel with the gold-liveried rider was at the other end of the line by a man in blue on an older gelding.

The ribbon fell.

With a cheer from the onlookers, the horses lunged forward, dirt and grass flying from their hooves.

Rafe didn't push Pems, but let him move into the third position, two lengths back from the gray.

The boy raced into the lead, pushing too hard off the start. His horse would be winded long before he reached the final sprint. Following the yellow flags that marked the course, the boy raced into a lane beside the entry gates and came into the first jump too fast. Luckily it was a low fence, but still, his bay balked, almost unseating his rider. As the other horses surged around him, the animal collected himself and went at the jump again and made it.

Pembroke cleared it easily and continued at a relaxed gallop.

After the first mile, and three more easy jumps, the field began to string out. The horse in front of Pems tired and fell back. At the fifth jump—a low rock wall—Pems passed him and settled in behind the gray. The rider in gold kept pace at the far side of the rough lane, his attention divided between the course, Pems, and Brantley's gray.

The sixth obstacle was a narrow stream with a steep down-ward approach. Rafe edged Pems to the outside and left of the gray, but close enough to see the other horse take the jump.

Out of fear, Pems overreached, clearing the water by several yards and coming down hard, but he recovered quickly and charged up the opposite slope on the heels of Brantley's horse.

The course funneled into a narrow draw. The gold rider angled his sorrel toward Pems, then shied away when the boy in green surged up between them. Two other horses crowded behind Pems and he lurched forward until Rafe brought him back down to a steady gallop. He settled, still moving well, his neck slick with sweat, but not yet foamy, his wind holding.

Over a rail fence and another rock wall, then they whipped past the halfway flag, hoofbeats rolling like thunder, dirt clods flying as the draw opened into a wide field. Several riders sent their horses racing ahead, vying for the lead position. But Rafe held Pembroke back, remembering from his reconnoiter with Ash that the next jump had a lower landing side than the takeoff side, and needed to be approached cautiously.

When the lead horses bunched up, Brantley's rider reined his horse to the left to avoid the tangle. Rafe followed, clearing the ninth obstacle a pace behind the gray. As they headed into the tenth jump—another water hazard—the boy was in the lead again, then the gray, with Pembroke a close third. The gold rider stayed in the trees on the right side of the course.

Pems refused to cross the water. If Rafe hadn't expected the balk and locked his feet under the straps Thomas had added to the saddle, he might have come off. Without letting the stallion think about it, he brought him around and sent him forward again. This time he made it.

Grinning, Rafe leaned forward to praise him, then flinched when something slammed across his back. Gasping in pain, he twisted to see the gold rider swinging his cane whip at him a second time.

He ducked to the side. The whip whistled past, narrowly missing his head and knocking his Stetson into the brush.

Reining Pems hard into the sorrel, Rafe kicked out, catching the gold rider in the hip and almost driving him out of the saddle.

The horse veered away.

Pems raced ahead.

Teeth clenched against the throbbing in his back, Rafe hunched low, alert and ready, knowing the gold rider would try again.

The next jump came up before they were ready. Two horses were close behind them, and rather than cause a collision by stopping Pems, Rafe bent low over the stallion's neck and let him go.

Huge muscles bunched beneath him as the horse lunged up and over the wide tangle of downed trees. His back hooves clipped the last log when he came down, but he didn't stumble. The two horses behind them did, then the rider in blue plowed into them and they all went down.

Four racers left. The gray had taken the lead from the boy, then Pems, with the bastard on the sorrel a close fourth.

An easy jump, then another open stretch.

Rafe stroked the stallion's neck to settle his nerves. The biggest test was coming up around the next turn . . . the river.

Remembering that on the approach there was a two-foot drop down to the water, Rafe slowed the stallion in the turn so he could see it coming. Instead, they almost crashed into the boy on the bay, who was fighting the bit and dancing tight circles along the bank's edge.

"Move," Rafe ordered the boy.

The young rider gaped at him, his eyes round with fear. "I can't swim."

"Your horse can. Let him do the work." Pems hopped and twisted. Rafe could sense his fear building.

Halfway across, where the river had cut a narrow, deep channel, Brantley's gray sank until only his head and part of his neck rose out of the sluggish water. Head bobbing, he began to swim across the current.

The man in gold raced past and sent his horse into the water.

"Jump or move!" Rafe shouted at the boy. "You're blocking my horse."

"What if I fall off?"

"Hold on to his mane. Stay off his head and away from his legs. Now get out of the damned way!"

Pems shoved past and, at Rafe's kick, leaped down into the shallow water. He tried to turn back. Rafe urged him on, water splashing up from the churning hooves, dampening his boots and trousers.

Rafe heard a splash behind him as the boy sent his bay into the water.

Pems was starting to panic. Reaching down, Rafe gripped the crest of his neck, squeezing hard to remind him to drop his head and think.

The stallion struggled on.

Then the bottom dropped from beneath his hooves.

Rafe leaned forward, letting his body float partially out of the saddle, one hand clutching the loop Thomas had braided into the stallion's mane, the other gripping the horse's neck. He spoke into the animal's ear, keeping his voice calm, his tone relaxed. "You can do this, boy. Just a few more feet. I'm here with you. You're almost there."

Downstream, the gold rider's sorrel struggled out of the river and up the muddy bank. Soon he was racing after the gray into the trees.

The stallion's breathing was a hoarse rasp. The muscles in his shoulders pumped too fast, fueled by fear.

Rafe kept talking, trying to reach through the panic, then felt a jarring bump when the stallion's front hoofs hit bottom again. Sinking back into the saddle, he let go of the loop and gathered the reins.

Pems lurched forward, hind legs digging for purchase, front legs slipping on the muddy bank. With a final lunge, he scrambled onto solid ground, then stood shaking, his sides heaving.

The bay clambered up the bank behind them, so winded his head hung and every breath sounded like a raspy cough.

No sign of the boy.

*Hell.*

Rafe looked back and saw him bobbing in the current, arms beating the water. With a curse, he rode downstream, tracking the young rider.

The boy grabbed frantically at a passing shrub, but the current pulled him back into the deeper channel. Rafe jumped off Pems, looped his reins over a downed log, and leaped, boots first, into the water.

When he reached the deep channel, the boy sank, rose coughing, then sank again. Reaching down into the murky water, Rafe grabbed a handful of hair and yanked him back to the surface.

"Don't fight me," he shouted, batting away the flailing arms.

After what seemed an endless struggle against the current, he felt firm ground beneath his boots. He dragged the boy up onto the bank and dropped to his knees beside him, his lungs on fire as he gasped for air.

After a moment, the boy stopped coughing and sat up.

Rafe struggled to his feet and staggered over to where he'd left Pems. "If I find your horse," he called back, "I'll tie him by the trail."

He was relieved to see the stallion had relaxed enough to eat snatches of grass poking up around the log where he was tied. The bay stood nearby, still trembling and breathing hard. Rafe quickly tied him.

After making sure the stallion's girth was secure and tight, he vaulted into the saddle and raced down the trail marked with yellow flags.

Precious time had been lost. But the field was down to three horses now and only two jumps left before the long final sprint. If they could make up half the distance they had lost by the time they reached the straight run, Pems might still have a chance.

The first jump posed no problem. Pems was calming down again, his stride losing the jerkiness of panic and settling into a smooth, fluid rhythm. The last obstacle was trickier because of its height, but at Rafe's signal, the stallion collected, then lifted off, clearing it without difficulty. A bit of a hard landing, but he never broke stride.

Ahead was the home stretch. It was now or never.

Bending his knees so he could slip his boots into the higher straps Thomas had made, Rafe crouched above the saddle, shifting his weight off the stallion's back and distributing it evenly along his sides. In addition to anchoring Rafe more solidly to the horse, the straps also allowed him to bend low over the horse's neck, creating less of a wind barrier for the animal to overcome. A modified race rider's saddle. But since a hunt course was rougher terrain than a flat course, balance was more precarious, so Rafe held the reins in one hand, and slipped his other through the braided loop. Now safely anchored by the straps and the loop, he leaned over the stallion's neck and urged him to a faster pace.

The blow came out of nowhere, almost knocking him from

the saddle. Before he could recover, another blow hit him across the shoulders. He looked to the right to see the gold rider sliding a long, thin blade from his cane. His arm swung back. But instead of coming at Rafe, the blade swooped low, toward Pems.

Rafe struggled to turn the galloping stallion.

The tip of the blade caught the stallion's chest. Another swing narrowly missed the horse's face, but sliced into his neck.

Reaching down, Rafe frantically dug for the leather bat that Ash had slipped beneath the skirt. Yanking it free, he raised it just in time to deflect another swipe of the blade.

"You bastard! What are you doing?"

The sorrel veered in, close enough for Rafe to see the vicious grin on the rider's face as he drew his arm back again.

His boots still anchored in the straps, and holding on to the loop with his left hand, Rafe leaned as far toward the other horse as he could. With all his strength, he whipped the flat side of the leather bat across the gold rider's face.

With a cry, the man tipped to the side, barely hanging on as the sorrel bolted through the brush.

Pems ran on.

Rafe righted himself and looked back, but saw neither the sorrel nor his rider. But he didn't slow, knowing they were still out there somewhere.

He couldn't tell how badly Pembroke was hurt. Blood covered his neck, splattered Rafe's trousers and jacket. He couldn't see the cut on his chest, but the stallion wasn't limping. The gash in his neck was bleeding badly, but not spurting as it would have if an artery had been cut. Rather than pulling Pems in and giving the gold rider another try at him, Rafe let him run.

The gray was closer now, clearly visible through the trees.

They still had a chance.

Sound dimmed. Vision narrowed to the light at the end of the trees where pennants atop the tents fluttered in the morning sun. They inched nearer to Brantley's horse. Dirt kicked up by the gray's hooves pelted Rafe's face.

Pems stretched out, his muscles bunching and reaching in long, churning strides. Wind whipped through Rafe's sweat-and-blood-dampened hair. He could almost reach out and touch the gray's haunches. Then his rider. With every stride, the gap narrowed. He could hear the gray's breathing, the shouts of his rider urging him on. Flecks of foamy sweat flew back into Rafe's face.

Above the pounding hooves, he heard the shouting of the crowd grow louder. They were almost there. Nearly blinded by the sudden glare of bright sunlight, they burst out of the trees.

Nose to nose now. Necks straining. Ahead, the ribbon stretched above the grass like a flat yellow snake.

"Go!" Rafe shouted over the screams of the crowd.

Pems dug in and, a second later, bounded past the watchers.

It was over. Done. The sudden release of tension was so great Rafe's arms shook as he gradually pulled Pems back to a lope, then a trot, and finally to a walk. The shouts of the crowd grew dim. Movement slowed. Panting, he sagged in the saddle, his body shaking.

"You did it, boy," he murmured to the spent horse. "Everything I asked."

Dimly, he heard the hoofbeats of an approaching horse. Whirling, he saw Brantley's rider coming toward him.

"Excellent run," the man said, stopping the winded gray a few feet away. "Outstanding horse." His affable expression changed to horror when he saw the blood. "Good God, man! What happened?"

Fury made Rafe's voice shake. "The gold rider had a blade in his whip."

"A blade? He cut your horse?"

Rafe nodded, too enraged to speak. His body trembling again but for a different reason, he turned Pems back toward the tents. He would kill the bastard. Break his neck. Snap his bones with his bare hands.

Thomas met him before he reached the crowd, Ash close on his heels, Gordon limping behind. Rafe slid down. "Take Pems to his stall," he told Thomas. "And Josie, too." He didn't want her to see what he was about to do. "Gordon, see if Brantley has a horse doctor. If so, send him to the stable as soon as you can."

"What the bluidy hell happened?" Ash demanded.

"The bastard cut him." Rafe shoved past the Scotsman and charged toward the sorrel just crossing the ribbon. Without a word, he yanked the rider from the saddle and slammed his fist into his face. A crunch as teeth broke. "You son of a bitch!"

Another swing, another crunch as the nose flattened beneath Rafe's knuckles. Before he could swing again, Ash and several other men pulled him back from the man bleeding on the ground.

Voices rose around him, but Rafe was still too furious to hear their words.

"I say! What's going on here?" Brantley shoved through the men gathered around Rafe and the gold rider.

"He has a blade in his whip," Rafe accused. "He cut my horse."

With the help of his employer, the gold rider struggled to his feet, blood streaming from his nose and mouth. Both eyes were almost swollen shut.

"What whip?" the horse's owner demanded. He pointed at Rafe. "He's the one who injured my man here. He hit him in the face with his bat, the bloody bounder!"

"Did your rider have a whip, Haverton?" Brantley demanded of the owner.

"Do you see one?" Haverton shot back.

Brantley directed two men to check the sorrel's saddle.

As Rafe had expected, they found nothing. "He probably threw it into the brush." Pulling his arms free of the restraining hands, he turned to Ash. "You saw it. Tell them."

"Did you see a blade, Lord Kirkwell?" Brantley asked.

"I saw a cane that probably held a blade."

"That's absurd," Haverton argued.

Brantley waved him to silence. "But did you actually see the blade, Lord Kirkwell?"

"I dinna need to. I ken it was there."

Haverton pointed an accusing finger at Rafe. "That man shouldn't have even been allowed to race. He's an accused criminal awaiting deportation and should be disqualified. He attacked my rider."

"That's a lie!"

All turned as the boy in green trotted his spent bay across the ribbon on the ground. "It were just the opposite." Reining in, he scowled at Haverton's rider. "I saw 'im do it, just a'fore he tossed this into the brush." Reaching under his saddle skirt, he pulled out the gold rider's cane and showed the blade hidden inside. "'E's the attacker. The man on the stallion saved me life, so 'e did."

And as quickly as it had turned against him, the mood of the crowd swung back in Rafe's favor.

He didn't care. Now that the fury had bled away, he just wanted to check on Pems. Without a word, he turned and strode stiffly toward the stable.

Ash fell in beside him. "Brantley sent down his horse doctor."

Rafe walked on, trying to ignore the muscles cramping in his back.

"The cuts dinna look that deep."

He hoped not. To have Pems needlessly hurt again just to amuse his owner sickened Rafe. It sickened him even more that, this time, he had had a part in it.

"By the way," Ash said as they entered the stable and hurried toward the small group of people gathered outside Pembroke's stall. "Congratulations."

Rafe looked at him.

"You won the race."

An hour later, feeling drained and shaken, Rafe led the bandaged stallion from his stall. The injuries weren't as bad as he had feared, and he knew horses could tolerate a lot of pain, but watching the animal suffer through the doctor's ministrations had been difficult to bear.

The cut on his neck wasn't dangerously deep but did require ten stitches. The one on his chest took three. Because the blade had been clean, and the wounds had bled freely, there was only a small chance of infection. Still, to be safe, Rafe intended to carefully follow the horse doctor's instructions: a flush with a mild saline solution, a topical salve, and a new bandage every day. When the wound healed, Rafe could cut out the stitches—maybe in a week or ten days.

Pems would be fine. But that didn't lessen Rafe's guilt that he had exposed the valiant, trusting horse to more injury. He could hardly look at Josie when he stepped into the aisle, aware of how miserably he had failed to protect her beloved horse. "I'm sorry."

She didn't say anything, but stepped forward and slipped her hand in his. That simple show of understanding was a balm to his aching heart.

"Can we leave now?" she asked.

He nodded, as eager to be on their way as she seemed to be. "Get Jamie and meet me at the Kirkwell carriage."

She gave his hand a squeeze, then hurried from the stable.

Lord Brantley, who had been talking to Ash and Thomas, turned to Rafe with a look of concern. "How is he?"

"He'll make it. Thank you for sending your doctor so quickly."

"A hellish thing. Puts a blight on the entire sport. Be assured Haverton will be blacklisted from ever racing again." Brantley sighed and shook his head. "Apparently the man bet heavily on his horse to take second, but you stood in the way. I would have brought his rider up on charges, but he's long gone." He held out a hand. "You have my apologies, Mr. Jessup. And my deepest regrets."

Rafe accepted the handshake and the apology. "I appreciate that." He didn't want to appear brusque, but he was anxious to get moving. "Thank you for your hospitality, but I'd best hurry if we're to sail today."

"Of course, of course." Brantley stepped back. "Safe travels, Mr. Jessup. On your way, then."

"On your way where?" Cathcart asked, walking toward them. "And where do you think you're going with my horse?"

Rafe frowned. Josephine's father showed none of the remorse or concern over Pembroke's injury that Brantley had exhibited—in fact, there was a glint of malice in his dark eyes. "What are you talking about, Cathcart?"

"I'm asking you what you're doing with my horse."

"He's not your horse."

"No?" With a look of innocent confusion, the older man pulled a fat leather pouch from his pocket. "Then why did Lord Brantley present me with these winnings as the horse's owner?"

"Because that was our arrangement."

"Arrangement?" Brantley stepped forward. "Is there an issue here? The horse doesn't belong to you, Mr. Cathcart?"

"Not since noon today," Rafe snapped, never taking his eyes from Josie's father. "And I have the Bill of Sale to prove it."

"Excellent." Spreading his hands in invitation, Cathcart looked innocently at the other men watching the exchange. "Then by all means, produce it."

# *Twenty-eight*

R afe felt a chill in his gut.

Had Cathcart stolen the Bill of Sale? Was he the one who had gone through his trunk earlier that morning? Was that why he looked so pleased with himself?

A bitter taste rose on his tongue. "It was witnessed by Hammersmith, your own head groom. And Gordon Stevens, as well. Even if the bill is lost—or *stolen*," he added, glaring menacingly at Cathcart, "they can vouch for it."

"This is most confusing." Brantley frowned from Rafe to Cathcart. "I'm afraid, Mr. Cathcart, that until this matter is resolved, I'll have to rescind my offer on the stallion."

Rafe swung toward him. "He tried to sell you the horse? But Pembroke isn't his!" Whipping back to Josie's father, he tried to keep the panic from his voice. "You signed the Bill of Sale over a month ago!"

"Prove it."

Rafe started toward him.

Ash's hand fell on his arm, his green eyes carrying a silent warning. "Here comes Stevens. Let him verify that he witnessed the sale."

Seeing the smug smile on Cathcart's face, Rafe knew the worst had happened. The Bill was gone. He stood shaking, his mind churning with fury.

"Stevens," Ash said as Gordon limped up. "Did you witness

a document drawn up between Mr. Cathcart and Mr. Jessup, concerning ownership of Pembroke's Pride?"

Gordon shifted his weight off his bad leg. "I think so, milord."

"You *think*?" Cathcart laughed, playing to the onlookers.

Brantley ignored him. "Did you, or did you not, witness the signing of the document?"

"I had just broken my leg, sir. I was taking laudanum. Things were a bit muddled at the time." The beleaguered groom shot Rafe an apologetic look. "I'm fairly sure I did."

Cathcart sneered. "*Fairly* certain is not the same as *absolutely* certain."

"What about the other witness?" Brantley asked. "Hammersmith, I believe you called him."

"He's at the docks," Ash said, "loading my horses for transport." He turned back to Gordon. "Where is Jessup's trunk? Perhaps the document is in there."

"On the cart. But . . ." Another worried look at Rafe. "This morning before the race, it seems someone went through Mr. Jessup's things. That's why I'm late. I was checking with Lord Kirkwell's grooms to see if they had seen anyone loitering about during the race."

"And had they?" Brantley pressed.

"No, milord."

Cathcart grinned nastily. "There you have it then. No Bill of Sale. No reliable witnesses. Just the word of a felon against an upstanding English businessman."

Rafe glowered at him. Maybe they had missed it. Maybe they didn't know he'd slipped it in the back of the tablet. He asked Gordon if he'd seen a tablet when he'd packed his belongings. "It would have been on the bookshelf by my cot. 'Thomas's Story' was written on the front page."

Gordon shook his head. "I couldn't go up into the loft because of my leg. The master sent one of the footmen to pack your belongings."

A footman. With loyalty to his employer, not a banished wrangler. Rafe would have hit something, if not for the muscles clenching into knots in his back. He couldn't let Pems go back to Cathcart. It would be the horse's death warrant if he did. Rafe would put a bullet in Pembroke's brain before he'd let Cathcart abuse him again.

"Bollocks," Ash muttered. "It must be somewhere."

"If it even exists." Cathcart's smile broadened. Greed flashed in his dark, feral eyes.

"If what exists?" Josie came up, caught sight of Rafe, and her smile died. "What's happened?" she asked, looking at the faces of the men crowded around the stallion in the stable aisleway. "Is it Pems? Has he taken a turn?"

Rafe couldn't answer. Couldn't even look at her.

A flush darkened Lord Brantley's face. It was obvious he wished himself anywhere but caught in the middle of this mess. "There seems to be confusion about ownership of the horse," he said when no one else responded to her question. "A missing Bill of Sale."

"Missing?" Shock flared into anger. She glared at Cathcart. "What have you done, Father?"

"I've done nothing, girl. Go back to the house. This doesn't concern you."

"But I—"

"Now, daughter!"

Rafe stepped toward Cathcart, hands fisted.

Ash pulled him back as Josie fled the stable. "Dinna make it worse, lad."

Worse? The worst had already happened.

The argument continued around him, but Rafe couldn't hear anything over the buzzing in his head. Gone. Josie. Pems. Everything. He'd been played like a fool.

"Stevens," Ash prodded, "are you verra certain you dinna remember signing the paper as witness?"

"What do you expect him to say?" Cathcart broke in before Gordon could answer. "Stevens is now in Jessup's employ. Of course he'll back his employer if pushed hard enough. It means nothing unless we have the bill in hand. Which can't be found—*if* it ever existed." He turned to Brantley and the other men standing around them, as well as those who had wandered in from outside when word of an altercation had spread. "The horse is mine."

Thomas stepped forward, but Ash stopped him and murmured something into his ear. The object of this discussion stood quietly, head drooping as if he knew the future that awaited him with Cathcart.

Rafe wouldn't let that happen. "Send for Hammersmith," he said in desperation.

"Give it up, Jessup," Cathcart jeered. "You've been caught. Someone send for the magistrate."

Whispers swirled in the still air. Men who had congratulated Rafe only a short while ago now avoided his eyes. Several of the owners didn't bother to hide their disgust. Titled men. Protected by wealth and privilege. Affronted that a foreigner would cause a ruckus in their elite company. Even Lord Brantley began to edge away, apparently fearing condemnation by association.

Rafe's back spasms escalated, making it hard to take a breath, hard to concentrate. Cathcart had well and truly boxed him in. As long as Rafe couldn't produce the Bill of Sale, it was his word against Cathcart's. And Cathcart had the right of it: who would believe a common wrangler—an American already accused of poaching and facing deportation—over a presumably wealthy English businessman?

"I will fix this, Rayford Jessup," Thomas murmured beside him.

"How?"

Despite the thin smile, savagery showed in the Cheyenne's dark eyes.

"No, Thomas. We're already in enough trouble."

"You will let him take your horse?"

"I'll think of something." But Rafe didn't know what. He could hardly even think, much less come up with a coherent plan.

Hicks elbowed his way through the murmuring crowd of men still filling the aisleway. "Ready to go, fellows?" he asked in a low voice, eyeing the finely dressed men standing around. "I told the Constable I'd get you aboard ship this afternoon." When neither Rafe nor Thomas made a move, he leaned closer to add, "Do I need the manacles?"

Too stunned to argue, Rafe told Gordon to put Pembroke back in his stall. "Maybe something will come up before we leave." He could send for Hammersmith. Try to buy Pems from Brantley. He had to do something.

A high-pitched voice rose above the low male chatter. "Excuse me. Step aside, please."

Turning stiffly, he saw Josie push her way into the tight circle around Pembroke. Shame twisted in his chest. He had failed her. How would she ever forgive him for losing her horse? How could he forgive himself?

She shoved a piece of paper into Lord Brantley's hands. "Is this what you're looking for?"

Rafe froze, his heart drumming. Had she found it?

Brantley studied the paper. His frown deepened. "What is this, Cathcart?"

"It's a Bill of Sale," Josie cut in before her father could respond. "Conferring ownership of the stallion listed as Pembroke's Pride to Rayford Jessup. Stevens?" She motioned Gordon closer. "Is this your signature?"

The groom limped over and studied the paper. "It's a bit wobbly, but that's my mark. Hammersmith's, too."

Rafe's legs started shaking. He saw Josie's smile of triumph and felt the knot of fear in his throat loosen.

"Well, there you have it then, lads." Ash clapped Brantley's back—the only man there who dared such familiarity, since they were of equal rank. "A foolish mix-up." He swung his gaze to Cathcart, his smile spreading into a menacing show of teeth. "Right, Cathcart?"

When Josie's father tried to stammer an excuse, Ash waved his words away. "I understand, Horatio," he said in a robust voice. "As a man ages, he verra often forgets events of a week past, so he does. No ill intent, I'm sure. No doubt it will happen to all of us someday, right, fellows?"

Strained smiles. Nods of sympathy.

Cathcart's face paled. His darting gaze scanned the faces around him.

Rafe waited to see if he would accept Ash's insulting explanation, or try to bluster his way out of the fix he'd gotten himself into. Whichever tack he took, he would look the fool. Harsh punishment for such a prideful man.

"Just so," Cathcart finally mumbled, wiping a hand over his sweating brow. "A mistake. Completely forgot. Been in such a rush these last few days . . ."

But men were already wandering away, glad to separate themselves from the taint of either attempted theft, or advancing senility. Cathcart was ruined either way.

"Carry on, then." With forced joviality, Lord Brantley thrust the Bill of Sale at Rafe. "Sorry about this, Jessup. Dashed embarrassing." Leaning forward, he added, "We'll have to keep an eye on him, what?" He straightened and offered Rafe his hand. "Excellent ride today, my good man. Excellent horse. Would have made a wonderful addition to my stable."

"Thank you, sir. Now if you'll excuse us."

"Quite. Safe voyage and all that. Off you go, then."

Rafe handed Pembroke's lead to Gordon, hoping the groom didn't see the tremble in his hand. "Tie him to the back of Kirkwell's carriage. We'll be in the constable's wagon behind you, so I can keep an eye on him." He followed Thomas and Hicks out of the stable, half-afraid his legs wouldn't hold him.

He'd won. It was over. Pems was safe.

A slim hand slid into the crook of his arm. Sudden emotion clogged his throat. Josie didn't speak. Didn't offer excuses or platitudes or words of comfort. Just walked beside him. God love her.

"How did you find it?" he asked after he'd gotten himself in hand.

"I snooped in your room after the constable took you away."

At his curious look, she smiled sheepishly. "I wanted a memento. Something to cling to until you returned. I found the Bill of Sale in the tablet, and knowing it was too valuable to leave lying about for sticky fingers to find, I decided to keep it safe for you."

His chest swelled with pride. "You can cross the river with me any day, sweetheart." Seeing her puzzlement, he added, "That's a cowboy expression. It means I know you'll always have my back, even when I make foolish mistakes and disappoint you and cause you worry. It means I trust you. And love you."

"Oh?" That impish smile. "Do cowboys say that often to one another?"

He gave a wobbly laugh. "Only if they're smitten."

When they reached the wagons that would take them to the docks, she pulled back. Looking up into his face with a tremulous smile, she said, "I'm so sorry, Rafe, for what my father tried to do to you."

He took in a deep breath and let the anger go. He loved this woman too much to let her father's actions come between them. "I know."

"But he's still my father. And I need to tell him good-bye."

"But you'll come back?"

"Always."

Reaching out, he brushed his fingertips over her cheek,

needing the contact, wanting the goodness and strength of character within this remarkable woman to drive out the ugliness and pain of these last turbulent hours. "Want me to go with you?"

"No. You've suffered enough at his hands. But if your watchdog could wait a few minutes, you can get Jamie while I talk to Father. He's in Henny's room. It would be a great comfort to him to know that you and Pems are all right. Also," she added with a small frown, "he has a kerchief he wants to give you. I'm not sure what that's about."

Rafe smiled. "I'll get him. You do what you need to do."

After Josephine walked back to the stable to find her father, Rafe gripped the edge of the wagon with both hands as muscles tightened like a vise around his back. He'd suffered back pain before, after a fall from a horse. This was no worse. With rest, it would pass. All he had to do was get to the ship.

"Load up," Hicks said, climbing into the driver's box.

"I need a minute," Rafe said through clenched teeth.

"And I need to get home before the wife locks me out. She's a stubborn wench with an evil tongue, but a bloody fine cook. I'd hate to have to start over with someone else."

Ash pulled something out of his carriage and walked back toward the cart. "Would a wee bottle of Highland nectar make the delay worth your while, Private?" He held up a half-empty bottle of his famous brew.

Hicks's eyes lit up. "The whole bottle?"

"Whatever's left."

The guard smacked his lips. "Don't mind if I do."

Relieved, Rafe headed toward the house to get Jamie.

When Josephine went looking for her father, she saw that most of the crowd had dispersed and were now strolling toward the tents on the front lawn.

One figure walked alone. Father, head down, angling toward the terrace, the square set of his shoulders an indication of the anger and humiliation that still gripped him. She tried to be empathetic. But all she felt was anger at what he had tried to do to Rafe, and a building dread of this last confrontation in a lifelong troubled relationship.

Still, he was her father. She would probably never see him

after this day—in truth, she didn't want to see him again—but she did owe him a good-bye.

He was ruined now. Within a matter of days, all his possessions, collected over decades of hard work and unfettered ambition, would go on the auction block. He might even be sent to debtor's prison. A sad end for a man who had once had the vision and strength to claw his way out of the dark and into the light of a better life. How sad that he hadn't the courage or character to find contentment there.

Still, he was her father. And she wouldn't allow her anger at him to cast a pall over her new beginning with Rafe. She owed herself that.

His pace slowed as he went up the terrace steps. At the top, he paused, one hand braced on the stone railing, his head hanging.

"Father," she said, coming up the steps behind him.

He turned. His face was alarmingly pale and tears glinted in his reddened eyes. Pushing away from the railing, he straightened. "Come to gloat, have you, daughter?" he asked in a quavering voice.

He had once been the strength in her life. The indulger of her every whim. A mostly benign tyrant who had no one else in his life but a lost, motherless girl. Now he was the one who was lost—a broken, frightened man bolstered by the last remnants of angry pride.

"No, Father. I've come to tell you good-bye."

"Good-bye, then." He waved her away, head turned as if ashamed to show his weakness even in front of the daughter who knew all of his faults. "Don't worry about me. I crawled out of the black pits once, and I can do it again."

She doubted it. But that wasn't why she had come. "I wanted to give you this." She handed him her reticule, weighted again with the money she had received from her pawned jewels. She had no intention of giving him her winnings, but by rights, this money belonged to him. She didn't want to leave him completely without funds.

"What's this?" Spreading the drawstring, he peered inside. A look of shock came over his face. "Where did you get this?"

"From you."

"Me?"

"I sold all the jewelry you gave me. Now I give it back to you in the hope that it will keep you out of debtor's prison."

His mouth worked. He blinked hard.

Fearing some lingering shred of fatherly pride might force him to refuse her offering, she quickly added, "Please take it, Father. With my blessing. And my thanks for all you've done for me and Jamie."

He looked up, his face a mask of despair, not even bothering to hide the tears rolling down his cheeks. "I never meant to hurt you, Josephine. You must know that. But when I saw the way of it . . ."

"I understand, and I harbor no animosity toward you. I just wish . . ." She faltered, not sure what she wished. For things to be different? For him to be a more loving father, and for her to be a more deserving daughter? They had each done their best, but sometimes that wasn't enough. "I just wish you well, Father."

He gave a wobbly smile. "Perhaps we'll meet again in America."

"Perhaps." They stood in awkward silence for a moment. "Jamie will want to tell you good-bye. Shall I get him?"

"No." He swiped a trembling hand over his damp cheeks. "I don't want him to see me like this. You tell him good-bye for me."

"But—"

"Perhaps I'll come by the docks to see you off," he cut in. "It's not far from the train station. Now go." He pulled her into a rough hug—the first he'd given her in many a year—then abruptly let her go. "Take care of yourself, child."

"You, too, Father."

As she watched him walk away, she felt a surprising mix of emotions. Relief, regret, a deep sense of loss . . . not only because her father would no longer be a part of her life, but because the girl who had been his daughter, and who had worked so hard to please him, was gone forever, too.

But mostly she felt . . . free.

When she approached the servants' wing a few minutes later, she saw Rafe coming down the back staircase with Jamie in tow. Seeing her son's look of concern, and the stiff way Rafe held himself, she wondered if all was well. Then they spotted her, and bright smiles broke over their faces.

"Is Pems truly all right?" Jamie asked, rushing toward her.

"Yes, dearest. A bit banged up, but he'll be well soon."

"I saved an apple from breakfast. Do you think he'll like it?"

"I'm certain of it." As they walked toward the entry, Josephine glanced worriedly at Rafe over Jamie's blond head, saddened by the weary strain on his face. But it was over now. Nothing ahead but a bright, shining future and a new start for all three of them.

Jamie's steps slowed. He looked out the terrace doors. "What about him?"

Josephine looked over to see William standing with his hands tucked behind his back, staring down into the rose garden and two reflecting pools. He was dressed for travel, his fur-trimmed overcoat adding to his bulk, his top hat resting on the balustrade beside him.

Another sad, lonely man. Another life ruined by foolish choices.

On impulse, she bent down in front of her son. "Would you like to tell the baron good-bye?"

She watched him study the solitary figure, saw resistance in the small frown creasing his brows. Then he surprised her by nodding. "I suppose I should."

Motioning for Rafe to wait, she rose. Holding Jamie's small hand in her own, they stepped through the terrace doors. "Good afternoon, Baron Adderly."

With a start, he turned, saw Jamie, and gave a stiff smile. "Good afternoon. On your way to America, are you?"

"We are. But first, we wanted to say good-bye." Resting a hand on her son's shoulder, she gave a squeeze of encouragement.

"Good-bye, sir." Jamie held out his hand.

After a look of surprise, William took the small hand in his own, gave it a gentle shake then released it. "Good-bye, Jamie. I enjoyed meeting you. I know Neddy enjoyed meeting you, too."

"Perhaps I shall write to him. Do you think he would like that?"

"I'm sure he would."

A moment passed in awkward silence, then Jamie said, "Thank you for the horse, sir. I'm sorry I won't be able to take Thunder to America with me. Perhaps if I come back to visit someday, I'll be big enough to ride him."

"I'm certain you will be."

Another awkward pause. Then William cleared his throat and said, "I wish, Jamie, that I had done things differently. Come to see you sooner and spent more time with you. I regret that, and am sorry for it. Even so, I want you to know that I think you are a fine boy, and I shall always be proud to call you my son. And . . . and I hope you will not forget me."

"I shan't, sir."

Seeing the conversation had reached its end, Josephine nodded to Rafe. As he came forward, she gave Jamie's shoulder a pat. "Why don't you and Mr. Jessup go feed the swans? I shall only be a moment."

She and William watched them go down the steps toward the ponds, then William turned to her with a wistful smile. "Mr. Jessup is very good with him."

"Rafe is a kind and honorable man. He cares deeply for Jamie and will treat him well."

"I'm glad. I only wish . . ." The words trailed off on a deep sigh. "I did love you, you know. Had I been a different man . . . a better man . . . I would have done right by you, rather than bowing to my father's edicts."

"I know. I should have made wiser decisions, as well. But how could I resist?" she added, smiling sadly at the memory. "You were quite the grandest thing that had ever come into my sixteen-year-old life."

"So you don't hate me?"

"Admittedly, I did for a time. But no longer. We are vastly different people now, William, and it avails us nothing to cling to the past."

"Quite." He nodded and looked away, regret still showing in his eyes.

For some reason she didn't fully understand, even after all the pain this man had once caused her, she didn't want to part from him in bitterness. Perhaps because she was the one walking away the better person. No regrets. No remorse. She had Jamie, and Rafe, and a new life awaiting her, and all he had was an empty title, a lonely future, and a dying son.

"William, I know this has not ended as you'd hoped. But you must put that aside and think of Neddy now. He needs his father. Save for you, he has no one to turn to in the difficult trials ahead. I urge you to enjoy the time you have left together, rather than spending precious energy worrying about the barony. Take him to a warmer clime. See other doctors. Medical advances are made every day. Don't give up on him yet. Or on yourself."

For a long time, he didn't speak, but watched the man and the boy down at the pond, trying to lure the birds to the bank. Jamie's childish laughter drifted up to them as a swan rose partway out of the water, flapping its great wings. William sighed and turned to her with that wistful smile again. "You're correct, of course. I fear I've been blinded by duty. Hurt so many for the sake of a title."

"It's not too late to change."

"I hope that's true." He took her hand in his. "Thank you, Josephine. For your understanding. For your kindness toward Neddy." His gaze returned to Jamie, one arm across the shoulder of the man hunkered on his heels by his side, their blond heads catching the late afternoon sun. "And for your gentle care of Jamie. You have done well with him."

"He's a fine boy." Pride and love swelled within her, so intense it brought a sting to her eyes. "I think he will be a good man someday."

"I have no doubt of it." Releasing her hand, he brushed back his thinning hair and picked up his hat. "Well . . ." His gaze sought Jamie again. "Tell Mr. Jessup . . ."

She saw him falter and wondered how difficult it must be for a father to put his son in the care of another. To never see him again. To know that another man would raise his child—nurture and protect him and teach him all the things a father teaches a son.

A precious gift put in a stranger's hands.

She doubted she would have had the strength to do it.

On impulse, she reached out and rested her fingers on his arm. "If it's any comfort to you, William, know that Jamie will be dearly loved. And someday, somewhere in this world there will be a fine, strong man with Adderly blood in his veins, who will carry the best of both of us within his heart."

Tears formed in his eyes. "Thank you for that, Josephine. You're a forgiving woman." With a nod, he donned his hat, turned, and walked away, the sag in his shoulders making him look a good bit older than his thirty-some years.

# Twenty-nine

The Liverpool docks were only eight miles away, but it took them well over two hours because of Pembroke. Rafe didn't want to push him too hard.

Besides, with his back a mass of cramping muscles, the less jarring he suffered in the unsprung cart, the better. By the time they arrived at the pier, the Kirkwell horses were already aboard and seamen were loading the last of their provisions onto the ship.

After saying their good-byes, Thomas took Pems up the lower gangplank into the hold where the other horses were already penned, and Gordon and Henny took Jamie up the gangplank to the upper deck where a uniformed sailor stood ready to greet them and show them to their quarters.

Moving stiffly, Rafe rummaged through his trunk in the back of the constable's cart, collected the tablet, then stepped back so the sailors could carry the trunk aboard. Sending Hicks on his way—wearing a nice flush and a happily befuddled look on his stubbled face—Rafe joined the countess and Josie, who were watching Ash bark orders at the men loading his carriage and team onto his channel freighter for the trip back to Scotland.

"He does so love ordering others about," the countess mused, smiling fondly at her shouting husband.

"But not you," Josie guessed.

"Not usually. Although sometimes . . . but never mind that. Ready to go, Rayford?"

Guessing the nature of the orders Ash gave his countess, Rafe bit back a smile. "I am. But I wanted to ask a favor before we board." He handed over the dog-eared tablet. "This is Thomas's story. Could you please see that your publisher gets this? It's not finished, and I know it's not what Chesterfield expects, but I think it's good. If he likes it, we can send the rest after we reach Heartbreak Creek."

"I'm sure it's wonderful. I shall see that he gets it right away."

After carefully tucking the tablet into the traveling case at her feet, she studied the two of them with tear-bright eyes. "I wish I could photograph you just as you are. But Ash won't let me near my emulsion chemicals. He's afraid I'll blow everyone up. Understandable, I suppose, considering his past military experiences." She paused to dab gloved fingertips at her leaking eyes. "Do tell Luce and Tait and the Brodies and Audra and Ethan . . ." Her voice broke. Reaching out, she gripped each of their hands with surprising strength. "Tell them I miss them terribly and hope to see them soon."

"We will," Josephine said in a quavering voice.

Rafe nodded and, fearing they would both burst into tears, quickly added, "And you'll send word when the prince arrives?"

"Viscount." Releasing their hands, Maddie dabbed at her eyes again. "I'm sure Ash will be crowing it from the rooftops. I just pray he doesn't have him swinging a toy claymore and fitted for pipes before he leaves the cradle."

No one mentioned the possibility that the child would be a girl.

Thomas suddenly appeared, startling the three of them. He handed the countess a crumpled envelope. "You will send this to Prudence Lincoln."

"Of course. But aren't you seeing her on your way through Indiana?"

"Yes. But we will travel slow and this must reach her before I do. You will see that it does."

Tucking the envelope into her coat pocket, Lady Kirkwell nodded. "I will."

Thomas never requested or asked. He instructed. Rafe hadn't

been able to break him of that habit, nor was he sure he should. That unwavering confidence was part of who the Cheyenne was.

Maddie was pulling a parcel from the case at her feet when Ash walked up. After issuing last-minute instructions to Thomas about the horses, the Cheyenne nodded, gave a long, meaningful look to the countess, then without a word, turned and went back to the freighter.

Picking up the case, Ash slipped an arm around his wife's shoulders. "Come along, lass. The tide is turning, and if we're to see Scotland before the first snows, we'd best leave now." It was obvious to Rafe that the Scot was anxious to get back to his beloved Highlands.

Maddie gave Josie one last hug, then pressed the parcel into her hands. "For your wedding. I wish we could be there, but hopefully these will bring you luck."

New tears filled Josie's eyes. Rafe had never seen so much crying over a simple good-bye. "Thank you both for all you've done for Jamie and me."

"You're part of our Heartbreak Creek family now."

"Aye. So prepare yourself, lass, for the welcome you'll receive from the rest of the family when you arrive in Colorado." He grinned at Rafe.

Rafe grinned back. Josie had no idea what awaited her.

"I shall write to them of your arrival," Maddie promised.

"All aboard that's coming aboard," a gruff voice called as sailors rushed from one bollard to the next, loosening the mooring lines that anchored the tall oceangoing steamer to the pier.

Fearing more tearful good-byes, Rafe urged Josie up the gangplank just as the ship's steam whistle pierced the salty air. Henny and Gordon and Jamie joined them on deck to watch the ship drift away from the pier.

"Look!" Jamie cried, waving wildly. "It's Grandfather! See him waving? He came to see us off, Mother. I knew he would."

Rafe saw the tears in Josie's eyes, and took her hand in his. "Maybe he'll come see us in Colorado," he offered halfheartedly.

"Oh, I pray not," Josie murmured, lifting a hand in farewell. "You would be at each other's throats in a week."

Rafe couldn't argue the truth of that.

Knowing this would be a difficult parting for Josie, he stood with her at the rail, watching the lights of Liverpool dim. By the time the dark silhouette of England and then the green shores of Ireland faded into mist, the captain, a Scot named Andrew Stewart, came to welcome them aboard.

"Lord Kirkwell said I was to perform a marriage ceremony."

"You're licensed to do that?" Rafe had to ask. Ash might be honorable, but he was also slippery.

A twinkle came into the Scot's eyes. "Aye. Since I'm also an ordained Presbyterian minister. Kirkwell dinna tell you?"

"He forgot to mention it." Relieved, Rafe suggested later in the evening after dinner for the ceremony.

Captain Stewart grinned through a tangle of teeth half-hidden behind a bushy red beard and mustache. He could have been Hammersmith's twin, except Stewart had a full head of hair, as well. "The sooner, the better, eh, lad?"

Rafe grinned. Josie looked down at her shoes.

"So it is, then. We dine in an hour. A seaman will show you the way."

As Josephine stepped through the narrow doorway into their quarters, she looked around. Rather cramped, but serviceable. A table and chair bolted to the floor. A bed big enough for two bolted to the wall. A lamp bolted beside it, and another bolted to the table. Their trunks were stowed under the bed, with straps to keep them from sliding, and several clothing hooks were spaced along the wall beside the bed. There was one tiny, salt-crusted porthole.

Definitely not the *Oceanic*. But Josie felt a thrill of excitement, nonetheless. Two weeks in this cozy nest, alone with Rafe. She needed nothing else.

"You can't stay," she told her betrothed, pushing him back into the hallway. "It would be bad luck. But if you see Henny, please send her to me."

After the door closed behind him, she opened Maddie's parcel.

It was filled with treasures. A beautiful paisley shawl. A lacy blue garter, a cameo, a dried blossom of some sort, and a sixpence coin. There was also a note.

*'Dearest Josephine,'* Maddie had written.

'*Since I cannot be there to share this wonderful moment, please accept these small tokens of the great admiration I feel for you. In the tradition of Scottish weddings, I have included . . .*

*Something old—the pressed thistle blossom I carried in my own wedding.*

*Something new—the paisley shawl made of Kirkwell wool and woven by our talented Irish weavers.*

*Something borrowed—a cameo of our Queen, to remind you of home.*

*Something blue—what wedding would be complete without a blue garter?*

*And finally, a lucky sixpence in your shoe—to ensure a prosperous future.*

*I am certain you will be a beautiful bride. A shipboard wedding sounds quite romantic, but don't be surprised if the ladies of Heartbreak Creek insist on a more traditional church wedding after you arrive. Hopefully, they will wait until I return to enjoy the festivities with you.*

*Your new sister,*
*Maddie Kirkwell*'

Josephine almost burst into tears. Having been an object of pity and scorn for so long, this simple act of friendship was almost more than she could bear.

The wedding was brief and simple. Facing Rafe as they spoke their vows, flanked by her son, witnessed by Thomas and Henny and Gordon, and wearing the shawl and other items Maddie had given her, Josephine felt like the most blessed bride in the world.

Rafe fought an undercurrent of panic. Not regret. Never regret. But he'd suffered failure before in his life, and now as he faced the prospect of being a husband and father, his confidence wavered.

But not for long. When he looked at his wife, he realized it didn't matter what quirk of fate had brought them together—if it was divine providence, or blind luck, or whether a man like him deserved a woman as fine as Josie. He just knew that beside her was where he was supposed to be. Needed to be.

After the short celebration——Captain Stewart wouldn't accept recompense for officiating, but seemed quite appreciative of the bottle of Northbridge Whisky Ash had sent along—— the wedding party went on deck to look at the stars that cast a shimmering dome from one watery horizon to the other.

Jamie was especially enthralled, more so when Thomas took the time to point out the North Star and explain the Indian origins of several constellations. Rafe hoped the stories weren't as grisly as his other native legends.

The night was cool, a sharp breeze filling the auxiliary sails stretched overhead, sending the ship skimming over gentle swells. He hoped the weather held. He hoped the horses would adjust quickly. He hoped his back would quit hurting soon. He had plans.

Trying to ease it, he leaned against the rail, caught Josie's worried look, and quickly straightened. But the longer they stood in the damp air, the more his muscles tightened. Worried that he might not be able to perform his duties later, he considered breaking the seal on the other bottle of whisky Ash had sent along. But if he dosed himself with enough alcohol to deaden his pain, he would probably deaden everything else as well. Not a risk he wanted to take.

When they finally went to their quarters, he left Josie in their cabin to change—hopefully not into that voluminous nightgown—and went down to check on Pems.

He seemed to be resting well, eating and taking water. Thomas had come down, too—after changing back into his Indian attire—and he assured Rafe that he would check on him during the night as Ash had ordered.

"What is wrong with your back?"

Rafe gave a wry smile. "Is it that obvious? I strained it during the race. It's spasms in the muscles. I've had it before. Eventually it fades."

Thomas went to the medicine trunk Hammersmith had sent with them, pulled out a familiar brown bottle, and handed it to Rafe. "Lift your shirt."

"Horse liniment? Are you joking? She won't come anywhere near me if I put on that stinking stuff."

Thomas smirked, dangling the bottle like a lure. "Do you want her or not?"

Rafe sighed. "I'll take it with me. If I still need it, I'll use it."

"Put her on top. That will make it easier."

*Hell.* Now he was receiving instructions in bedding his wife from a loincloth-wearing savage. It was humiliating.

But a fine idea. An image formed in his mind. Josie bouncing above him, that dark mane of hair flying, her pert breasts jiggling as she rode him to bliss.

Anxious to get started, he slipped the bottle into his jacket pocket and hobbled up the narrow metal ladder to the deck where their cabin was.

Josephine nervously paced the center of the small room, wondering when Rafe would return. She had felt him withdrawing all evening; he had hardly spoken a word through dinner or during their walk on the deck.

Something was wrong.

Was he having regrets?

She thought for a moment, then discarded the notion. She had seen the desire in his blue eyes whenever their gazes had met. He loved her. She didn't doubt that. He was happy they were going with him to America.

Then what?

A knock, then the door opened and Rafe stepped in. "Sorry to be so long. I went to check on Pems."

"How is he?"

"Doing well. Thomas is keeping an eye on him."

As he crossed to the table, she studied his face, saw the lines of tension around his eyes and mouth, and her bravado faded. He wasn't wearing the expression of a man anxious to claim his bride. In fact, he hadn't even noticed her standing there, wearing little more than a quilt and a nervous smile.

Bracing one hand on the table, he turned stiffly. And finally, he noticed her. His eyes went wide, his gaze sweeping from the loosened hair fanning over her bare shoulders to the toes showing beneath the quilt wrapped around her naked body.

"I've been waiting," she said, and let the quilt drop.

"Josie." He took a step, then stopped, his face twisting into a grimace. "Damn." He braced his hands on the tabletop. "Damnit to hell."

Mortified, she grabbed for her robe, hanging on a hook. She had disgusted him with her wanton behavior. Made a fool of herself. *Silly woman.*

"No," he ground out, raising a hand. "It's not that. It's not you, Josie. It's my back."

She clutched the robe closed over her breasts. "What's wrong with your back?"

"Muscle cramps. I thought it would get better, but it hasn't." He gave that crooked smile. "And if seeing you naked doesn't do the trick, nothing will."

Relieved that she hadn't ruined everything, she quickly belted the robe, tossed the quilt on the bed, and went to him. "Let me see." She gently eased the jacket from his wide shoulders.

Something clinked against the table. Curious, she reached into the jacket pocket and pulled out a dark bottle. Liniment. Setting it aside, she helped him pull off his shirt. "Shall I put the liniment on you here at the table, or would you rather lie down?"

"It'll stink up the whole room."

"I'll open the porthole."

"You don't have to do this, Josie."

"Oh? And how will you apply it to your back? Pour a puddle on the floor and roll around in it? Sit."

"I . . . don't think I can."

"Then brace yourself." She filled her cupped palm with the evil-smelling liquid and clapped it to his back.

He sucked in air. "That's cold."

"Stand still." Eyes watering from the fumes, she quickly smeared oily liniment over his back, recapped the bottle, then set it in a safe nook so it wouldn't roll off and break. "Now turn around."

When he did, she unbuckled his belt, striving to be as matter-of-fact about his body as he was with hers.

"It's my back that hurts. Not my front."

"And yet, look how swollen you are," she quipped nervously as she slipped his drawers over his . . . parts . . . and down his hips. "Perhaps I'll find a way to ease that, too."

"Not with hands covered in liniment, I hope."

"No, not with my hands."

*Mercy.* Had she truly said that?

Perspiration damped her brow. In fact, she felt damp everywhere, and entirely too warm. She quickly opened the porthole, then trying not to stare at the tall, strapping, completely *naked* body of her husband, she ushered him to the bed and told him to stretch out on his stomach.

Nudity always made her feel vaguely ashamed. Not so, Rafe. Her watchful presence seemed not to bother him a whit as he climbed into bed, adjusted himself, then settled facedown on the pillow.

More muscles, lean hips, rounded buttocks . . . *oh, my*.

Hiking the hem of her robe, she climbed on top of him, her bare bottom straddling his bare thighs. It felt odd and immodest and delicious. "Am I hurting you?" she asked, settling her full weight on him.

"You're killing me," he mumbled into the pillow. "Let me turn over and I'll show you."

"Later." She began to work his back, massaging the liniment into knotted muscles, using long strokes, then gentle circles with the heels of her hands. She tried to remember all she had seen him do when he'd massaged Pems. Instead, she thought of those strong hands moving across her own body.

"Am I doing it right?"

His answer was a deep sigh, and a mumbled "Don't stop."

As she kneaded and stroked, she marveled at the strength and masculine grace in the body beneath her hands. Long, firm muscles spreading out from the dip of his spine. Broad shoulders tapering to a narrow waist. Skin tinted a golden brown by the sun . . . except for those lovely, firm buttocks. Sculpted marble, heated from within. The only things that marred his perfection were the three bullet scars.

Her hands began to ache, but she kept at it until she heard a faint snore. Careful not to wake him, she climbed off and rinsed her hands in the bucket of water hanging from a hook. After opening the porthole wider to draw out the lingering stench of the liniment, she blew out the lamp on the table then took off her robe. Moving quietly, she climbed in beside him and pulled the quilt over their naked bodies.

Not a memorable wedding night. But she felt closer to him than she'd ever felt before. He had let her see his pain, and then allowed her to help him. There was trust in that. And what could be more compelling to a woman than to be needed by a strong, capable man? His vulnerability touched her in a way nothing ever had. She felt truly married now. Needed. Loved. A partner.

Cuddled against his side and lulled by the distant throb of the steam engines belowdecks and the gentle sway of the ship, she drifted into a deep, dreamless sleep.

Rafe awoke to an acrid stench and the sensation of movement. He tried to roll onto his back, couldn't, and twisted to see a warm body pinning him to the mattress with an arm over his shoulders, and a leg twined with his. Josie.

He blinked in drowsy befuddlement. The stench was liniment—the motion was because they were on a moving ship—and the spasms in his back had dwindled to a dull ache. By the faint dawn light showing through the porthole, he could see they were both nude.

Excellent.

Gently extracting the arm trapped between them, he rolled onto his side facing her, and ran his hand down her bare back. Her skin was as smooth and warm as a new colt's belly—but without the hair.

When she didn't respond, he stroked her again.

On the fourth stroke, she sighed and rolled onto her back.

He happily set to work on her breasts, trailing his fingertips over the soft mounds, tracing the rounded contours in decreasing circles until he reached the puckered tips. He gently tugged.

She sighed again.

Rafe watched her come awake under his touch. She was so beautiful. So responsive and trusting. He prayed she harbored no regrets, or second thoughts, or doubts about the dramatic change he had asked her to make in her life. He was determined to make this work, and would gladly spend the rest of his years making it up to her for all that she had left behind.

Leaning down, he drew his tongue over her nipple.

Back arching, she stretched, arms over her head. Then she relaxed and opened her eyes. "You're awake."

"I am." He nibbled his way to the other breast.

"How's your back?" Her voice was husky with sleep. Unbelievably arousing.

"Better." He continued to caress her, learning again what made her shiver and sigh. When he thought she was ready, he said, "Roll toward me."

She did, lying half across his chest. "Like this?"

"Exactly like that. Now put your leg over my waist."

"I wouldn't want to hurt you."

"You won't." When she complied, he pulled her the rest of the way on top of him. "I'll let you do all the work."

Seeing her puzzled look, he told her to sit up, then positioned her knees forward against his sides so that she straddled him. "How's this?"

Understanding dawned. She watched him, her beautiful eyes growing dark with passion as he reached down to stroke her. Soon she was squirming against him, until finally she reached between their bodies to position him, then slowly took him inside.

Her lips parted. Her eyes fluttered closed.

"Now ride me," he ordered.

It was better than he had imagined . . . Josie rising above him, head thrown back in abandon, her beautiful body gilded with dawn light and open to his touch.

He didn't question how he had won this remarkable woman. He simply embraced the gift that she was, and vowed in his heart to love and cherish and protect her for all of his life.

# *Epilogue*

She should have been prepared.

She had seen paintings in London galleries, tintypes in books, even several of Maddie Wallace's artful photographs. In addition, Rafe had spoken at length about the sheer scope of Colorado's Rocky Mountains.

But after over a month of flat prairies and bison-dotted grasslands, and two entire days of watching a distant jagged silhouette that never seemed to grow closer, Josephine's anticipation had begun to wane.

Then just as they neared the town of Pueblo, when she had almost convinced herself that the lofty descriptions of the majestic Rockies were simply another American exaggeration, suddenly there they were, rising like a wall before them.

The closer they grew, the more inspiring they became. Giant, towering peaks. Stately firs, limbs bowed under a burden of snow. Ice-crusted boulders rising out of white-water brooks—which Rafe called "cricks." She saw sheep poised on sheer rocky outcroppings—"bighorn"—herds of enormous deer grazing in wooded meadows—"elk"—and once, foraging in the brush alongside the tracks, a huge late-hibernating bear—a "griz"—that would have outweighed a horse and stretched almost ten feet into the air when it rose on hind legs to glare at the train rolling by.

The Highlands were impressive. The Rockies were frightening. Definitely a world away from the manicured estates and carefully tended fields of home.

"How much longer?" Jamie asked for at least the hundredth time over the last few hours.

"Around the next bend we start into Heartbreak Creek Canyon."

"Why is it called Heartbreak Creek?" Henny asked, sitting beside Jamie on the couch opposite Rafe's and Josephine's in their private compartment. With Gordon remaining in the drovers' car to oversee the unloading of the horses when they arrived at Heartbreak Creek, she had joined them for this last leg of their journey. Josephine was grateful for the moral support.

"Probably because of the water. Or maybe a disgruntled miner gave the place the name. This used to be silver country, but the mines are mostly played out now."

"What's wrong with the water?" Josephine wondered what other surprises awaited them. Like snow. There seemed to be a great deal of it, even for December. How soon before it began to melt and this dreadful cold abated.

"Nothing's wrong with it now," Rafe explained. "Thanks to the Rylanders and the sluice they commissioned, we have all the sweet water we need."

*We.* Even though Rafe had spent only a short while in Heartbreak Creek before traveling to England, he already thought of it as home. So she would, too. These people were all part of what Maddie called her "Heartbreak Creek family," and Josephine was determined they would be her family, as well.

Assuming they accepted her as readily as the earl and countess had—or Maddie and Ash, as the Kirkwells preferred to be called when in America. It was all rather confusing.

The locomotive ahead gave a long whistle blast, followed by several shorter blasts. The train began to slow.

Her heart beat faster.

"There's the church." Rafe pointed to a distant small, steepled structure situated in a broad open stretch blanketed with snow. Through the glare of sunlight bouncing off all that white, Josephine saw people coming out of the open church doors and walking in the same direction the train was headed.

"Looks like we'll arrive in time for Sunday dinner," Rafe

said. "Let's hope it's not at the Brodies' this week. His wife's not much of a cook."

Josephine looked at him in alarm. The *wives* did the cooking?

Maddie had told her about the Sunday dinners—rowdy family gatherings that rotated each week between the different households. She had assumed they all had cooks. If not, she was in dire trouble.

Henny must have seen her panic. Struggling against a smile, she mouthed, *I'll teach you.*

Mollified, but still hoping for a reprieve, Josephine gave a deep sigh. "I suppose with the horses to unload, we'll miss the family dinner today."

Rafe laughed. "You won't get off that easy, sweetheart. Since the Rylanders own this branch line and have connections with several of the main lines, I'm sure they've been tracking us for the last thousand miles. In addition to the men coming to help with the horses, I know the women are chomping at the bit to welcome the newest Heartbreak Creek bride. They'll wait for us."

Josephine smiled weakly. "Well, that's a relief."

He leaned over and gave her a quick kiss. "Relax, Josie. I know you dislike the attention, but they want to meet you and I'm raring to show off my beautiful wife and handsome son." Had his accent become more pronounced the farther west they'd traveled?

"Are those the boys you told me about?" Jamie pointed to two youngsters racing beside the slowing train.

Rafe nodded. "The middle Brodie boys. The blond is Joe Bill. Lucas is the smaller one with brown hair. That tall one by the cowboys is the oldest, R.D. The youngest is still a baby."

The train rolled slowly up to the platform, where a small crowd waited.

Gripping her gloved hands tightly in her lap, Josephine hiked her chin and strove for serenity.

"Don't do that," Rafe murmured, putting his big hand over hers. "There's nothing to be afraid of, honey. Just give them a chance."

Give *them* a chance?

But seeing his concern, she put on a smile. The people

waiting on the platform were Maddie's dearest friends. If they were anything like the countess, they would soon be enveloping her in hugs, whether she knew them or not. Exuberant people, these Americans.

Brakes squealed. Billowing steam curled around their railcar, reminding Josephine of a thick London fog.

The train jerked to a stop.

"Finally!" Jamie bounded off the couch.

Rafe rose. Bending beside the window, he tipped his Stetson to the people waving and grinning on the platform.

Josephine peered through the coiling mist, struggling to put faces with the names Maddie had mentioned.

The tall, broad man with the toddler bouncing on his shoulders must be Declan Brodie, the cattle rancher and sometime sheriff. The blue-eyed woman clinging to his arm and displaying an abundance of ruffles beneath her coat must be his Southern mail-order wife, Edwina—or Ed, as most called her.

The more sedate couple beside them were probably the wealthy Rylanders—Tait, handsome in an austere way, and Lucinda, his beautiful, very pregnant wife, and the owner of the town's only hotel.

The third couple must be the newlyweds—an architect named Ethan Hardesty, and his wife, Audra, who was the editor of the local paper. There were also several cowboys, one with a wooden leg, Josephine noticed, a grinning Negro couple dressed in their Sunday best, and beside them, an older woman with a cane she used to menace the boys running by. Lucinda's guardian and Pringle's previous employer.

"Hurry, Mother," Jamie called back as he rushed after Henny down the narrow aisle of the railcar.

She rose. "I'm coming." Her voice sounded tinny in her own ear. Hoping to ease the sudden constriction in her throat, she took a deep breath, then another, yet couldn't seem to fill her lungs. Grateful for Rafe's hand on her elbow, she left the compartment on wobbly legs.

But when they reached the door to the rear platform, he pulled her to a stop. "I love you, Josie."

She looked up, saw the warmth and pride in his eyes, and her anxiety faded away. She could do this. She could face all these strangers. She would make a home for herself and Jamie here in this harshly beautiful place. With this strong, loving man by her side, she could do anything.

"I love you, too, Rafe."

"Then smile." With a quick kiss, and taking her hand firmly in his, he guided her out onto the platform.

Tiny pellets of frozen mist pricked her cheeks and eyes, momentarily blinding her. The air was so cold it seemed to sear her throat. She faltered, the leather soles of her traveling boots slipping on the icy boards.

"I've got you, honey," Rafe murmured in her ear.

Clinging to his sturdy arm, she started down the slippery steps.

"There she is!"

"She's so pretty!"

"Quit staring, Declan."

"Welcome to Heartbreak Creek!" several voices called.

A blush warmed her cold cheeks. She looked at the faces smiling back at her, and suddenly the challenge awaiting her no longer seemed so intimidating. This was going to work. They would be happy here.

"Thank you," she called back. And putting on her brightest smile, Josephine stepped boldly off the train and into her new life.

Their grand adventure had begun.

Read on for a special preview of the next

# HEROES OF HEARTBREAK CREEK NOVEL

Available soon from Berkley Sensation

Squinting against bright morning sunlight, Prudence Lincoln stood at the library window of the Friends School and studied the letter in her hand.

". . . rise from your dreams, *Voaxaa'e*, and together we will fly away."

What did that mean? She knew *Voaxaa'e* was the Cheyenne word for eagle, a fanciful name Thomas had given her months ago. But "fly away" where? Back to Heartbreak Creek?

Their last meeting had been horrid. When she had told him she still had work to do here at the school and needed to stay longer in Schuler, he had allowed his anger and frustration to show. It was the first time Thomas had ever raised his voice to her and it had frightened her, awakened old memories she fought hard to keep buried. She had reacted without thinking. When he had seen her cowering before him, arms raised in defense, he had been stunned. Then hurt. And without allowing her to explain, he had walked out the door and never came back.

Pru's half-sister, Edwina, had written from Heartbreak Creek to tell her he had gone with Ash and Maddie—the Earl and Countess of Kirkwell—and Ash's horse wrangler, Rayford Jessup, to England to purchase thoroughbreds.

But she hadn't heard a word from Thomas.

Terrified that she would never see him again, she had written to him in England, trying to explain her fears.

And now, months later, he responded with this? Bemused, she read again the words written in the familiar bold script she had taught him back in the one-room schoolhouse in Heartbreak Creek, Colorado Territory.

"Look for me, Prudence Lincoln. When the wind blows cold and the Long Nights Moon rides in the sky, I will come to you. Listen for my voice in the shadows. Then rise from your dreams, *Voaxaa'e*, and together we will fly away."

She didn't know whether to laugh or cry.

"Are you ready?" a voice said behind her.

Turning, she saw Cyrus Marsh standing in the doorway beside her valise, one gloved hand on his hip, holding back his overcoat, the other gripping the brim of the hat he impatiently tapped against his leg.

"I-I can't go, Mr. Marsh." As she spoke, she slipped the letter into her coat pocket, not sure why she didn't want him to see it. She disliked Mr. Marsh, and had from the moment she had met him. Despite his practiced smiles and polite words, she sensed an undercurrent of coldness within him.

"Oh?" His blond brows rose in arcs above eyes of such a pale hazel they seemed yellow against his sallow skin. "I'm sorry to hear that, Miss Lincoln. We've gone to a great deal of trouble to make arrangements for you to join us on this trip. May I ask why, at the moment of our departure, you feel you can't go?"

"I'm expecting a visitor. He's coming a long way, and I wouldn't want to miss him."

"Your Indian friend." His voice carried no emotion, but she saw the disdain in his eyes and the slight curl in his thin lips.

"Yes. Mr. Redstone."

"I see." The hat tapped harder, faster.

Behind him, a small figure moved silently through the hall.

Lillie. Eavesdropping again. Pru reminded herself to have another talk with the girl. Not that it would help. The child had little enough to keep her insatiable curiosity and bright mind occupied, and listening in on the lives of others was her dearest pastime. At least the girl was honorable enough not to repeat the things she heard.

"When do you expect him?" Mr. Marsh asked.

*When the wind blows cold and the Long Nights Moon rides in the sky.*

"Mid-December," she guessed. "I'm not sure of the exact date." Possibly around the twenty-first, since that would be the longest night of the year. Thomas's colorful speech was often difficult to decipher.

"Perhaps you could write back and ask him to delay the visit."

"I don't know where to reach him, sir." Pru clasped her hands at her waist so they wouldn't betray her nervousness. She hated confrontation. Bad enough Mr. Marsh ordered Brother Sampson around as if he were still a slave, but to have him interfering in her life was intolerable. Still, as trustee of the school that employed her, he deserved at least a show of respect. "He's traveling from England, you see."

At least that's what Maddie's latest letter had said. The freighter carrying the Kirkwell thoroughbreds, Mr. Jessup, and Thomas were scheduled to arrive in Boston near the middle of this month. From there, they would travel by rail to Colorado, with stops along the way to rest the horses, which would drag out the journey for several weeks or more. Maddie had concluded by saying she assumed Thomas would stop to visit her on his way through Indiana, and for Pru to expect some changes.

Changes? In Thomas? He was solid as a rock. As sure and steadfast as any man she had ever known. He certainly had no need to make changes.

"If he's not due until mid-December," Mr. Marsh said, regaining her attention, "that would still leave us ample time to accomplish our purposes in the capitol. I see no problem." Looking pleased, he set his hat on his head. "I'll instruct the school administrator to send word if your Indian arrives before we get back. But should he do so, you can leave a note, telling him you'll return shortly. Schuler is only a four-hour train ride from Indianapolis."

"But things could have gone more smoothly than anticipated," Pru argued. "He might arrive any day. I would like to be here if he does." And being Thomas, if he did arrive and found her gone, he might simply leave. He had a habit of disappearing when things weren't to his liking.

"Miss Lincoln." Marsh paused as if struggling with words—or his temper. "You know how important this trip is. Not only for Brother Sampson, but for your education initiative, as well."

"Yes, but—"

"And with backing from important key people in Indianapolis," he went on, ignoring her protest, "the two of you can advance equality and education for blacks more than the Quakers have ever done."

"I understand that, and I—"

"He could be a state senator, Miss Lincoln! Or even governor. Isn't that what you want? What we all want?"

"Certainly, but—"

"For God's sake, why are you defying me, woman? Do you think I'll allow you to ruin everything because of a damned Indian?"

Pru shrank back, old fears flooding her mind. Breathe. Show no fear.

"Christ." Dropping his hands to his hips, Marsh let go a deep breath.

Moments passed. Tension weighted the air while Pru stood locked in fear, waiting to see what he would do next.

Stay or run.

When he finally spoke again, his voice was flat and as cold as the glint in his near-colorless eyes. "I didn't want to have to resort to threats."

Threats?

Tipping his head to the side, he said in an almost conversational tone, "I know what you've been up to, Miss Lincoln."

Fear ballooned into an almost overwhelming urge to flee. How could he know? How did he find out? She fought to keep her voice steady. "I-I don't know what you're talking about."

"Don't you?" His smile showed small pointed teeth. A predator's smile. "I know the Underground Railroad has started up again. Only this time, it's not to aid runaway slaves seeking freedom, but black felons and agitators escaping into Canada. The misguided fools helping them could go to jail. Or worse. I know you're involved, so don't bother to deny it."

"They only want to live free, Mr. Marsh. Instead of being brutalized in the name of Southern Reconstruction."

He waved a hand in dismissal. "Save your speeches. If I could, I would turn the lot of you over to the authorities today."

Perspiration gathered under her arms. "Why do you care if a few desperate colored people seek a better life?"

"I don't. But I do care about Brother Sampson, and he cares about you and your initiative." He leaned toward her, that icy gaze stripping away her courage. "And I especially care about the people who flock to hear him speak and who believe in the both of you. Voters, all."

The hairs on the back of her neck lifted. This was about votes?

"You're an intelligent woman, Miss Lincoln, especially for one of your race. Surely you're aware that you and the good Brother are my stepping-stones to the real power in Washington. I've invested a great deal of time and effort toward that goal and I will not allow scandal to jeopardize those plans."

He stepped closer, his yellow eyes burning with the fervor of a fanatic. It took all her strength not to step back.

"So be warned, Miss Lincoln. Behave. Stop this foolish business with the railroad. Because if you persist, I will exact a terrible price, if not from you, then from someone dear to you. One of your students, perhaps. Or your Indian. Maybe even Brother Sampson. But rest assured, someone will pay. Do you understand?"

Pru fought to drag air into her lungs. He's insane. Evil. Like Satan is evil. Just being near him made her feel unclean.

Another step. "Have I made myself clear, Miss Lincoln?"

Pru nodded.

He studied her for a moment, then stepped back, his smile once more in place. "Then we'll speak no more of it." Bending, he picked up her valise. "Write that note to your Indian while I put this in the carriage. When I return, I'll take it to the administrator along with my instructions to wire us if Mr. Redstone arrives before we return. And do hurry, Miss Lincoln. Brother Sampson is waiting and you know how the cold aggravates his hands."

Light-headed and shaking, Pru watched him leave the room. Terror careened through her mind, muddled her thinking. But one thought kept surfacing. After she finished this last rescue through the railroad, she would tell Brother Sampson about Marsh's motives. Perhaps together they could find a way to stop him. But for now, and for his own safety, she had to send Thomas away.

And there was only one way to do that.

The pain of it almost doubled her over.

On wooden legs, she went to the desk by the window and extracted a piece of paper from the drawer. Struggling to keep her hand steady, she wrote . . .

*Dear Thomas,*

*I fear you misunderstood my last letter to you. I am not seeking a reunion. Our last visit made it clear to me that despite the deep feelings I have for you, we come from such different worlds we could never build a solid future together. I am sorry. Please give everyone my regards when you return to Heartbreak Creek.*

*I will always remember you fondly.*

*Prudence Lincoln*

# *One*

With an unaccustomed twinge of nervousness, Thomas Redstone paused at the gate in front of a large brick building on the outskirts of Schuler, Indiana. He studied the words on the sign planted in the front yard. With the help of Rayford Jessup, his reading had improved, but it was still troublesome, and he wanted to be certain the name had not changed since his last visit.

The Society of Friends School for Colored People.

It was the same.

From inside the building came the distant voices of children chanting their numbers. He pictured her standing before them, smiling as she had once smiled at him, her oldest pupil.

Had she received his letter? Would she welcome him? Or would she choose these strangers over him once again, and send him away with more excuses? If so, it would be the last time. He could not spend the rest of his life waiting for Prudence Lincoln to accept him. If she turned him away this time, he would not come back.

He did not want to think about how empty his days would be if that happened.

Pushing the thought aside, he brushed back his shoulder-length hair and tugged the collar away from his neck so he could breathe, then opened the gate. As he walked toward the front porch, he looked around.

The yard was bare except for a leafless willow tree by the front fence. There was no snow on the ground and few clouds hung in the sky. The breeze off the Ohio was cold but so gentle it felt like a cool hand against his cheek. It was much warmer here than in Colorado. For a moment, the horizon beckoned, and the call to return home was strong in his mind. He had been gone many months and had traveled far. He wanted to go back to his snowy mountains.

But first he had to see Prudence Lincoln.

When he started up the steps, he saw a black-skinned girl child sitting in a chair on the far end of the porch, staring in his direction, her head tilted to one side. She looked small and thin beneath her worn coat, and probably had less than a dozen years. She was darker than Prudence Lincoln, and tiny ribbon-tied braids sprouted from her head like raven feathers from a war bonnet. He wondered why she was not at her lessons with the other children.

"Mornin'," she called. "My name Lillie. It really Lillian, but everybody only call me Lillie."

He nodded without speaking. Setting down the leather pouch holding his extra clothes, he stared at the closed door, that uneasiness rising in him again. He did not like it. Did not like the feeling of doubt that came with it. Irritated at such weakness, he smoothed a hand down the front of his jacket. He did not like this fancy suit the Scotsman had bought for him, either. Or the boots he had to wear instead of his moccasins. He missed his topknot and eagle feather.

But to honor his white grandfather—and Prudence Lincoln—this was the path he had chosen. For now. But once he returned to his mountains, he would cast aside these foolish trappings and become Cheyenne once again.

"Ain't you gonna knock?" the girl called.

He scowled at her for interrupting his thoughts.

She seemed not to notice and continued to stare, her head cocked.

He took a deep breath, let it out, then lifted his fist and pounded on the door.

Footsteps approached. He stood stiffly as the door opened and a stern-faced old woman in a plain, brown dress looked out at him. He did not recognize her from before, when he had left

Prudence Lincoln in anger and sailed across the wide water with the Scotsman and his wife and Rayford Jessup.

"Who are you?" he asked.

"Friend Laudner. How may I help thee?"

A Quaker. He remembered the strange way they spoke. "You will take me to Prudence Lincoln." Seeing the woman's mouth tighten, he added, "Please."

"Miss Lincoln isn't here."

The woman tried to close the door.

Thomas stopped it with his hand. "Where is she?"

She blinked round, dark eyes, reminding Thomas of a tiny brown wren. "I was told they went to the capitol."

They? And what was this capitol?

This time, she shut the door before Thomas could stop her. "*Noxa'e!* Wait!"

The footsteps faded into silence.

Muttering, he turned to find the girl rising from her chair.

"I know you." She reached out to touch the porch rail. "You her Indian, ain't you? Thomas Redstone." She walked closer, one hand on the railing, the other pointed his way. "You a Cheyenne Dog Soldier."

He saw nothing familiar in her face, or in the odd way she looked toward him, but not at him. She spoke like other black skins he knew who had once been slaves. Except for Prudence Lincoln. She had never been a slave, and her white father had raised her to speak in the white way. The proper way, she called it.

Thinking this girl—proper or not—might be more help than the Quaker woman, he put on a smile. "I did not see you when I came here before."

"I not see you, neither," she said and giggled.

Then he understood. Her careful gait. That blank stare. The intent way she listened, head tilted to one side to catch every sound. "You are blind."

"Scarlet fever. Three years back when I was eight. You sound tall."

"If you cannot see me, how do you know who I am?"

She continued toward him. When the fingertips of her outstretched hand brushed his coat, she stopped and let her arm fall back to her side. "You talk different from the Friends. Or

Miss Pru. Or anybody." She smiled at his chest. "Can I feel your face?"

He drew back. "Why?"

"That how I see what you look like."

Forcing down his natural wariness around those marked by the Great Spirit, Thomas bent to within reach of her hands.

Her touch was as soft as a moth's wings. And ticklish. But he stood motionless while she felt everything, even his ears and lips and eyes. When she finally took her hands away, he straightened, glad the ordeal was over. He was not comfortable with such touching, except with Prudence Lincoln. He liked to keep people far enough away that he could see all of them at once and be ready should a threat come. "What do you see?" he asked.

Another giggle, showing a gap where a front tooth had been. "You gots a big nose and you eyebrows very stern. What color you eyes?"

"Black, and my nose is not big. What is this capitol?"

"Indianapolis. I go there 'fore I blind. It a big place, sho' 'nuff. What color you hair?"

"Black. Why did Prudence Lincoln go there?"

"To raise money for Reverend Brother Sampson." A spark of excitement lit the blankness in her brown eyes. "You fetchin' her? She 'posed to come back long time ago, but she ain't showed."

Thomas stared past her, plans already forming in his mind. If he fetched Prudence Lincoln, it would not be to bring her back here.

"Oh. Well." A deep sigh. "They not let you take her, anyways."

He glared down at her dark head. "Who would stop me?"

"Mistuh Marsh. He say Reverend Brother Sampson need her."

"Tell me of these men."

Leaning over the rail, she groped until her hand brushed a shrub planted alongside the porch. Plucking a withered blossom, she sniffed it, then slipped it into her coat pocket before moving down the rail to another plant. "Reverend Brother Sampson a preaching man. He a slave in Kentucky 'fore he come here on the Underground Railroad. Now he preach the holy gospel to folks in a big tent. He nice. Always bring me peppermints."

"And the other man?"

She plucked another dead blossom, sniffed, then put it in the pocket with the first. "Mistuh Marsh. He white." Her voice changed. Held a trace of . . . fear? "Usually he take Brother Sampson around so he can preach, only this time, he take him to a big tent meetin' in Indianapolis. Miss Pru say folks there maybe send him all the way to Washington to talk to the president."

Thomas snorted. He knew what a talk with the White Father in Washington meant. More treaties, more broken promises, more trouble for the People. "Why do they need Prudence Lincoln to do this?"

"'Cause she smart. Mistuh Marsh say with her by his side, folks maybe like Reverend Brother Sampson 'nuff to make him a leg-a-slater. I ain't sure what that is. Nobody tell me nothin' 'round here. They think 'cause I blind, I stupid, too."

Thomas felt a jolt in his chest. "And Prudence Lincoln? Does she like Reverend Brother Sampson, too?"

"'Course. Everybody do. Even the Friends."

A coldness gripped him. Did that mean she had chosen this man over him?

He did not want to believe that. Prudence Lincoln was his heart-mate.

But why, then—after he wrote to her that he was coming—was she not here? What was he to do now? Wait for her until he grew old and his days ran out?

He could not do that. He would not live his life that way. Better to walk away now than to be sent away later.

Fury burned away the chill. But it also awakened that part of him too stubborn to give up . . . not even when he hung in agony from the ropes during the Sun Dance Ceremony . . . or when he saw his chief killed and the People driven from their lands onto government reservations . . . or when he searched tirelessly, despite his wounds, to find Prudence after Lone Tree took her.

He would not walk away this time. He would go to this other place—this Indianapolis. He would find Prudence Lincoln and tell her what was in his heart. Then he would go back to his mountains. If she chose to stay here, that would be the end of it. He would put her from his life forever.

If he could.

He looked down at the girl staring blankly across the yard,

her thin fingers tugging at a loose thread on her worn cuff. "Where is this place called Indianapolis?"

She looked up.

Her eyes might be blank, but he sensed a sharp intelligence hidden behind them. This girl was not stupid.

"You go after her? 'Cause I tell you how to get there. I even get you a map." She leaned closer to whisper at his jacket. "But you gots to take me with you. Miss Pru need both us to get her away from Mistuh Marsh."

Thomas almost smiled, amused that she thought he needed help from a blind girl who probably weighed little more than his pouch of extra clothes. "I cannot take you with me."

Chin jutting, she crossed her arms over her chest. "Then I ain't helping."

"Good-bye, Lillian." He picked up his leather bag.

"Where you goin'?"

Ignoring the panic in her voice, he started down the steps into the yard.

"You cain't jist leave me!" She stumbled forward, hands clutching at air. "A po' blind black girl who ain't got nobody to look out for her, not even a dog to lick away her tears!"

"Go inside, Lillian," he called over his shoulder.

"Don't go!" She flung herself toward him.

With a curse, he dropped the bag and caught her before she flew headfirst down the steps. "You foolish *katse'e*," he scolded, setting her back on her feet. "You could have hurt yourself!"

Behind him, the door swung open. A man in a dark collarless coat over a plain white shirt stepped onto the porch. "What's going on out here? Lillie, what mischief have thee done this time?"

When she tucked her head without answering, the Quaker turned his attention to Thomas. "I'm Joseph Matthews," the older man said. "Administrator of the school. Who might thee be?"

"Thomas Redstone."

"The man seeking Miss Lincoln?"

Thomas nodded.

"Didn't Friend Laudner tell thee she was in Indianapolis?"

"Yes, but she did not tell me when she would be back."

"We don't know when she'll be back."

Thomas thought for a moment. "She knew I would come. She left no message for me?"

"None that I'm aware of. I'm sorry, friend." Turning to the girl, he held out his hand. "Come along, child," he said, gently.

"No." The girl fumbled until she found Thomas's hand. Taking it in both of hers, she grinned at the Quaker's stomach. "I'm going with Daddy."

Ten minutes later, Thomas walked back toward the Schuler train station, this time with two bags of clothes and a beaming little black girl by his side.

"I know'd you catch me 'afore I fall down the steps," the girl said, clinging to his arm as they walked along the rutted road. "You a good daddy. Gots any other chilrin 'sides me?"

"No. And I am not your father." He had spoken those words many times . . . to her, the Quaker, and anyone else who would listen before they shoved them both out the door of the school. They all seemed eager to send the girl away with him. He could guess why.

"I knows you ain't."

"Then why did you tell them I was?"

"'Cause I need a daddy and they wouldn't let me go with you if you wasn't. Slow down. I'm just a po' little blind girl, 'member?"

More like *heavoheso*—a devil—in pigtails. Reining in his temper, Thomas slowed his pace. He did not know what to do with this strange child. He was not a nursemaid. "Where are your parents?"

"You mean 'sides you?"

"I am not your father."

"Don't know where my other daddy is. He sold off 'fore I born. Mama gone to Jesus. Drowned. Up and walk out the field one day, straight into the river. Overseer find her floatin' in the weeds. You know skin turn white and come off you stay in the water too long?"

Thomas kept walking, not sure what to say. The girl had lied about him being her father. Maybe she lied about this, as well. He hoped so.

"Mama always want to be white," she said after a while. "Guess she got her wish. She make a pretty white lady, sho' 'nuff. Miss Pru pretty?"

"Yes."

"That probably 'cause she half white."

Thomas smirked at the notion. "It is not the color of her skin that makes her pretty. It is the goodness in her heart." And her smile. And the way she looked at him when he touched her. Would he ever hold her against him again?

"After your mother died, who took care of you, Lillian?"

"Whoever around. Then after the fightin' stop, the Friends come and bring us to freedom land. Been here since. They nice, even if they talk funny."

They talk funny? Thomas wondered what Prudence Lincoln thought about the way this girl spoke. He remembered how she had sat beside him, pointing out the letters in her book and teaching him to speak in the proper way. He had not been a good student. It was hard to think about words when she sat so close.

"Hey," the girl said, giving his hand a yank to get his attention. "Since I be your little girl, my name Lillie Redstone now?"

Thomas did not answer.

After a while, they turned onto a side road that ran along the tracks. Up ahead, the depot squatted like a beetle beside a water tower balanced on eight skinny wooden legs. A beetle and a hungry spider. He felt caught in a web, too. He still was not sure what to do when the train came. He could not leave the girl by the tracks. And he could not take her back to the school. Maybe when he found Prudence Lincoln . . .

"She not forget."

He looked down at her. "What?"

"Miss Pru. She not forget you comin'. She leave a note for you, but Mistuh Marsh don't give it to Friend Matthews like he say he do."

Thomas felt a warmth spread through his chest. She had remembered.

"And he mean to Miss Pru. Take her to Indianapolis when she want to wait for you. Say she better behave. He a mean one, make Miss Pru cry like that."

Cry? Thomas's steps slowed. *Eho'nehevehohtse* never cried. Not even after he freed her from Lone Tree. Or when she tended him after he was shot, and he heard her awake from night terrors. Who was this man and why did he warn her to behave? Prudence Lincoln always behaved. When Thomas was with her, that was his hardest task—to convince her not to behave. But maybe the girl was lying about this, too.

He stopped and looked down at her bent head. "How do you know all this?"

"I listen. A shadow on the wall, that me. And I hear Miss Pru say, 'Here the note.' And he say, 'I take it to Friend Matthews right now.' But he don't. And he don't tell him you comin', neither. Mistuh Marsh, he a damn liar."

"Like you, *okom*?"

"No, I better'n him." She frowned. "What *okom* mean?"

"Coyote."

Lost in thought, Thomas resumed walking, the girl close at his side, her hand on his arm. If Prudence was in trouble, he would help her. But if he had to take this strange child with him, she must obey him so he could keep her safe.

Stopping again, he hunkered onto his heels and gripped her thin shoulders. "Listen well, *katse'e*."

"Cat see what?"

"*Kat-se'-e*. It is the Cheyenne word for little girl."

She frowned, her gaze fixed on a distant horizon her eyes could not see. "Cats is sneaky. I like dogs better. And horses. Chickens, they—"

"Never mind that," he said more harshly than he should have. "Heed my words. From this day, there will be no more lies. You will speak only the truth to me, Lillian, or I will send you back to the school."

"They not take me."

"Then I will leave you by the tracks with your bag of clothes."

"Would you really?"

"I would," he lied. "Do you understand?"

"I 'pose." A sniff. "But you not being a very nice daddy."

The quaver in her voice left him unmoved. And unconvinced. "Now you will make your promise to me. You will tell no more lies."

She huffed out a deep breath. "All right. No more lies."

"And you will do what I say."

"That two promises."

"And you will do what I say," he repeated through gritted teeth.

"All right! But we ain't got time for no more promises, Daddy. The train coming."

Behind him, a locomotive whistle blew. With a sigh, Thomas rose. If Prudence Lincoln sent him away again, he would leave this devil-child with her. It would serve them both right.

Several hours later when the sun began to slip behind the trees, their train reached Indianapolis. The girl had been talking when Thomas dozed off, and was still talking when he awoke. She had strong lungs.

And she was right. Indianapolis was a big place. Not as big as the city where the English queen lived and people spoke with a strange accent. But bigger than Schuler. With the girl anchored in one hand, and their bags of clothes gripped in the other, Thomas stepped outside the depot and looked around.

People rushed along the street as if they had someplace important to be. Many stared at them as they went by. Thomas wished he had brought his war axe instead of sending it on to Heartbreak Creek with Rayford Jessup. But he had his long knife under his jacket, tucked into his belt at his back. That would be enough if danger came.

"We just stand here all day?" the girl complained.

Probably hungry after so much talking. He was, too.

"I will find food," he announced, and led her in the direction most of the people were headed. Before they had walked far, they came to a place that had a strong smell of cooking meat. He led the girl inside.

A worried-looking woman with fox-red hair rushed to meet them. "Coloreds ain't allowed," she whispered, looking around at the other tables and the white people sitting there.

"Allowed to do what?" he asked.

"Eat here. Roy, you better come."

A big man with hair on his face and angry eyes came around from behind a counter where a brass moneybox sat. "Look here, mister—"

"Don't hurt him!" Lillian shrieked in a loud voice, pressing against Thomas's arm. "He only tryin' to find my mama 'cause I a poor little blind girl and cain't find my way! He mean no harm!"

The man called Roy looked at her in surprise. Thomas did, too. The white people watching from the tables muttered to each other.

"We leavin'," Lillian cried, almost yanking Thomas off balance and into the branches of a plant in a pot beside the door. "Please don't hurt us, mistuh. We just hungry, is all. Don't mean no harm."

"Roy, let me take them around back," the woman whispered. "Cook can give them something and send them on their way." When the man hesitated, she gave his arm a shake. "For heaven's sake, Roy, the child is blind, and people are looking."

"I can pay," Thomas said.

A few minutes later, he was carrying the girl with her box of food across the tracks toward a grassy field.

"You promised no more lies," he reminded her.

"Somebody gotta do something. You just stand there like a big lump while my belly scream for food."

Setting her down beside a stump, he dropped the clothes bags and looked around. In the distance, a big white tipi stood in the middle of a grassy meadow. People went inside. Others hurried to follow.

Perched on the stump, the girl dug through the box of food. "'Sides, it not a lie. We lookin' for my mama, sho 'nuff."

"You said your mother was dead."

"That my other mama. You hungry?" She pulled a chicken leg out of the box, sniffed it, then took a bite. "Mm. Tasty. Got biscuits in here, too. Want some?"

Taking a share of the food, Thomas settled beside the stump. While he ate, he watched people go into the big tipi. None came out.

The girl finished eating, then wiped her hands on the rock. "Where we sleep? Not outside. Chilrin ain't 'posed sleep outside. Specially blind ones."

Thomas took a bite of chicken.

From inside the tent came the sound of singing.

"You Injuns not talk much."

Voices drifted across the field. Thomas recognized the tune as one he had heard in the Come All You Sinners of Heartbreak Creek Church.

"How long we sit here, Daddy? I gots to pee. And it cold." With a shiver, the girl pulled her coat tight around her thin body. "I liable freeze dead we don't find Miss Pru soon."

Tossing his chicken bone into the brush, Thomas smiled. "We just did."